KISS AND SAY
GOOD SPY

Book 12 of the NEVER SAY SPY series

Diane Henders

KISS AND SAY GOOD SPY

ISBN 978-1-927460-49-8

Copyright © 2017 Diane Henders

PEBKAC Publishing Inc.
P.O. Box 67, Station Main
Qualicum Beach, BC V9K 1S7
www.pebkacpublishing.com

This book is a work of fiction. Names, characters, places and incidents are either the product of the author's imagination or are used fictitiously, and any resemblance to actual persons, living or dead, business establishments, events or locales is entirely coincidental.

First printed in paperback August 2017 by PEBKAC Publishing Inc.
v.5

Books in the NEVER SAY SPY series:

More books coming! For a current list, please visit
www.dianehenders.com
Or sign up for my New Book Notification list at
www.dianehenders.com/books

Humour by Diane Henders

Since You Asked...

People frequently ask if my protagonist, Aydan Kelly, is really me.

Yeah, you got me. These novels are an autobiography of my secret life as a government agent, working with highly-classified computer technology... Oh, wait, what's that? You want the *truth*? Um, you do realize fiction writers get paid to lie, don't you?

...well, shit, that's not nearly as much fun. It's also a long story.

I swore I'd never write fiction. "Too personal," I said. "People read novels and automatically assume the author is talking about him/herself."

Well, apparently I lied about the fiction-writing part. One day a story sprang into my head and wouldn't leave. The only way to get it out was to write it down. So I did.

But when I wrote that first book, I never intended to show it to anyone, so I created a character that looked like me just to thumb my nose at the stereotype. I've always had a defective sense of humour, and this time it turned around and bit me in the ass.

Because after I'd written the third novel, I realized I actually wanted other people to read my books. And when I went back to change my main character to *not* look like me, my beta readers wouldn't let me. They rose up against me and said, "No! Aydan is a tall woman with long red hair and brown eyes. End of discussion!"

Jeez, no wonder readers get the idea that authors write about themselves. So no, I'm not Aydan Kelly. I just look like her.

Oh, and the town of Silverside and all secret technologies are products of my imagination. If I'm abducted by grim-faced men wearing dark glasses, or if I die in an unexplained fiery car crash, you'll know I accidentally came a little too close to the truth.

I hope you enjoy the book!

For Phill

Thank you for being my technical advisor and the most tolerant husband ever. Much love!

To my beta readers/editors, especially Carol H., Judy B., and Phill B., with gratitude: Many thanks for all your time and effort in catching my spelling and grammar errors, telling me when I screwed up the plot or the characters' motivations, and generally keeping me honest.

To Cassie at Crowe Photography: Thank you for coming all the way up here from Victoria! Your flexibility and expertise made the photo shoot easy, even for a camera-hater like me.

To everyone else, respectfully:
Canadian English is an unholy hybrid of British and American English, so I apologize if spellings in this book look odd to you. But if you find typos, please send an email to errors@dianehenders.com. Mistakes drive me nuts, and I'm sorry if any slipped through. Please let me know what the error is, and on which page. I'll make sure it gets fixed as soon as possible. Thanks!

CHAPTER 1

Driving through the cold grey November morning, I belted out an off-key version of 'My Own Way To Rock' along with the radio. Burton Cummings's bouncy tune might have been enough to energize me for a day at the office, but it couldn't dissipate the perpetual current of low-level anxiety buzzing in the back of my mind.

I stopped murdering the song and switched to foolish optimism instead.

No need to worry. I could just relax and be myself: Aydan Kelly, ordinary middle-aged bookkeeper. My undercover assignment had dragged on for months with no discernible progress, so maybe my potential arms buyer had lost interest. Or gotten arrested. Or better yet, killed.

Or maybe he'd seen the error of his ways, repented, and joined a monastery to spend the rest of his days ministering to the poor and infirm...

The ring of my burner phone shattered my fragile bubble of wishful thinking.

Heart thumping, I swerved over to stop by the side of the road. After a single deep breath that was supposed to be calming, I thumbed the Answer button and barked, "Arlene Widdenback" in my best hardass-bitch voice.

"Good morning, Ms. Widdenback." Frederick Labelle's rich radio-announcer's tones oozed through the small speaker like warm butterscotch syrup, stirring queasiness in the pit of my stomach. "I hope you are well."

"Fine," I said shortly. "I'll be even better if you finally have a deal for me."

"Not quite yet." He infused the words with all the synthetic regret of a weatherman predicting hail, tornadoes, and plagues of locusts. "However, you'll be pleased to hear that our client will be coming to Calgary soon, and he'd like to meet you face to face."

Fear tightened my throat, and I held onto Arlene Widdenback's no-bullshit voice with an effort. "You're supposed to be my broker, so do your job and bring me a deal. I don't do face-to-face meetings."

Annoyance chilled his voice, congealing its former sweetness into something quite a bit less pleasant. "That's what I told him. I've been working on this deal since August, and I don't appreciate being cut out at this late date."

"So tell him to go piss up a rope," I snapped.

"Unfortunately, it's not that simple. He was quite... insistent."

Mentally agreeing that gangland bosses could be remarkably persuasive, I sat in silence that I hoped would radiate disapproval.

Should I just repeat 'I don't do face-to-face meetings' and hang up?

But the last time I'd refused a meeting, Labelle had sent a very cranky man with a gun to collect me. And if a middleman arms broker like Labelle kept a cranky gun-toter on staff, a high-ranking gang member like Benoit Riel probably had a whole stable of cranky gun-toters.

And even that thought didn't scare me as much as what the Department might do to me if I bungled this mission.

"He hasn't given me an arrival date yet," Labelle said into the silence. "Likely early next week. I do hope you'll be able to meet him. I think his visit is a positive sign that he's ready to move the deal forward."

Stall.

I grunted, putting as much contempt into the sound as I could. "Maybe. Call me if he actually shows up."

I pressed the disconnect button and collapsed back in my seat, willing my pulse back down into normal range.

After a few moments of fruitless yoga breathing I abandoned the effort and activated my small bug-detecting device. Its indicator light glowed a green 'all-clear', and I pulled out one of the Department's secured phones and hit the speed-dial.

As usual, Director Charles Stemp answered on the first ring with a crisp, "Yes?"

"It's Aydan," I said, trying not to sound as anxious as I felt. "I have a development. Benoit Riel might be coming to Calgary to meet with me in the next few days."

"Excellent. Briefing at zero nine hundred."

I checked my watch. Eight thirty. My civvie clients would have to wait.

I held in my sigh. "Okay. I might be a few minutes late, though."

"Very well. I'll inform your partner."

The click of his disconnect sounded before I could utter the words, "Wait, what partner?"

Uh-oh.

As I jogged across the frosty parking lot to the entrance of Sirius Dynamics, my heart thumped in a rapid rhythm that had nothing to do with exertion. Who would I get? Please, let it be someone I liked and trusted...

Dammit, I didn't want a new partner; I wanted my first and best one back. A vision of John Kane's steady grey gaze and reassuringly broad shoulders warmed my mind. If only he hadn't resigned...

I puffed out a harsh breath as I hurried into the building. Too late for that. Get over it.

The security guard gave me a cheerful 'Good morning, Aydan', and I managed a smile while I jittered through the sign-in procedure. I took the stairs two at a time, then paused at the top to dry my sweaty palms on my jeans and give myself a mental pep talk.

I could do this. I was getting closer to being the experienced agent I'd been impersonating for the past year. I'd taken some courses, and I had a few missions under my belt. And despite turning forty-eight a couple of months ago I was in the best physical shape of my life. Everything would be fine. Piece of cake.

I headed for the meeting room with my feet dragging as though I was already knee-deep in doom.

Outside the door, I plastered on a smile that I hoped would look convincing, then stepped inside.

"Hi..." I began. My greeting faltered at the sight of the occupants of the room, and I faked a cough to cover my dismay before continuing, "...Greg; Ch..." I added another strangled cough when my attempt to force Stemp's first name from my lips failed. "'Scuse me; something in my throat," I croaked. "Director." I nodded to Stemp and slid into the nearest chair, hoping I hadn't sounded as idiotic as I felt.

"Hey, Kelly!" Greg Holt greeted me, his steel-blue eyes glinting like broken glass in the craggy landscape of his face. "Long time no see. Team Anger-Management, boo-yah!"

Forcing a laugh, I reached across the table to reciprocate his proffered fist-bump. His gaze flicked behind me and I spun, but let out a pulse-calming breath at the sight of Clyde Webb's beanpole figure.

Thank God. At least I could count on Spider.

"Hi, Spider!" My relief burst out on my face in a wide smile and I jumped up. "Here, take this chair. I'm going to-"

"...sit with your back to the wall," he finished along with me, his mischievous grin making him look more like a high-school kid than a twenty-seven-year-old techno-genius. Then he turned a repentant expression toward Stemp. "I'm sorry I'm late. I got, um..." His cheeks went pink. "I was a little late leaving the house this morning..."

Holt guffawed. "Three months married and the honeymoon's still not over, eh?"

Spider blushed scarlet. Dropping into the chair I'd just vacated, he mumbled, "Sorry, it won't happen again," with a guilty glance at Stemp.

Stemp's impassive façade eased enough to allow a quirk at the corner of his mouth. "You're forgiven. Agent Kelly just arrived moments ago, too."

"Oh, good..." Spider gave me a flustered glance. "I mean, um... not that I'm glad you were late, too, just... I'm glad you weren't waiting on me."

Giving him a smile and a pat on the shoulder, I rounded the corner of the table and sat down with my back to the protection of the wall.

"Now that everyone is present..." Stemp began.

Shit.

I had been clinging to the hope that my real partner would arrive at any moment. But no; apparently I was getting Holt.

Good God. As if I wasn't already scared enough.

I dragged my attention back to Stemp's voice as he brought Holt up to speed.

"...Agent Kelly has been posing as Arlene Widdenback, a dealer in arms of all kinds, but particularly in technologically advanced designer weapons. Three months ago Frederick Labelle, a former broker for Fuzzy Bunny's now-defunct arms empire, initiated contact on behalf of one Benoit Riel, who is high in the gang hierarchy in Montreal."

Holt glanced over at me. "What did you sell him?"

"Nothing, yet." I slouched a little lower in my chair. "It's been frustrating as hell. Labelle keeps hinting that Riel will put in a big order, but it hasn't happened. Then this morning he called to tell me Riel is planning to come to Calgary and wants to meet me." Hiding my fear at the thought, I added, "Who knows, though? He doesn't know when Riel is supposed to arrive, so it could be just talk. He's been oozing butterscotch-flavoured bullshit for months now."

"That's weird," Holt said. "If Riel's using Labelle as his broker, why would he want a face-to-face?"

"No idea. I told Labelle I didn't do face-to-face meetings and he should do his job as a broker and bring me a deal."

Holt raised an eyebrow. "Huh. Are you going to stick to that if Riel shows up?"

"Probably not," I mumbled.

"Good call," Stemp said. "Keep playing hard to get, but you should definitely meet with Riel if he comes. Holt will be your backup."

Holt's lips tightened, and I could almost see the thought-bubble above his head. He was a top agent. He should have the leading role.

Stemp continued smoothly, but I knew he hadn't missed Holt's reaction. "The analysts have uncovered a complex web of interrelationships, so it will be ideal that Holt is unknown to Labelle, Riel, Tawny Harchman, and James Helmand."

I blinked. "I see the potential connection with Tawny Harchman since we know she had ties to Fuzzy Bunny, but what does Helmand have to do with this? He's in prison, and he never even knew about my Arlene Widdenback cover. He only knew that Fuzzy Bunny wanted me as Aydan Kelly and he was going to make a tidy profit by handing me over."

I didn't bother to add 'after he beat me and tried to rape me', but memories of pain and terror stirred darkly in the back of my mind nonetheless.

"Helmand was incarcerated with the former members of Fuzzy Bunny and they got to know each other," Stemp replied.

My mouth went dry. Oh, shit...

Stemp went on, "The latest intel indicates that Tawny Harchman also had contact with Helmand through her connections with Fuzzy Bunny; and we've discovered that Helmand knows Benoit Riel through his gang connections."

My heart thudded to the bottom of my belly. "They all know each other. Great. Absolutely fu-" I bit off the incipient f-bomb and substituted, "...fine. Marvelous." I massaged my temples, where a tension headache was already throbbing.

Stemp nodded. "Not ideal, I agree. Now that Helmand has been released-"

"*What?*" My voice came out in a strangled squawk, and I cleared my throat and forced a level tone. "It's only been a year."

Stemp gave one of his infinitesimal shrugs, his mouth flattening into a sour line. "We couldn't prove he had intent to jeopardize national security, so the money laundering and assault cases were tried in civilian court and the charges were plea-bargained. He has been a model prisoner, and yesterday he completed two thirds of his sentence and was released on parole."

Oh, God. That vicious bastard was free. Sick fear flooded my belly at the thought of him coming after me.

But at least I was armed. What about Nichele? He knew where she lived. After brutalizing her once, he wouldn't hesitate to do it again.

Shit, I had to call her right away.

"So do we know where he is?" I tried to hold my voice steady but it quavered slightly despite my best efforts.

"He's in Calgary, but the conditions of his parole prevent him from contacting his victims, including you, your friend Nichele Brown, and Helmand."

Holt frowned. "Helmand? Isn't that who we're talking about?"

"James Helmand is the parolee," Stemp replied. "I was referring to his younger brother, Arnold Helmand. For clarity, let's refer to them by their first names."

"Arnold... oh. Hellhound?" Holt asked. "Big ugly bearded guy covered in tattoos; sniper and weapons specialist?" Stemp nodded and Holt's frown deepened. "His brother is a gang kingpin? Isn't that a hell of a security risk?"

"Arnie would rather die than even give James the time of day," I snapped. "He doesn't associate with James at all."

"Arnold's loyalty isn't in question, nor is it relevant to this briefing," Stemp said. "But it is relevant that James knows your cover story and your subsequent dealings with Fuzzy Bunny. He'll think that Arlene Widdenback's connections with corrupt law enforcement were what resulted in his arrest."

"Great," I muttered. "So not only is he going to be pissed that I escaped and he didn't get his money from Fuzzy Bunny, he's going to be super-pissed that I got him arrested."

"Very likely," Stemp replied, as though he wasn't the least bit concerned that I was the target of a murderous lunatic with a vendetta.

And why should he worry? He thought I was an experienced agent who could easily handle the situation, not a bookkeeper scrambling just to stay alive...

"Inform me as soon as your meeting with Riel is scheduled," he went on. "Webb, get wiretaps on Riel's and Labelle's phones as soon as possible. Holt, I've given you security clearance to access the complete dossier on Arlene Widdenback and the developments in this case to date. Questions?"

Mute headshakes were his only reply, and he rose with a nod. "Dismissed."

As he strode out the door, I sprang up and followed him.

Hurrying down the hallway, I tried to pluck some reasonable arguments from the storm of fearful protests hurtling through my brain. Why did I get saddled with Holt? How could I request somebody I trusted?

"Yes?" Stemp inquired, and I realized I had trailed him into his office and he was regarding me with a quizzical eyebrow raised.

"Oh. Um... I was wondering if Carl Germain might be

available for my partner. Or maybe Jill Francis?"

"No, they're both assigned to other missions." Stemp's eyes narrowed. "Why?"

"I, uh... I just... I haven't worked with Holt very much, and, um..."

"So this will be an excellent opportunity to remedy that," Stemp said. "Was there anything else?"

I nearly blurted, 'Yeah, he scares the shit out of me.'

But that would only make me look like a coward and a whiner. And besides, Holt wouldn't have been reinstated to active duty if his psych evaluation didn't show he was over his anger issues.

Theoretically.

Although if he knew how to game the evaluations like I did...

Defeated, I mumbled, "No, nothing else," and plodded out the door.

CHAPTER 2

Creating mental priority lists, I hurried back to my office. First, call Nichele and warn her about James Helmand. I dropped into my desk chair and hesitated, hand hovering over the phone.

No, maybe calling Nichele should be the second thing.

I picked up the phone and dialled, then sat jiggling my knee up and down while the ringtone sounded over and over. At last a clipped but welcome voice came over the line.

"Dave's Trucking, Dave here."

"Hi, Dave, it's Aydan," I began.

"Hi!" The shortness in his tone vanished and I could hear his smile when he spoke again. "Good to hear your voice! How the heck are you?"

"I'm fine, but there's a bit of a situation..."

The phone made a hollow sound as though he'd cupped his hand over the mouthpiece, and he dropped his voice. "Where are you? Do you need help?"

Thankful as always for his unhesitating loyalty, I replied, "No, thanks, I'm okay. Where are you?"

"Moncton, New Brunswick. What's wrong?"

"Shit, you're days away..."

I hadn't meant to speak that thought aloud, and a crackle from Dave's end sounded as though he'd clenched the phone in his fist.

"What the hel... heck's going on?" he demanded, tension vibrating in his voice.

"Sorry, Dave, I didn't mean to scare you. It might be nothing to worry about, but James Helmand has been released on parole and even though he's not supposed to contact Nichele I wanted to make sure she was being careful. I was hoping you were in town with her."

"Shit!" I knew how upset he was when he didn't censor his language. His voice rose. "I'm hauling in the Maritimes this week and even if I start home right now it'll still take me four days! You gotta protect her! Promise me you'll..."

He bit off the words and the sound of his deep breath hissed on the line.

"Sorry," he said tightly. "I know your duty's gotta come first, but..."

"No, this time it doesn't," I interrupted. "I'm going to call her as soon as I get off the phone with you, and then I'm going to drive down to Calgary right away. I'll make sure she's okay."

"But... you're still in Silverside?"

At my 'uh-huh', he muttered, "Two hours away..." He hesitated. When he spoke again, I understood why he had wrestled with the decision. "Can you get Hellhound to go over and stay with her 'til you get there? I still think he's a jerk, but... you trust him, don't you? And he knows how to handle himself..."

"I'll call him right away. Don't worry. Arnie won't let anyone get to Nichele. He hates James as much as we do, probably more. And James's parole conditions prevent him from contacting either of them, so he won't risk getting sent back to jail."

"Yeah, right."

On that dubious note, I offered one last feeble attempt at reassurance before disconnecting to dial Hellhound's cell phone.

He picked up on the first ring with a brusque, "Helmand."

"Hi, Arnie, it's Aydan," I said cautiously.

His tone changed to a warm and cheerful greeting. "Hey, darlin'! How ya doin'?"

"Hey, yourself," I said, smiling in spite of my worry. "Why are you all bright-eyed and bushy-tailed? It's only nine-thirty. Usually I get nothing but a groan if I call you before noon."

"Had an early job."

He didn't elaborate as to whether the job involved killing people, and I didn't ask. Instead, I got to the point. "Can I hire you?"

His gravelly chuckle tickled my eardrum. "Hell, darlin', ya know how easy I am. Gimme a kiss an' I'm yours." He added hurriedly, "I mean, s'long's ya ain't askin' for a commitment."

"Bite your tongue," I chided, grinning at our long-standing joke. My smile slipped away as anxiety overcame me again. "No; I just found out that James is out on parole, and I'm worried about Nichele. She'll be at work by now, so could you please go over to her office and stay with her until I get there in a couple of hours?"

"Fuck, I can't." His chagrin came through loud and clear. "I'm outta town an' I ain't gonna be back 'til late today even if everythin' goes slicker'n shit through a tin horn. If anythin' fucks up, well..."

He trailed off and I shivered. He hadn't specified

location or details, so I knew exactly what kind of 'job' he was doing. If anything fucked up, he might not come back at all.

Dammit, now I was worried about him, too.

"But I thought you'd know Jim was gettin' out," Helhound added. "Didn't ya get your call from the Parole Board?"

"No..." Memory dawned and I smacked my forehead. "Shit! I remember you telling me to register with them for notifications, but I got tied up on a mission right then and didn't get a chance. And by the time the mission was over I'd forgotten. So, no, I didn't find out until this morning. And Nichele doesn't know either, or she would have called me."

"Well, try not to worry about it," he comforted. "Jim's smart, an' he ain't gonna take a chance on goin' back to jail. Nichele ain't got anythin' he wants. I'm more worried about you. If Jim thinks there's still a price on your head..."

I let out an unladylike grunt in an attempt to clear the large hairy lump of fear clogging my throat. "That's the least of my worries. Intel says James thinks I got him sent to prison. Never mind profit; he'll be out for revenge."

"Fuck." Before Hellhound could speak again, I heard a crackle that sounded like a radio command at his end of the line. "We're buggin' out; gotta go," he said rapidly. "Watch your six. I'll call ya soon's I can. Be safe. Love ya. 'Bye." The connection went dead.

"Shit," I muttered into the silent receiver before slapping it back onto the cradle.

My nerves twitched with the need to run to my car and drive as fast as possible to Calgary, but I forced myself to draw a deep breath.

Kane was living in Calgary. If anybody could protect Nichele, he could. But was it fair to ask him to put himself in danger after he'd quit the Department?

I drew another deep breath. Let him decide for himself.

I dialled.

The phone rang a couple of times at the other end before the connection clicked open and a deep but wary voice said, "Kane."

"Hi, it's Aydan," I said, attempting a light tone.

"Oh... Hi. How are you? It's been a while." He still sounded cautious. "I didn't expect you to be calling from the office."

"Um. Yeah, sorry about that..."

Guilt squirmed in my belly. This was just sleazy, asking him to risk his safety when I hadn't even had the grace to call and say hi for weeks.

I couldn't do it. Resolve squared my shoulders and I kept my tone warm and casual. "I just realized I hadn't talked to you for ages, and I had a few minutes so I thought I'd call. How's everything down there?"

"Oh." His voice warmed and deepened, smoothing into his usual velvet baritone. "It's nice to hear from you. Everything's... fine."

His tiny hesitation set off my alarm bells. "That's not the word I expected you to use," I probed gently.

"Well, no, I meant... it's good. Really good. Great."

"What's wrong?"

The sound of his exhalation carried clearly over the line. "Nothing. I'm still adjusting. So are Daniel and Alicia. It'll just take time." His voice firmed. "Now, are you going to tell me what's wrong at your end?"

"Nothi-"

"What's wrong, Aydan?" he demanded.

I blew out a breath of my own. "You're 'way too good at

reading me. Sorry, it's just that... I just found out James Helmand is out on parole and I'm worried about Nichele even though he's not supposed to contact her. I'm leaving in a few minutes to drive down but-"

"I'll stay with her until you get here. Will she be at work today?"

Gratitude swamped me, putting a catch in my voice. "Th- Thank you. But... I don't want you to put yourself at risk. You promised Daniel you'd always be there for him, and it's not fair to-"

"It's all right, Aydan, I want to," he interrupted. "And it's not going to be dangerous. If James shows up, I'll just call the police like any other citizen. Tell Nichele I'm coming, and then call me back with her location."

I drew a breath of relief. "Thanks. I'll call you right back."

When Nichele answered the phone a few moments later with a crisp, "Nichele Brown, how may I help you?" I slumped with relief. She was still okay. Thank God.

"Hi, Nichele."

"Aydan!" Her business voice vanished, replaced by her usual squeal of delight. "How are you, girl? Long time, no talk!"

"Um, yeah, sorry about that..." I mumbled. "Look, Nichele..."

Her voice went flat except for a faint vibration like an electrical current. "What's wrong? Is it... ohmigod, *Dave...?*"

"No, no, Dave's fine, I just talked to him," I reassured her with slightly too much heartiness.

"What is it, then? I can tell it's bad by the sound of your voice. Spill it."

"Um..." I couldn't think of any good way to say it.

"James Helmand is out on parole."

If not for the tiny squeak at the other end of the line, I would have thought we'd been disconnected.

"But he's not allowed to come near you," I added hurriedly. "If he even thinks about it, they'll throw him right back in jail. I'm coming down to stay with you, I'm leaving right now, and John will stay with you until I get there..."

"Aydan..." Her voice was breathy with terror. "Ohmigod... what... what... how could he be out? So soon?"

"I'll explain when I get there," I said firmly. "I'm leaving now. Tell your secretary to cancel your meetings for the day. Tell her you're working on an important investment plan. Close your door and don't open it until you hear the secret knock."

A puff of air that might have been a sob or a giggle floated over the line. "Girl, we made up the secret knock when we were five years old. Everybody knows shave-and-a-haircut. And you can't do anything to stop him if he comes for me." Her voice firmed into the determined Nichele that I knew. "Don't come. You'll be safer if you stay away from me. There's no point in giving him two targets for the price of one."

"I'm coming," I snapped. "I'm not going to leave you to face him alone. John will be there as soon as he can, and I'll be there in two hours. Wait for the secret knock." I hung up on her protests, wishing I could tell her about Kane's deadly martial arts skills and the Glock strapped to my ankle. But I couldn't blow my cover, not even for my best friend since childhood.

I sighed and called Kane before jogging out to the parking lot.

Fifteen minutes later I was scurrying around my

bedroom, stuffing overnight essentials into my small backpack while fearsome images of James's grinning face flashed in my mind's eye. His fists balled and dripping with Arnie's blood. Nichele's small body blackened with bruises from those same brutal fists.

What if he was stalking her right now? What if he was armed and I'd just sent Kane into the path of his bullets? Dammit, I shouldn't have involved Kane...

Muttering worried obscenities, I locked my front door, raking my usual glance over the farmyard and fields beyond in case of snipers or spies. Hurrying into my garage, I almost skipped checking the car for tracking devices. After all, I'd checked it before I left Sirius only half an hour ago...

I hissed out a breath between my teeth and did it anyway.

Check everything, every time. My new mantra. I would get good at this spy stuff, dammit.

The reassuring green light glowed on my detection device, and I slid into my car and headed for the highway.

CHAPTER 3

Despite the knowledge that Nichele and Kane were probably perfectly safe, my heart thudded faster than it should have while I fidgeted in the elevator up to Nichele's highrise floor. When I charged into the reception area, the heavy glass entrance door rebounded on its hinges with a crack of protest.

The receptionist twitched behind her polished granite desk, snatching her wide-eyed gaze off Kane to face me.

"Hi," I said anticlimactically. "I'm Aydan Kelly, here to see Nichele Brown."

"Oh..." She patted her chest with trembling fingers. "My, you startled me. Please have a seat. She's with a client now, but she'll be with you in a few minutes."

With a client? Dammit, I'd told her to cancel. And what the hell was Kane doing sitting in the reception area instead of guarding her?

"Thanks," I muttered, and strode across to confront Kane.

He rose from one of the sumptuous leather chairs as I approached, and my feet stumbled involuntarily to a halt while I fought to keep my jaw from sagging.

Holy... shit!

He had always been delicious eye-candy; but where he

had been magnificently muscled before, now he was spectacularly ripped. His black T-shirt strained across his chest and mountainous shoulders, sleeves stretched to their limits around biceps carved from stone. Before I could prevent it, my gaze travelled greedily down his body, taking in the ripples of his abs and the iron thighs filling his jeans to perfection.

And speaking of filling jeans to perfection...

I jerked my gaze up from his crotch.

"Hi," I croaked. "Wow, you look..." I swallowed and tried again, but my brain hadn't re-engaged yet. "Wow," I repeated stupidly. "Have you been working out extra-hard lately?"

My voice trembled on 'extra-hard' and I was pretty sure my eyes had glazed over with X-rated memories.

Dammit, get it together...

He grinned, a wicked spark kindling in his grey eyes. "Nice to see you, too."

He held out his arms and I stepped into them, managing with a supreme effort to keep the hug short and G-rated instead of sinking my teeth into that luscious ridge of shoulder muscle and humping his leg.

Pulling away, I dropped into the nearest chair to put some distance between us and kept my gaze firmly fastened on his face. Changes were visible there, too, his square jaw even more defined and...

"You dyed your hair," I blurted.

He flushed and ran his fingers self-consciously through the short dark hair at his temples where the silver used to be. "Yes..." His gaze wavered before meeting my eyes again. "I've been volunteering at Daniel's school, and the other parents of six-year-olds are so... young. I'm old enough to be *their* father, for God's sake."

"Well, you look amazing either way," I said. "And you could run circles around all of them. You don't have anything to prove."

His face softened into a smile. "Thank you." His smile faded and he sank into the chair beside me. Dropping his voice, he murmured, "Nichele has cancelled the rest of her appointments for the day but she said she needed to keep this one since it's a new client. I have a direct sightline to her door, and she has my number on speed-dial so she only has to press one button on her cell phone to alert me if there's anything wrong."

I sagged back in my chair, following his gaze down the hallway to Nichele's door. "That's great. Thanks. And thank you for dropping everything to come here. I didn't want to involve you but..."

"I really don't mind," he insisted. A rueful smile twisted his lips. "I'm finding civilian life a little... tame."

"I can imagine. I hope..." I began, only to break off when Nichele's door opened. A shock of adrenaline blazed into my veins at the sight of the pleasant-faced ponytailed-and-business-suited man with her.

I lunged forward, seizing Kane by the back of the neck and dragging him into a kiss.

He reacted instantly, pulling me into his lap to devour my mouth.

I heard Nichele bidding her client good day, and when the door hinges gave their distinctive crack I pulled away from Kane far enough to peek over his shoulder.

Shit!

The ponytailed man was standing in the lobby waiting for the elevator, watching us with interest through the glass door.

Shit, shit, shit!

I dove back into Kane's enthusiastic embrace.

A few seconds later Nichele's amused voice came from beside us. "I like my clients to get excited about their investments, but you two are carrying it a bit too far."

"Is your client gone?" I mumbled against Kane's lips.

"Yes." Her voice sharpened with worry. "Why?"

I pulled away from Kane and rose, smoothing my hair and trying to look nonchalant under the receptionist's scandalized and distinctly envious gaze. "Um, I know him, that's all. Blind date a while ago. It sucked, so I didn't want him to notice me."

Nichele laughed. "Girl, you were making out like a teenager, in the middle of a brokerage office. Trust me, he noticed. But you must've mistaken him for somebody else. He's from Montreal and he's only been here a couple of days."

Shit, of course he would have had to give her his home address if he was pretending to hire her as his stockbroker. I should have thought of a better lie, but now I was committed, dammit...

Willing the heat out of my face, I tried again. "I know, but I dated him last year when he was here visiting. I thought he'd go back to Montreal and I'd never see him again." I attempted a chuckle. "Stupid small world, right? Anyhow, I didn't want him to recognize me."

Nichele plopped down in my vacated chair, her eyes sparkling with amusement. "You're such a goofball. How many women have long red hair like yours? If you dated him, of course he recognized you. But..." Her salacious grin widened as she waggled her eyebrows at us. "...if you wanted to make him jealous, you probably nailed it."

"Great," I muttered.

"Well..." Nichele bounced to her feet. "I need a new dress for my business retreat tonight, and I'm starving! Let's go to the mall for lunch and some retail therapy!" Her act was almost convincing, but her gaiety rang false and her hands were trembling.

"Um, I don't know..." I objected, but Kane caught my eye and rose to herd us toward the door.

"That's a good idea," he said firmly. "It's a public place with video surveillance, and James wouldn't expect you to be there on a workday. Take Aydan's car and leave yours in the underground parking."

An afternoon at the mall was approximately as attractive as a colonoscopy, but Kane's logic was sound. And the sooner I got Nichele out of here, the better. My nerves still sizzled with adrenaline and my fingers itched to draw my Glock.

"Text me when you get there," Kane added with a significant look at me as he pressed the call button for the elevator. "I'm due at the school in half an hour to volunteer during lunch period, but I'm free after one o'clock if you need me."

"You could come shopping with us." Nichele batted her eyes up at him mischievously. "We could use a big strong guy to carry all our shopping bags."

Kane had obviously caught my tiny nod. He swept her a gallant bow as the elevator doors opened. "As milady commands."

She flushed and giggled, eyeing him appreciatively as I said, "We'll be at Chinook Centre. We'll meet you by the Dairy Queen in the food court. Would one-thirty work?"

He nodded, and we watched the illuminated numbers counting down in silence while I tried to get my heart rate under control.

When the elevator doors opened in the underground parkade, I kept my tone casual as I halted in the lobby. "Sorry, I just need to make a quick call before we go."

Kane responded with a nod and engaged Nichele in a conversation about stocks while I drifted a few paces away and dialled Frederick Labelle, my heart in my mouth.

When his unctuous tones rolled out of my phone, I said, "This is Arlene. Have you heard anything from our client yet?"

"No, he hasn't arrived. I'll be sure to contact you as soon as he does."

"Okay, thanks."

I disconnected, turning away so Nichele couldn't see me extracting a secured phone from my waist pouch. At the sound of Stemp's crisp greeting, I muttered, "I just saw Riel in Nichele Brown's office. Labelle says he hasn't arrived yet, but I'm positive it was him. Is our wiretap working?"

"Not yet. I'll inform you as soon as it's active."

I disconnected and rejoined the other two. Kane walked us to my car, where he stood watching until we had navigated the exit ramp.

Nichele giggled again from the passenger's seat. "So... you and Hot John! You've been holding out on me!" She poked a teasing knuckle into my ribs. "Girl, he's got it *bad* for you! Why didn't you tell me you two were together?"

"We're not." I signalled and made the turn to take us out of downtown, watching to be sure we weren't followed.

Nichele snorted. "Yeah, I can tell you can't stand each other by the way you were polishing each other's tonsils.

Seriously, girl, you're crazy if you don't hit that! And don't give me any excuses. You know you want to, or he wouldn't have been the first person you called for help."

"He wasn't." I concentrated on driving and watching my mirrors. "I called Arnie first, but he was out of town."

"You..." Words apparently failed her for a moment before she sighed and spoke with resignation. "Seriously, girl, I don't know what to do with you. That's like eating broccoli when you could have chocolate-dipped strawberries. I know you keep saying Arnie's great in bed, but sooner or later you need to find the right guy and settle down..."

My bark of laughter interrupted her. "Says the woman with every eligible male over thirty in her booty-call speed dial."

She tossed her head. "Not anymore. When you find the right guy..."

"Yeah, yeah," I groused. "You settle down after all these years and then right away you try to convert everybody else. And anyway, Arnie isn't broccoli. Far from it. He's more like..."

I checked the vehicles around us yet again. Damn that white SUV. Was it following us?

"...lobster," I finished absently, eyeing the rearview mirror.

"Yeah, the cockroach of the sea," Nichele gibed with a theatrical shudder. "So hideous you don't even want to touch it. Brrr!"

"Be nice, you jerk. I'm not talking about appearance." The SUV in question turned off down a side street and I relaxed and returned my attention to Nichele. "I'm just saying there's great stuff inside the shell."

"Nuh-uh." She shook her head. "Too much effort to get

past all that ugly. Especially when you've got Mr. Tall-Dark-and-Delicious waiting in the wings."

Even though I knew she liked Hellhound and was only teasing, I had to fight down irritation. Pasting on a smile, I closed the discussion with our time-worn but affectionate taunt. "You're so shallow."

She grinned and settled back in her seat with her stock reply. "You have no standards, girl."

I changed the subject. "So tell me about your business retreat."

"Oh, it'll be..." She considered for a moment. "Either a blast or a total snorefest; I don't know which. But all the high-rollers are going to be there, so it's a great opportunity to schmooze. I was just lucky I got the last ticket! It's at a swanky resort spa and there's a champagne reception tonight at eight for ticket-holders. The public panels and seminars run all day tomorrow, and then there's a private windup dinner. And we can stay at the spa for the weekend, too, if we want. How decadent is that? So..." She grinned. "I need a new dress. Or two. And shoes, and a matching handbag. And maybe a bit of new bling to go with it. And a new swimsuit, and..."

"Shopaholic." I shook my head in mock reproof before adding, "But better you than me, 'cause my idea of hell would be a never-ending business networking event. And at least James won't be able to find you in your posh hideaway."

We were halfway through lunch when Nichele's phone belted out the chorus of "I'm a Road Hammer". My heart warmed at the sight of her eager flush as she hastened to accept the call.

"Hi, honey," she purred. After a short pause, she added, "Yes, I'm fine. Aydan and I are at the mall where there are lots of people... No; no sign of James... Yes, we're being careful..."

She fell silent, listening while her expression faded from pleasure to a dubious frown.

"Okay..." she said slowly at last. Then she nodded and adopted a smile and a cheery tone. "Of course I am, it'll be fun! Just like an early honeymoon... Okay, I'll be packed and ready. See you soon, honey... I love you, too. 'Bye."

She hit the disconnect button and her hand drifted down to her lap, still clutching the phone as if she'd forgotten she was holding it.

I eyed her troubled face with rising worry. "What's wrong?"

"N... Nothing..."

"Bullshit."

She sighed. "Nothing. Really. It's just..." She sighed again and stirred her coffee, watching the stick swirl through the liquid as if it required her full attention.

I waited.

"That was Dave," she said.

"I figured. Unless you've got another honey I don't know about," I teased.

"No," she mumbled as though my words hadn't registered. After a moment she added, "He changed his schedule. He was supposed to be in the Maritimes until the middle of next week, but he's coming straight home now. He'll be here by Monday, and then he has a quick turnaround out to Ontario where he's got a bunch of short hauls lined up. And he wants me to come with him. We could be on the road for two or three weeks, depending on how his loads work out."

"Perfect," I said with relief. "You'll be safe when you're out of town. James doesn't know Dave so you'll be impossible to find."

"Well... that's true..." She frowned and stirred her coffee harder.

"But..." I prompted.

She blew out a breath. "But I feel like such a coward running away. And it won't solve anything. James will still be around when I get back and I can't hide forever. And..."

From the way her fingertips whitened on the stir stick, I knew she was about to divulge the true reason for her reluctance.

"And..." She gave me an imploring look. "This means Dave and I will be together 24/7. For *weeks*."

I failed to suppress a smile. "Well, yeah. Is this a bad time to point out that you're marrying him in less than two months and you'll be together 'til death do you part?"

"I know... Together... but not *together*-together." She fiddled nervously with the stirrer, bending it back and forth. "I mean... we get along great as long as he's on the road most of the time. But what if..." The stick snapped between her fingers, splattering coffee over the tabletop, and she grabbed a handful of napkins and scrubbed up the droplets with far more vigour than necessary.

"What if we can't stand each other when we're together all the time?" she burst out. "What if this is all a big terrible mistake and we hate each other after three weeks and he just dumps me and drives away forever?"

My heart squeezed at her tragic expression. "He won't, Nichele. Trust me, Dave's crazy about you. You're the best thing that's ever happened to him, and you're going to love being together." I hesitated, reluctant to dilute my pep-talk with inconvenient facts. "Um... what about your work?"

"No big deal." She waved a dismissing hand. "I've got my laptop and phone. I can easily work in the truck. But... but what if..."

Her voice faded from my attention as I glimpsed a ponytailed man leaving the food court. My blood chilled.

He was wearing jeans instead of a business suit, and I couldn't see his face. Was it Riel?

A moment later he vanished around the corner.

I turned back to Nichele, who was eyeing me with a supplicating expression. Damn. I hadn't heard a word she'd said.

I blew out a breath. "Look, you know I'm the queen of fucked-up relationships so I'm not qualified to give anybody advice, but I will tell you this for absolutely certain. Dave loves you, and you love him. Together you can figure out anything." Desperate, I invoked the only magic spell at my disposal. "Come on, you need your stuff for this weekend as well as a whole new wardrobe for your road trip with Dave. We need to start shopping."

CHAPTER 4

By the time Kane joined us at the mall, Nichele was fully engaged in retail therapy and I hadn't seen the ponytailed man again despite my nervous vigilance. The afternoon dragged interminably while Nichele foraged through store after store, loading Kane's arms with a burden of shopping bags that would have bowed a lesser man.

At last the ordeal was over and we grabbed an early dinner in one of the restaurants attached to the mall. When the bill was paid, Nichele rose to her feet without her usual energy. "Well, I guess I'd better go home and get my game face on. I have to leave by seven and we still need to pick up my car from the office."

"You should rent a car," I urged. "You're too easy to spot in that red Miata."

"It won't matter." Nichele's voice trembled just a bit. "I have to go home to get my suitcase and James knows where I live. All he has to do is wait there." She tossed her head, putting on a confident act. "He won't anyway. Why would he? Last time he only wanted me as a way to get money transferred to his offshore account. He's too smart to try the same thing again, and he probably wouldn't violate his parole anyway. I'll be fine."

"I'll take you home," I argued. "You can get your stuff

and then I'll drive you to the car rental place. You can leave in a different car from there and fly under the radar."

"But then my car will still be at the office..."

"No problem," Kane said. "Aydan will drive you home to get your things and then bring you to the car rental place. I'll park my vehicle at your office and drive your car to the rental office, and then Aydan can drive me back to pick up my vehicle from your parkade."

"But that's 'way too much trouble!" Nichele gave an uncertain laugh. "Aren't we getting a little paranoid here? We're not spies on some secret mission!"

Somehow I managed not to glance at Kane. "I know, but wouldn't you like to have a hot new ride?" I coaxed. "Wouldn't it be fun to show up in a Ferrari or Lamborghini or something? And then you could just relax and enjoy your retreat without worrying about looking over your shoulder all the time."

"Oooh..." Nichele's eyes lit up. "Well, when you put it that way... but it's pretty short notice to rent an exotic car..." She rummaged in her purse and pulled out her phone. "Maybe they'll still have something available. After all, it's November and it's the middle of the week. It should be past their peak time..."

We waited in silence while she dialled, and moments later she was the proud lessee of a Lamborghini.

"Perfect," I said with relief. "Let's get going."

With Nichele safely on her way an hour and a half later, I pulled into the office parkade and turned off my car with a long breath. "Thank goodness. She should be safe for the next couple of days, anyway."

"Yes." Kane turned a piercing gaze on me. "So now are you going to tell me what's really happening?"

My worry over Riel's presence returned full force, and I swallowed to hold my voice steady. "Um..."

How much should I tell him? A glance at my wristwatch showed it was nearly seven-thirty, and I opted for procrastination.

"Do you have time?" I asked. "You've spent the whole day with us and I don't want to take you away from Daniel."

"I appreciate that." Kane consulted his watch, too. "His bedtime is eight o'clock. There's just enough time to go and get him tucked in, so let's talk afterward."

"Okay, should we meet at your condo? What time?"

Kane shrugged, a twitch of his shoulders that looked uneasy. "You might as well come with me to Alicia's. I shouldn't be long."

"Okay..." I said slowly, but he didn't seem inclined to elaborate.

"I'll see you there," he said instead and got out of my car.

Just as he backed his Expedition out of its parking stall, my phone vibrated. Stomach clenching at the sight of 'Private' on the call display, I accepted it. This likely wasn't good...

"Hey, darlin'." Hellhound's weary rasp answered my cautious 'hello'.

"Arnie!" My initial gush of relief was rapidly staunched by worry over the obscured phone number. "Where... um, how are you?"

"I'm okay. Still outta town. Didn't get a chance to do the job today, but we're gonna try again tomorrow. How 'bout you? Did ya get to Nichele okay?"

"Yes, she's fine and leaving town for a business retreat

right now. She'll be out of danger for a couple of days at least. And John came to help us out."

"Good." Relief warmed Hellhound's voice, and he added, "Can't talk long, darlin', but I just wanted to make sure you're okay. Maybe we can catch up if you're still in town tomorrow."

"That'd be good. I might stay at your place tonight even if you're not there." I stifled a cavernous yawn. "I'm bagged and I don't feel like driving home."

"Go ahead an' crash at my place," he urged. His voice deepened to a sexy tease. "I'm gonna have hot dreams of ya naked in my bed tonight."

"Not as hot as if you were there," I teased in return. "Stay safe. I love you. With zero commitment," I added hastily.

He chuckled. "Love ya, too, darlin'. G'night."

Warmed, I put the car in gear and headed for Kane's ex-wife's house. When I pulled to a stop at the curb, Kane sprang out of his SUV and hurried over.

"Sorry." I forestalled his anxious look with an explanation as I got out of the car. "Arnie called, and I didn't realize you'd be waiting outside for me."

"It's all right." He turned and strode up the walk. Rapping lightly on the door, he turned his key in the lock and let us in without waiting for a response.

Bloodcurdling screams made me snatch my Glock from my ankle holster, my heart jackhammering my ribs.

Kane gripped my wrist. "No, it's all right," he muttered. "Put that away." After I had obeyed, he called out jovially, "Hello, there! Who's making all that racket?"

The shrieks stopped as if switched off, and a moment later Daniel pelted around the corner in pajamas, his blotchy crimson face dripping tears and snot. *"Daddy-Daddy-Daddy-Daddy!"* he wailed.

A harried-looking Alicia trailed him, and she jerked to a halt at the sight of me. Her hostile glare bounced from Kane to me and back to Kane again. "Nice of you to show up," she snapped.

"I'm sorry," Kane said as Daniel thumped into him and flung his arms around his father's legs. "I got here as soon as I could." He stooped to swing the child effortlessly up into his arms.

Daniel clung and buried his flushed face in Kane's shoulder, leaving a glistening trail on the black T-shirt.

"Hey, Daniel," Kane murmured in a soothing singsong. "We talked about this. Remember I said I might be a little late today? Remember you promised you'd let Mommy tuck you in?"

Daniel's only response was a juicy sniffle as he tightened his grip, his chubby fists bunching in Kane's T-shirt.

"Come on, then, let's get you settled," Kane added in the same reassuring tones. "Which bedtime story would you like tonight?"

Daniel mumbled unintelligibly into Kane's shoulder as they headed down the hallway with Alicia behind them, leaving me standing there like the fool I was.

After a few minutes of awkward hovering, I quietly let myself out.

When my phone vibrated twenty-five minutes later, I picked up at the sight of Kane's number.

"I'm sorry about that," he said to my 'hello'. "Are you on your way back to Silverside?"

"No, I'm at the Tim Horton's down the street. It's been a long day and I wanted a few minutes of downtime and a quiet cup of tea."

His sigh was clearly audible on the other end of the line. "That sounds wonderful. Do you still have time? I can be there in five minutes."

"I'll be here."

Precisely five minutes later he strode in, garnering appreciative glances from the female patrons and dark looks from the males. Shortly afterward he joined me at my table, carrying a cup of coffee for himself and placing a small box of doughnut holes in front of me.

"Yum! Thank you!" I popped open the box and surveyed the tempting assortment of sugar-coated spheres. "I shouldn't, but I'm going to." I selected a glazed chocolate morsel and popped it into my mouth. "I'll regret this later," I added, my words slightly muffled by sweet greasy goodness.

Kane smiled. "You work out hard enough to make up for it. And you won't regret it much."

"You know me too well." I grinned and chomped down an apple fritter and a strawberry-filled Timbit before pushing the box toward him. "Take these away before I eat them all."

He peeked into the box. "Aha. You left the old-fashioned sugar-coated ones for me."

"Of course. For you, no sacrifice is too great." Hand over heart, I sketched a bow before adding, "Also, old-fashioneds are my least-favorite."

"I'm touched by your selflessness."

"I know; right? And, hey, here's another happy thought," I added. "Now that you're a civvie, nobody's going to crack any lame jokes about cops and doughnuts."

"For which I am truly thankful. This will be the first time

I've been able to eat a doughnut without feeling like a cliché."
He popped a doughnut hole into his mouth and I tried not to
have a hot flash while he licked off the sugar clinging to his
fingers.

Dammit, I could still feel the touch of that tongue and
those fingers in places that were aching to feel them again...

I jerked my hormones to an unceremonious halt as Kane
plied a napkin and leaned back with a sigh, cradling his
coffee cup. "I'm sorry about that scene at Alicia's," he said.
"Apparently we haven't made as much progress as I'd
thought."

"No problem." I sipped my tea, firmly transferring my
attention to the conversation at hand. "All kids get cranky
around bedtime, don't they? But he settled down the instant
you got there. You're a great dad."

Kane grunted, hunching his shoulders. "Don't be fooled.
It was nothing to do with my parenting skills. If I'd been the
one trying to put him to bed, he would have screamed just as
frantically for Alicia. That scene plays out every night."

"Oh." I surveyed him over my cup. "Well, it hasn't been
that long since he was kidnapped. He'll gradually realize he's
safe and you'll both always be there for him; it'll just take
time."

"I certainly hope so." Kane sucked in some coffee as
though the mug contained life-giving elixir. "This has been a
nerve-wracking time. It's gotten a little better since I started
volunteering at the school, but still, every morning it's an
emotional bloodbath when we leave him in his classroom.
Every night he has a meltdown if both of us aren't there to
tuck him in. He has night terrors and wakes up screaming.
After being toilet-trained for years, he's now wetting the bed
regularly..."

He made a gesture of resignation, his hand dropping to the table. "The pediatric psychologist says it's all part of the process and it should improve soon, but..." He sighed. "I don't know, Aydan; I just... I didn't expect it to be easy, but... having a child is nothing like I thought it would be."

I reached over to squeeze his hand. "Said every parent since the dawn of time. You're doing fine. He goes to you for comfort and he trusts you. Any parent would struggle with the kind of issues Daniel's having, and you've been dropped into it cold without any chance to get to know him as a happy stress-free kid, and without a supportive partner."

"That's the other thing." Kane's hand tightened on mine. "Alicia is pressuring me to move in with them. Saying that if I truly cared for Daniel I'd make a stable home for him. That's why I wanted you with me tonight, to disrupt her usual attempts. And I just..." Muscles rippled in his jaw, his lips pressing into a thin line. "I..."

He hissed out a breath. "Aydan, I'm so furious with her, I can barely contain it! She willfully cheated me out of six years of my son's life! I never got to hold him as a baby. I wasn't there for his first laugh or his first step or his first tooth. I don't know what his first word was. I didn't get to teach him to ride a bicycle. I wasn't there for his first soccer game. I didn't get to walk him to school on his first day..." He broke off, his hand clenching mine, his breath coming hard. "I've missed so much," he gritted. "Precious memories that I'll never have. Because of *her*!"

I clutched his hand in both of mine, my heart breaking. "Oh, John, I'm so sorry! I can't imagine how awful that must be."

"And do you know what the hell of it is?" He stared across the table, the storm raging in his eyes. "I want to hate her; but if not for her, I wouldn't even *have* a son. This wonderful, frustrating, frighteningly complex little person who is both of us and neither of us... he wouldn't exist. How the hell do I deal with that?"

"I don't know." I swallowed against the tightness in my throat. "I wish I could do or say something that would help."

The tension went out of him on a long breath and he released my hand with a gentle squeeze. "You've helped just by hearing me out. And I'm sorry for dumping on you. I usually work out those feelings at the gym."

I gave him a wry smile and gestured at his rippling muscles. "I can see how upset you've been."

He twitched his shoulders in a self-deprecating shrug. "It seemed like a better solution than murdering my ex."

"Yeah... I guess. Although to be honest, I feel like murdering her myself."

Kane gave me a twisted smile. "I've got a couple of free gym passes if you like."

"I might take you up on that."

"So..." He leaned his elbows on the table, closing the distance between us and lowering his voice to a soft rumble that sent tendrils of warmth tickling through my belly. "Much as I enjoyed kissing you this afternoon, I'm not flattering myself that it was because you suddenly found me irresistible. What's going on?"

CHAPTER 5

Extricating myself from the pull of Kane's sexy grey eyes with an effort, I declined to mention how close I had come to ripping his clothes off in the middle of Nichele's office.

"I'm working on a case," I said. "And Nichele's client is it."

Kane waited.

The silence lengthened and I suppressed the urge to squirm.

Shit, I should never have involved him. He was a civilian now. He'd be safer if he didn't know.

"I just didn't want him to recognize me," I added lamely.

Kane maintained his expectant silence.

"For shit's sake," I burst out as though he'd actually been arguing with me. "You're a civilian now. Go home to your son and be safe!"

Hurt flashed in his eyes, quickly vanishing into the impenetrable expression I called his 'cop face'. "It's a little late for that," he said evenly. "Your mark spotted you, and what's more, he spotted you making out with me. You've already involved me, and I'll be safer if I know what might be coming my way."

"Oh, shit." I let my forehead fall against the table with a thud. A little too much of a thud. "Ow," I added, sitting up and rubbing the sore spot. "Dammit! I'm sorry, I'm an idiot. I wasn't thinking; I was just..."

Just getting so caught up in ogling a hot hunk of man that my already woefully inadequate spy skills deserted me altogether. 'Idiot' didn't even begin to describe the depth of my incompetence.

I clenched both fists in my hair. "Shit, what a moron I am! All I had to do was get up and wander away with my back to him, and he'd never have given me a second glance! I'm so sorry!"

"It's all right." The wicked glint was back in Kane's eyes. "So you're saying you were just looking for an excuse to kiss me." A tantalizing whiff of his spicy aftershave made all the moisture in my mouth migrate to more southerly regions of my body as he leaned closer. "Maybe you should kiss me some more. Just to keep up appearances."

Sucking in an inadequate breath, I leaned away from his gravitational pull. "I thought we weren't doing that anymore."

"You started it." Half teasing, half challenging, he gave me a slow grin that raised my body temperature several degrees.

"And I'm finishing it," I said, my words far more decisive than the husky voice that came from my lips. "You're a dad now and your responsibility is to Daniel. I'm a bullet magnet, and you can't afford to be close to me."

"Which would have been a valid argument before you dragged me into this." Kane gave me the commanding stare that reminded me all over again what a good agent he had been. Hell, still was. "I need a full briefing, Aydan. If you've potentially endangered me, that threat might extend to Daniel by proxy, and *nobody* threatens my son."

Defeated, I blew out a breath of frustration before leaning forward and keeping my voice low. "Okay, fine. The man in Nichele's office was Benoit Riel. He's one of the higher-ups from a gang in Montreal and I'm supposed to meet him in my Arlene Widdenback cover, but he's not supposed to be here yet. I recognize him from the dossier, and I have to assume he recognized me if he's anywhere near as smart as we think. And it was definitely no coincidence that he was in Nichele's office, because he's also friends with James Helmand, who knew Fuzzy Bunny's minions in prison."

"Oh." Kane's voice went flat. His gaze flicked around the coffee shop before he leaned in and matched my quiet tone. "So let me be sure I understand this. James and Riel are potentially connected to Fuzzy Bunny's original arms empire; they both know you by sight; and they both think you're Arlene Widdenback the arms dealer. And they both know that Nichele is your friend, and Riel just proved how easily they can get to her. And now they both know that I'm a little more than your friend, too. So if they're looking for leverage on you, they've found it."

"Yes," I mumbled, staring at the table and damning my own stupidity. "I'm sorry. The smartest thing you could do is shoot me right now. If I'm dead, Riel will leave you alone."

"I turned in my weapon when I resigned. But I could throttle you slowly with lots of screaming."

I gulped. "Um... You 'could'? Or you 'want to'?"

"I'm deciding."

Edging back in my seat, I managed a sickly smile. "Well, I guess I'll be the first to know when you make up your mind."

He chuckled. "I'm kidding. Of course I'm concerned;

but I'm actually glad things worked out this way. At least now I know what's coming. If Riel has connections to Fuzzy Bunny, he'll already know that you and I acquired their secret weapon last winter. And even if by some miracle he doesn't know that, I'm a target anyway because James knows we were together last fall."

"But he only glimpsed you at that bar, and I never told him your name..." I began.

"Aydan." Kane gave me a 'you-aren't-thinking' look. "James has known me since I was six years old."

"Oh..." The enormity of my mistake rose like choking bile in my throat. "Oh, *shit!* I forgot you'd grown up together."

"Not really," Kane corrected. "He's eight years older, and although my parents did make an effort to get to know Arnie's family, they quickly figured out that even as a young teen James was nothing but trouble. Neither Hellhound nor I made any effort to stay in touch with James as adults so he won't know anything about my law enforcement career. But he definitely knows who I am. In fact..."

He stared into space for a few moments. "Yes..." he muttered. "That adds up..."

"What? What adds up?" I jittered on the edge of my seat, the domino-fall of connections still echoing in my brain.

Arnie, John, Nichele...

"Oh, Jesus, no!" I groaned and thudded the heels of my hands against my temples. "John..." I had to stop and swallow to steady my voice. "Does... does James have a photographic memory like Arnie's?"

Kane's eyes narrowed in thought. "I don't know. But when Mom and Dad were still trying to help Arnie's family, they arranged for all the kids to have IQ tests. Arnie and

James scored highest, in the genius range. So it's certainly possible."

"Shit, shit, *shit!*"

"What is it?" Kane demanded.

"Dante." I thumped my aching forehead. "When we were in the bar last fall I told James you were my ex. So if Riel tells him we were kissing today, he'll think we're back together. That's bad enough; but last fall James also saw me going home with Dante. If he thinks Dante and I are still close, too..."

Kane sighed. "One more tool for leverage. And if James has the same phenomenal memory as Arnie, he'll remember Dante's last name, where he works, and any other tiny detail Dante might have mentioned. And even if he didn't know those things, he'd remember that Dante is an underwear model. That's impossible to forget." There was a slight edge to Kane's voice that might have been jealousy, but I didn't have time to analyze it before he went on, "If he wanted to track Dante down, it would be as simple as calling the local modelling agencies."

"Oh, God." I wallowed in despair for a few more seconds before pulling myself together. "Okay. You need to take Alicia and Daniel and move to a safe house. I'm sure Stemp will agree to that, at least for the short term. Arnie's out of town so he'll be safe until he gets back. I'll warn him as soon as I can. I'll get Holt to watch Dante-"

I broke off at the sight of Kane's negative headshake.

"What do you mean, 'no'?" I demanded, tension winding up in my shoulders.

"I'll be safe, and I'll make sure Alicia and Daniel are, too," he said calmly.

"Safe? How do you figure you're *safe*?" My voice rose on

the last word, and I reined myself in with a glance around the nearly-empty restaurant. Nobody seemed to be paying attention, and I returned my attention to Kane with a glare. "Didn't we just agree that you're a prime target?"

"No, we agreed that I would be a prime target if anybody actually knew how to find me."

I flung out a hand in frustration, gesturing at his mountainous six-foot-four frame. "You're not exactly hard to spot!"

Kane gave me a thin smile and I glimpsed the steely resolve that had made him the best agent in the Service. "Not hard to spot, but very hard to follow. That's what I meant earlier when I said 'it adds up'. I dropped over to Hellhound's place yesterday for a little while. When I left, a white Ford Explorer tailed me. A single male driver wearing dark glasses. I evaded him and then turned the tables. I got behind him in traffic and confronted him when he stopped. It was James."

My throat went dry. "And...?"

Kane's lips turned up in a predatory grin. "I told him to get lost, and if he ever followed me again I'd make sure he got lost permanently."

I gulped. "Oh, shit. John..." I leaned in and lowered my voice again. "You're a civilian now. You can't just go around killing people who piss you off. Even if they really, really deserve it."

Kane gave me an affronted look. "You know perfectly well that even as an agent I could never kill for my own convenience. Or are you forgetting the mountains of paperwork and performance evaluations and psych assessments after a serious incident? We..." He hesitated as if suddenly remembering he'd quit the Department, then tried again. "Agents have to hold themselves to a higher standard of behaviour than any civilian."

"I know; I didn't mean that," I muttered. "I'm just saying you shouldn't have threatened him. It'll only piss him off. What if he decides to kill you before you can kill him?"

Kane shrugged, a dangerous light in his eyes. "Let him try. Then I can claim self-defense. When the police investigate they'll find out James was a dangerous criminal with gangland ties who was just released from prison, and I'm an innocent civilian. I'd be shocked if it even went to trial, and even if it did no jury would convict me."

I clapped my hands over my ears and hummed. "La, la, la, la... I can't hear you... Not going to be an accessory before the fact..."

He grinned and pried my hand away. "Don't worry, it won't happen. James is a coward and a bully, and he won't take a chance on crossing me. And anyway, nobody has followed me since."

I started to ask 'are you sure', but stifled myself before the words came out. If he said nobody had tailed him, I was damn sure nobody had. Even as a civilian he was a better agent than I'd ever be.

"My condo isn't registered in my own name," he went on. "Thanks to Alicia's pettiness, nobody knows I have a son; so nobody would expect me to be going to or from an elementary school. Unless they pick up my trail via you or Hellhound, there's no way to find me."

"But what if..." I began.

"At this point I have only three options," Kane interrupted. "One, take Alicia and Daniel and hide in a safe house. For how long? Until you stop being Arlene Widdenback the arms dealer? How many years will that be?

Stemp won't go for it, and in any case Daniel doesn't need any more disruption in his routine. We've finally gotten him to the point where we can leave him in his classroom after the obligatory morning meltdown and he settles down and participates in class."

"It'll be a fucking big disruption to his routine if you end up dead," I snapped.

"I won't. And that brings me to option two, which would be to go underground by myself until this is resolved, leaving Daniel to deal with my abandonment and my broken promise. I told him I'll always be there for him, and I won't break that promise. Not for anything."

"You're missing the point," I argued, worry making my tone harsher than I'd intended. "You won't be *there* for him if you're *fucking dead!*"

"Even if they captured me, which they won't, they wouldn't kill me. Leverage only works if the hostage is still alive. I'm no good to them dead."

"Until they decide they don't need you anymore," I insisted. "And then they pretty much have to kill you. That still adds up to *fucking dead.*"

"Or there's option three," Kane went on imperturbably. "Which solves all the problems at once. I can be there for Daniel twenty-four-seven, I'll be absent from my condo even if somebody does figure out where I live, and I'll be able to protect my family in the unlikely event that I'm traced back to them." He drew a deep breath and let it out slowly. "I'll move in with Alicia and Daniel."

Shock struck me speechless, my jaw flapping uselessly on strangled protests. "You wha...? What? That's... that's..."

"The best possible solution," Kane finished, and rose. "Keep me in the loop. Have you got a burner phone I can borrow?"

"But... but... you just finished saying how much you hated Alicia!"

"And I love Daniel more than anything. He's my top priority. If this is what it takes to keep him safe, I'll do it."

"But..." My useless syllable hovered in the air, unsupported by any viable rebuttal.

Shit.

I pulled out the spare phones I carried in my waist pouch and we wrote down each other's numbers in silence. Then he pocketed his phone, leaned down to kiss me hard, and vanished out the door.

After a few stunned minutes I trailed out in his wake, finally returning to full mental capacity when the cold night air slapped me in the face.

"Well, that's just fucking *fine*," I snarled, aiming a vicious kick at a lone paper cup that lay on the sidewalk, rolling gently in the chilly breeze.

Shivering, I slid into my car and cranked up the heater before pulling out a secured phone. A moment later, Stemp's crisp "Yes?" sounded through the speaker.

"It's Aydan." I drew a deep breath to organize my thoughts before explaining the situation.

"So you briefed Kane on your mission." Stemp's voice was completely without inflection.

A chill trickled down my spine.

Shit, I hadn't even considered the potential repercussions of confiding in Kane. Even though I kept thinking of him as an agent, he was officially a civilian. If the chain of command wanted to get picky about it, I'd just breached security.

"Only in general terms," I hurried to explain. "I didn't

mention any of the updated protocols and I didn't tell him any identities that he didn't already know..." I gulped as I realized that wasn't actually true. "Um... except Riel; but Kane had already seen him, so the only new information he got from me was that Riel was a gang member who was potentially involved in my current mission. That's it."

After a short disapproving silence Stemp said, "Very well. Continue."

I resisted the urge to babble more excuses. File that as 'lesson learned' and do better next time.

Assuming my most professional tone, I laid out my theory and its connections. "...so I'd like Holt to come here and guard Dante," I finished.

"Using Holt to guard your friend would be a waste of resources." As if anticipating the furious words boiling up to the tip of my tongue, Stemp softened his tone. "Even if you are correct in your assumption that Riel and James are attempting to gain leverage on you for some unspecified reason, they are almost certainly only gathering data at this stage. Hostages are an encumbrance and a last resort, and the danger to your friend will be negligible when they realize you haven't had any contact with him for a year."

Clenching my teeth to hold in the anger, I tried a different tack. "But if James was watching Arnie's apartment and following John, that's too much of a coincidence. Dante would be the logical next step. And if he's watching Dante he won't expect to be watched in return, so it's a perfect opportunity to see what else he's up to."

"That is a tenuous link at best. Both Kane and Hellhound are well-known to James and there are many reasons why he might be watching them. I don't believe that indicates a threat to your friend. In any case, James's activities are outside the scope of your current mission; and we are not in the bodyguard business."

Fury boiled into my veins. "Listen, d-"

Fortunately Stemp interrupted before I could complete the word 'dickhead'. His cool impersonal voice went on, "...However, if you are in Calgary tonight anyway and Riel has yet to make official contact, there is nothing preventing you from watching over your friend. And if you include his name and address in your report we can be prepared to act if he does become involved."

I drew a deep breath. Do *not* call him a dickhead. He'd offered me a loophole, and if I pissed him off he might forbid me to do anything to protect Dante. Then it would just get ugly when I defied him...

"Okay." I thought fast. "Um... I'll file my report in the morning. For all I know Dante may not even be in the country. He travels a lot. I'll confirm his whereabouts first. Are our wiretaps active yet?"

"Yes, and the analysts are monitoring them. No useful intel so far. Is there anything else?"

"That's it." I hung up, congratulating myself on successfully concealing the fact that I couldn't even remember Dante's last name, let alone his address.

My smugness was short-lived when I realized I was going to have to call Nichele to find out.

Shit.

That led to another thought that spiked anxiety into my heart. I should have made her leave her cell phone with me. James probably had the resources to trace it. Damn, damn, damn!

After a moment of furious self-recrimination, I let it go with a long breath. She wouldn't have parted with her phone without a life-or-death struggle, and I couldn't break my cover to explain why it might actually be life or death.

I considered retreating to the comfort of Hellhound's apartment before making the call, but it was getting late and delay wasn't going to lessen the humiliation. I emitted a brief but heartfelt groan and dialled.

"Aydan!" Nichele's greeting was as enthusiastic as ever. "Hey, girl, are you calling to check up on me?"

"Hell, yeah. Somebody has to keep you in line," I bantered, delaying the inevitable. "How's the party?"

"Oh, it's fabulous!" Music and conversation were suddenly muted in the background as though she'd stepped out of a party room. She lowered her voice. "It turns out this whole thing is publicity for a new app they're launching. The app presentation before the reception was a total snore, but tomorrow's panels are going to be great. And I'm making some amazing connections tonight! These people are the real big-money movers and shakers, the ones you never get to meet socially. I'm so glad Benoit got that ticket for me!"

My heart stopped. "Wh... Who got you the ticket?"

"Benoit Riel."

CHAPTER 6

When I wasn't able to force a response from my suddenly-constricted throat, Nichele teased, "You remember... Benoit Riel? The guy you dated and were trying to avoid in my office this morning? Have you got early Alzheimer's or something, girl?"

"N... no..." As if making up for lost time, my heart restarted, rattling like a machine gun in my chest. I clenched the phone in a deathgrip and held my voice steady with all my might. "Nichele, where are you?"

"At my business retreat," she said cautiously. "Did you forget that? Are you feeling okay?"

"No, I know that, I meant... where is your retreat being held?"

"Oh, it's at this giant estate near Priddis. You should see it, Aydan, it's spectacular! It's got a full spa and this super-deluxe guesthouse and a manmade lake and fountains and-"

"And a two-storey gazebo with wet bars on both levels that seats about a hundred people," I finished in a strangled voice, doom squeezing my lungs like a toxic cloud. "It's Lawrence Harchman's place, isn't it?"

"Yes, do you know him?"

Goddammit.

"Yes. We're not on good terms." Understatement of the

century. "So don't mention my name," I added. "And stay away from Benoit, too, okay? He's creepy. In fact, you should just leave now. Come back to Calgary and-"

"Oh, Aydan, you're such a social misfit. He's perfectly nice. I'm having a fantastic time, and I'd be crazy to walk away from this kind of business opportunity. I have to get back to the party now; Benoit's been teasing me for checking my phone all evening. Did you want something, or were you just making sure I'd gotten here okay?"

"Both..."

My mind whirled uselessly, failing to come up with a plausible reason to tell her to leave.

I tried anyway. "Look, Nichele, I didn't mention this before because I didn't want to worry you, but Benoit is friends with James. He might have just lured you out there..." I trailed off, not even wanting to speak my fears aloud.

"Oh..." Nichele sounded as though the wind had been knocked out of her, but she rallied fast. "Well, there's nothing I can do about that." Her decisive business voice trembled only slightly. "And I guarantee I'm safe from James while I'm hobnobbing with the cream of society here. You should see the security, Aydan; there are guys in cheap suits and radio headsets everywhere. This is the safest place for me."

Stifling a groan, I thumped my forehead against the steering wheel. I couldn't tell her that Harchman's wife was a criminal and the security might not be for the protection of the guests.

Damn, damn, damn...

Nichele interrupted the downward spiral of my thoughts. "So... I'd better get back to the party. What were you calling about?"

"Well, stick with the bigwigs, and be careful," I warned. "Keep your phone on you and be ready to call-"

"Aydan, relax! You are so paranoid, girl! Now hurry up and tell me what you really want."

"Right. Um... so... the reason I was calling was, um... what's Dante's last name and address?" I asked in a light tone that sounded false even to my own ears.

"Aha!" Her triumphant chortle made me wince in anticipation of the ribbing to come. "Aydan, you booty-licious babe! Are you going to make an Aydan sandwich with Dante the Inferno and Hot John? Wheee-ooo!"

"No, I just, um..." A fortuitous fount of bullshit erupted in my brain and I spouted it gratefully. "You remember Lola and her sex shop? She's looking for a model for one of her ads and I thought of Dante."

"Thought of Dante first thing," Nichele teased. "Uh-huh. Purely for business purposes. Nothing to do with the way he fills out his undies in those ads."

"Come on, Nichele."

"Okay, okay. His last name is Olivieri. Hang on while I grab his address..." Her voice faded as she moved the phone away from her ear and she added, "But I'll only give it to you if you promise to apologize to him and then go for some smoking-hot makeup sex. I can't believe you ran out on him last time."

"Uh, yeah, that was, um... a mistake."

And impossible to explain without divulging a whole lot of classified information.

"I'll definitely apologize," I added. "But I'm not going to sleep with him."

"Seriously, Aydan..." Her voice resumed its normal

volume.

She did sound serious. Shit.

"...why did you run out on him?" she asked. "Climbing out his bathroom window was severely weird. All you had to do was tell him you'd changed your mind. He's a nice guy. He would've taken you home or called you a cab, whatever you wanted."

"Can we please not talk about this again?"

She didn't reply, just waited on the line with her usual terrier-like tenacity.

I sighed. "I told you before; it was just one of those stupid things you do when you're drunk."

"Girl, crank-calling your ex or getting a tattoo would be 'one of those stupid things you do when you're drunk'. Climbing out a guy's bathroom window and disappearing into the night is a whole 'nother level of weirdness."

"I just... I freaked out, okay? It was easier to climb out the window than explain that I didn't want to sleep with him after all..."

"Only you would think it was easier to dismantle a window than have a simple conversation," she said with resignation. "Never mind; you're still my favourite oddball. Here's his phone number and address." She reeled them off, then added, "Tell him I said hi. And, Aydan, if it was the size of his package that scared you, don't worry. He goes really slowly and he's so gentle-"

"Well then, thanks, Nichele!" I interrupted with desperate heartiness. "Call me tonight when you get settled in your room, and call me again tomorrow morning before you go into your discussion panels so I know you're safe, okay?"

"You bet I will," Nichele said sweetly. "'Cause I want all

the dirt on you and Dante."

"It's just a modelling job," I gritted. "I'm not planning to sleep with him."

"Then you should change your plans. Go get him, girl! Bye-bye!"

After a few minutes of fervent swearing, I slumped back in the seat and stared out the windshield into the darkness. Then I hissed out a breath between my teeth and hit the speed dial on another secured phone.

When Stemp answered with his usual briskness, I said, "It's Aydan. Sorry to bother you again."

"You're not bothering me; this is my job."

"During the day. You shouldn't have to work 24/7."

His impersonal tone softened. "Perhaps not, but I would rather sleep soundly between calls than lie awake worrying that my stand-in might make decisions that would jeopardize a mission, or worse, cause harm to one of my agents."

A small pocket of warmth settled in my chest. "Well, it means a lot to me that you're always there. Thanks."

"You're welcome."

A brief awkward silence hovered between us and I hurried into my update.

"...so I'm going out there tonight," I finished with determination.

Stemp's clinical tone was back. "Is that a personal or a professional decision?"

No point in lying to him. He knew me too well.

"Both. I know you said they won't likely take hostages this early in the game and I trust your judgement, but... Nichele is my best friend and I can't leave her unprotected. That's the personal part. But on the professional side, this is directly mission-related. It's a good opportunity to scope out the connection between Riel and Tawny Harchman, and maybe I can even follow up on the intel about James and Tawny cozying up. If Nichele's there, it gives me a perfect excuse to crash the party and sniff around."

"Very well, if you can do so without arousing Ms. Harchman's suspicions."

"No problem. I'll avoid her." My lips peeled back from my teeth in equal parts revulsion and dark humour. "I'll just pop in and say hello to Lawrence, my old buddy and business partner. I didn't get a cheque for my share of the porn-video proceeds last month, so I'll jog his memory. That'll make him very eager to tell me anything I want to know so I don't make a scene at his fancy party. He's all about keeping up appearances."

I considered for a moment, my heart pounding at the thought of going into an unknown situation with no backup. What if my worst imaginings came true? What if I got captured? I was pretending to be an experienced agent, but would it betray my inexperience more to request backup or not to request it?

I swallowed hard and added, "Could you please send Holt down in case anything goes sideways at Harchman's? I don't want him with me out there, but it would be good to have him closer than Silverside."

I held my breath.

"Very well," Stemp agreed as though it was normal procedure.

I eased out my breath of relief silently before adding, "Tell him I'll text him..." I considered for a moment. God only knew what time I might finish there. "...sometime tonight. If he hasn't heard from me by morning I might need help."

"And what would you like him to do in that case?"

I clenched my fist in my hair and tugged, hoping to dislodge some useful plan from a brain completely devoid of ideas. "Um..."

Nothing came to mind except 'come and rescue me', and my stupid pride wouldn't let those words out.

"I'll have to leave it to his best judgement," I said lamely. "I really don't know what I might find. If it's anything out of the ordinary I'll report in as soon as I can so he'll have a better idea of what he's going into." Then my evil twin spoke up. "And if Holt's going to be in Calgary anyway, he might as well watch Dante's place while he's waiting for me to check in."

"Very well." Stemp's dry tone might have held a flicker of amusement. "Give me the address and I'll inform Holt." I read it off to him and he confirmed it before adding, "How do you propose to get into this event? You mentioned that it required tickets which were sold out...?"

"I'll sneak in through the creek at the back. There's only one camera back there and I've avoided it before." I didn't bother to mention that they might have updated their surveillance perimeter since then. Worry about that later.

"Very well. Holt will be en route within the hour. I'll text you the number of his burner phone. Good hunting."

"Thanks."

After I hung up, I sat frowning through the windshield. Should I call Kane? I sat eyeing the burner phone in my hand.

No. By now he'd be settled into Alicia's... The green-eyed monster in my brain tried to say 'bedroom', but I firmly diverted it. He hated her. He'd be settled into her *spare* room.

And even if I asked for his help, he wouldn't put my needs ahead of Daniel's. He had made it clear from the start where his priorities lay. He hadn't given a second thought to nearly getting me gang-raped and tortured in his attempt to rescue Daniel.

I shook my head, denying my hurt feelings as well as the terrifying memories. Kane hadn't dragged me in there. I'd gone willingly.

Because I had trusted him to keep me safe, a small sad voice whispered.

"Shut up," I muttered. "I knew damn well it was dangerous, and he was treating me as an equal partner. It was the highest compliment he could give me."

Pushing aside my mood, I refocused.

I couldn't show up at a snobby champagne reception in my faded jeans, hiking boots, and waist pouch unless I wanted to attract a lot of attention. That might throw Harchman off-balance enough to quickly tell me what I wanted to know...

Scowling, I considered that scenario. Nope, bad idea. He'd just have his security guys chuck me out on my ass. I needed to blend in with the rest of the well-dressed crowd so he wouldn't be able to throw me out without causing speculation among his fancypants guests.

So I needed dress-up clothes.

Shit.

I didn't have time to get my formalwear from home, but all the stores were closed already. And if I used my key to Nichele's place I could borrow one of her stretchy dresses and pretend it was meant to be worn micro-short, but her tiny shoes were out of the question for my size-ten feet.

Double-shit.

Another note for the spy manual: Always keep a wrinkle-proof black dress and high heels in the trunk. With a matching handbag, appropriate jewellery, and a holster I could strap to my inner thigh.

I swore loudly and put the car in gear.

By the time I parked in the visitor's lot at Hellhound's condo building, my clenched jaw was aching and my head was pounding. Hauling myself out of the car, I made for the door.

If only Hellhound had been home, I could have briefly set aside my deadly reality under an erotic massage from his magic hands, followed by a glorious temporary oblivion induced by one of his other magic body parts. But no; he was off in some undisclosed location dealing with his own potentially deadly reality.

I stifled a self-pitying whimper.

When I pushed my key into the lock, Hooker's serenade of raspy meows floated to my ears. Cautiously cracking the door open, I crouched to scoop up the large furry body when he made his usual determined attempt to escape into the hallway.

"Nice try, buddy," I murmured as I stepped inside and locked the door behind us. "How's my big guy?"

After a moment of standoffish inspection in which he made it clear that he was disappointed I wasn't Hellhound, the big cat philosophically leaned into my fingers for a chin-scratch. Eyes squeezed shut in bliss, his purr rumbled like an outboard motor. Heavy tufted paws kneaded my shoulder for a few moments before he squirmed up to plant a paw on either side of my neck in a hug, nuzzling his moist nose under my hair.

Grinning, I massaged his scruff while I kicked off my shoes at the door and carried him to the small kitchen, knowing the next step in the dance.

Right on cue, Hooker withdrew from the shelter of my hair and braced his paws against me in the universal 'put-me-down' gesture. I lowered him to the floor where he paced beside his dish, gazing up at me with hungry yellow eyes and emitting short demanding meows.

"Here you go, you big freeloader." Scooping a few crunchy treats from the bag in the cupboard, I sprinkled them into his dish and stood watching while he devoured them, his fluffy tail making ecstatic figure-eights in the air.

Wishing I could just crack open a cold beer and curl up in my usual spot on the couch, I blew out a sigh and eyed the living room wistfully.

Hellhound's guitar slumped like an abandoned lover beside his empty chair. Despite Hooker's purring presence, the apartment seemed too quiet, a desolate place pining for the return of Arnie's warmth and music and laughter.

I shivered. What if this was a premonition? What if his mission went terribly wrong? He always seemed so indestructible, but even his strength was no match for bullets. My mind filled with nightmare images of flesh brutally torn, crimson blood leaking out like red ink draining from his tattoos...

"For shit's sake, cut it out!" I snapped, and headed for the bedroom.

With only a slight qualm about rummaging through his things, I helped myself to a black duffel bag and a black hooded parka large enough for two of me.

Hooker had padded into the bedroom to observe, and I

reassured him, "I'm not stealing these. I'll bring them back."

The cat gave me a quizzical look before twisting to sit on the base of his spine, one hind leg extended skyward while he licked an indelicate place with evident satisfaction.

"Nice," I told him. "Thanks for sharing that."

I left him to his ablutions and departed, locking the door behind me and trying not to dwell on the fact that right now normal people were curled cozily on their sofas watching TV and looking forward to a blissful snooze in their safe comfortable beds instead of getting ready to commit a crime or two before sneaking through a creek bed in the cold darkness.

"Fuck my life," I muttered, and headed for my car.

CHAPTER 7

Driving slowly through an empty shopping mall parking lot, I surveyed the storefronts and weighed the chances of making a successful smash-and-grab.

"This is stupid," I said aloud. "I can't even buy shoes and a purse and dress in less than two hours when I'm *not* under pressure. How the hell am I going to break in and steal something that looks decent in three minutes before the police show up?"

For the umpteenth time I counted the friends I knew well enough to show up at ten PM asking to borrow clothes. It was a short list, literally. They were all several inches shorter than I, and their shoe sizes were correspondingly smaller. Not a chance.

Sighing, I cruised past a few more stores. This was going to be ugly. And noisy.

I added another note to my mental to-do list: Learn to pick locks. And maybe there was some kind of super-spy course on how to bypass security systems...

Okay, quit stalling. Should I try to grab everything at one store, increasing the amount of time I spent inside, or break into a shoe store here before moving on to another mall to grab a dress?

And how the hell was I going to find anything even

remotely suitable in the dark with a burglar alarm blaring?

I was near the end of the parking lot when a glorious sight made me jam on the brakes and stare.

A mannequin posed in a brightly-lit display window, wearing the perfect black cocktail dress and necklace with matching shoes and purse. The shoes probably weren't size ten, but they looked like eights at least, and they were slingbacks. I'd look like a doofus with my heels hanging out the back of the shoes, but I wasn't planning to stick around and dance the night away.

My heart vibrated in my chest, halfway between hope and fear.

I could smash the plate glass window with my crowbar, grab the goods all in one place and get the hell out...

My breathing short-circuited as a car bearing a security logo turned into the parking lot. Trying not to look guilty, I drove out of the parking lot at a decorous pace, turning down a side street.

On autopilot, I turned right at the next intersection. That brought me around the back of the mall and I slowed, eyeing the rear delivery entrances of the shops. Heart thumping, I pulled into a parking spot under a conveniently burned-out streetlight.

Could I do this?

If I ran out the store's back door, I should be able to jump the short concrete retaining wall and hit the embankment fast enough that my momentum would carry me easily up to my car. And the car would be out of range of their security cameras, too. As long as I kept my hood up they couldn't identify me.

And I'd spotted the security car cruising away in my rear-view mirror. They'd be on their way to a routine patrol of their next site, wherever that might be.

Now or never.

The guilt of breaking into the store made my stomach twist, but it was either commit larceny or risk losing Nichele.

"No contest," I said aloud, and pulled on Hellhound's giant parka.

Leaving my car unlocked, I strode away with the hood up and my crowbar tucked inside the floppy sleeve, trying to look nonchalant while my knees trembled.

Wouldn't it be just my stupid bad luck to have my car stolen now?

I determinedly banished the mental image of myself bursting out of the store with my ill-gotten goods only to find my getaway car gone.

No; this would work. I'd have time to grab everything and vanish before the police arrived.

Really, I would.

Unconvinced by my feeble assurances, my heart galloped as if attempting a getaway of its own.

I strode along the side of the mall and rounded the corner. A fast survey showed no cars, no people. Perfect. Before I could second-guess myself, the crowbar scythed up in a wide swing.

The glass shattered into sparkling rubble and the shriek of the alarm slammed a burning rush of adrenaline into my veins.

A couple more sweeps with the crowbar cleared my way, and I lunged up onto the dais that held the mannequin.

Hell, what was I going to do with the crowbar? I might need it later...

Hiking up the back of my parka, I stuffed the crowbar into the waistband of my jeans, wincing as it ripped a fiery trail down my lower back.

I snatched at the mannequin.

Purse over my arm. Necklace...

Fuck, it had a tiny clasp. My hands were shaking so hard I couldn't have managed it even if I hadn't been wearing gloves. I jerked fruitlessly at the mannequin's head, hoping to pull it off and grab the necklace.

The too-close whoop of a siren sent icy fear down my back.

"Fuck-fuck-fuck!" I yelped, sounding like a deranged hen laying a particularly unwieldy egg.

Dress and shoes. Just get the damn dress and shoes.

The siren was approaching fast.

The dress was secured to the mannequin with clips. The shoes were attached with nylon ties...

"GODDAMMIT!" My shout was nearly drowned out by the siren, almost on top of me.

Desperate, I jerked the mannequin off its stand and fled through the store with it clenched under one arm. One of its legs swung loose, swivelling and flopping against displays as if trying to save itself from my frantic abduction.

Stay on, you fucker, I can't lose that shoe now...

Charging into the stockroom at the back, I spotted the exit door, equipped with a panic push-bar and a large sign saying "Emergency Exit Only – Alarm Will Sound".

"No shit," I gasped, the alarm punishing my ears as I stiff-armed the door and burst through. The crowbar fell out of my pants and clanged to the pavement, advertising my location as effectively as an alarm bell. Beyond logical thought, I wasted a precious second snatching it up, then turned and ran.

Three fast strides brought me to the retaining wall and

my fourth stride took me over it, my legs pistoning up the embankment.

My foot slipped.

A frantic lunge, feet pedalling like a berserk cartoon character...

The grass that had looked brown and dry was slicked with invisible frost, a fact that I discovered when I slammed face-first into it.

"Fuck-*umph-ow-shit!*"

The vindictive mannequin jabbed painful plastic fingers into my side while I scrabbled for purchase on the slope. At last I managed a graceless scramble on my knees, driving the crowbar into the turf to pull myself to the top.

Panting like a steam engine, I hooked the crowbar around the mannequin's neck to ransack the pocket where I'd stowed my keys.

Oh, please God, please let my keys still be there...

My fingers clamped around them as I staggered to my feet. Yanking open the driver's door, I slung the mannequin toward the back seat, crowbar and all.

The fucking dummy wedged between the seats, its feet angled across the headrest and sticking out the door.

My frenzied swearing rose to an even higher pitch while I jerked and shoved at the recalcitrant legs. A loud crack might have been its back, mine, or some formerly important part of my car, but it didn't matter. Its legs folded and thank-you-Jesus, its feet cleared the door.

Flinging myself into the driver's seat, I nearly lost an eye to the spiked heel of one of the shoes, but I didn't have time to swear. My shaking hand jabbed the key fruitlessly at the ignition.

Missed. Missed again...

Oh, God, that was a police car racing to the front of the mall, lights and siren splitting the night.

At last the key went in and I twisted it savagely. The car roared to life, my foot already on the gas. I slapped it into gear and accelerated toward the first cross-street.

Just as I rounded the corner I glimpsed a flash of red and blue lights in my rearview mirror, but I used every ounce of self-control to stay at the speed limit while I wound my way through a few more side streets.

Nobody pursued.

Whimpering gasps escaped me, sweat pouring down my face while my body vibrated like electrified jelly. The giant black parka felt like my own personal sauna, but I didn't dare stop to take it off until I was farther away from the scene of the crime.

I kept driving, my wild panting slowly giving way to hysterical giggles.

What a clusterfuck.

Only I would get locked in a life-or-death struggle with a plastic dummy. Kane would never do something so clumsy and boneheaded. He'd pick the lock in seconds flat, do backflips to bypass the infrared security camera beams, and seduce the clothes right off the damn dummy.

Hell, forget that. He wouldn't need to break in and steal clothes at all. He probably kept a super-compact wrinkle-free tux rolled up and concealed in his pants at all times.

My snuffles of laughter faded at the memory of what he did keep in those ever-so-well-filled pants.

And I wasn't going to get any of it.

I heaved a martyred sigh and headed for the city limits.

Slightly over an hour later I was stumbling through the darkness along a half-frozen creek bed, enveloped in Hellhound's parka with the duffel bag of purloined formalwear swinging from my hand. A stingy cloud-shrouded moon provided just enough illumination to keep me headed in the right direction, without allowing me to avoid the scratchy diamond-willow twigs that seemed intent on removing most of the skin from my face and hands.

Teeth grinding, I added another mental note to my spy-manual: Keep night-vision goggles in the car. I could roll them up in the middle of my emergency blanket and nobody would ever know. And at least I wouldn't end up blinded by...

"Ow! Fucking twigs!" I snarled, rubbing a smarting scratch on my cheek.

My slow progress made the trip seem much longer than the last time I'd come this way almost a year and a half ago. But then I'd been following Kane, and I'd been feeling much safer than I did now...

I blew out a short sigh and peered into the darkness. Why wasn't I there yet?

Dammit, I couldn't be going in the wrong direction. And I couldn't possibly have overshot the estate. I would have seen the blackness of the cutbank looming up against the paler sky.

Trudging forward again, I tried to ignore the small anxious voice in my head that assured me that I had indeed overshot the estate, and I was doomed to fight my way down this godforsaken creek in the darkness until I finally fell into the Elbow River ten miles to the west.

"Shut up," I muttered. "Just shut up."

I sucked in a breath as I finally identified the welcome

bulge of the cutbank blocking the sky. Thank God. Now I only had to sneak past the night-vision surveillance camera.

I was pretty sure I remembered the route to avoid it.

But just in case...

Heart thumping, I prepared to implement the second part of my plan. The guards should be accustomed to animals triggering their camera down here. Deer, moose, elk, bears; any of those were likely to make frequent appearances on their monitors.

So I'd just be a bear.

Pulling the parka hood over my head, I bent over and stuffed the duffel bag into the gaping front of the parka to make a convincingly pendulous belly.

At least I hoped it would be convincing, as long as I kept enough shrubs between me and the camera. Just an amorphous black shape moving aimlessly along the creek...

"Be the bear, be the bear," I chanted softly as I moved forward on all fours, head down beneath the hood.

The defect in my plan was immediately obvious. I couldn't see where the hell I was going.

Using the soft mud at the edge of the creek to provide direction, I pushed through the shrubs. Weaving back and forth and occasionally backtracking when I encountered a particularly impassable thicket, I hoped my erratic progress looked bearlike. After all, erratic was part of my plan. A dark shape moving purposefully in a straight line would arouse suspicion, right?

"Right," I muttered, and ran headfirst into what felt like a very solid tree. "Ow, dammit."

At last I chanced a quick peek from under the edge of the hood, and drew a breath of relief at the sight of the cutbank behind me. As long as they hadn't added any more cameras,

I should be safely inside their surveillance perimeter.

I was slowly straightening my aching back when a flashlight beam blazed over the willows and a male voice crackled out of the woods directly to my left.

"A bear!" The voice rose to an agitated pitch. "Shoot it, shoot it!"

Shit!

CHAPTER 8

Dropping back to all fours, I fled in the opposite direction. Apparently my crashing progress through the undergrowth was convincingly bearlike. The voice behind me rose to the edge of hysteria.

"Omigod! Hurry up, shoot it, shoot it!"

Frigid mud sucked at my hands and feet while I barrelled through the icy creek, praying the duffel bag wouldn't fall out of my parka. Redoubling my efforts as I charged into the shrubs on the other side, I prayed even more fervently.

Please, after surviving a year and a half while people intentionally tried to kill me, please, please, don't let me get shot by some fucking moron who thinks he's the Great White Hunter...

"Settle down, Simpkin." A deeper, calmer voice made me suck in a breath of relief. "This is why we don't give sidearms to rookies like you. It's illegal to shoot it; and anyway, the poor damn thing's more scared of you than you are of it."

"But it's a *bear*..."

"And it's probably in the next county by now," the second voice said in long-suffering tones. "Come on. By the time we finish this circuit it'll be midnight and we can sign off-shift. My feet are killing me."

"But it was a *bear*, it could have killed us..."

Their voices faded, and I fought the urge to collapse on the ground and quiver for a while.

Get it together.

If anything was happening to Nichele, I needed to get in there. And even if she was perfectly safe, the party might be winding down soon if everybody was planning to attend the seminars tomorrow. My chances of buttonholing Harchman were rapidly diminishing.

Suppressing a groan, I turned to splash and slither back through the creek.

The woods were a fresh misery. The inadequate moonlight only penetrated in small patches where a few deciduous trees raised their autumn-bare branches to the sky, and the rest was stygian blackness. Following the sound of distant music, I blundered uphill, making frequent and painful acquaintance with roots, rocks, and low-hanging tree branches.

By the time I reached the edge of the trees by the guesthouses, sweat was trickling down my backbone despite the chill. My jeans and parka sleeves were soaked and icy cold, and I could feel mud drying on my hands and face. I didn't dare use my muddy hands to check, but the way my scalp was prickling I probably had twigs in my hair, too.

Dress or no dress, I couldn't join the party looking like this.

Nerves vibrated in my belly. Running out of time.

Through a gap in the trees, the lights of the guesthouse glowed a welcome to those who weren't mud-covered and marinated in stale sweat. A tantalizing finger of warm light reached toward me as the doorman swung the door wide, offering his usual half-bow and smile to the tux-and-gown-clad couple who strolled inside. Their well-bred laughter mocked my hopeless inability to join them.

The closing door cut off their voices and the doorman resumed his position outside.

Dammit, I needed to get into that guesthouse and get cleaned up.

Rapidly shedding the parka and stripping down to my bra, I turned the parka sleeves inside-out, hoping their wet insides would be cleaner than their mud-caked outsides. My breath plumed in the frosty air while I smeared the soggy ice-cold fabric over my arms and hands.

I finished the job by scrubbing my hands vigorously against my jeans, then transferred my gun to the mannequin's purse along with the essentials from my waist pouch. With a few jerks of my hairbrush, I dislodged some tangles and stray twigs from my hair.

Halfway to hypothermia, I peeled off my wet, clinging jeans and shivered into the cold fabric of the dress. The icy weight of the necklace added the crowning touch to my goosebumps.

Shivering violently, I stuffed my boots and clothes into the duffel bag and slung it under the nearest large spruce tree, where it melted into the darkness. I did my best to memorize the duffel bag's position relative to the guesthouse door, then turned back to study the doorman.

I needed a distraction.

Teeth chattering, I glared at the man, willing him to take a break. Go for a smoke or go to the bathroom or something, dammit.

He remained in place, as stiff and solemn as a Buckingham Palace guard.

Hell, he probably didn't even pee until his shift was over.

What if I screamed, and then circled around to sneak in while he came to investigate?

No, he'd likely stay put and call security. That was the last thing I needed. A generic security guard would be bad enough, but if one of them remembered me from last year my plans could go south in a hurry.

At last common sense kicked in. I muttered, "Idiot," and pulled out my cell phone to dial Nichele. She would let me into her room for a quick cleanup with no more than some fond eye-rolling and teasing. Thank God my weirdness was already firmly established.

The ring tone sounded again and again before finally going to voicemail. Nichele's perky recorded voice made my throat constrict.

Oh, God. She always answered her phone. It was never outside her arm's reach.

Something bad had happened.

I punched the disconnect button and charged out of the woods.

As I lurched onto the illuminated walking path in my ill-fitting slingbacks, a brown-haired woman let out a startled cry from a few feet away, her hand flying to her bejewelled chest. "Oh! I almost shit a brick! Where did you come from?"

Dammit, I hadn't even seen her on the path behind that big cedar hedge. Her jewellery, dress, and shoes looked classy to me, but what the hell did I know? I couldn't imagine a high-society matron saying something like 'shit a brick'. Was she friend or foe?

Even more rattled than before, I mumbled, "Sorry," torn between the burning need to charge straight up to the main house waving my gun and the urge to keep a low profile.

And double-damn, the doorman had caught sight of me now, too. He offered his usual smile, but it wavered when he took in my appearance.

The woman's brows drew together, too, as her gaze travelled from my head to my toes.

Almost afraid to look, I glanced down at myself.

Oh, shit, it was worse than I'd thought.

The protection of my hiking boots had only served to emphasize the stark line between my clean feet and ankles and my mud-streaked calves. My hands and wrists were filthy up to the forearms, with deep black crescents of mud under my fingernails.

I didn't even want to know how my face and hair looked.

"I... uh, I slipped and fell down by the pond," I lied rapidly. "I was trying to sneak back into the guesthouse and get cleaned up before anybody saw me."

"Are you all right?" the woman inquired with concern.

"Cold and grumpy, but fine."

Humour twitched at the corner of her mouth. "Okay, I'll pretend I didn't see you, then. Come on; you look half-frozen." She gestured toward the guesthouse door with a smile.

"I can't," I blurted, urgency hammering at me. Find Nichele...

The frown was back between her eyebrows. "I hate to point out the obvious, but you need to. My grandsons come home cleaner than that after running wild outside all day long."

"Um, no, I meant..." An excuse popped out of my mouth as if I'd actually rehearsed it. "I'm bunking with my friend and she has the room key. I just tried to phone her but she's not answering..."

"Well, you can't go to find her looking like that," the woman said firmly. "Come on, you can clean up in my room. I was just on my way to change to a more comfortable pair of shoes anyway." She indicated her elegant pumps with a rueful grimace before extending her hand. "Lois Butler."

"Uh..." I half-extended my filthy paw, hesitating. Give her my real name or my alias?

"Aydan Kelly," I said in a split-second decision. "Sorry, I don't think I'd better shake your hand." I turned it toward her, grubby palm up, and she laughed.

"A little mud never hurt anyone." She gave me a firm handshake. "Hurry up; you're shaking like a leaf. Don't you have a wrap?" She herded me down the path to the guesthouse door as she spoke.

"Nothing that's not soaking wet and muddy," I replied truthfully as the doorman bowed us inside, his expression professionally pleasant again.

"I have a spare sweater you can borrow," Lois offered as we hurried down hallway.

"Oh, no, I don't want to impose..."

She slid the cardkey into its slot. "Nonsense. I'm not using it, and you can give it back to me tomorrow."

"Uh... I don't know if I'll be here tomorrow," I muttered, and made a beeline for the bathroom before any more inconvenient questions came my way.

The sight that confronted me in the mirror was enough to make even a strong woman blanch.

I faked a jocular tone. "Omigod," I called through the door. "You weren't kidding. This is horrible."

Her laughter carried back to me. "I told you so."

Heart pounding, I surveyed the damage. What terrible things might be happening to Nichele while I stood here wasting time?

I forced myself to take a breath and marshal all my hard-earned spy skills. Rushing off without a plan could get us both killed. I needed to schmooze and fit in. No swearing or gun-waving, no matter how attractive the prospect seemed.

I yanked off the pinching shoes and began at the top, shaking a few more spruce needles out of my hair and cleaning the muddy smudges off my face. I couldn't do anything about the angry red scratch on my cheek, but some diligent scrubbing returned my hands to more-or-less presentable condition.

Hoisting each leg in turn up to the sink to sluice off the mud, I gave thanks that there was nobody to witness my skirt riding up to my waist in the process.

My cleanup felt far too slow, but it couldn't have been more than a few minutes later when I did a rapid clean-up of the sink and floor with wads of toilet tissue.

I pasted on a smile and emerged from the bathroom. "Thank you so much. I'll get out of your hair now. I really appreciate you taking me in."

Lois rose from the soft leather loveseat that graced the small grouping of furniture in front of an impressive stone fireplace. "You look a lot better. Here..." She delved into her purse and handed me a small tube. "Put some concealer on that scratch and you'll be as good as new."

Chafing at the delay, I followed her instructions. All part of the plan to fit in, I admonished myself. Stay calm. Stay professional.

When I returned the concealer, she held out a black sweater. "Here, put this on. You're still shivering."

"Oh, no, it's okay. Thanks, though." I held onto my smile and moved not-too-subtly toward the door. "I'll be fine as soon as I get back to the party. You know how warm it is in a crowd like that."

Lois nodded and slid her feet into a flat-heeled version of the pumps she'd worn earlier. "Okay, if you're sure." She sighed and followed me to the door. "I can hardly wait to call it a night." She pulled the door closed behind us and added, "I hate these parties. I thought I'd be done with them when I retired, but I got roped into this by a charity I volunteer with."

"Mm-hm," I mumbled, my mind fully engaged in worrying about Nichele.

A moment later I repressed the urge to smack myself in the forehead when I realized Lois had given me a perfect opportunity. Instead of slinking into the party like the pariah I was, I could be Super-Spy Jane Bond, strolling in chatting with an invited guest as though I belonged.

Tuning back into the conversation, I used my best party manners to draw out Lois's love of music, gardens, and grandchildren on the way back to the main house, thankful that her sarcastic wit made for easy banter.

When we stepped laughing into the grand ballroom, a waiter bearing a tray of wineglasses descended on us immediately. "Would you care for some Chardonnay?"

Lois gave him a smile and accepted a glass. "Thank you. My favourite!"

"Um, sure. Thanks." I took a glass, too, pretending to sip while I studied the party with my heart pounding.

A middle-aged woman hailed Lois, who turned to engage in the conversation. As soon as her attention was elsewhere I eased out a breath.

The wineglass was trembling in my fingers, and I willed it to steady. Get with the program. Jane Bond would be coolly cataloguing the situation in a single blink of her sophisticated eyelashes; not standing here shaking in her too-small shoes and trying not to spill wine down the front of her stolen dress.

Then again, Jane Bond wouldn't have bumbled around kidnapping dummies and impersonating bears, either. And she probably didn't have any friends as dear as Nichele...

I pushed away the babblings of my nervous brain and squared my shoulders. Focus.

With a pleasant shock, I realized I actually had been analyzing the situation while the foolish part of my mind was occupied. Thank God. Maybe I was getting better at this spy stuff.

I already knew the physical layout of the house, and the surveillance cameras were still where I remembered them. And Nichele had been right about the security personnel.

In the ballroom alone there were six goons in dark suits, blending into the cultured crowd approximately as well as toads in a bowl of cream. I'd seen another pair patrolling the path on the way over, and there were likely more of them down by the gazebo and pond. All this in addition to Harchman's regular uniformed security guards.

Wow. Either somebody was really paranoid, or...

An iron hand closed around my upper arm, not painful enough to make me yelp, but tight enough to mean business. My heart leaped up to vibrate in my throat as the giant owner of the hand leaned down to growl in my ear.

"Please come with me. Don't make a scene."

CHAPTER 9

Heart hammering, I glared up at the mountain of business-suited gorilla attached to my arm and spoke just below a pitch that would attract instant attention in the hum of polite conversation. "Total screaming meltdown launching in three... two..."

He unhanded me, scowling, and spoke into his comm link. "Mr. Harchman? She says she's going to make a scene."

"Give me that." I snatched the link, stretching the curly cord behind his ear to its limit as I stood on tiptoe to snarl into it. "Larry, you slimy little bastard, get your ass out here before I tell all your fancy friends about your porn empire and how you're screwing me-"

The gorilla recoiled, jerking the link out of my grasp and staring open-mouthed.

"...out of my share of the profits," I finished for his benefit, and added, "Trust me, I wouldn't screw that pencil-dicked little shitbag if he was the last man on earth."

"Uh... okay..." His gaze darted sideways as though he'd just discovered a scorpion and was deciding whether to flee or crush it.

Apparently the intellectual challenge was too great, and he spoke into the link again. "Uh, Mr. Harchman, what do you want me to...? Okay, I'll tell her."

He returned his attention to me. "He said, don't make a scene, he's coming."

"He'd better not be," I growled. "I've seen him do that, and it nearly made me puke."

"Uh..." The gorilla's prominent brow ridge furrowed. "But you just finished telling him to c- ...Oh." A tide of red surged up his cheeks all the way to the tip of his nose. "Gross! I mean, uh..." He pulled himself together, giving me a curt nod. "He'll be right with you." He turned on his heel and strode away.

"Is everything okay?" Lois's voice penetrated my adrenaline rush. "What was that all about?"

"Uh..." Rapidly shifting gears, I put on a smile and turned to face her and her companion. "Yes, everything's fine. He was just making sure I was all right after my fall."

"Oh, good." Lois's smile returned. "Aydan, this is Gwendolyn Kennedy. She's the owner and CEO of..."

I glimpsed Lawrence Harchman hurrying into the ballroom, his tubby little body straining upright as if attempting to add a few inches to his inadequate height. He stalled momentarily beside a group of well-dressed men, offering handshakes and backslaps that seemed more tolerated than welcome, and I refocused on Lois in time to hear her name the second-largest petroleum company in Calgary.

Gwendolyn offered me a gracious smile that made her look like an older and happier Princess Diana, complete with a gown and jewellery worthy of royalty. Feeling inferior, I plastered on a smile of my own and accepted her handshake just as Lois continued, "Oh, and there's Miles. Miles!" She waved, and a distinguished-looking man strolled over, smiling.   His immaculately-tailored suit and classic tie probably cost more than my car.

"Lois, nice to see you again." He gave her a warm handshake.

"You, too," Lois agreed. "Aydan, this is Gwendolyn's husband, Miles. He's the 'Kennedy' in Kennedy, Quade, and Harkness."

I managed not to choke. Holy shit, the biggest law firm in Calgary. And his wife was a petroleum magnate. High-rollers indeed.

"And Miles, this is Aydan Kelly," Lois said just as Lawrence Harchman arrived, his obviously-expensive tux and ostentatious diamond shirt studs looking déclassé beside Miles and Gwendolyn's understated elegance. Lois went on, "Aydan owns a bookkeeping firm."

I gave her a grateful smile. She'd made it sound more prestigious than it really was, and better still, she'd cued Harchman to the name I was currently using.

"Nice to meet you, Miles," I said with my best smile and handshake. Harchman was eyeing me with barely-concealed hostility, and I included him in my smile with an effort. "I suppose everyone here knows Lawrence, our host?"

"Don't believe we've had the pleasure," Miles said, triggering a fresh round of introductions.

A few minutes of chitchat ensued, with Harchman alternately fawning and backslapping after learning the identities of our companions. The Kennedys were far too well-bred to show any obvious distaste, but I could read their aversion in the subtle pinching around their eyes.

"And how do you and Lawrence know each other?" Miles asked me, seizing a momentary break in Harchman's latest self-aggrandizing story.

I gave Harchman a pointy-toothed smile that made him stutter to a halt. "Lawrence and I share some business interests."

"Yes," Harchman interrupted hurriedly, paling. "And we won't bore you with them, but Ar-" He bit off the name and substituted, "...Aydan and I do have some business to discuss tonight, so we'll have to excuse ourselves. It was very nice to meet you, Gwendolyn, my dear..."

He took her hand and kissed it, and I marvelled at her self-control. When he'd bestowed his moist grip and slimy kiss on my hand last year, I'd nearly gagged. Gwendolyn's pleasant smile didn't even waver; but then again, maybe he hadn't slipped her the tongue.

I nearly gagged all over again at the memory.

Apparently concluding that Lois wasn't of sufficient social standing to merit his attention, Harchman excluded her from the hand-kissing. Considering the dangerous glint in her eye, that decision probably saved him some discomfort.

"Miles..." Harchman offered him a handshake combined with a chummy squeeze of Miles's upper arm that caused a miniscule twitch in the other man's eyelid.

Oblivious, Harchman released him with a hearty backslap. "So nice to meet you." He turned to include Gwendolyn in his smarmy smile. "Please have another drink, both of you. Have lots! Mi casa es tu casa," he gushed, using the overly-familiar pronoun either out of ignorance of Spanish or complete disregard for courtesy. Babbling on, he racked up even more boor-demerits. "And make sure you try that Almas caviar. I imported it straight from Iran. It costs over thirty thousand dollars a kilo, but nothing's too good for my guests, and after all, what good is money if you don't spread it around? You can't take it with you, ha, ha..."

He linked his arm through mine in a show of friendship and I leaned down and hissed, "Off!" in his ear.

He released me as if my arm was red-hot. "Well, it was nice to meet you all," he repeated nervously. "Please excuse us..."

I took my time with the parting pleasantries to my new friends.

When we drifted away from the threesome at last, Harchman shot me a venomous look. "What the hell are you doing here? How did you get in?"

"Why so rude, Larry? Aren't you glad to see me?"

He drew himself up to his full unimpressive height, nearly half a foot shorter than me in my heels.

"You know I prefer Lawrence," he said stiffly.

I gave him a sorrowing look and rested my hand fondly on his shoulder, close to his throat. He flinched, sweat dewing his upper lip.

"Larry," I repeated. "Larry, Larry, Larry. My old buddy. My honest and dependable business partner." I leaned down to look him in the eye, smiling, and dug my thumb into the sensitive spot above his collarbone. "You can pay thirty grand for stinking fish eggs, but you can't pay me on time? Where the fuck is my cheque?"

He twitched and squeaked, casting a panicked glance around the room.

The gorilla who had accosted me earlier moved in our direction, but Harchman waved him off, apparently still trying to maintain the appearance of a powerful man in control of his own destiny. Little did he know he'd been Fuzzy Bunny's puppet for the past decade or so.

Speaking of which...

My heart sank at the sight of Tawny Harchman giggling and wiggling through the crowd. Her bottle-blonde hair cascaded down her back in a rat's nest of artful tangles that had probably taken hours to achieve, and her freakishly overinflated lips were painted brilliant scarlet. The resemblance to a baboon's ass was striking, and if I hadn't feared for both Nichele's life and my own, I would have choked on a snicker.

But I didn't feel much like laughing as she squirmed sensuously up to us in her skintight dress, batting thick false eyelashes at every male within range.

"Hi, Pookie-Poo," she cooed at Harchman. "Remember me?"

"Of course, my darling. How could I forget?" He leaned in and they rubbed noses, making 'ootsie-cootsie' noises at each other.

"Hi, Tawny," I said, hoping to make them stop.

Harchman wrapped an arm around her and shot me a triumphant 'see what you're missing' look, as though I should be properly chagrined by my inability to land a man of his obvious attractiveness.

Tawny gave me a blank stare, her vapid baby-blues wide. "Have we met?"

"Just once before," I assured her. "And only for a few seconds."

"Oh." She batted her eyelashes at me. "Wow, you've got a good memory! I don't remember you at all. But..." She giggled and wiggled some more. "I've had a little too much champagne and it always makes me..." She tilted her head and assumed a little-girl lisp. "A wittle silly."

"But I love you anyway, sweetums." Harchman patted

her bottom indulgently, utterly blind to the calculating manipulation behind her bubble-head act.

"Awww, I wuv you too, Pookie-Poo!" She wrapped herself around him, squashing silicone-enhanced boobs that looked in imminent danger of exploding.

Her boobs; not his. Though his man-boobs did seem even rounder and fuller than the last time I'd seen him...

Tawny interrupted my distasteful reverie with a breathy giggle. "Pookie, where are your manners? Aren't you going to introduce me?" She extended a scarlet-taloned hand. "I'm Tawny. Pookie-Poo's wife."

I didn't bother to point out that I'd just finished addressing her by name. "Nice to meet you, Tawny. I'm Aydan."

"*Aiding?* That's a funny name. Do you help people a lot?"

"Uh-huh," I said straight-faced. "All the time. Right, Larry?"

Harchman gave me a stiff smile and an even stiffer nod.

"As a matter of fact," I went on, "I was just aiding Pookie-Poo here with his memory. He must've had a bit too much champagne tonight, too."

"Oh, Pookie." Tawny made a sad face. "Did you forget something important?"

"Nothing important at all, my dear," Harchman said, sending a quelling glance my way. "Arlene and I were just finishing up."

"Arlene?" The bimbo-blues narrowed for just an instant before clouding over in her ingenuous act again. "But I thought your name was Aiding."

"Arlene is Pookie's pet name for me," I explained with a vindictive glance at Harchman. "We were very close... before he married you. But even now he still calls me by my pet name, just for old time's sake. Don't you, *Pookie-Poo*?"

Red suffused Harchman's face and a vein bulged in his forehead. "Tawny, sweetums, why don't you go and get another glass of champagne?" he asked in a strangled voice. "*Aydan* and I are just finishing up our business. We'll only be a minute, and then she's leaving."

"But Pookie..." Tawny went into her little-girl act again, eyes wide and lower lip sticking out like some grotesque scarlet tumour. "You *pwomised* I could sit in on your business deals. You *pwomised* you wuvved me for my mind as well as my body."

Aha, so she had wormed her way into his business deals. Clever girl. I kept my expression bland while Harchman attempted to extricate himself.

"And I do love you for your mind, Sweetums, I do!" The vein in his forehead throbbed in a rapid rhythm. "But you already heard what nasty lies Aydan tells, and I don't want you to hear such unpleasantness. You can sit in on my next business deal as usual, I promise. Okay, Sweetums?"

She blew out a breath, lower lip still protruding like a disappointed little girl, but something sharp and ugly glittered in the look she shot me from under her false eyelashes. "Okay, Pookie," she cooed. "I know you're always right. I just *wish* I could be as smart as you!"

Harchman puffed up his repulsive chest with a triumphant glance my way, and the two parted with another exaggerated show of affection.

As soon as Tawny was out of earshot, Harchman turned to me with a huffy expression that didn't quite mask the twitchy nervousness in his eyes. "How dare you trespass on my private function? These people are my dear friends and valued business associates..."

"And I'm sure they'd all be very interested to find out how we know each other," I agreed. "Wouldn't they be shocked to find out how you faked porn videos of an innocent woman and then sold them for your own profit..."

"Innocent!" he interrupted. "That's a laugh, after you and your accomplice tried to steal the last app I released! You're just a common criminal-"

"Just like you," I snapped. "You're lucky I decided to share the profits instead of calling the cops and pressing charges. Now where's my cheque? And where's Nichele?"

"Nichele?" He sniffed. "I have no idea who you're talking about. I certainly wouldn't have anything to do with any of your... *associates.*"

I threw a friendly arm over his shoulders and leaned close, slowly tightening my grip as I ground out, "Listen, you disgusting little blob of scum on the cesspool of humanity, one more crack like that and I'm going to pop your head off your shoulders like the pus-filled zit it is. Now *where's Nichele?*"

He let out a squeak, his sweaty neck disgustingly slippery against the bare skin of my arm. "I'm sorry, I'm sorry, I honestly don't know who you're talking about!"

I sighed and eased my grip. He wasn't smart enough to fake that kind of confusion. Damn. Maybe I should lean on Tawny. But she wouldn't be nearly as easy to bully...

Harchman was still babbling. "...and I'm sorry about your cheque, I'll write it out right away; it's just that when the videos went viral, I made... I mean, you and I... *we...* made a lot of money but they aren't very popular anymore so I'm... we're not making that much off them..."

"Right, whatever," I growled. "Cheque. Now. And then

I'm going to go and socialize, so don't piss me off or I'll make a big scene."

"I rue the day I set eyes on you," he muttered, slipping a chequebook out of the inside pocket of his tuxedo jacket to scribble out a cheque.

"Trust me, the feeling is mutual." Tucking the cheque into my purse, I turned to survey the thinning crowd in the ballroom and added, "You're just lucky I've never decided to audit your books to see if you're cheating me."

He went sheet-white. "Of... of course I'm not," he stammered, dabbing at fresh beads of perspiration that dotted his brow. "I would never..."

"Of course you would," I said tiredly. "You'd screw your own mother out of her last penny. Hell, never mind that; you'd screw your own mother, period. You make me want to puke."

As I turned away from him, I spotted a tuxedoed Benoit Riel coming through one of the french doors, laughing over his shoulder at an unseen companion as he slipped a cell phone into his pocket.

A metallic red cell phone with a pattern of rhinestone-studded high-heeled shoes.

Nichele's phone.

CHAPTER 10

My heart thudded to the bottom of my belly, leaving a desolate hollow in my chest.

Frozen, I stared at Riel's laughing face while rage rose like magma from the centre of my being.

Nichele. He had Nichele.

The tiny human firecracker who had been my best friend since childhood. One of the few who had stuck by me even when my disastrous first marriage became a prison of isolation...

I was across the room before I even realized I was moving, my gun hard inside the purse I was clenching in one fist.

Control. Don't shoot him in front of all these witnesses...

Riel turned, surprise flashing across his face before he relaxed into a smile.

"Ah, Ms. Widdenback," he said in a French-Canadian accent that might have been delightful if I hadn't been moments away from pumping him full of lead. "'Ow nice that we meet."

He extended his hand, but his smile wavered at the sight of my expression.

"Where is she?" I hissed.

"Give that back, you big goof!" The cheeky admonition

was delivered in a familiar voice that made my heart clutch with fierce relief. An instant later Nichele scurried into the ballroom and made a beeline for Riel.

"Ah-ah-ah!" He returned Nichele's grin and extracted her phone from his pocket to dangle teasingly a couple of feet above her head. "Non, chérie, I won it square and fair."

"You cheated!" she teased in return. Then she caught sight of me and her mouth dropped open. "*Aydan?* What are you doing here?" She recovered quickly and a devilish sparkle lit her eyes as her gaze bounced between Riel and me. "Well. I guess there's no need for an introduction here," she added.

Riel's eyes narrowed for a bare instant, summing up the situation. "Of course not," he said smoothly. "*Aydan* and I were just catching up on the old times." He gave the name a slight emphasis and moved closer as if to gauge my reaction.

"Well, yeah, um... great to see you again," I mumbled, backing away. "Sorry to take Nichele away from you, but I just need to talk to her for a minute."

"Of course." He inclined his head graciously. "I 'ope we can talk again soon. Nichele, ma chérie, I shall keep this phone as a trophy until you return."

She pitched her voice to a ridiculous bass and assumed an Arnold Schwarzenegger accent. "I'll be back!"

He smiled and wiggled the cell phone at her. "Soon, I 'ope."

I clamped a hand on Nichele's arm and dragged her away, trying to look nonchalant.

"Aydan, what are you doing here?" Nichele demanded. "And whose clothes are you wearing? Those shoes are, like, two sizes too small! I swear, girl, I can't let you out of my sight! I thought you hated dressing up, hated business parties, hated Benoit, and hated Lawrence Harchman." She wrinkled her nose. "But you're right about Icky-Lawrence. Ew!"

My heart still thumping too fast, I managed a squeaky chuckle. "I know; right? What a slimeball." Fighting the adrenaline-jangled nerves that made me want to take her by the arms and shake her, I kept my tone casual. "I tried to call you earlier. Why didn't you answer?"

"That was you?" Nichele grimaced. "Why were you calling from that weird number? You made me lose the game."

Shit, of course; I'd called from the burner phone.

"What game?" I inquired, hanging onto my patience.

"After I finished talking to you earlier, Benoit and I started a contest that whoever looked at their cellphone first would have to give it up for the rest of the night. At least if I'd known it was you I would've picked up. Instead I rejected the call but he said he'd won anyway because I looked at it."

My pulse picked up and I shot a glance over my shoulder at Riel. Was this a ploy to somehow steal data from Nichele's phone? Oh, God, if he downloaded all her contacts, how could I possibly protect everyone?

He appeared absorbed in conversation with another man, but as I watched he glanced up, meeting my eyes in a cool appraisal. Then one of his eyelids twitched in a fractional wink and he returned his attention to his companion.

Nichele nudged me, grinning. "Go on, you can't take your eyes off him, can you? Admit it. He's hot. Hottie-Benoitty."

"Oh, come on, Nichele!" I objected. "He's just an ordinary middle-aged guy. Even a suit-slut like you can't be that blinded by expensive clothes."

"It's not just the suit. It's the suit *and* that French charm *and* that sexy accent!" She flung a dramatic hand to her forehead and faked a swoon. "Oooh-la-la!" She straightened and leaned closer. "And he's still interested in you, I can tell. What was so bad about your blind date, anyway? He's a lot of fun; I can't imagine why you didn't have a good time."

"We just didn't click," I mumbled.

She sighed. "Seriously, you've got Hot John and Dante the Inferno and Hottie-Benoitty on a string and you're still shagging Mister Ugly? What am I going to do with you?"

As if sensing my irritation, she sobered, staring at me as though seeing me for the first time. "Aydan... You're really in love with Arnie, aren't you? That's why you won't even look at anybody else." She threw her arms around me. "I'm sorry, but you had me fooled with that whole no-commitment thing. It's great that you and Arnie are together. You've been alone for 'way too long."

"We're not together," I protested, feeling what little control I had over the conversation slipping away. "Anyway, it doesn't matter. Forget it." I hugged her back, worry and affection making my embrace tighter than usual. "Can I bunk in your room tonight? My buddy Lawrence didn't offer me a place to stay."

"Well hell yeah, girl!" She drew back, her smile dissolving into a mock-serious frown. "Which brings me back to my original question. What are you doing here? How did you get in without a ticket?"

"Um... I was worried about you, so I sneaked in."

Nichele's eyes danced. "You're such a goofball! How did you get past the guards in the gatehouse? And where did you get a pair of too-small Manolo Blahnicks and a Valentino evening gown?"

Dammit, only my shitty luck would make me rob some fancy designer place. I had been hoping it was just an anonymous little hole-in-the-wall with suitably nameless clothes.

"Tell you later," I whispered as another dark-suited gorilla lumbered purposefully toward us.

Shit, what did he want? Was he going to throw me out despite my threat of a screaming meltdown?

I held my breath as he strode up, but instead of grabbing my arm he offered me a deferential inclination of his chin. "Mr. Harchman was concerned that you couldn't find your friend so he has authorized me to take you to the security control room. We can check the closed-circuit cameras and see if we can spot her."

Yeah, right. And as soon as I was separated from the hoity-toity guests, Harchman had undoubtedly also authorized the gorilla to pitch me out on my ass.

I smiled up at him, radiating goodwill. "Oh, thank you, that's so kind of you and Lawrence! But you can tell him it's okay, I've found her."

"Oh." He shuffled his feet. "Um... Okay. Good..."

He drifted away, muttering into his comm link, and Nichele's face softened into fondness. "You really were worried about me, weren't you? And look at you, all dolled up even though I know how much you hate it. You're such a good friend!" She gave me one of her trademark bearhugs. "Come on, let's go get my phone back from Benoit."

"Yeah, let's," I agreed, trying not to let the grimness show in my voice.

I obviously didn't succeed.

Nichele laughed. "Come on, you can make polite

conversation with an ex-date for a few minutes. It's not like you're facing a firing squad."

"Let's hope not," I muttered, and followed her through the few remaining clusters of guests.

My heart sank at the sight of Tawny and Riel with their heads together. Comparing notes; and it didn't take a genius to figure out the topic of their conversation.

Tawny glanced over at us and laughed, her brassy giggle rising over the music and conversation.

"Aiding!" she greeted me enthusiastically as we arrived. "I was wondering where you went! Come on, let's have some girl talk!" She linked arms with me and headed for the door.

"Whoa, slow down," I protested, hanging back and grasping at the first plausible delay that came to mind. "Nichele, have you met Lawrence's wife Tawny?"

"Yes," Nichele replied. "Hi again, Tawny..."

"Hi," Tawny interrupted. "Come on, Aiding, let's go!"

Short of wrestling her to the ground, I couldn't see any way to avoid going with her. And while I was damn sure Riel knew I'd recognized him, I was equally damn sure that Tawny didn't know I was clued into her criminal connections. Playing along was my best bet.

Assuming, of course, that she wasn't luring me away so she could have her goons kill me and quietly dispose of my body...

With a feeble wave to Nichele, I let Tawny drag me away.

Apparently instant death wasn't on the agenda. We had barely cleared the door of the ballroom when Tawny turned to me, eyes glittering. "Are you putting the moves on my Pookie-Poo?"

The question was so unexpected that a bark of laughter escaped me. "God, no! I wouldn't touch him with a..."

Belatedly recovering, I cut off the insult with a cough and finished, "...devoted wife like you on his arm. That would just be sleazy."

"You'd better not." Her eyes slitted. "He's mine, and I don't share."

Nodding gravely, I agreed, "I totally get it. I wouldn't either if I was married."

"Oh..." Slightly deflated, she squinted at me as if trying to figure out what other evil designs I might have on her Pookie-Poo.

I had to admire her act. I almost believed she was just a conniving bimbo trying to hang onto a rich husband.

Almost, but not quite.

"What did you mean when you said earlier that you and Pookie were close?" she demanded.

I made a split-second decision to stir the pot and see what surfaced. "I meant he faked porn videos of us together and sold them on the internet. That kind of close."

"*You made porn videos with my Pookie?*" Her shriek of outrage would have done any actress proud. Her fingers crooked into scarlet-tipped claws.

"No, I said he faked them!" I backed away, afraid I'd lose an eye if she came at me with those talons. "I never touched him." A demon of vindictiveness seized me and I lowered my voice. "But he damn well touched me. Groped me all over, and he was married at the time. You'd better watch him."

"You're lying! My Pookie would never do that!"

"Yeah, he would." I took a chance. "You know what men are like."

Something flared deep in those baby-blues; a flash of something bitter and angry that wasn't directed at me.

An instant later it was gone, replaced by bimbo-Tawny's

wide-eyed indignation. "My Pookie isn't like that."

I shrugged. "Maybe you're right. People change. And you're much nicer to him than his previous wife."

A self-satisfied smile spread across her face. "I'm the best wife *ever*. And Pookie wuvs-wuvs-*wuvs* me! So is that what your business was about tonight?"

The pointed question didn't quite fit her air of innocent ditziness, but I went with it anyway.

"Yeah. He pays me part of the money he makes every month on the porn videos."

Tawny crossed her arms and stuck out her chin as if she'd won an important round in the conversation. "See, I *told* you my Pookie was a good man."

"Uh, yeah. Right. Well, nice talking to you, Tawny, but I want to get back to the party now-"

"How did you get in?" she interrupted. "Pookie didn't invite you, and I sure didn't."

Uh-oh.

I widened my eyes and went for ingenuous. "I sneaked in. I'm sorry, but when I called Nichele earlier she told me what a great party it was, and I really wanted to come."

True, if not complete. At least Riel could confirm that Nichele had talked to me earlier.

A frown fought the botox between Tawny's eyebrows. "You can't just *sneak in*. We have security guards. The only way in is past the gatehouse."

"Yeah, I know..."

I sure as hell wasn't going to point out the weak spot in their security. My pulse thumped in my ears while I cast about for a convenient lie, but nothing came immediately to mind.

"Um... that's the way I came in, though," I added lamely.

"Past the gatehouse."

"You're lying." As if realizing her bimbo act had slipped, Tawny batted her false eyelashes at me and backpedalled. "Come on, Aiding, tell me how you did it! I love playing hide-and-seek with the guards!"

"I wasn't playing hide-and-seek," I insisted. "I just came in through the gate like everybody else..." Inspiration struck, and I added, "With a man. I found a single man and got him to bring me in."

"Which man?"

"I don't know. I wasn't interested in his name; I just seduced him long enough to get through the gate in his car."

Tawny let out a contemptuous snort. "You're far too old for that to work. Look at you. You've got wrinkles around your eyes and mouth and grey in your hair..." Her critical gaze tracked downward. "Your boobs are pretty good for your age, I guess, but they're not big enough. You should get a boob job like mine." She thrust out her chest and I suppressed the urge to throw up my hands in self-defense when her prominent nipples took aim at me.

"It did work, though." I shrugged and took another potshot at the bitter creature behind her eyes. "You know what men are like; they don't care what you look like as long as they get some."

"You have to look good if you're going to get anything out of them long-term," she snapped. As if realizing she'd slipped out of character once too often, she scowled. "It's time for you to leave." Pressing a button on the intercom beside us, she assumed her little-girl voice again. "Hello, secuwity? Will you pwease come and help my wittle fwiend back to her car? Thank-you!"

"I have to tell Nichele I'm leaving or she'll worry," I

argued, sidling toward the ballroom door.

Tawny gave a brittle laugh as another suit-clad goon materialized in the doorway. "Nice try. You can call her when you're outside the gate." She turned to the goon. "Aiding left her car outside the gate. Will you pwease dwive her back to it?"

He nodded and gestured toward another door, effectively blocking the door to the ballroom with his bulk. "This way, please."

Dammit.

Heart thumping, I gave him a pleasant smile. Should I kick up a stink or just go quietly? What would a real agent do?

What would Kane do?

Kane would stay cool. He'd never blow his cover this early in a mission.

Cool. Stay cool.

"Thanks." I widened my smile to include both Tawny and the goon. "Tawny, it was nice talking to you, and thanks for the escort. See you later."

"Oh, I *hope* so!" Tawny gave me a theatrical hug and air-kisses on both cheeks. "You know I like seeing you just as much as my Pookie-Poo does!"

No doubt that was true.

"Right," I agreed.

"And have a safe dwive home. We wouldn't want anything to *happen* to you," she added with a smile that glittered like ice.

Shit, was that a code phrase telling the goon to *make* something happen to me?

Clutching my purse with the gun inside it, I breathed through a surge of adrenaline as the goon touched my elbow and escorted me out.

CHAPTER 11

As we wound through the labyrinthine house, my pulse pounded. Was the goon taking me into some soundproofed room where he could kill me unobtrusively?

Drawing a deep breath, I countered my own nervous speculation. So what if he did take me to a soundproofed room? It just meant I'd be able to shoot him without attracting unwanted attention.

And anyway, if he'd been intent on mayhem, wouldn't he have searched me for weapons? Any hitman with half a brain would have confiscated my purse, finding my gun in the process.

Dammit, I really needed to get a holster I could strap to my thigh under a dress...

"Ma'am?" the goon inquired politely, touching my arm. I twitched violently and he snatched his hand back. "I'm sorry, I didn't mean to startle you."

Patting my heart back into place, I attempted a light laugh. "It's okay, I was just a million miles away. Thinking about... um... accessories for this dress."

He nodded without interest and opened a door for me, revealing a six-car garage containing several gleaming black limos. He hurried ahead to open the rear door of the nearest one, then handed me in before closing the door softly and rounding the car to slide into the driver's seat.

I eyed the exposed back of his head. Either he was stupidly confident about his abilities to subdue me, or else he had no intention of trying. And I was pretty sure no assassin would be dumb enough to expose his back to his mark.

Easing into the leather upholstery, I pulled the burner phone out of my purse and dialled Nichele's cell phone. Even if Riel was still holding it hostage, maybe he'd let her answer...

"Hello, this is Nichele Brown."

Her voice made me suck in a breath of relief. Thank God.

"Hi, Nichele." My throat was dry and I had to swallow before my voice came out in the light tone I'd intended. "Guess who just got busted and escorted out?"

Her laugh bubbled over the phone. "Seriously, girl? Your buddy Lawrence threw you out?"

"Seriously," I agreed, declining to mention Tawny's involvement. The less Nichele knew about Tawny's real identity, the better. "I told you he didn't like me. So thanks anyway, but I won't be bunking with you tonight." Aware that my chauffeur was listening, I raised my voice just a fraction. "But call me when you're turning in for the night, and again in the morning, okay? And call Dave, too. He'll be expecting to hear from you."

There, that was the best I could do to ensure her safety. If they knew she'd be instantly missed maybe they wouldn't try anything...

"I will," Nichele promised. "But you're worrying for nothing. I couldn't be safer here."

"I know, but indulge me. Have fun, and I'll talk to you soon. Call me at this number; I accidentally left my own phone in Calgary."

"Okey-dokey. Have fun driving home in disgrace in the middle of the night," she teased.

Grinning in spite of myself, I gave her a fond, "Shut up", and hung up on her laughter.

"Ma'am?" The chauffeur eyed me in the rearview mirror. "Where did you leave your car?"

I hesitated.

It was cold and pitch dark, and I was in ill-fitting high heels with no jacket. Already I had blisters on my feet and I was shivering. If I didn't get him to take me directly to my car, I'd end up hypothermic, crippled, or both by the time I walked there. But did I want him to know where I'd parked?

"Ma'am?" he prompted.

"Sorry... it's dark out and I came in with a friend," I stalled. "I'm just trying to figure out where I left my car. It was a turnoff around here somewhere..." I peered earnestly out the tinted window at the black-on-black landscape.

Fuck it. I was exhausted and my night was far from over. If he tried anything, I'd just shoot him.

"There!" I pointed to the gravelled road that led to the small clearing where I'd parked.

He took the turn at a decorous pace and moored the giant limo beside my Subaru Legacy. Opening the door for me again, he remained standing beside the limo.

I slid into the Legacy and gave him a wave, hoping he couldn't see my fingers trembling in the headlights. "Thanks for the ride!"

"You're welcome." He gave me a deferential half-bow but didn't get back in the limo. Clearly I was to be supervised until I was on my way.

Suppressing a sigh, I put my car in gear and headed for

the highway.

The limo's headlights followed me, then remained stationary at the intersection while I turned east toward Calgary.

Shit. Watching me out of sight.

Letting out a small whine of tension and exhaustion, I kept driving until a hill hid his headlights behind me.

Damn, damn, damn.

How long would he wait to make sure I didn't come back? I'd have to find a different access to the creek and get back inside the security perimeter to retrieve my duffel bag.

I hissed out a slow breath between my teeth, considering. Could I get Nichele to grab it for me?

No. She might be able to sneak it into her room tonight; but when she checked out, a muddy black duffel bag beside her fashionable designer suitcases would attract far too much attention. And anyway, Riel might have bugged her phone.

And speaking of bugs...

Pulling over, I activated my scanning device and let out a breath of relief at the sight of its green light. Okay, so at least they weren't tracking me.

Well, probably not...

Unless they were tracing my burner phone now that they'd gotten the number from my call to Nichele. And dammit, I had to carry it because I wouldn't get Nichele's goodnight call otherwise...

Unleashing a string of profanity, I thumped my fist against the steering wheel.

Was I being too paranoid? Or not paranoid enough?

A deep longing filled me. If Kane were here, I could defer to his expertise...

"Let it go," I muttered.

Should I call Holt? He had the field experience I needed.

I weighed the phone in my hand.

But did I dare reveal my lack of confidence? Bad way to start an already-shaky mission. If it had been a life-threatening situation, maybe, but it was just a simple decision that any experienced agent would make without a second thought...

No.

And I wasn't going to call Stemp in the middle of the night to tell him I'd gotten chucked out on my ass before I could discover any useful mission-related intel, either, dammit.

Hissing out a harsh breath, I stuffed the phone back in my purse and put the car in gear.

After a frustrating hour of driving up and down dead-end roads, I finally discovered another clearing where I could park my car within hiking distance of the creek. Turning off the ignition with a sigh, I leaned my aching head against the headrest for a moment.

If anybody was tracking my burner phone they'd know by now what I was doing, and I could expect an unfriendly reception. Not only that, but I'd lose the advantage of my secret access point.

Groaning, I hauled myself out of the driver's seat and plodded to the trunk. Too late to worry about it. I'd just have to trust to luck.

And so far luck seemed on my side, more or less. At least I had my winter-driving emergency kit in the back so I didn't have to make the trip in high heels and an evening dress. Shivering, I hauled the kit out and surveyed my resources glumly.

The parka and ski pants were bright green.

Mental note: Invest in some Jane-Bond-approved basic black cold-weather gear.

My boots would be far more comfortable than the too-small slingbacks, but they were giant Sorels rated to 60 degrees below zero. Trekking the muddy creek would be like wading through quicksand wearing a concrete block strapped to each foot.

I sighed. No choice.

Hiking up the ski pants under my dress, I slid my feet into the boots, donned the parka and set out.

Only a few paces away, I slapped my forehead and turned back to transfer my gun, phone, and keys into my parka pockets.

God, how much dumber could I get?

I hovered beside the car. What other sleep-deprived idiocy might I be committing?

After a few minutes of intense thought, I popped the trunk again and dumped out my sleeping bag before pocketing its storage sack. At least the sack was navy blue. I could use it to conceal my head and some of the green parka for my next bear impersonation.

With any luck the guards watching the security cameras would be as tired as I was. They might not look too closely at a bear, especially if they'd already heard there was one in the area. I offered a silent thank-you to the ursaphobic guard who had undoubtedly told everyone who would listen about his near-mauling.

After only ten minutes of hiking, my shivering was nothing but a fond memory.

Sweat tickled unpleasantly in my cleavage and dribbled down my temples and backbone. The heavy boots dragged at my feet and the swish-swish of my strides in the nylon ski pants sounded loud enough to alert the whole county.

I was peering anxiously around me when the nerve-shattering ring of the burner phone nearly stopped my heart. Snatching the phone out of my pocket, I muted it with a glance at the display before accepting the call.

"Hey, girl, it's Nichele. Just checking in on your paranoia."

I smiled in spite of myself. "My paranoia's alive and well. Are you calling it a night now?"

"Yep. All locked into my room."

"Alone?"

"Of course I'm alone!" Hurt and indignation fought for ascendancy in her tone. "I'd *never* cheat on Dave!"

"No, no, I know! That's not what I meant," I said hurriedly. "No; I just meant... you're by yourself and in for the night, right? You're not going to pop over to anybody's room for a nightcap, or let anybody in...?"

"No, you goof." Fond indulgence had returned to her voice. "I'm done like dinner. My makeup's off, and you know I'd never let anybody but you and Dave see me like that."

"Okay, good. Sleep tight, then. Call me before you start your seminars in the morning."

"I will. Are you home, too?"

"Almost," I lied. "I'm staying at Arnie's place tonight."

"Okay. Goodnight, Ms. Paranoid."

"Goodnight, Ms. Party Animal."

After I disconnected I stood straining my ears for a long moment. Nobody lunged out of the wilderness waving flashlights or firearms, so I resumed my tedious progress through the darkness.

By the time I had slogged along the cutbank and crept through the camera perimeter on all fours, I was so exhausted I couldn't have crawled in a straight line even if the thickets of diamond willow had permitted it.

Just a little farther. Then I could finally straighten up...

I blundered head-down along the creek, half-stifled by the nylon sleeping-bag sack. I was almost to the place where I'd been spotted by the foot patrol last time. Please, God, let them be on the other side of the property this time...

My hopes were dashed by the sound of male voices approaching. Dammit, they must have several teams rotating through the patrol.

Heart pounding, I crouched in the undergrowth with the sack over my hanging head.

Just a dark lump in the woods. Nothing to see here, guys. Just keep walking...

The flashlight swung my way. "There's that damn bear again!"

Oh, Jesus, no.

A gunshot shattered the silence of the night, catapulting me into frantic flight. Hunched over like Quasimodo with a bellyache, I crashed through the thickets and lurched across the creek.

Another shot rang out, followed by roars of laughter.

"Scared the shit out of it! Look at it go!"

"Gonna be a big pile of bear shit there tomorrow morning!"

More laughter, mercifully fading as they walked away.

Sucking air, I sank to the ground in a puddle of my own sweat.

"Mother... fucking... asshole..." My quiet invective hissed out between gasps. "Shove... that gun... right up... your..."

I froze at the sound of more distant voices approaching.

Christ, were they having a fucking party down here?

Snatches of conversation reached me.

"...discharging your firearm..."

"...bear... only fired in the air..."

"...get the dogs..."

Oh, no. No, no, no.

I'd forgotten about the goddamn dog patrol.

I couldn't remember the real name of this crummy little watercourse, but if they brought out the dogs it was Shit Creek to me; and I was far up it with no paddle to be found.

The thunder of my heart almost drowned out the voices.

"...Fish and Wildlife in the morning..."

The voices receded again, leaving me trembling in the undergrowth and straining my ears for the sound of barking.

Should I run?

Wouldn't that attract more attention?

But, shit, if the dogs caught my scent it wouldn't matter. I couldn't outrun them at the best of times, and with my giant boots and fatigued muscles I couldn't even outrun a crippled snail.

For long moments I sprawled panting on the ground. Gradually I got my breathing and heart rate under control. No barking disturbed the silence of the woods, and after a few more minutes I dragged myself into sitting position and took stock.

Maybe they weren't sending the dogs after all.

Or maybe the dogs were on the far side of the property and it was taking them a while to get here.

I drew a deep breath. Relax. They were looking for a

bear, not a human. The dogs wouldn't have any reason to hone in on an unidentified human scent.

My shoulders had just begun to ease down from around my ears when a horrid thought clenched my muscles into quivering knots all over again.

If they found my duffel bag, the dogs would have a scent to follow.

Shit!

Hauling myself to my feet, I staggered back across the creek and struck out uphill.

Trying to balance stealth with speed, I pushed my protesting muscles into an ungainly jog. The clumsy boots slipped on fallen trees and caught on unseen projections, and after a couple of hard falls I gave up and shuffled forward with more caution.

Despite the slower pace I was out of breath by the time the mellow light of the guesthouse glowed between the intervening tree trunks.

Panting as quietly as possible, I eased toward the tree where I'd left my duffel bag.

The doorman was still in position, and I spared a moment of sympathy for him standing out in the cold darkness all night long.

A moment later my charitable feelings evaporated.

The duffel bag was gone.

CHAPTER 12

Muttering violent profanity, I knelt beside the tree patting frantically over the prickly bed of spruce needles beneath it.

Gone. They'd found the goddamn bag.

Were they letting the dogs sniff it right now, committing my scent to memory before they hunted me down like an animal?

A shaft of warm light fingered through the trees as the doorman admitted a late-night guest, and I hunkered lower.

Wait a minute...

The door closed and I straightened, staring.

Then I squeezed my eyes shut in equal parts chagrin and relief. That beam of light had gone in a different direction than I'd expected.

Wrong tree, idiot.

I crept forward and to the left, and a moment later my grateful hands found the rough canvas of the bag.

Nearly weeping with relief, I skinned out of my inappropriate garments and exchanged them for my jeans, hiking boots, and Hellhound's big black parka. Wrestling icy wet denim up over my gooseflesh-pebbled legs was an exercise in misery, but at least my return trip would be quieter than my arrival.

The re-packed duffel weighed down my tired arm as if it was loaded with bricks, and I shifted it from hand to hand while I stumbled back down the hill.

A dog's distant bark froze me to the spot.

I flung up my head, listening with every cell of my body. My rapid breathing plumed silver in the cold air. Goddamn moon, pouring down light like a fucking lantern now that I *didn't* want it...

The barking sounded again.

Was it closer?

I couldn't tell.

"And don't hang around to find out, dipshit," I muttered, and turned to plunge down the hill at the fastest pace my aching muscles would allow.

I slowed as I approached the guards' usual patrol circuit and eased forward trying to stifle my panting.

No voices. No flashlight beams or gunshots.

Yet.

The back of my neck prickling, I scurried across the path and into the undergrowth by the creek.

A voice boomed out of the night. "Hey, was that the bear?"

Oh, God, not again.

Suppressing a whimper as a flashlight beam bored through the willows, I curled into a ball around the duffel bag.

"Nah. Too fast and quiet. Probably a deer."

The beam stabbed the bushes again but the crunch of approaching footsteps didn't slacken. When the second man spoke again, it sounded as though he was close enough to touch.

"Base, this is Team Three. Seen any bears on camera

lately? Over."

The crackle of a radio responded. "Nope. Didn't even see the one Vilquist said he scared off. Damn fool, discharging his weapon like that. You see any bears? Over."

"Nah. Just the usual bunch of deer." The crunch of footsteps receded along with the voice. "Vilquist's gonna get sacked for that, and good riddance. It's a friggin' miracle he hasn't shot one of us yet. Team Three out."

Silence fell again and I dared to move at last.

So they hadn't spotted the 'bear' on camera. Good.

Now I only had to follow the same route on the way out...

By the time I stumbled out of the creek bed the moon was sinking on the horizon, leaving velvet-black sky spangled with frosty stars. Clammy with cold sweat, my legs numb in the soggy denim, I shivered in the knife-like breeze while I tottered over to the car. Easing my protesting body into the driver's seat of my car, I cranked the heat on high before texting 'Clear' to Holt and hitting the road.

My dashboard clock read five AM when I pulled into the visitor's lot at Hellhound's condo at last. Moaning quietly, I persuaded my stiffened muscles to unbend, and limped toward the door.

When I shivered into the warmth of the apartment, Hooker yawned and stretched in his cozy nest of blankets on the sofa. Then he jumped down and padded over to the mud-caked duffel bag I'd dropped beside the door, his nose tracing its contours with rapt interest.

"Enjoy," I growled, and made a beeline for the bathroom where I dove into the shower and trembled under the hot spray until I felt sufficiently thawed.

I was almost to Hellhound's bed, eyes half-closed, when duty prodded me to check my cell phone and the burner phone I'd left behind. The message light was blinking on the burner phone, and I sighed and pressed the voicemail button.

My heart lurched at the sound of the smug voice oozing from the speaker. "Good evening, Ms. Widdenback, it's Frederick Labelle. I just had a call from our client. He arrived this evening and would like to arrange a meeting with you first thing tomorrow morning. Let's meet for breakfast at seven-thirty AM at the Petroleum Club. I'll look forward to seeing you there."

Thoughts of bed and sleep evaporated as I stared at the phone.

"What the hell?" I demanded of Hooker, who twitched an ear from where he had resumed his snooze on the sofa. "Does this mean it's only about my original mission after all and Nichele is safe? Or does it mean they kidnapped her tonight after she called me?"

My fingers clenched on the phone. Oh, God. What if they were holding Nichele as a trading piece?

Hands trembling, I checked the time on the message. It indicated nine PM, before I'd even known Riel was at Harchman's.

Scowling at the display, I growled, "Okay, I really hope that means she's safe, but there's no way they'll let me into the Petroleum Club wearing these..." I prodded the heap of wet filthy denim on the floor with a weary toe. "...or any jeans for that matter. So that means I'm going to have to go back to the goddamn mall first thing in the morning to buy business clothes, and there's no way I can make a seven-thirty meeting." Exhaustion and stale adrenaline exploded into violent irritation. "And who the hell does Labelle think he is, anyway, just expecting me to hop to his bidding whenever he calls? Asshole!"

After a few minutes of pacing and swearing, my fear and anger subsided enough for me to take stock.

I collapsed onto the sofa and offered Hooker a chin-scratch. "Here's something interesting," I said over the rumble of his purrs. "Labelle said Riel arrived this evening. But I know Riel was here this morning. So he lied to Labelle. I wonder why. And I wonder how long he's really been here..."

I trailed off, staring into space for a few moments before dialling Spider's office number. "Hey, Spider," I said to his voicemail. "Could you check to see whether Benoit Riel flew on a regular airline into Calgary, and if so, when? Thanks. 'Bye."

I weighed the secured phone in my hand. Should I call Stemp with the latest developments?

A cavernous yawn made up my mind. "No need to wake him," I told Hooker. "This isn't an emergency."

The cat opened both eyes to give me a penetrating stare, and I shivered with a spooky sense of premonition. Would a real agent delay a non-urgent report? What if these trivial facts somehow spelled the difference between life and death?

And how the hell was I supposed to know?

"Don't look at me like that," I said. "Stemp's fast asleep like a normal human being right now, and nothing's going to change in the next..." I consulted my watch and groaned. "...two hours. And if it does, I'll call him right away. And great," I added. "Now I'm arguing with a cat."

Hooker yawned, pink tongue curling up and whiskers quivering, then tucked his nose under his front paw and closed his eyes as if to say, "It's your funeral."

A real agent wouldn't second-guess herself. And she wouldn't go running to the director of ops with every tiny detail like some little kid seeking approval.

Fine.

I hauled myself to my feet and trudged off to nosedive into bed only to toss and turn, expecting a catastrophe at any moment.

The sound of a key in the lock jerked me to wakefulness. My heart rose as Hooker bounded eagerly toward the door, and I rolled out of bed to follow. Hellhound must have finished his mission last night after all...

The door opened and my cheerful greeting died on my lips.

The frail elderly lady froze with Hooker in her arms, her eyes widening. "Oh! Excuse me, I didn't realize Arnold had returned."

"Um... Hi, Miss Lacey. He hasn't," I stammered, my head-to-toe blush abundantly obvious since I was wearing nothing but a mortified expression. "He was hoping to be back today, but he said I could sleep here last night..."

I shuffled my feet. Should I stand here and brazen it out? Grab the afghan from the couch in a belated attempt at modesty? Or just die on the spot from sheer humiliation?

Miss Lacey solved the dilemma for me. "Oh, how nice. It's lovely to see you again, Aydan," she said as though we were both clothed in our Sunday best complete with gloves and pearls. She lowered Hooker to the floor with an affectionate pat. "Well, John Lee, I can see that you are in good hands." She returned her attention to me, keeping her gaze politely above my chin. "I would be most grateful if you would give John Lee his breakfast, and I shall return around six PM to provide his evening meal. Have a pleasant day, dear."

"Thanks. You, too," I mumbled as she tactfully withdrew, locking the door behind her.

Shivering, I hurried for the bathroom, only to pull up short at the sound of the burner phone vibrating on the bedside table.

I dove for the bed, snatching up the phone and burrowing under the still-warm covers as I punched the Talk button. Then I hesitated. Shit, was this the phone number I'd given Kane, or the one I'd given Labelle? Was I Aydan or Arlene?

I settled for a noncommittal, "Hello?"

"Ms. Widdenback, it's Frederick Labelle." His deep smooth voice practically dripped sweetness. "I hope I'm not calling too early."

I glanced at the bedside clock. Seven-fifteen AM.

Asshole.

"What do you want?" I demanded, missing graciousness by a wide margin but mentally congratulating myself for not ripping a strip off him after only an hour of crappy sleep.

"I didn't hear from you last night, so I'm just calling to confirm our meeting this morning with our client at the Petroleum Club."

Arlene Widdenback wouldn't put herself at his beck and call. And I couldn't go even if I wanted to. I needed business clothes.

"Can't do it," I said shortly. "I have other meetings. The earliest I could do is eleven."

And that would be cutting it pretty damn close, since the

malls didn't open until ten...

"Make that eleven-thirty," I amended.

"That won't work." Labelle didn't sound nearly so sweet now. "The client wants a morning meeting."

"Then he should have arranged it more than eight hours in advance," I snapped. "I'll see you at the Petroleum Club at eleven-thirty." I punched the disconnect button and sat quietly hyperventilating for a few moments.

What if they had Nichele? What if they decided to persuade me to attend their meeting by sending me one of her fingers or toes? Or worse...

With shaking hands, I grabbed my cell phone and hit the speed dial for Nichele.

It rang once on the other end. Then twice...

"Hey, girl, what are you doing calling so early?" Nichele's usually-perky voice still held a fuzzy overtone of sleep. "I haven't even been up long enough to put on any makeup yet."

Breathless with relief, I did my best to match her lighthearted tone. "Sorry, but I've got a morning meeting and I wanted to talk to you before I got into it. All set for a big day of business seminars?"

Her yawn carried clearly through the speaker. "Not yet, but I will be. And there's no sign of James, and Hottie-Benoitty didn't break into my room and ravish me last night, so you can stop worrying."

"Okay, good," I began, but she wasn't finished.

Her tone slid into a sly tease. "So how did it go with Dante? Did you call him?"

"Um, no. It was too late when I got home last night."

But, damn, I needed to call him this morning and make sure he was okay. And find out if Holt had spotted anybody hanging around his place...

"It wasn't too late when I gave you his number yesterday evening," Nichele persisted. "Why didn't you call him then?"

"Um... I decided it would be too weird. So don't mention the modelling job to him, okay? I hadn't said anything to Lola about it yet, either; so no harm, no foul," I said, secretly congratulating myself on avoiding an embarrassing future in which Nichele casually mentioned the 'potential job' to either Lola or Dante.

She began, "But you should..."

I kept talking. "You're right, though, I probably need to call him anyway just to clear the air. I'll do it this morning. Unless... do you know if he's in town?"

"He didn't have any trips planned the last time I talked to him. And he's a morning person; he'll be up by now. So call him right away, okay? At least you can tell him you and Arnie are together and that's why you ran out on him. He was really hurt, you know? He thought you liked him."

I groaned. "Okay, okay, I already said I'd call him. And I did like him; I just..."

Giving up on a complicated and ultimately futile explanation, I finished, "...whatever. I'll call him, I promise. Have a good day, and call me this afternoon, okay? I've got a lunch meeting but I should be done by one."

"Okay." I could hear the smile in her voice. "Have a good day, too. Thanks for watching out for me."

"You're welcome. 'Bye."

Before I could lose my nerve, I punched in Dante's number and squeezed my eyes shut while I listened to the ringing on the other end. When the call went to his voicemail I almost chickened out and hung up, but my Jane Bond persona kicked me in the ass. Instead, I clenched the blanket in my fist and attempted a breezy tone.

"Hi, Dante, it's Aydan... um... Aydan Kelly... from last fall? Nichele's friend...?" Mentally cursing myself for not preparing better, I fumbled on. "I was just calling to, um... catch up; well, to apologize actually. I'm sorry for the way I acted and I wanted to..."

Wanted to what? God, what if he thought I was angling for Round Two?

"...um, just wanted to apologize," I finished lamely. "Could you please call me?"

I left my number and disconnected before jamming my face into the pillow with a moan and a heartfelt hope that I'd smother to death before he called back.

CHAPTER 13

After a few moments of humiliated profanity muffled by the pillow, I sat up and shook off my mood.

Okay, fine; so I was embarrassed. If it saved the life of an innocent man, it was a small price to pay.

Hauling myself out of bed, I dressed in the spare jeans and T-shirt from my backpack and responded to Hooker's demanding meows by dumping a few crunchies in his dish. Then I wandered around the living room, both hoping for and dreading Dante's return call.

After a few minutes I decided to do something useful, and scooped up Hellhound's muddy parka, the duffel bag, and my dirty clothes for a trip to the laundry room.

At the door, I hesitated.

The parka and duffel bag alone would make up an entire load. And the laundry basket in Hellhound's closet had been half full. No point in running the coin-operated washer and dryer for only my jeans and T-shirt.

Tossing my clothes on top of his, I hoisted the laundry basket and headed down the hall.

By twenty to ten I'd grabbed a couple of fitful naps between laundry cycles and the clothes were clean and dry;

mine tucked into my backpack and Hellhound's folded and stacked on his dresser.

I hesitated, eyeing the tidy pile of clean jeans and T-shirts.

Was this a kind gesture or an invasion of his space? What if he came home and thought I was playing housewife, and his commitment-phobia took over?

Muttering at my own stupidity, I scooped his clothes off the dresser and back into the laundry basket, stirring them into a convincing tangle.

My phone vibrated as I straightened, and I drew a deep breath and braced myself for an embarrassing conversation with Dante.

Instead, a text from Stemp glowed on the screen: "Call home. Urgent."

Anxiety prickled the back of my neck. Urgent? In all the times he'd texted me, Stemp had never used that word.

I rapidly scanned the apartment with my bug detector before punching the speed dial button on a secured phone.

Stemp's 'Yes?' was as crisp and precise as always, but I thought I detected a subtle edge of tension. Or maybe that was just me.

"It's Aydan," I said.

"Return immediately for a briefing. How soon can you get here?"

"Two hours, but I'm supposed to be meeting Labelle and Riel at eleven-thirty."

"This takes precedence. Briefing at eleven-forty-five."

He disconnected without another word.

Heart thumping, I switched to my burner phone and dialled Labelle. The call went to voicemail, and after his smooth voice had delivered its recorded message I said, "It's

Arlene Widdenback. I'm sorry, I won't be able to make it at eleven-thirty after all. I have to deal with an urgent matter this morning. I might be able to meet later..."

I did a rapid mental calculation. Four hours round trip to Silverside and back, but who knew how long the briefing might take; or whether I'd even get back to Calgary today at all?

"...Maybe around three," I went on. "But it will depend on the outcome of my meeting this morning. I'll call you as soon as I know."

Imagining Labelle's annoyance and hoping it didn't make him send another gunman after me, I shouldered my backpack and hurried out to my car.

When I strode into the meeting room at Sirius Dynamics on the dot of eleven-forty-five, Stemp, Holt, and Spider were already seated around the table.

"Please close the door," Stemp said as I crossed the threshold.

I obeyed and slid into the nearest chair as Stemp began the briefing.

"This morning a terrorist threat was sent to the news media, indicating that upcoming Remembrance Day services may be attacked with a new and devastating weapon that is capable of killing large groups of people instantly, without leaving any visible injuries."

My heart froze in my chest.

"That's only three days away!" Holt snapped. "Which services? Where?"

"Unknown."

I got my voice working with an effort. "P-Please tell me

that prototype ultrasound weapon isn't missing from our lab again..."

"The weapon is secure," Stemp replied. "Except for the few days that I carried it, it hasn't left the lab since you and Kane retrieved it nearly a year ago."

I was just beginning to breathe again when Holt shot Stemp a hard-eyed look. "Well, the technology's obviously out there now."

Even though accusation had tinged Holt's words, Stemp's response was as emotionless as always. "Apparently. However, Dr. Chow and his staff underwent lie-detector tests and they all passed, so it was not leaked from the R&D lab."

"Did *you* do the test?" Holt's tone made me eye him warily. Pretty belligerent for a guy who had supposedly overcome his anger problem.

Stemp remained impassive. "I completed it this morning at zero nine thirty, fifteen minutes after the report came in. Due to our involvement with the weapon last year, Kane and I were at the top of the list to be tested."

"What about Kane?" Holt demanded. "Has he done his yet?"

I smothered my small stab of defensive irritation. Holt was right to ask hard questions if somebody was about to unleash a death ray on innocent civilians.

"Kane passed his lie-detector test ten minutes ago," Stemp said.

Wait, Kane was here?

I suppressed that train of thought and returned my attention to the meeting as Holt dialled his attitude back to something a little less confrontational. "Oh. So I suppose you'll want Kelly and me to get tested, too."

"Yes; and also Webb. Dr. Travers will see you as soon as you complete this briefing." Stemp surveyed us before continuing, "The testing is only a formality. I do not believe we have a leak in the Department. We knew when we captured the weapon that it might not be the only working prototype."

"But…" I spoke up as a thought occurred to me. "…the prototype we have uses a targeting system. You have to aim it at somebody to kill them; you can't just wipe out a crowd with one press of the button."

"True," Stemp agreed. "I raised that point with Dr. Chow. He said it would only take a small modification of our weapon to produce a continuous ultrasound ray that would disrupt brain tissue as it passed over multiple targets."

My guts twisted. "So they'd only have to wave it back and forth like a flashlight to kill everybody its beam touched."

"Yes." The single word was grim.

"Any luck tracing the origin of the threat?" Holt asked. "How did the media find out before we did?"

"It was a laser-printed letter on generic paper mailed to a newspaper in Montreal; and the postmark indicates it was mailed from within Montreal yesterday." Stemp's customary emotionless façade didn't change, but his disgust was palpable nonetheless. "The newspaper opened the letter this morning and immediately broadcast the news. We had no prior intel."

Spider's face was a mask of worry. "I've reviewed all the analysts' reports and checked with Brock and Tammy, too. There was no chatter in advance; nothing that even hinted at anything like this. And it'll be virtually impossible to trace a paper letter. I've already put Brock and Tammy on it to see if they can find anything floating around the internet."

"Good. You will oversee the investigation as soon as you complete your lie-detector test," Stemp agreed. "Civilian counter-terrorism units across the country are taking the primary role so you will coordinate with them. Kelly, you'll be following up our other lead."

Slow suspicion welled up, clenching my guts. "The threat came from Montreal," I said, holding my voice steady. "That's not a coincidence, is it?"

Stemp's mouth flattened. "Unlikely."

"Shit."

"So Riel might be involved," Holt said. "Maybe that's why he's here for a face-to-face meeting. If he suddenly needs a deadly ultrasound weapon and he doesn't trust Labelle enough to use him as a middleman..."

I swallowed the sick lump in my throat. "Maybe."

"But it doesn't make sense for Riel to be the terrorist," Spider objected. "He wouldn't be so specific about the way the weapon works unless he actually had one. And if he already had one, he wouldn't need Arlene Widdenback to supply it. And if he's coming here now to order it from her, he's cutting the timing pretty close if he's planning to use it on Remembrance Day."

"Riel may be fishing for information," Stemp said. "If he is aware of the existence of the weapon, he may have issued a hoax threat to see how Arlene Widdenback reacts."

"But we can't take that chance." Spider's voice trembled. "All those innocent people..."

"Agreed," Stemp said. "We'll bring in the weapons expert Kane consulted last fall and administer the lie-detector test to determine whether he leaked the technology. Kelly, you'll go ahead with your original mission to meet Riel.

If he is our terrorist and is planning to acquire the weapon, he should reveal his motive soon. If he does not appear to be behind this threat, simply proceed with your original mission."

Holt thrust out his chin in an action-hero pose. "I can coordinate with the military units..."

Stemp shook his head. "No, you'll be backing up Kelly. You'll both return to Calgary immediately."

Holt's jaw clenched, but he gave a single short nod and didn't argue.

When Stemp dismissed us and hurried out, I turned to Holt. "How did it go at Dante's? Did you see anybody? Did you check the area for bugs or surveillance?"

"Of course!" Holt barked. "I'm not a fucking rookie!"

"I know." I held my voice level despite my spurt of reciprocal anger. "I'm just making sure the bases are covered. I hope you'd do the same if our positions were reversed."

"Damn right I would." After a brief silence, he drew a breath and added, "Sorry I snapped at you." I acknowledged the grudging apology with a nod as he went on, "I've got motion-sensor cameras on his place. No activity so far."

Worry tightened my shoulders. Was that good or bad? Maybe Dante was out of town and everything was fine...

"Okay, thanks," I said, and rose. "I have to check in with Labelle. I was supposed to meet him and Riel today at eleven-thirty, but..." I consulted my wristwatch. "I'll see if he'll go for three o'clock at the Petroleum Club. I won't want you with me, but if you could stay in the area that'd be great."

"Fine." Holt strode out, his stiff shoulders still radiating irritation.

I sighed and gave Spider a 'what can you do?' shrug

before following.

There was no sign of Kane in the lobby or parking lot. He must have left already, hurrying back to be with his family.

Ignoring my disappointment, I slid into my car and dialled Labelle. Though his tone was shorter than usual, he nevertheless made a show of graciously accepting the three o'clock meeting, and I texted 'we're on' to Holt before heading back to my farm to pack some business clothes that would satisfy the Petroleum Club's dress code.

Worry squirmed in my belly while I drove. What if Riel really was behind the terrorist threat? Did he intend to kidnap me and force me to hand over the weapon? Or did he have one already?

A shudder shook me at the thought of scores of innocent civilians collapsing into instant death, never even knowing what had hit them.

And just to add to my worries, Dante still hadn't returned my call.

Was he out of town?

Still too hurt and angry to return my call?

Or suffering horribly at the hands of captors who had yet to reveal themselves to me?

CHAPTER 14

Blowing out a long breath in an attempt to slow my pulse, I turned into the parkade closest to the Petroleum Club and paid the exorbitant fee.

I had barely seated myself in the understated luxury of the club's reception area when Frederick Labelle strode out to meet me.

"Ms. Widdenback." He extended his hand for a warm handshake, apparently over his earlier pique. Or hiding it well. "How nice to see you."

His gaze flicked over my clothes before returning to my face, and I suspected he was remembering the last time we'd met face to face; he in grievously-torn designer businesswear and I in filthy jeans accessorized with foul temper and a loaded Glock.

"Benoit is waiting at our table," Labelle added, gesturing toward the restaurant door. "After you."

With the uncomfortable feeling that he was studying my back to determine the best place to stick a knife, I preceded him to the table where Riel rose with a smile and a fractional bow.

"Allô, *Arlene*." He gave the name a teasing emphasis. "'Ow nice to meet you at last."

I nodded and mumbled, "Nice to meet you, too," as I slid

into the chair he had politely withdrawn for me, my knees weak with nerves.

After settling me in it, he resumed his seat with a smile while Labelle took the other chair, frowning as though he knew he'd missed some important exchange but didn't quite know how to demand clarification.

Riel immediately took charge of the conversation, steering us into an innocuous discussion of Calgary's tourism highlights and best restaurants interspersed with witty comparisons to his native Montreal, a city he clearly loved.

I forced myself to laugh along and volley banter back to him, wondering when the axe would fall; but our friendly conversation continued until our meals arrived.

After the waiter departed, I turned to Riel, holding onto my friendly demeanor. "So, Benoit, are you in town for business or pleasure?"

"Ah, for me they are... 'ow shall I say it? The same and one?" He inclined his head graciously in my direction. "Especially when the company is so delightful."

"One and the same," Labelle corrected.

Riel gave him a smile and nod. "Yes, both." He sliced off a small piece of beef medallion and chewed. "Ah, delicious. The Alberta beef, it is always so tasty, is it not?"

"Yes." I tried again. "Do you come to Alberta regularly on business?"

"Not regularly, no. This is a special trip for me. I 'ave been enjoying the dining and the sights. Today I spent at the Glenbow Museum. They 'ave the most interesting exhibit..." He steered the conversation into generalities again.

As the meal wore on I made a few more attempts to guide the conversation; but short of pinning him to the table and threatening to geld him with a butter knife, I couldn't think of a way to force him to talk business. Labelle made a few attempts of his own, but Riel parried them with equal skill and the conversation remained light. I did my best to look relaxed, and Labelle ate in silence with the strained smile of the odd man out.

When Riel and I ordered dessert, Labelle rose with poorly-simulated regret. "I do apologize, but I have another appointment," he said. "Please take your time. It's my pleasure to buy your meals."

Riel demurred and attempted to share the bill, but Labelle prevailed by claiming it was his privilege as a club member. He withdrew amid effusive thanks from Riel and a half-hearted attempt at gratitude from me.

As soon as Labelle disappeared through the door, Riel leaned back in his chair with his ever-present smile. "Ah, alone at last," he murmured.

My heart gave a thump. Finally.

"So, *Aydan*, ma chérie, tell me more about this date we 'ad last year." He put on a sorrowing expression. "Surely I was not so boring as you told Nichele."

Dammit.

Despite my best efforts, I could feel heat rising on my cheeks. Not knowing what else to do, I went with it. "Sorry about that. What did she tell you?"

"Only that you said we didn't... 'ow did she say it..." He cocked a quizzical eyebrow at me. "...'click'? And that she thought you still liked me even though you pretended not to." He made big imploring eyes at me, humour glinting in their depths. "Please tell me you still like me, even just a little. Or my 'eart will be broken into tiny pieces."

"Give it up," I admonished, smiling at his charm despite myself.

"But 'ow can I give it up when we were so close?" He was still joking, but seriousness lurked behind it. "'Ow will I know what to say around you? 'Ow to act?" His smile faded. "What name to call you?"

"Uh. Yeah. There's that." I sighed. "It doesn't really matter. The people who know me as Aydan just assume it's mistaken identity if somebody calls me Arlene, and vice versa. But you'd better call me Aydan in front of Nichele." Summoning some fake righteous indignation, I added, "I was doing just fine keeping my identities straight until Lawrence Harchman released those damn porn videos last summer. That asshole."

Come on, talk to me about the Harchmans...

"Ah." Riel leaned back in his chair, eyeing me seriously. "Yes, the sexy movies." He shook his head. "But they were fake, no? That plastic woman, she was not you."

In spite of the knowledge that he was a ruthless criminal, my heart warmed with gratitude. "No, she was definitely not me. You couldn't pay me enough to get naked with Lawrence Harchman." A shudder shook me. "God, I don't know how Tawny does it."

Wariness flickered in his eyes and vanished. "She is his wife," he said smoothly. "She loves 'im."

I mumbled a noncommittal 'mm' and took a bite of my key lime pie to forestall any other response. Maybe he'd keep talking if I stayed quiet.

He didn't. Instead, he savoured a sip of coffee in reflective silence, studying me.

"You are not what I expected," he announced after a long moment.

"Oh? What did you expect?" I took another slow bite of pie, trying not to look too interested.

Wicked humour sparkled in his eyes. "The famous Arlene Widdenback, they say she is... 'ow shall I say it? The stone-cold bitch. Lawrence 'Archman, he is nearly peeing in his pants when you come close. Our friend Monsieur Labelle, he tells me he would not cross you. Those who do, they vanish without a trace or die in accidents or go to prison only to die in fights. Or..." He eyed me gravely. "...they live on and suffer as a warning to others." His charismatic smile came back. "And yet, here I find une femme belle et sympathique... a woman beautiful and pleasant with a sense of humour and a love of fine food. Where is this stone-cold bitch?"

I shrugged, trying not to be disarmed by his appeal. "You haven't crossed me yet."

He chuckled and raised his coffee cup in a small salute. "And I shall not. I greatly prefer to make friends instead of enemies. This is why I like to do business face to face."

"Right. And speaking of that..."

"Yes, let us speak," he agreed. "It 'as been a long wait."

His tone was still polite, but there was a hint of reprimand in it.

I eyed him steadily, wondering whether to unleash Arlene Widdenback's legendary temper at the implied accusation.

No. Fish for a bit more information.

"It has been a long wait," I agreed. "In August Labelle was pretty pushy about arranging a meeting, and then nothing happened for months."

Riel's eyes narrowed. "Monsieur Labelle said you were not ready to discuss business yet."

"That's funny, because he told me the same thing about you."

We stared at each other in silence.

"Most interesting," Riel murmured. "So. The news this morning, they say someone is threatening Remembrance Day services."

My pulse accelerated and I drew a slow breath. Stay cool.

"Yes, I heard that." I ate another forkful of pie.

"It is most odd," he said.

I raised an eyebrow and diminished my pie by another bite.

He took a reflective sip of coffee. "Usually the terrorists are not so... 'ow shall I say it?   ...honest... about their weapons."

"I thought that, too," I agreed.

Riel sat up a little straighter.   "Did you?   Most interesting. So this weapon they describe, does it exist?"

I chose my words carefully. "If it didn't exist, why would they be so specific about how it works?"

"That is what I thought, too." He sipped some more coffee, his gaze laser-sharp over the edge of the cup. "A woman of your... connections; maybe you would know where such a weapon might be found?"

This is it. Don't screw up...

I eyed him in silence for a few moments, hoping I looked like a badass arms dealer considering whether to do business.

"Maybe," I said at last, and shovelled in another mouthful of pie to prevent myself from babbling.

"And if you did know, 'ow long might it take to get such a thing?"

My surging adrenaline turned the pie to tasteless mush in my mouth, but I took my time as if enjoying it. After two tries I managed to force it down my throat, but I surveyed him without speaking until I was reasonably sure my voice would come out steady.

"Not before Remembrance Day, if that's what you're asking."

Riel jerked back in his chair as if I'd slapped him, his face twisting in disgust. "Most certainly not! Whoever would kill innocent people is..." He spat a tirade of French before drawing a breath and adding, "...'ow shall I say it in English? I do not know enough bad words."

"I got the gist," I assured him, hoping I'd hidden my surprise. "I didn't mean to insult you; I just wasn't sure where you were going with that question."

"Where am I going...?" He frowned as if trying to puzzle out my meaning.

"I didn't know why you were asking," I amended.

"Ah." His brow cleared. "I asked because I thought you might know."

"I might," I hedged. "But we might not be talking about the same thing. I don't know of anything that works exactly like that. I've only heard of a single-shot."

"Only one target; not many targets at once?"

"Right."

His pleasant business façade vanished, his eyes turning cold and penetrating. "That is what I want. Get it for me."

The sudden revelation of the true nature behind his charming façade sent a shock of fear through me. I gulped another mouthful of pie, hoping the trembling of my fork wasn't too noticeable. "Not so fast. I didn't say I could get it; I just said I'd heard of it. And we haven't talked price."

The waiter arrived with a coffee refill, and Riel resumed his charming act. "Maybe if you can get it we may talk again...?" He gave one of his expressive shrugs. "I regret that I must depart for another meeting soon. But I find myself without accompaniment for une petite fête I must attend this evening. I would be most honoured if you would come with me." His smile widened to teasing humour. "Please allow me to make things better after our disappointing first date."

Shit, how was I supposed to handle this?

Tell him to stick his party up his ass, or go along with his 'let's be friends' act? What would he do if I didn't play his game?

Stemp's advice echoed in my mind: *Keep playing hard to get.*

I ate my last mouthful of pie, stalling. Then I leaned back to mirror his relaxed posture, and went for coolly polite.

"I'm a businesswoman. I'm not looking for a date." I softened the statement with a slight smile. "No matter how charmingly it's offered."

"Ah. My 'eart is broken."

His expression conveyed exactly the right amount of disappointment to be flattering. This guy was good. If not for the brief glimpse of his true nature I'd be fooled.

He inclined his head with a lift of one eyebrow. "Then per'aps may we attend as business associates? I promise you I will not... 'ow shall I say it? Step over the fences...?"

"You mean 'overstep the boundaries'."

His face lit with that disarming smile again. "Yes, overstep the boundaries. I shall not be un malotru..." He hesitated as if searching for the right English word. "...ah... a rude man...?"

"Pig," I supplied. "Jerk; creep; asshole..."

Riel laughed. "Yes, those."

I laughed, too, stalling while I tried to decide whether to accept the invitation. "Is that 'yes, I'll be a creep' or 'yes, I won't be a creep'?" I teased.

"I will not be a creep," he replied, grinning. "I like this word, 'creep'. It sounds like... some... low creature..." He made a moue of distaste. "...that crawls upon the ground. Like a snake."

"Usually leaving a slime trail," I agreed.

"I will not do that," he assured me, eyes wide with sincerity.

Dammit, despite my stalling I knew I had to accept his invitation.

At least if I was with him, he couldn't stalk Nichele or torture Dante. And maybe he knew where James Helmand was, too. Who knew what information I might gather after he'd downed a few drinks and lowered his guard?

"All right, if you promise not to be a creep," I said, hoping I wasn't making a fatal mistake. "Where and when would you like to meet?"

"I would be pleased to pick you up..."

"Not necessary." I bared my teeth in a semblance of a smile. "Just tell me where the party is and I'll meet you there."

"D'accord; as you wish, of course." He withdrew a gold pen from the inside pocket of his blazer and jotted an address on one of the paper napkins. "It is at the house of a friend. Let us meet at eight PM. I will wait for you outside, in the front."

"Okay." The keenly humiliating memory of the stolen dress and too-small shoes prompted me to add, "Um... is it... a formal party? What should I wear?"

As soon as the words left my mouth, I regretted them.

Prime opportunity for him to tell me to dress like a hooker...

He offered me a gallant bow from his seated position. "Whatever you wear, you will be the most beautiful woman there. But most will likely be dressed... so." He indicated our business wear with a graceful gesture.

"Oh. Good. Okay." Before he could divert the conversation again, I added, "By the way, I was surprised to see you at Nichele's office. Have you been working with her for long?"

"Ah. No, that was our first meeting." He smiled. "She is charming, your Nichele. Such a brightness."

"Yes. How did you discover her?" My question came out a little more edged than I'd intended, and I added, "You must be special. She rarely takes on new clients these days except by referral."

Riel made a self-deprecating face. "I am not so special at all. Tawny Harchman is Nichele's client and she referred me."

A chill slithered down my backbone. How long had Tawny been Nichele's client? Nichele was one of the top-rated stockbrokers in Calgary and the Harchmans certainly had the assets to qualify, but that one degree of separation from James Helmand made my blood run cold.

"You're lucky to be working with her." I managed to keep my tone casual. "But Montreal is pretty far away. I'm surprised you couldn't find a stockbroker there."

"I do have one there. But I may be returning to Calgary frequently, so this is most convenient." He consulted his wristwatch. "And speaking of business, I regret now that I must go. But I will count the hours until this evening."

I took the hint and stood. "Well, it was nice to officially meet you."

He rose, taking my hand and bowing over it. "The pleasure was all mine." As I retrieved my hand and turned away, he added, "Say allô to Nichele for me."

Did I imagine a sinister inflection in his tone? I whirled, surveying him, but his expression was as pleasant and guileless as ever.

"I will," I muttered, and left before I could seize him by the throat and demand what the hell he meant by that.

CHAPTER 15

As soon as I slid into my car, I checked my bug detector. Green light.

Next I checked my cell phone. Neither Dante nor Nichele had called, but I had a text message from an anonymous number: 'Call home'.

Tension knotted my shoulders as I pressed the speed-dial for Stemp.

When I identified myself after his curt 'Yes', he said, "Webb found Riel's airline records as you requested. Riel flew into Calgary on a regular Westjet flight, arriving at nineteen-twenty hours on Tuesday."

"Hm. So he was here for a day and a half without telling Labelle. That fits, since I've just found out Labelle has been playing us both. Riel must have gotten suspicious and that's why he wanted to meet me without Labelle as an intermediary. Anything on the wiretap?"

"Only a brief conversation confirming the time for your meeting today. But Webb has activated remote monitoring on their phones so they act like audio bugs, and we're also receiving all their text messages. No relevant intel yet. The analysts will inform you immediately if anything comes through."

"Okay, thanks." I gave him a brief summary of my

meeting with Labelle and Riel and finished, "...so for a guy who's in the market for a lethal classified weapon, that was a lot of indignation over 'killing innocent people'. It was probably an act, but still... I'm not convinced he's behind the terror threat. When I told him it wasn't the mass killing machine the threat described, he specifically said our single-shot version is the one he's looking for. I'm going to a party with him tonight to see if I can get more information. If I tell him I can supply the weapon, maybe he'll talk price and delivery."

"Very well. Keep me posted."

As soon as the connection clicked closed I dialled Nichele. After several rings she answered, her voice low and hurried.

"Hi Aydan. Sorry I didn't call but I'm right in the middle of this seminar. Can I call you later?"

"Sure, but wait, do you have another number for Dante?" I asked rapidly, wondering whether to be relieved that she'd answered or worried that she sounded so distracted. "He hasn't called me back."

"No, that was his cell and he always answers it, even if he's travelling. Sorry, gotta go, okay?"

"Okay. Call me as soon as you can. 'Bye."

She disconnected, and I stared blankly out the windshield, fear rising like a cold tide.

Of course Dante always answered his phone. He wouldn't want to miss a call from his modelling agency or any other potential job. So why hadn't he called me back?

Had he really been that hurt by my abandonment?

Or had he been abducted because of me?

"He's a gorgeous underwear model, for chrissake," I muttered. "He can have any woman he wants, and he's sure as hell not going to mope for a year over some middle-aged bag who ran out on him. This is bad. This is really bad."

A quick call to Holt confirmed that there had been no activity on the cameras at Dante's house. The queasy conviction that something was wrong expanded in my belly, making me regret the key lime pie.

Bringing up my cell phone's browser with trembling fingers, I searched 'Dante Olivieri' and was rewarded with a gallery of delicious photos, and, more importantly, the name of his modelling agency.

I dialled the number with my heart thumping. Please, please, let him be on a photo shoot in some exotic location where he can't answer his phone...

The voice that answered the phone was professionally pleasant, and I drew a deep breath to steady my voice. "Hi, I'm calling because I'm looking for Dante Olivieri..."

"Oh." A waver of uncertainty in the receptionist's voice made my pulse quicken even more. "I'll... let you speak to his agent. Please hold."

Oh shit. Shit, shit, shit...

A brusque voice snapped onto the line. "Francine Belmont."

I cleared my throat so my voice wouldn't come out in a dry croak. "Hello, my name is Aydan Kelly, and I'm looking for Dante Olivieri-"

"Well, if you find him, tell him he's fired," she barked. "We've got lots of other talent who are actually capable of showing up when they're scheduled."

"Wait!" I implored, afraid she'd hang up. "I think something might have happened to him. When did you hear from him last? When was he scheduled to work?"

"Who did you say you were?"

"Um..."

Shit, I couldn't tell her I was a secret agent.

"I'm Aydan Kelly. A friend of Dante's. It's not like him to miss a job," I babbled, hoping that was actually true. Hell, I hardly knew him. Maybe he was an arrogant prima donna who delighted in making people wait on him. "When did you hear from him last?"

A sharp hiss of breath on the other end of the line pumped my blood pressure even higher. Was she going to hang up on me?

When she spoke again, her voice was tight and worried. "I'm sorry; this week has been a total gong show and I'm pretty stressed. You're right, I've never known him to be late, let alone not show up. He left me a voicemail late Wednesday evening and said he was sick. He sounded terrible then, but he didn't call in yesterday so I expected him to be at his shoot this morning. He didn't show, and he hasn't returned my calls. I've been trying to find talent to cover for him but the client wants the wonderful Dante Olivieri..." She broke off. "Never mind; not your problem."

"What do you mean 'he sounded terrible'?" I demanded. "How did he sound? Hoarse and stuffed up like he had a cold?"

"No; weak and shaky. Like he had the flu or something. You said you're a friend; do you have a key to his house? Can you go and check on him?"

"I'll check on him and let you know," I promised. "Don't fire him, please. I'm sure he'd have been there if..." My throat closed and I swallowed hard. "...if he was capable of it."

"Dammit. Call me if you find him. Thanks." The line went dead in my ear.

Fingers trembling, I extracted a secured phone and punched the speed dial button. Stemp's brisk "Yes?" felt like a reassuring pat on the back.

"It's Aydan again," I said. "Dante called his agency late Wednesday night and left a message saying he was sick, and nobody's heard from him since. He didn't show up for a job this morning and he hasn't returned his agent's calls. Holt says there's been no sign of life since he got there. I'm going to go over to his place now and see..." My throat went dry. "...see what I can find."

Please don't let me find his body.

After a fractional pause Stemp replied, "Very well, as long as it doesn't divert resources from your mission."

His dispassionate tone brought a surge of anger all the way up from my toes. An innocent man might be dead or dying, and all he could say was 'don't waste time on it'?

Clenching my teeth on a retort, I reined in my temper. He had the weight of hundreds, maybe thousands, of civilian lives on his shoulders. I should be glad he hadn't outright ordered me to abandon Dante and concentrate on the mission.

Then again, he knew me well enough to realize what would happen if he did.

Gratitude replaced my irritation. He was looking out for me, communicating a warning but not issuing a direct order that would get me arrested for insubordination.

"This won't take resources away from the mission," I assured him. "That's still my top priority, but I've got about three hours before I have to start getting ready for the party."

"Very well," he repeated with exactly the same inflection, and a smile eased the stiff corners of my mouth as I hung up.

Then I dialled Holt again.

When he answered, I said, "I'm coming over to search Dante's house. I'll meet you two blocks west of his house. See you in twenty minutes."

"No, park in front."

"Uh..." Well, what the hell. He was an experienced agent. Surely he knew what he was doing. "Okay."

When I parked on the quiet street in front of Dante's house, there was no sign of Holt. About thirty seconds later a shiny red Audi Quattro rounded the corner and pulled up behind me. Holt stepped out, leather briefcase in one hand and Starbucks coffee cup in the other.

As I walked back to meet him, I spotted magnetic 'Greg Holt Real Estate' signs on the Quattro's doors. Holt himself was dressed in expensive-looking business clothes, and he gave me a broad smile as he strode toward me.

Tucking his briefcase under his arm, he offered me a hearty handshake. "Excellent, you made it," he said, still smiling. "I'm Greg Holt. We spoke on the phone earlier. My card..."

He delved into his blazer pocket and produced a professional-looking business card that matched the signs on his car.

"Thanks," I said, slightly overawed, and accepted the card.

"Shall we?" Holt inquired, gesturing toward Dante's house.

"Uh... sure."

On the front step, he produced a ring containing several keys. "Stand here," he muttered, nudging me into a position that would conceal what he was doing from anyone passing on the street.

He pulled on vinyl examination gloves before trying the keys in the lock one after the other. When one slid in, he produced a screwdriver from his pocket. While I watched in puzzlement, he held the key in the lock with one hand while rapping the end of the key briskly with the screwdriver handle. After only a couple of taps the key turned and we stepped into Dante's front foyer. Holt nonchalantly closed and relocked the door behind us.

I gaped at him. "How did you do that?"

He frowned. "It's just a cheapo lock, and these are standard bump keys from Stores. Don't you have a set?"

Shit, something else I should have known about. Would've been damn nice to have known about it last night before I smashed the store window.

"Yeah," I lied. "But I can't get in nearly that fast."

Holt didn't quite smirk, but I could tell he was pleased. "This is the secret," he confided, showing me an ordinary rubber O-ring around the base of the key. "With the O-ring in place you only have to hold a gentle twist on the key and it rebounds automatically. No pulling it out again between taps."

"That's amazing."

I studied the key. It didn't look like anything special; just a standard house key with the projections cut low and spaced evenly along it.

Shaking myself back to reality, I filed 'bump key' into my memory to research later and pulled my own gloves out of my pocket.

"Expecting something messy?" Holt inquired grimly, comparing his unobtrusive clear vinyl to my bright blue nitrile.

"I hope not. But I keep them in my toolbox so nobody gets suspicious about why I'm carrying a bunch of them. Mechanics use blue nitrile."

"Okay. Where do you want to start?"

I sighed. "With the obvious, I guess." Raising my voice, I called, "Hey, Dante! It's Aydan! Are you here?"

Silence was my only reply, and I tried again a little louder. "Dante! Hello! Are you okay?"

After a few more moments of silence, I turned to Holt with a tense shrug. "Let's see if we can find anything."

It didn't take long.

When we rounded the corner into the kitchen, we both froze.

"Shit," Holt growled.

My heart motionless in my chest, I stared at the overturned kitchen chair and the doormat scrunched into the corner. A few brownish smears and droplets of dried blood led to the back door.

"Didn't kill him here," Holt muttered. "Not nearly enough blood..."

My heart resumed beating again, banging frantically in my chest. Oh God, no. I had so wanted to be wrong...

Without moving from the doorway, Holt's keen gaze scoured the kitchen. "There." He pointed to a spray of droplets across the end of the kitchen counter. "Looks like somebody came in the back door and hit him. Didn't beat the hell out of him, though. Not enough blood or signs of struggle. And he must've let them in because there's no sign of forced entry; and he was still walking when he left. No drag marks through the blood. So he went with whoever hit him."

He turned back to me. "Your boyfriend have any

enemies?"

I had to try twice before I could get my voice to work. "He's not my boyfriend. Just a poor innocent guy who had the misfortune to kiss me in public a year ago. I don't even know him well enough to know if he's got enemies; but I'd be willing to bet this is because of me."

"Huh." Holt eyed the kitchen again. "Hell, who knows if that's even his blood. Maybe he attacked somebody who came in, and now he's lying low."

"Maybe..." I tried to reconcile that with my memory of Dante's anxious expression when he'd asked if Kane was dangerous last year. He didn't seem like the type to attack anybody.

"Well..." Holt shrugged. "Let's check the rest of the place and then call the cops."

I drew a breath of relief. Thank God one of us knew what to do.

"I'll start in the basement," I croaked, and headed for the stairs.

Touching as little as possible, I gave it a once-over. Everything seemed in order, at least as far as I could tell. But I'd never been in his basement before so how would I know?

My knees trembled as I crept back up the stairs.

They had Dante. Was he dead?

Would it be worse if he was still alive and suffering?

And who were 'they'? Riel hadn't been acting suspiciously earlier. Surely if he'd beaten and abducted a man for leverage on me he would have given some indication. But he'd never even met Dante, so he likely wasn't involved.

James, on the other hand...

I could easily imagine him ringing the doorbell and

pushing his way in when Dante opened the door to him. And when Dante protested, I could see James hitting him viciously across his handsome face just for spite; then jerking him to his feet and forcing him outside, maybe with a knife at his throat or a gun in his back...

My breath caught.

What if James had killed Dante for revenge on me?

What if Dante's mutilated body was lying in the back yard?

CHAPTER 16

"Find anything?" Holt's voice made me start violently.

I turned to face him. "Jesus, you scared the shit out of me," I complained, hoping he'd mistake my funk for surprise. "No. Did you?"

He shook his head, and I steeled myself and added, "Have you been watching the back yard?"

"Yeah." He produced his phone and turned it toward me, displaying a camera view of Dante's back yard. "No activity."

There were no visible bodies in the camera's field of view, and I drew a deep breath. "Guess we'd better call the police, then. We've been in here too long already."

Holt nodded. "I'll put some fingerprints on the front doorknob." He removed his gloves and stuffed them down the front of his pants with a quirk of his mouth. "Don't think they'll strip-search us."

"Let's hope not." I followed suit, removing my gloves and sliding them down my pants into my underwear.

Holt's eyes kindled with ribald humour. "You're having a bit too much fun there, Kelly."

"Shut up," I growled, still trying to tuck the last nitrile finger under a scrap of fabric and lace that was never designed to contain anything besides what was already in it.

"Trust me, life is easier when you're a guy wearing tighty-whities."

"Actually, I'm a boxer-briefs guy," Holt said.

"Too much information."

He grinned. "Can you do some hysterics or something?" he asked as he punched 911.

"Oh, hell yeah." I dropped unceremoniously to the floor, curled into a ball, and released all the fear I'd been bottling up.

Over the sound of my sobs, I caught snatches of Holt's report to the police as he casually drifted to the front door and handled the doorknob and deadbolt lock on both sides.

He explained he was a realtor whom Dante was considering hiring; that Dante had arranged for me, his friend, to let the realtor in to do an estimate of the property's value; how we had found evidence of foul play and I had collapsed in hysterics.

In minutes sirens swelled outside the house. My storm of emotion had subsided and I had to fake my continued weeping and hyperventilating, but my trembling was real as Holt and a police officer helped me out of the house and onto the front porch.

After taking our statements and instructing us to go to the police station to supply fingerprints so ours could be eliminated from those found at the scene, the uniformed officer strode away.

As I slumped on the front step, arms wrapped around myself and head hanging, Holt knelt solicitously in front of me. "Was it a good idea to point them at James Helmand?" he asked quietly.

I shrugged. "Why not? They'll be all over him for a possible parole violation. If he looks even a little bit guilty they'll lock him up and save us the trouble, and if he's innocent we need to be looking somewhere else anyway."

Holt grunted assent, or possibly resignation. "Come on, I'll buy you a coffee," he said, just loudly enough for the bystanders to hear. "You look like you need one."

I let out a convincing sniffle. "O-okay..."

Hand under my elbow, he helped me down the stairs and past the police cordon. A news crew lunged through the knot of onlookers, and Holt shoved a palm in the camera's lens and tucked me into the passenger seat of his car.

Then he turned and faced the camera with a giant shit-eating grin. "Greg Holt, Realtor, at your service," he proclaimed. "I can sell your home no matter how undesirable it might be!" He gave the camera a sly wink. "Even if there's been a murder in it!"

The reporters pressed closer, salivating, and Holt proceeded to ignore all their questions and trumpet his own services for the next ten minutes until finally the last reporter gave up in disgust.

Still grinning, Holt slid into the driver's seat and pulled away. "Won't be seeing us on the six o'clock news," he said smugly.

"That was slick," I agreed with sincere admiration. "But... what if somebody actually tries to call Greg Holt, Realtor?"

Holt shrugged. "Then I'll sell their house. Or hand it off to one of my associates. I have a real estate broker's license in every province. It makes a great cover. After I knock on a few doors and flog a few complimentary property assessments, everybody in the neighbourhood ignores me and I can hang around as much as I want without anybody getting suspicious." He snickered. "And I give everybody handouts telling them to protect themselves by checking the credentials of anyone claiming to be a home inspector or realtor. I like irony."

Sobering, he added, "And I like knowing that maybe they'll be wary of the next asshole like me that shows up on their doorstep."

"That's absolutely brilliant." I gazed at him with new respect.

He shrugged, scowling out the windshield as if to hide his appreciation of the compliment. "It works. Nice job on the hysterics, by the way. I almost believed you myself."

"Thanks." After an awkward moment of silence, I added, "So that's how you got away with installing the cameras? Hanging around pretending to be a realtor?"

"No. I came by in a panel van with Enmax logos so I could fiddle with the utility boxes and set up the surveillance cameras. I've set them up with a motion sensor and real-time video feed to my phone so I'll get a ping anytime the camera picks up movement. Speaking of..."

He handed over his phone. "Keep an eye on Dante's house. If our perp sees the police action he might decide to go and do a little rubbernecking. Maybe we can spot him. Let's figure out our next move while we grab a coffee, then go back and get your car and do the fingerprint thing at the police station."

Belatedly, I realized he'd completely taken charge of what was supposed to be my op.

It chafed me to let him get away with it, but I suppressed my injured pride with the knowledge that I wouldn't have been nearly as well-prepared and professional.

Hell, the more I learned, the more I realized how little I knew. If I had been assigned to watch a house, I probably would've parked on the street and hunkered down in my car, and some nosy neighbour would have reported me to the police in ten minutes flat.

"You okay?" Holt's voice penetrated my gloomy reverie.

"No. I suck." The words popped out before I could stop them, and Holt snickered.

"Good to know, but I'm not in the market just now. Save it for your next porn video."

"Fuck you."

He guffawed, and somehow I felt just a bit better.

We drove in silence for a few minutes before he said gruffly, "Don't beat yourself up. You can't protect everybody. You can only do the best you can."

"Not good enough," I muttered.

"That's the hell of this job," he agreed, and we didn't speak again until we were reseated in his car, hot beverages in hand.

Holt reclined his seat a few degrees with a sigh and leaned his head back. "Okay. So which one of your enemies do you think it is?"

I embraced my cup of tea as though its heat could dissipate the chill around my heart. "My money's on James Helmand. He's exactly the kind of asshole who'd go after my friends to get at me. He's vicious enough to enjoy beating up an innocent person just for the hell of it, and it makes sense for him to go after Dante because nothing in his parole prevents him from contact."

Holt snorted. "If he just committed assault, kidnapping, and forcible confinement, I doubt if he was that worried about breaching the no-contact terms of his parole."

"No." I sighed. "But he's smart, and I'd be willing to bet he's got some plan to make his hands look clean. He wouldn't take a needless chance on getting spotted somewhere he shouldn't be."

"Still, though, abducting somebody is a dumb move," Holt argued. "It's messy, it attracts attention, and hostages are high-maintenance. And controlling you by threatening the hostage only works if he wants you to do something specific in a short timeframe. But if he was going to do that he probably would've contacted you with his demands already. Especially if he's had the guy since Wednesday."

I sank my forehead onto the top of my cardboard cup, folding over the emptiness in my chest. "I doubt if he intends to keep a hostage. This is revenge. Dante's probably already dead." I shuddered. "For his sake, I hope so."

"This guy's a real sicko, eh?"

I spoke without raising my head. "He'd delight in torturing someone for as long as he possibly could without actually killing them, and then he'd take whatever was left of them to where he'd know I'd find them and lay them out there to strike the killing blow. So I'd know exactly how much they had suffered. I'm going to be afraid to even go around a corner until this is over." Sickness climbed the back of my throat. "And that's exactly why he would choose Dante. He was... is... so beautiful. It would be a desecration..."

A sudden horrible thought struck me and I bolted upright. "Shit, it's after four o'clock and I haven't heard from Nichele yet!" Thrusting my cup at Holt, I snapped, "Hold this", and scrabbled frantically at my phone. "She sounded weird when I talked to her at one." My voice rose despite my efforts to control it. "Dante sounded weird right before he disappeared..."

I punched the speed dial and waited, fingers clenched so

tightly on the phone that my knuckle popped in protest.

Listening to the ringing at the other end, I muttered, "If she doesn't answer, I'll hunt that fucker down and kill him with my bare h-"

"Hey, girl, sorry I didn't call you." Nichele's blithe apology made me fall back in the seat, quivering with released tension. I must have made some sound, because she added, "Seriously, I'm really sorry. This was a great seminar series, and I was so involved I just lost track of time. I didn't mean to scare you."

"It's okay," I croaked. "I'm just glad you're all right."

"I'm fine. Just finished the last seminar and now I'm getting ready for the windup dinner. The food here is amazing! I'm so glad Benoit got me a ticket! I'll have to buy him a bottle of something as a thank-you. Do you know what he drinks?"

"Um... no." I nearly said, 'I'll soon find out', but fortunately stifled myself. No need to create more questions in her mind. Instead I added, "Was he... um, did you see him today?"

"No, he wasn't attending the seminars; he just got invited to the champagne gala because he's staying with the Harchmans. So..." Her salacious grin was clearly audible in her voice. "How did it go with Dante?"

Gut-punched anew, I couldn't speak.

"Aydan? ...Hello! Your cell phone cut out. Are you still there? Hello?"

"I... I'm still here," I whispered. "Nichele..." I didn't know how to say it. "I... I have some bad news."

Her gulp carried over the line. "H-how bad?"

"It might be... really bad." I swallowed and tried to steady my voice. "Dante is missing. The police are at his house now, and it... doesn't look good..." Drawing a deep breath, I spoke into the tense silence. "There are signs of a struggle and some blood."

"Ohmigod!" I could hear the tears in her voice. "Ohmigod. What... when...?"

"He left a voicemail for his agent on Wednesday night and said he wasn't feeling well. That's the last anybody heard from him."

"Oh... ohmigod..." The word trembled into silence. She swallowed audibly. "What... what can we do?"

"Nothing. Wait and hope." The words tasted bitter on my tongue. "Just go ahead with your weekend plans. If I hear anything I'll let you know right away."

"Ohmigod, Aydan. I just... I feel sick. What if..."

"Think good thoughts. And watch your back, even if you do feel safe there."

"I... I don't think I can do this," Nichele quavered. After a tremulous breath she went on, "I have to go to the windup dinner, but I think I'll just go home afterward instead of staying at the resort. I'm..." She gulped again. "...not really in a spa mood anymore."

I hesitated. Was she safer there or at home? At least if she was out of Harchman's clutches I had a better chance of keeping tabs on her...

"I don't blame you," I said slowly. "But I want to make sure you're safe if you come home..." In a split-second decision, I added, "John and Arnie are both busy right now, but I've got a friend who used to be a security guard and I'm going to get him to watch your place. Just call me when you're on your way home, okay?"

"O-okay..." She let out a long breath and her voice firmed. "Okay. I'm thinking good thoughts. He's fine; I

know it. This is all a big misunderstanding and everything
will be okay."

"Good. Keep thinking that," I encouraged, my stomach
curdling with guilt. "I'll talk to you soon. 'Bye."

Thumbing the disconnect button, I leaned my head back,
squeezing my eyes shut to hold back the burning of incipient
tears.

Holt said nothing, and I was grateful for his silence.

After a moment I blew out a harsh breath and sat up to
extract a secured phone from my waist pouch.

Stemp answered on the first ring, as usual. "Yes?"

"It's Aydan." My voice came as though from a great
distance. "It looks as though Dante has been abducted,
probably Wednesday evening. There's blood and signs of a
struggle in his house. The police are there now. I suspect
James."

After a fractional pause Stemp spoke, pain vibrating in
his voice. "I was wrong. I am sorry."

Heart squeezing, I said, "It's not your fault. It was too
late before I even asked you about it. I should have been
paying attention to James's release date and taking steps to
protect his potential targets." I drew a deep breath. "But I'm
not going to make that mistake again. I'm assigning Holt to
watch Nichele, and I'm going to find Dante. The police don't
know we're agents, so please ask Spider to keep an eye on
their investigation and keep me posted."

"I will monitor the investigation." Stemp's dispassionate
tone was back. "However, your assigned mission is still your
top priority. Let the police investigate your friend's
disappearance. And Holt's role is to support you in your
mission, not act as a bodyguard-for-hire. As much as I
sympathize with your situation, if you delay or compromise

your mission for your own personal reasons I will not be able to shield you from the consequences."

I bit down my instinctive surge of fury and concentrated on the concern I could detect behind Stemp's warning. If the chain of command decided they couldn't trust me to do my job, the consequences for me would be life imprisonment.

And, as much as it sickened me, saving Dante at the cost of hundreds or thousands of other innocent lives was both illogical and irresponsible no matter what my heart told me.

I cleared my throat but my voice still came out in a strangled whisper. "Okay."

I disconnected and turned to face Holt's glower.

"What the fuck?" he barked the instant I lowered the phone. "I'm a top agent, not some fucking pansy-ass rent-a-cop! This is bullshit! I should be-"

My frayed nerves snapped and my fist shot out to clamp onto his nice tie and jerk him toward me.

He reacted instantly, twisting my hand into a submission hold that jabbed red-hot knives of pain through my arthritic thumb.

Refusing to give him the satisfaction of wincing or yelping, I pushed my face within inches of his and spoke very quietly. "You *should* be protecting innocent lives. If you want glamour, go do something that doesn't have 'secret' in the job title."

He glared at me from close range, his lantern jaw clenched and steely gaze boring into mine. Slowly, he eased the pressure off my hand and settled back in his seat. Staring fixedly out the windshield, he took a couple of long breaths, in through his nose and out through his mouth. On the third one, he spoke stiffly.

"Sorry. You're right."

My muscles turned to jelly and I flopped back into my seat, cradling my throbbing thumb and whimpering, "Ow, ow, ow, fuck, ow, *fuck!*"

"Don't be such a fucking wuss, Kelly. I didn't break it."

Hissing pain through my teeth, I glared at him. "Next time I'll just shoot you."

He sneered. "You can try."

Rage veiled my vision in a red haze. Fighting the burning urge to just draw my gun and end him, I closed my eyes and breathed.

In through my nose, out through my mouth.

In... out...

In... out...

"Sorry." He didn't sound quite so grudging this time. "I was out of line."

I drew another breath and opened my eyes. "I was, too. Sorry."

His shoulders relaxed, and he grimaced. "What the hell was Stemp thinking, making us partners? If we don't kill each other before this is over, it'll be a fucking miracle."

I gave him a shaky smile and extended my undamaged fist, palm down. "Team Anger Management."

He snorted and gave me a fist bump. "Boo-yah."

CHAPTER 17

"So what next, oh mighty leader?" Holt inquired, but his tone wasn't too snarky so I let it go.

"Stemp says I can't use you as a bodyguard for Nichele..." I began.

"Fuck, why didn't you say so?" He scowled. "I wasted a perfectly good tantrum."

"Sorry," I apologized insincerely. "But even if you can't actually follow her around, do you have some spare cameras you can put on her place? I'm going to want you available to back me up, but I won't want you actually with me so you'll have time to keep an eye on her, too."

"No problem. I can just add the extra cameras onto my monitoring software."

"Thanks. Here's her address..." I brought it up on my phone and passed it over. He glanced at it and handed it back, and my estimation of him rose another notch. Memorized, just like that. "And this is what she looks like," I added, scrolling through the photos on my phone to find a clear one of Nichele.

When I handed it to him, his eyebrows rose and he let out an appreciative whistle. "This is going to be a lot more fun than watching some pretty-boy model. I'd better get a camera in her bedroom just to make sure she's really safe."

"Jeez, you're a pig," I said without heat. "Didn't you get any sensitivity training as part of your whole 'top agent' schtick?"

Holt grinned. "Yeah, but it didn't take. I like rattling cages." He sobered and passed my phone back. "You think it's a good idea to carry your friends' photos and addresses with you?"

"No." I sighed. "I usually don't, but..."

My heart sank even lower. No buts. Carrying that kind of personal data was criminally negligent. If my enemies found it on me, it could cost the lives of every one of my friends.

I had a memory-flash of Kane's, Stemp's, and Hellhound's homes. All of them barren of personal photos.

"But what?" Holt prompted.

"Never mind," I muttered, cursing my own incompetence yet again. "Take me back to my car. We can go separately to the police station and then you can get set up at Nichele's place."

"What about you?"

I grimaced. "I'm going to a party."

Holt said nothing, and after a moment I glanced over to find him regarding me expectantly.

When I gave him a blank look, he scowled. "Fuck, you really are used to working alone, aren't you?" He made exaggerated gestures, pointing first to me, then to himself. "You. Me." He wagged his hand back and forth between us. "Partners. As in, 'working together'. *Where* is the party, dipshit? When is it, why are you going, who do you expect to meet there, what do you expect to gain from it, and do you want backup?"

"Oh." I stared at him, equal parts irritated and grateful.

Grateful won. "Thanks. Sorry. The party is here." I passed him the scribbled napkin. "I'm meeting Riel there at eight. My original plan was to tell him I could supply the weapon and see if he'd discuss price and delivery, but now I'll be fishing for information about James and Dante, too."

Holt nodded and memorized the address before handing the napkin back to me. "Okay, I'll be..." He fiddled with his phone, zooming and panning across a satellite map. "...here." He tapped the screen. "This Starbucks is only a few blocks away so I can get to your location in about a minute and a half."

"But what about Nichele?" I demanded. "What if somebody tries to abduct her in the meantime?"

"I'll have the cameras set up by then. If anything happens I'll call the cops." He met my half-voiced protest with a silencing scowl. "Priorities, Kelly. Don't let your personal shit get in the way of the mission."

I bit my tongue to hold in my angry retort, and he went on, "Put me on your speed dial. If I get a call from your number and you don't say anything, I'll get there as fast as I can. If you need me to do anything else you'll have to say something on the call. Check in via text every hour or so. After you're clear of the party, meet me at the Starbucks and we'll debrief."

I drew a deep calming breath. Backup. What a concept. And at least he'd still be watching Nichele.

"Okay," I agreed.

Holt patted me patronizingly on the head. "Very good, Kelly. That wasn't so hard, was it?"

"Don't be a prick."

He grinned. "But it's what I do best."

By the time we finished at the police station it was nearly six-thirty. I drove to the nearest fast-food restaurant and inhaled a greasy burger and fries, then steered toward Hellhound's place with slightly more optimism.

My hopes were dashed at the sight of his still-empty parking stall, and I trudged up the stairs worrying. Was he in a place where he couldn't call me, or did he see no reason to call? Or... I swallowed the tightness my throat. Had he been so badly injured he couldn't call? Or... worse?

"Think good thoughts," I muttered as I unlocked the door.

Miss Lacey had undoubtedly fed Hooker at six as she'd promised, but he made such a fuss at his dish that I dropped in a few more crunchy treats to satisfy him.

"Emotional eating doesn't solve anything, you know," I informed the cat as I tore open a bag of Cheezies from Hellhound's junk-food stash. After gobbling numerous handfuls of crunchy comfort, I rinsed the bright-orange cheddar dust off my hands and closed the depleted bag.

"Shut up, I'm coping," I said to Hooker's accusing yellow stare.

Flopping onto the couch, I took out my cell phone, weighing it regretfully. Then I drew a deep breath and initiated the phone's reset procedure.

In only a few short minutes, everything was cleared. Happy photo memories, phone numbers and addresses, friends' birthdays, funny text messages. All gone.

Swallowing hard in an attempt to fill the void in my chest, I laid the device aside to punch Kane's number into my burner phone.

He answered with a cautious, "Yes?"

"Hi, it's me. Can you talk?"

"Just a minute." After a few muffled thumps in the background, he came back on the line. "You have news?"

"Yeah. Bad news." I tried to emulate Stemp's clinical tone, but I didn't quite manage it. "Dante is missing. Probably abducted from his home. There were signs of a struggle and some blood."

"Dammit. Any demands?"

"Not yet. We think he was taken on Wednesday night and forced to call in sick to his agent. That's a long time to hold a hostage without making a demand, so if he's not being held as leverage..." I drew a deep breath that hitched in the middle. Swallowing the sob, I finished evenly, "...it's likely revenge."

"Dammit! How about Nichele?"

"She was still okay when I talked to her around four-thirty, and I'm..."

I almost said, 'getting Holt to watch her' but thought better of it. Our phones were supposed to be secure, but...

Realizing with a jolt of adrenaline that I'd forgotten to check Hellhound's apartment for bugs, I snatched the bug detector out of my waist pouch and activated it.

"Are you still there?" Kane demanded.

I drew a shaky breath of relief at the sight of the bug detector's green light. "Yeah. Sorry. I meant to say, I'm taking precautions. She'll be safe. Everything okay at your end?"

"So far. Do you have time to meet?" The tightness in the question told me things weren't exactly peachy with him.

"I wish I could, but I'll probably be too late tonight. Sorry. I'd much rather meet you than do what I'm doing."

His voice sharpened. "Are you safe?"

I sighed. "Am I ever?"

A moment of silence stretched between us.

"Do you need me?" he asked.

Now there was a question fraught with meaning.

I took a little too long to formulate my reply. "Not as much as Daniel does. I have to go. Take care. Stay safe."

"You, too." There was an odd note in his voice, but I didn't have time to analyze it before he disconnected.

Feeling eighty years old, I dragged myself off the sofa and began removing the cat hair clinging to my slacks and sweater. While I picked off the stubborn strands, my mind circled gloomily around the events of the day.

What a travesty I'd made of my so-called leadership. Holt's smooth competence had reminded me all over again how little I knew; and then I had let him take charge and order me around. Twice, dammit; once at Dante's house and again just a little while ago. What the hell was the matter with me?

As though in response, my therapist's voice murmured in the back of my mind and I straightened my spine.

"Okay, fine," I said to Hooker's snoozing form. "I know it was just my old programming kicking in, but I don't have to knuckle under to keep the peace just because I'm partnered with an angry man... again."

A wave of sickening memories made my voice quaver on 'again', and I shook my head vigorously to dislodge them.

Fuck my ex-husband, and double-fuck my old conciliatory habits.

"I'm done with that shit," I said aloud. "And I *am* a good agent. Or I will be."

Resolutely turning my thoughts in more productive directions, I mentally reviewed my earlier meeting with Riel.

Except for that brief flash of his true nature, he had been a delightful lunch companion.

I knew he was a criminal. Why did I find him charming?

"It's the accent," I decided aloud.

Hooker opened one eye and emitted a long-suffering sigh before tucking a paw over his nose and resuming his interrupted slumber.

"Holt controls people with aggression and the threat of an explosion," I elaborated, feeling my way through the puzzle. "...but Riel controls people by smiling and agreeing and complimenting them... and pretending he doesn't speak English well..."

The memory of Riel's self-deprecating "'Ow shall I say it?" echoed in my mind, and I made the connection.

"That's it! He lets you feel superior when you supply words. It's a subtle way to flatter people so they like him and want to help him. God, he's good."

Hooker didn't even twitch an ear at that revelation, and I sighed. "And I'm talking to myself. And stalling."

Pushing myself into action, I turned toward the bathroom, where a glance in the mirror revealed a depressing sight. I couldn't do anything about the giant bags under my eyes, but I swiped on some tinted lip gloss in an attempt to look a little less haggard.

After checking my destination on the internet and surveying it in street view, I considered myself as ready as I'd ever be. I brushed my fingertips across the reassuring hardness of the Glock in my ankle holster before pulling myself up to my full height and heading for the door. There I paused, every exhausted cell in my body yearning to stay in the safety of the apartment.

But all those innocent people wouldn't be safe unless I

did my job.

Squaring my shoulders, I locked the door behind me and strode out into the night.

When I arrived in the upscale neighbourhood, it wasn't difficult to find the party. Sporty cars and expensive SUVs lined both sides of the street, and light and music poured from the open door and windows of the sprawling house. A few partygoers leaned against the garage, cigarette smoke rising in the cold air.

I finally found a parking spot nearly a block away. Sitting in the darkness behind the wheel, I texted 'Going to a party!' to Holt's burner phone, along with a silly grinning emoticon in a party hat. Then I drew a deep breath and eased it out slowly.

Stay calm. Be Jane Bond, superspy.

Gritting my teeth, I sat up straighter. Or be Greg Holt, supremely confident real estate salesman, relaxed and in control.

Aydan Kelly the bookkeeper whimpered and tried to convince me to put the car in gear and drive away as fast as possible, but I shoved her behind my Arlene Widdenback persona and got out instead.

I walked straight and tall, forcing an easy stride. In front of the house I slowed. Should I go in or wait for Riel outside?

My dilemma was solved when he hurried out the front door and down the walkway to meet me.

"Arlene." His infectious smile bathed me in warm admiration, and he bowed over my hand.

"Hi," I said. Not quite as effusive as I probably should have been, but my heart was rattling around in the vicinity of my tonsils so I didn't quite trust my voice.

"Please come in out of the cold," Riel encouraged, drawing me toward the house. "The winter, he is coming soon, I think."

I cleared my throat, hoping my voice would come out normally. "I hope not. I'm enjoying a snow-free November. That hardly ever happens in Calgary." I sounded much calmer than I felt. "How is winter in Montreal?"

"Ah... Cold; much more snow than here." He shrugged philosophically. "It is winter."

"Spoken like a true Canadian," I joked.

I thought something flickered in his eyes, but it might have been a trick of the light as we stepped into the house. His smile was as ready as ever. "Complaining of our weather. It is a national sport."

"Next to hockey," I agreed.

"Yes, of course. Do you like the 'ockey?"

"I'd rather play sports than watch them."

"Ah. Yes, you 'ave that look." His gaze skimmed me appreciatively before returning to my face. "May I get you a drink?"

"No, thanks; I don't drink if I'm driving," I said reflexively, realizing even as I said it that I shouldn't drink anything at all. Who knew if he might try to drug me?

"Allow me to bring you a soda then. What would you like?"

"Ginger ale, please," I murmured, with no intention of sipping anything he handed me.

He left my side to weave through the crowd, and I used the opportunity to drift farther into the house and survey the rest of the guests.

As Riel had predicted, most wore business garb; but a significant number of young women displayed plunging necklines with ultra-short skirts and sky-high stiletto heels. Apparently our host, whoever he might be, had deep enough pockets to hire professionals for the evening. While I stood considering the scene, one of the girls wrapped herself around a male guest in an unmistakable invitation.

He squeezed her ass, and she giggled and drew him through the door to another room.

As the door opened, I spotted sofas and a few couples in various stages of undress. The atmosphere of supercharged gaiety and the lines of white powder on the coffee table gave me a pretty good idea of what was happening in there.

The door closed, cutting off my view at the same time as Riel returned to my elbow bearing a heavy crystal tumbler of carbonated fluid that looked and smelled like ginger ale. I didn't intend to find out what it really was.

As I accepted it with simulated gratitude, another rent-a-date wobbled out of the party room on unstable stilettos and sashayed up to Riel. Letting her hand drift suggestively down his chest, she leaned toward him, her lips smiling despite the blankness in her eyes.

Riel captured her wayward hand and turned her in the opposite direction before giving her a gentle push. She staggered away without a backward glance and Riel shook his head, his eyes dark. "Drugs, I hate them. Such a waste. Come, let us find better company."

I raised an eyebrow at the pink drink fizzing in his hand. "That looks interesting. What are you drinking?"

He smiled. "Cranberry and soda. I do not drink alcohol. Please..." He gestured me forward.

We moved through the room, Riel guiding me with a light touch on my elbow toward a grand staircase.

Should I let him direct me upstairs, farther away from

the exit? This party could turn ugly fast; particularly if all the guests were criminals. With only ten shots in my Glock, I didn't like my chances if things went bad.

Hell, I wouldn't like my chances even if Holt was beside me.

Momentarily preoccupied with planning escape routes, I didn't identify the suit-clad figure descending the stairs until it was too late.

Each of his arms wrapped around a nubile young woman, the bulky hard-looking man stiffened at the sight of me. Then he roared and charged down the stairs, flinging the hookers away like discarded dolls.

As I registered his identity and processed the stream of obscenities pouring from his mouth, a searing wave of adrenaline wiped out all but my last pointless thought.

Too bad I didn't have time to signal Holt, because I'd just found James Helmand.

CHAPTER 18

My reflexes took over before my brain could offer a better solution. I dropped to one knee, snatching my Glock out of my ankle holster in a fast smooth arc.

My discarded glass rolled away on the hardwood floor as James froze only a few feet away, staring into the business end of my weapon. My attention fully focused on him, I vaguely registered shrieks and frantic bodies scrambling out of the way.

"Sit on the stairs. Slowly." My voice came out hard and dead-level. Just like my gun. Somewhere in the back of my mind, Jane Bond nodded approval.

James cautiously retreated a few paces and sat, his controlled actions completely at odds with the violent and barely intelligible invective spewing from his mouth. Even at this distance the alcohol fumes emanating from him were eye-watering, and his dilated pupils suggested drugs as well.

"...Fuckin' cunt!" he was bellowing. "...Right in my fuckin' house... Riel, ya fuckin' asshole, bringin' this bitch..."

As if suddenly recollecting that he had an audience, his slick persona subsumed the rabid animal. He straightened his expensive-looking suit jacket and smoothed a hand over his mouth and chin as if to wipe away the froth of madness.

When he spoke again, it was in the precise diction that

he usually affected. "Arlene Widdenback, I presume? Or is it Aydan Kelly tonight?"

I shrugged, conscious of Riel watching with interest beside me. The room had mostly cleared, but some pinpoints of light told me a few people were recording our little show with their phones. From somewhere behind me, I overheard snatches of a conversation that sounded like someone giving the address to an emergency operator. Or possibly to a gang of enforcers. I didn't intend to stick around and find out which.

"Where's Dante?" I snapped.

"How the fuck should I-" James began, only to stop and rephrase in more pompous words. "I have no idea, nor do I know why you and my parole officer apparently think I should know. I'm simply celebrating my release with a few good friends in my own home, where, I might add, you're currently trespassing."

"Where were you and what were you doing yesterday and Wednesday?" I demanded.

He smirked. "Perhaps you should take that up with my parole officer, since I was meeting with him at the time." His smirk faded into a scowl. "And thanks to you, I just finished meeting with him again. For several hours. At the police station, where I was told I was a suspect in your friend's disappearance, consequently making me late for my own party. Which I do not appreciate in the least."

"Cry me a river," I growled, and backed toward the door. "If I find out you had anything to do with Dante's disappearance, I'll make you wish you were back in jail."

The door was mercifully still open. I stepped out, considering and discarding the idea of backing all the way to my car with my gun at the ready. Once I was in the open I was a sitting duck anyway. If somebody took a shot at me, it wouldn't matter whether they hit me in the face or the back.

I turned and walked to my car as fast as possible without actually breaking into a run.

Sirens wailed, the sound swelling rapidly.

Sliding into the driver's seat, I holstered my gun before driving toward the sound. I rounded the corner just as the first police car turned in.

A block away I parked in a quiet cul-de-sac and pulled out a secured phone. My hands shook so violently that I had to steady the phone between my knees to press the speed dial button.

When Stemp answered with his usual brisk "Yes", I barely recognized the thin croak that issued from my mouth.

"It's Aydan. I had a run-in with James Helmand at his house and had to draw my weapon. There were a lot of witnesses and the police are on the scene..." I hesitated, hearing the distinctive beating of a rapidly approaching helicopter. "...and HAWCS is up," I added. "I'm only a block away and I'm sure lots of people saw my car so they'll likely find me soon."

"Did you fire your weapon?"

"No. James charged me, but I got him covered and he settled down."

"Very well. I'll advise the police to stand down after making a show of interviewing witnesses. Did you make any progress?"

I sighed. "Other than finding out James likes cocaine and hookers and really hates me; and Riel doesn't do alcohol, drugs, or hookers? No. I wasn't there long enough."

Stemp made a nondescript sound that might have been understanding, annoyance, or disgust. "Anything else?" he asked.

"No."

I disconnected and let my head fall forward onto the steering wheel.

What a clusterfuck.

I'd accomplished nothing, and now everybody knew I kept a gun strapped to my ankle. I hadn't exactly blown my cover, but I sure as hell hadn't done myself any favours.

"Well, it wasn't like I had a choice," I growled. "In another second he would've crushed me."

Replaying the action in my head, I groaned. Kane or Holt would have pulled some martial-arts move and had James on the floor in seconds.

Never mind that; Kane or Holt would have checked to see who owned the house before they went there so they wouldn't have been blindsided in the first place.

"What a fucking moron," I muttered.

Marinating in shame, I barely noticed the red and blue flashing lights until the police car pulled up behind me.

Heart pounding, I powered down my window, placed both hands on the steering wheel, and waited.

And waited...

Long suspenseful moments passed while I sat immobile in the driver's seat and the police officers sat in the car behind me. They must be cross-checking my license number for any outstanding warrants.

Please, God, let them find Stemp's stand-down order...

Just as I was beginning to consider calling 911 and telling them myself, the cruiser's doors opened and two uniform-clad figures strode toward me to take up positions on both sides of my car.

A powerful flashlight spotlighted me. There was a glint

behind it that looked a lot like a drawn weapon. Shit.

"Your name, please, ma'am?"

"Aydan Kelly."

Goddammit! I was carrying my Arlene Widdenback ID, not my own.

"I'm undercover as Arlene Widdenback at the moment," I added feebly.

The flashlight perused my features, making me blink and squint. "May I see your license and registration, please?"

"My license is in my purse and my registration is in the glove box. Would you like me to reach over and get it for you or would you rather get it yourself?"

"Please hand me your license and we'll get the registration." As I moved slowly and carefully to comply, the passenger door rattled.

"Sorry, it's locked," I said, passing my license over and hoping I looked non-threatening. "The lock controls are just down the side of my door. Would you like me to unlock it?"

"Yes, please."

I was still blinded by the flashlight. The voice was male and his tone was serious, but he didn't sound spooked, thank God. I kept my movements smooth and slow while I pressed the release button and then returned both hands to the wheel.

The passenger door opened and a female officer reached into the glove box to extract my registration. Heart pounding, I considered. Should I tell them I was armed in case they made me step out and searched me? Or was it better to stay put and shut up?

The officer's next question eased my tension. "Who's your commanding officer?"

"Charles Stemp."

The flashlight beam released me as the officer lowered it between us. "Your clearance note popped up when I ran your plates. It's okay, you can take your hands off the wheel now."

Afraid to relax too much, I obeyed. "Thanks."

The young officer leaned down, his eyes alight with curiosity. "So you're undercover, eh? Drugs? Or gangs?"

I lifted a cautious shoulder. "It's complicated."

"Ah. Special task force, then?" He handed my license back to me and straightened without waiting for a reply. "Well, good luck. Stay safe."

As his partner tucked the registration back into place and closed the door behind her, I croaked, "Thanks; you, too. Sorry I rocked the boat."

"No problem. Always nice to get a weapons call that ends safely." He tossed me an ironic salute and strode back to his car.

Quivering, I watched them pull out of the cul-de-sac, then leaned back in my seat and did some slow yoga breathing.

In... Out... Just like ocean waves...

After a few long breaths I sat up again. It was stupid to hang around here where I might be spotted. And Holt would have heard the police sirens. If he got antsy and showed up at James's house, I'd lose the advantage of his anonymity; and Lord knew I'd attracted more than enough attention myself.

Taking out my phone, I texted Holt, "Party sucked - leaving early." I almost added "See you soon," but thought better of it. No need to broadcast our plans, just in case...

I swore violently and yanked my bug detector out. My visit to the house would have offered a perfect opportunity for one of Riel's or James's cronies to tag my car with a locator beacon...

The steady green light glowed and I studied it with paranoid suspicion. Too easy. Why wasn't I being watched?

A sickening thought occurred to me. What if the bug detector was malfunctioning?

I got out of the car and walked around it, nervously eyeing the light. It still read all-clear, and I sighed and got back in the driver's seat. I had no choice but to trust it for now.

Watching my rearview mirror for signs of pursuit, I drove a complicated circuit around the neighbourhood. After driving ten minutes without spotting a tail, I turned toward the Starbucks.

When I entered the coffee shop, Holt wasn't there.

Tension rising, I dawdled over to the counter and ordered herbal tea, then made a production out of swishing the teabag around and around in the cup while I loitered.

A man came out of the lone washroom, dashing my hope that Holt had simply succumbed to a natural side-effect of too much coffee.

But if he wasn't in the bathroom, where the hell was he?

Oh, God, what if he'd been captured? What if Riel had been one step ahead of me all along?

My overstressed nerves frayed even farther while I surveyed the coffee shop with fresh vigilance. Nobody was paying attention to me, but what if they were watching from outside? They'd be invisible in the darkness while the illumination inside the shop made me frighteningly conspicuous...

My anxious scrutiny snagged on a car parked outside, its headlights on and a mist of vapour rising from its exhaust as it idled.

A shiny red Audi Quattro.

The realtor's signs had been removed from it, and Holt waited behind the wheel.

Biting back a curse at my own stupidity, I discarded the teabag and took a leisurely swallow of tea before snapping on a plastic lid and making my way outside.

Holt jerked his chin almost imperceptibly toward my car and I obeyed his instruction, not caring anymore who was commanding whom.

As I slid into my car he backed out of his parking spot and pulled away. Too exhausted to think, I focused on the twin red beacons of his taillights and followed. Car in drive; brain in neutral.

Face-splitting yawns racked me, and my hands wouldn't stop trembling. I shivered continually despite frequent sips of my tea.

Our drive was short, and when Holt steered into a crowded theatre parking lot I groaned aloud. Of course it was packed. Nearly nine o'clock on a Friday night. And he undoubtedly expected me to buy a ticket and follow him into a darkened theatre where we could converse unseen.

The thought of staying awake for another two and a half hours while being bombarded by a too-loud soundtrack was nearly enough to make me drive away and abandon Holt to his spycraft, but I plumbed some deep well of endurance and got out of my car instead.

Holt intercepted me in the shadow of a jacked-up four-by-four.

"The party sucked?" he inquired sardonically. "Would that be the kind of suckage that requires five police cruisers plus HAWCS?"

"Don't start," I growled. "Riel set me up."

"Well, duh.   Getting invited to a party at James Helmand's house should've been your first clue."

Hearing him confirm my self-recriminations out loud was the last straw. The evening's stale adrenaline exploded into violent irritation, clenching my fists and raising my voice.

"Fuck off with the attitude! You can damn well treat me with respect, asshole!"

His fists clenched, too, his chin thrusting aggressively forward. "I'll treat you with respect when you fucking earn it, bitch!"

The world went red.

He clearly wasn't expecting the sucker-punch I hammered up into his solar plexus. The air barked out of his lungs and he dropped.

Blind with rage, I fought the urge to kick him until nothing remained but a soggy sack of bruises and broken bones.

Fortunately better judgement prevailed and I jumped back as Holt scissored his legs in a sweep that would have brought me crashing down to the pavement beside him.

He rolled to his feet, murder in his eyes.

A voice from months ago spoke in my memory: "*...he's unstable... And he's almost as advanced in hand-to-hand combat as Kane...*"

I only had time for one word.

"Shit."

CHAPTER 19

Holt froze with his fists clenched, panting and glaring.

A memory surfaced from one of my outdoor survival courses.

Don't run. It activates the predator instinct.

Afraid to move, I stood staring at Holt.

"Hey, is everything okay here?" A booming voice made us both jump, and I turned to see a very large young man whose skin matched his dark hoodie, regarding us with a furrowed brow.

I could have sworn I actually saw Holt's secret agent identity click back into place. "Yeah, thanks for asking," he said easily. He grimaced and limped a couple of paces. "We're late for our movie. We were running, and I tripped over that fucking... thing." He jabbed a finger at the innocent concrete parking curb beside us. "Fucked up my ankle..." He limped a few more steps.

"Oh." The young man turned to me. "Ma'am, are you okay?"

I managed a smile. "Yeah. I didn't hit the ground." I cast a chagrined glance at my wristwatch. "But I think we've missed our show."

"Oh." My young saviour relaxed visibly. "Well, that sucks." He eyed Holt's ankle. "Do you need a hand getting back to your car?"

"No, thanks." Holt limped in a small circle. "I just need to walk it out."

"Okay. Well, I hope your night gets better."

"Thanks, and you have a good night, too. Thanks again for checking on us," I replied, my gratitude more genuine than he'd ever know.

The young man nodded and ambled away, leaving Holt and me staring at each other in silence.

"I'm sorry," we said simultaneously.

"No, really," I added, nausea swelling in my stomach as I realized I had attacked a fellow agent and devoutly wished severe injuries on him. "Oh, God. Greg, I'm so sorry." My trembling legs let go and I dropped onto the curb, head in hands. "I'll call Stemp," I mumbled. "Tell him I'm... out of control. He'll have to get somebody else..."

Despair closed my throat. He wouldn't just 'get somebody else'. He'd declare me unfit for active duty and throw me in jail for the rest of my life.

Holt lowered himself cautiously to the curb beside me. "Cut that shit out. It's no big deal."

"It *is* a big deal." I massaged my aching temples. "I completely lost it. I'm a danger to everybody, myself included."

"Hell, we all are. Hey, come on." He nudged my shoulder roughly with his. "I should've known better than to push you right after an op went to shit. I got what I deserved. I'm not going to go running to Stemp, so why should you?"

"Because one of us could have ended up dead."

Holt snorted. "Don't flatter yourself. It'd take a hell of lot more than a little rib-tickle like that to kill me."

"No; you're not getting it." I raised my head to scowl at him. "It's so easy to kill a person. A single bullet. A quick snap of the neck. And then it's all over; you can't take it back or make it better."

He frowned, his craggy face thrown into sharp relief by the unforgiving streetlights. "No, I do get it, but I don't think *you're* getting it. This is a test. You know Stemp; he's always got an angle. He put us together for a reason. I've been gaming the psych evaluations to make it look like I'm completely over my issues, and I bet you have been, too. But he can't prove it."

Unwilling to confirm his deduction, I eyed him in silence.

Holt studied my face and grunted. "Huh. Yeah, I thought so." The corner of his mouth lifted in a grim smile. "Don't look so surprised. Hell, we're spooks. Players; it's in our skin. I played that kid a few minutes ago without even thinking. You played me earlier with the bump keys. Giving me the big eyes and the 'oh, you're so smart, how did you do that' bullshit."

"I didn't..." I began, but decided to shut up instead.

Holt grinned. "Yeah. So, Stemp's testing us. If we get through this, we're golden. If he finds out we're at each other's throats every ten seconds, we're out on our asses."

"Or we kill each other before he gets a chance to give us the boot," I pointed out stubbornly.

Holt's steely gaze bored into mine. "I can think of a lot worse ways to die than quickly at the hands of a friend."

Sudden emotion clogged my throat, and I summoned a snarky tone to hide it. "Oh, trust me, I wasn't planning to make it quick."

Holt barked out a laugh and rose, reaching down to hoist

me up. "So tell me about your party."

I grimaced. "Nothing to tell. The usual booze, cocaine, hookers..."

"Damn, I knew I should've gone."

"Yeah, it was a blast," I said sourly. "Riel obviously wanted me to meet face to face with James and I don't have a clue why. If they're friends, Riel had to know that James would love to have my guts for garters. So either he was trying to piss off James or me. I'd say he succeeded in both." I sighed, fatigue throbbing in my bones. "So James took a run at me, I pulled my gun, somebody called the cops, and I left in a hurry."

"Pursued by half the Calgary police force."

Humiliation heated my cheeks. "Yeah. I had to call Stemp to explain everything to them before they hunted me down with the helicopter and got excitable with their weapons."

Holt shook his head. "Why didn't you just drop James with martial arts? It would've attracted far less attention."

"Not in my skill set as a bookkeeper," I said shortly.

"How about as a porn star?" Holt needled, then flung up both hands in a gesture of surrender. "Kidding, okay? You're an arms dealer so it made sense to pull a weapon. Anything else?"

"No. How about Nichele?"

"I got her on camera. She's safe." He gave me a mocking bow. "I'm only watching her exterior door; no bedroom shots. If you don't need me tonight, I'll get a hotel near her place so if anything happens I can be there fast. You didn't learn anything new about Dante's abduction?"

"No. James said he didn't know anything about it."

"There's a shocker."

"Yeah." I failed to stifle a cavernous yawn, still shivering. "Stemp will keep us updated on the police investigation. If they get a break, we'll know about it. And I guess I'll just have to keep trying with Riel." I kneaded the knotted muscles in my neck. "But he's too casual about this. Not in enough of a hurry. My gut says he's not the terrorist at all, dammit."

Holt grimaced. "We can only do our assigned mission. If it's not him, it's up to the rest of the team to figure out who it really is. Go get some sleep. You look like shit."

I flipped him a weary middle finger, and he grinned and added, "If you need to call me, use my Realtor number unless you need the secured system. Might as well save some phones if we can. I'm going to pitch this one as soon as I call in my report tonight, so here's my secured number for tomorrow."

"I called mine in already," I replied. "Here's my new one."

We entered the numbers into our respective speed dials and turned back to our cars without ceremony.

The drive back to Hellhound's apartment felt agonizingly slow. Hoping to see his SUV in its assigned place, I slumped in disappointment when I turned into the parking lot at last.

He still wasn't home.

Despite my exhaustion, fear quickened my pulse. Was this an abnormally long absence? I'd never stayed with him long enough to find out. Miss Lacey would know, but...

I consulted my wristwatch. Past ten-thirty. She was an early riser, and at ninety years old she probably went to bed early, too. No need to wake her just to share my worry.

Trudging into the elevator, I propped myself against the wall for the ride to the third floor and tried not to remind myself that Miss Lacey always climbed the stairs.

Hooker's meows began as soon as my key scraped in the lock, and I crouched to prepare for his imminent escape attempt. With him successfully snared I creaked to my feet and slipped into the apartment, locking the door behind me with relief.

"Yeah, yeah," I muttered fondly as the cat scrambled down from my arms to perform his starvation act beside the food dish. "You're such a drama king."

As I leaned against the counter watching him gobble the few treats I'd tipped into his bowl, my eyelids dipped and I swayed. Jerking myself upright again, I sleepwalked out of the kitchen.

Bed. Everything would be better in the morning...

The blinking voicemail light on my cell phone made me detour to the couch where I'd abandoned it earlier in the evening.

Nichele's was the first message: "Hey, girl, I'm safe at home. I didn't see your friend the security guard, but it's okay. This is a secure building and nobody's going to get up here. I've been phoning Dante but he hasn't answered. I... I hope..." Her gulp was audible. "Well, anyway... I'm going to bed early so call me tomorrow, okay?" She sounded tired and dispirited, and my heart smote me all over again.

Was Dante being tortured right now? Or was he already dead, mercifully beyond suffering?

The next message played, and Riel's appealing voice interrupted my dark thoughts. "Allô, Arlene? It is Benoit Riel calling. I am most sorry for this evening. I did not realize that you and my friend James 'ad this..." he hesitated as if searching for the right word. "...désaccord... ah... disagreement? I 'ope you will forgive me. Please let us try again and I will make... 'ow shall I say it? Make you up to it...?"

He made a sound that somehow managed to convey one of his expressive shrugs and went on, "...Make things better. I am staying at the 'Archmans' spa, and they 'ave invited you to spend a few days also. You would 'ave your own room and all the privacy you would wish, and I promise I would not be a creep. I 'ope you will come, and we can discuss our business in a nicer way. Please telephone me."

He followed up with a contact number, and after the click of the disconnect I sat frowning at the phone.

What the hell was he up to? How could he not know about the animosity between James and me? That had to be pure bullshit.

And now he wanted me to spend time with two more people who hated my guts. 'The Harchmans had invited me', my ass. The only sincere invitation I'd ever get from them would be to take a long walk on a short pier. So why had Riel coerced them into inviting me?

Was he testing me? What kind of reaction did he want? Or was he merely trying to get me killed in a way that didn't implicate him?

My mind felt as though it was struggling through thick syrup, bumping up against unanswerable questions only to churn sluggishly on to the next one. My eyelids drooped again, and I abandoned the effort.

Tomorrow.

Tomorrow I'd formulate some useful plan and return Riel's call, but tonight?

Fuck it.

I stumbled to the bedroom and fell fully-dressed into bed.

It was coming for me. I tried to run but my feet wouldn't move. The unnameable horror drew closer, its breath hot and fetid; its claws dripping gore. My bindings tightened, crushing my chest so I could barely breathe. The beast's bristly muzzle grazed my cheek and I gave way to blind terror, screaming and thrashing-

I jerked awake and let out an aborted cry at the sight of wide feline eyes inches from my face.

"Jesus Christ! Don't *do* that!" I shoved Hooker's considerable weight off my chest. "You scared the shit out of me."

He purred and nuzzled my cheek, and his tickly whiskers clarified the origin of the dream-beast's muzzle.

"Damn cat." I massaged his scruff, slowly relaxing as his purr vibrated through the mattress.

"Don'... do tha'... 'gain..." I mumbled as sleep reclaimed me.

...I was waist-deep in blood, screaming voicelessly at the sight of Dante's eviscerated body nailed to a cross...

The dream-beast's muzzle intruded again.

When Hooker's persistent nuzzling woke me from a third blood-drenched dream, I realized he wasn't actually causing the nightmares; he was waking me when I started to mumble and struggle in their grip.

"Thanks, buddy," I whispered, and cuddled him close. "You're as good as Arnie at guarding my dreams. Lucky thing, too, or I'd have screamed the whole damn building awake by now."

Dragging myself out of bed, I shucked off my wrinkled clothes and staggered to the bathroom for a drink of water. On my way back I paused in the bedroom doorway. The sight of the empty bed made me swallow hard.

Where was Arnie tonight? Sleeping safely somewhere, or creeping through the darkness in mortal peril?

Feeling foolish but unable to stop myself, I retrieved his big black parka from the closet and tucked it into bed beside me. Wrapping my arms around it and burying my face in the scent of his laundry soap, I drifted off again.

The sound of a key in the lock jolted me out of slumber. Hooker's hoarse meows rose to a crescendo as the door clicked open and then closed softly.

"Good morning, John Lee." Miss Lacey's voice dropped as she apparently noticed my shoes and jacket beside the door. "Hush now, John Lee, we mustn't wake Aydan. Hush now, hush now..."

The meowing receded to the kitchen and fell silent seconds after a cascade of clinks indicated food pouring into the bowl. Then scratching sounds from the front closet signalled the scooping of the litter box, followed by the quiet opening and closing of the door and the scrape of the key as Miss Lacey departed.

I burrowed back into the pillow, but slumber eluded me.

Was Dante still alive? Was Riel our Remembrance Day terrorist? Maybe I should have abducted James at gunpoint last night and forced him to tell me what he knew...

I flopped onto my back, grinding the heels of my hands

into my forehead. God, I was no better than James. Two years ago I would have been sick at the thought of using violence to extract information. Now it was the first solution that came to mind.

Groaning, I flipped over to bury my face in the pillow again.

But what else could I do? There was no point in duplicating the efforts of the police or the anti-terrorist teams, and I didn't have any super-spy skills at my disposal.

But a lot of innocent people might die if I didn't figure out Riel's game in time.

After a few more minutes of miserable contemplation, I dragged myself up to sit on the edge of the bed. Hooker appeared in the doorway, licking his chops and looking smug, and I glared at him as though it was all his fault.

"So; a gunrunner, a bimbo, a slimeball, and a spy walk into a spa," I growled. "Guess what the punchline is."

Hooker yawned hugely and began to launder a paw, and I muttered, "Yeah, I didn't think it was very funny, either."

CHAPTER 20

Hoping that Stemp would suggest a better strategy than going alone into a nest of enemies, I pressed the speed dial button on a secured phone.

When he answered, I drew a deep breath and told him about Riel's invitation to Harchman's.

"...so I was thinking of going," I finished. "I don't know whether Riel's inviting me because he wants to talk or whether he's just looking for a convenient way to get rid of me, but I don't know how I'll find out unless I show up." I didn't bother to add the part about looking for information about Dante.

Please tell me it's too dangerous and forbid me to go...

"Excellent," Stemp said.

Shit.

Over the clatter of my heart dropping to the bottom of my stomach, I barely heard his next words. "That ties in with another recent development. Please accept Riel's invitation and return here for briefing at ten hundred hours this morning."

"Ten hundr..." I glanced at the bedside clock. Seven thirty AM on a Saturday. Didn't the man ever sleep?

But then again, the whole Department was likely working 24/7 on the terrorist threat.

"Can we make it ten-thirty?" I asked without much hope. "That's cutting it a little fine."

"Very well. See you then."

Stemp hung up, and I fell back on the bed with a groan. Damn. Should have tried for eleven.

Avoiding frightening reality for a few more moments, I dialled Nichele's number instead of Riel's.

"Hey, girl." Her greeting lacked its usual buoyancy. "Have... have you heard anything... about Dante?"

"Nothing yet." My words came out sounding completely hopeless, and I injected some life into my voice with an effort. "But I'll let you know if I do. Like you say, it's probably just a big misunderstanding and he's fine."

"I h-hope so." Her gulp sounded clearly over the line, and when she spoke again I could tell she was fighting to sound positive. "I'm sure they'll find him soon. I'm going to work now, so call me if you hear anything."

"I will. And my friend the security guard is watching your building. He might follow you to work, too, so don't worry if it seems like somebody's following you."

"Okay. What does he look like?"

Shit. Should I describe Holt?

"He's short, bald, and chubby," I extemporized. "And he usually wears plaid pants."

Laughter rolled through the speaker. "Omigod, Aydan! That's just sad. Why couldn't you have a hunky security guard friend?"

"Maybe because hunky security guards attract too much attention? But he's good at what he does."

"Okay, I'll take your word for it." I could still hear the smile in her voice. "It's probably lucky he's a crappy dresser. I could never resist a hot guy in uniform. It's even better than an expensive suit."

"You're such a suit slut. Go to work and don't stop to ogle any hot guys," I admonished, grinning. "And... Nichele?" My good humour drained away and I had to swallow sudden emotion. "Be careful, okay?"

Her voice trembled. "I will. You, too. Call me at lunch so I know you're okay, too."

"Will do. 'Bye."

I fell back on the bed, heartsick at the thought of how little I could do to protect her. And how little I was doing to find Dante. Surely there had to be something...

Wait, maybe there was.

I punched in Spider's number.

When he answered with a cheerful, "Good morning, Webb speaking", I got straight to the point.

"Hey, Spider, would you be able to dig up some information for me?"

"Sure. What are you looking for?"

"Could you please get me a list of any real estate in and around Calgary that's owned by James Helmand, Benoit Riel, Frederick Labelle, or Lawrence or Tawny Harchman?"

"I'll get the team started on it right away. Anything else?"

"No, that's it for now. Thanks." We said our goodbyes and I disconnected, hoping he wouldn't mention it to Stemp. Or if he did mention it, that Stemp wouldn't figure out I was looking for places where Dante might be held.

Yeah, right. Stemp was far too smart to miss something like that. The only question was whether he'd rat me out to the chain of command.

Probably not.

Unless I totally screwed up my mission with Riel, and

the chain of command demanded answers. But if that happened, Command's disapproval would be the least of my worries. I'd have to answer to my own conscience for the death of innocents.

Please don't let me screw this up...

I stared at the ceiling, the phone heavy in my hand. Time to phone Riel. What should I say? Should I pretend to be oblivious to any potential threats? Suspicious? Defensive?

And shit, what if I made the call and then learned something in Stemp's briefing that changed what I should have said? Or what if I said something completely stupid and blew my cover?

"So don't say anything stupid," I growled, and punched in the number before I could lose my nerve.

At the sound of Riel's pleasant "Allô?" my heart thudded into overdrive.

I held my voice steady with all my might. "Hello, Benoit? It's Arlene. Thank you for the spa invitation. When are we expected?"

"Ah, you will come then?" He sounded sincerely delighted, and I had to remind myself that he might simply be delighted that I was walking into his trap.

"I'm considering it, but I'd like more information."

"Ah, naturellement; of course. If you would wish to attend, your room would be ready by eight o'clock this evening; and I would be honoured if you would join me for a dinner here in Calgary at six. I have discovered a wonderful restaurant downtown and it would be my pleasure to buy your meal. We could drive out to the spa together or separately, as you wish."

"Separately," I said. "I have other business and I might

get called away."

Or I might run away. Just get in my car and drive until I found a place where I could disappear and pretend none of this had ever happened...

Riel was speaking again and I shook myself back to the conversation at hand.

"We may stay at the spa as long as we wish, of course. We shall enjoy the delicious food and the massage and the mineral pool..."

"I can come tonight, but I may not be able to stay long," I said firmly. "What's the name of the restaurant? I'll meet you there."

He gave me the name and address and repeated his pleasure at my company before hanging up with a warm 'Au revoir'.

Quivering, I lay on the bed for a few more moments before rolling to my feet to groan my way through a too-short but gloriously hot shower. I was pulling on my jeans when the sound of a key in the lock made me straighten hurriedly and yank my T-shirt over my head.

Miss Lacey must have forgotten something. At least I wasn't naked this time.

Hooker made his usual beeline for the door and I followed, pasting on a smile.

The burly figure that shouldered through the doorway transformed my fake smile to a real one as the weight of world rolled off my shoulders.

"Arnie!" I flung myself at him, burrowing into his broad chest as his arms wrapped around me.

"Hey, darlin'." The soft gravel of his voice soothed my ears as his embrace soothed my heart. "Good to see ya."

"Good to see you, too." I gave him an extra squeeze

before pulling away to study him. "Are you... okay? Did you get done what you needed to do?"

"Yeah, I'm fine. Helluva long job, but it's done." He let out a tired breath and pulled me close again to murmur into my hair, "Damn, ya feel good, darlin'."

"You feel good, too." I cuddled into his arms.

Warm lips and tickly whiskers nuzzled my ear. "I can make ya feel even better," he growled.

"Mmmm, I know you can... *umph!*" I let out a grunt of shock as a heavy weight struck the middle of my back, followed by jabs of pain as the cat used me for a climbing post. Moments later Hooker launched himself off my shoulder at Hellhound.

"Shit!" Hellhound snagged the furry missile in mid-air, tucking the cat safely against his chest and glaring down at him with mock ferocity. "Goddam dumbass furball, how many times've I gotta tell ya? Don't climb the chicks!"

Unrepentant, Hooker planted a front paw on either side of Hellhound's neck and pushed his face into Hellhound's beard, his purr rumbling like freight train.

"Ah, ya big fuckin' dumbass," Hellhound muttered, tenderly massaging the cat's scruff. "Aydan, are ya okay?"

"Yeah, the bleeding should stop in an hour or two," I joked.

"Damn, did he get ya?" Hellhound inquired with concern. "Lemme see."

"I'm just kidding. It's no big deal."

"No, lemme see." Freeing a hand from the cat, he gently turned me around and lifted my T-shirt. "Fuck, he did get ya. That's it, no more lovin' for ya."

"Wha...?" I turned to protest before realizing he was talking to Hooker.

Hellhound stooped to jettison the cat, then kicked off his boots and shed his jacket. "Come on, darlin', let's get those scratches cleaned up." He guided me to the bathroom with an arm around my shoulders.

Inside, I lifted the back of my T-shirt and twisted to examine the damage in the mirror. "It's fine," I reassured Hellhound. "It's just a few surface scratches. The skin's only broken in those two little spots."

"Yeah, but ya don't wanna let a cat scratch go," he admonished. "Take off your shirt an' turn around."

"Oooh, kinky," I teased as I obeyed.

He lifted a bottle of peroxide out of the medicine cabinet, grinning. "This ain't my usual idea a' foreplay..." I shivered as he dabbed the cool fluid on my back. "...but maybe it'll do," he finished, leaning down to nibble whiskery kisses up my shoulder to the magic spot on my neck.

"Mmmm..." I pressed backward to gyrate slowly against the stiffening bulge in his jeans. Eyes half-closed, I watched in the mirror while his clever musician's hands lightly traced the curves of my hips, dipping in at my waist and moving unhurriedly upward to cup my breasts.

His gaze met mine in the mirror while the pads of his thumbs skimmed the lace of my bra in exactly the right places.

"Hot, darlin'," he growled against my neck. "You're so hot..."

Enjoying the rough slide of his jeans against mine, I purred wordless encouragement for a few more moments before turning to face him with a sigh. "Unfortunately I'm also a tease." I reached up to give him a long slow kiss. "I have to leave right away. I have a meeting with Stemp. I'm already going to be late."

"Well, hell," he rasped. "If you're gonna be late anyway, what's a few more minutes?"

"Mmmm... or a few more hours..." I lost myself in the artistry of his kiss for a long moment before pulling away. "I really do have to go. It's urgent, and I was just getting ready to leave."

Hellhound blew out a resigned breath. "Damn."

"But first I need the bathroom," I added.

"It's all yours." He withdrew while I did what had to be done.

A few minutes later I slipped into his bedroom to see the closet door standing open while he methodically packed away the gear from his rucksack. He looked up with a smile. "Thanks for doin' my laundry. Ya didn't hafta do that."

I gaped at him. "How did you know?"

"Hell, it ain't like I could miss it. I had a T-shirt in there I'd forgotten at the gym for a coupla weeks an' I could damn near smell it from the parkin' lot. Ya shouldn'ta touched it, darlin'; it mighta burned your hands off."

"I thought that one seemed gamier than the rest. Sorry I didn't fold everything for you. I thought... um... never mind. Um... you're not freaked out, are you?"

He laughed. "Nah. I ain't dumb enough to pass up clean clothes. But if ya start hangin' up curtains or puttin' a bow on the cat, we're gonna have a problem."

"You're safe from curtains, I promise. And Hooker would probably rip my hand off if I tried to put a bow on him."

He reached down to ruffle Hooker's fur as the cat wound between his ankles, still purring. "Nah, the big suck'd prob'ly love it. So, should I ask why my parka an' duffel bag needed washin', too?"

Post-larceny guilt struck me momentarily dumb. I cleared my throat. "Um... no, you shouldn't ask."

A short silence hovered between us while he surveyed me warily. "Okay. Any chance a' me gettin' any surprise calls or visits 'cause a' what I shouldn't be askin' about?"

"Nope, no chance."

"Anythin' that might show up with Luminol or a Geiger counter or a munitions swab?"

I laughed. "No blood, radioactivity, or explosives; I promise. I only had to wash them because they were muddy."

He smiled, relief warming his voice. "Okay, good. That's all I need to know."

"Thanks." I stepped over for another hug. "Um..." I pressed my cheek against his chest, not quite able to say the words face to face. "Thanks... for trusting me," I mumbled.

"No problem, darlin'." His arms tightened around me and he dropped a kiss on my hair. "So when're ya gonna be in town again?"

"Actually, I'm coming back this afternoon." I pulled away to give him a hopeful look. "I might have a bit of time before my next thing."

"Should I ask what your next thing is?"

I sighed. "No."

"Awright. I'll be here, so call me when you're gettin' close to Calgary again." His voice dropped to a sexy growl and he bounced his eyebrows suggestively. "I'll make it worth your while."

I shivered with hot anticipation. "Mmm, I know you will. I'll be back as soon as I can."

"Be safe, darlin'. See ya later."

CHAPTER 21

In the car, I gulped a fast-food breakfast sandwich that promptly turned to lead in my stomach while I anxiously second-guessed my conversation with Riel. By the time I arrived at Sirius Dynamics I was convinced I'd made the wrong choices, said the wrong words, and was quite possibly the stupidest person on the planet.

When I reported the conversation to Stemp, cringing inwardly, he leaned back in his chair with a nod. "Excellent. Well done."

I blinked. "Uh... okay. So, um... what did you want to brief me about?"

"We recently discovered that Harchman has resumed operating his 'wellness spa', which likely means he is once again operating a brainwave-driven virtual reality network. At first it seemed unrelated to the Remembrance Day threat; but now that Riel has invited you to the spa it warrants immediate investigation. Brock and Mellor haven't been able to locate it so if it does exist, it's a standalone network without internet access. And you are literally the only person in the world with the skills to infiltrate both the site and the network."

I hid a shudder at the memory of what I'd witnessed the last time I'd infiltrated Harchman's network, and held my voice level. "So you want me to check it out."

"Yes. If he's only using it to dupe the clients of his so-called wellness spa, we'll downgrade its priority and monitor it going forward. If not..."

I nodded, fighting the tension that gripped my neck and shoulders.

"You'll use your usual network key to access it," Stemp went on, and I tried not to wince at the memory of the brain-cracking pain that always accompanied my forays into cyberspace. "You'll also carry the remote network generator so you can link to our network," he went on. "See Webb for a full briefing."

"Okay. Anything else?"

"Not at this time, but when you make the connection Webb may relay other instructions. It will depend on what you discover in Harchman's network."

"Okay."

God, please let it be ordinary porn...

Stemp's tone softened, sympathy peeking through his customary emotionless façade. "Regarding your friend's abduction... the police have interviewed his friends, family, and co-workers, and they traced his last telephone call to a burner phone that had been discarded downtown. They're currently looking for witnesses who might have seen someone dumping the phone, and they're reviewing CCTV footage of the area. I'm personally monitoring their investigation and will notify you as soon as any relevant information surfaces."

Gratitude rose, warming my heart and thickening my throat. "Thanks," I whispered.

"You're welcome." His crisp business tone returned. "Also, our surveillance picked up this conversation from

Labelle at zero eight fifteen this morning. He must have received the call on a burner phone because the wiretap didn't pick up the entire conversation, but we did get his end of the audio from our makeshift bug." Stemp busied himself at the computer keyboard and a few moments later Labelle's smooth voice rolled out of the speakers.

"Yes?" There was a period of silence while his caller presumably spoke through the other phone. Then Labelle responded, "That's short notice. It'll cost extra." Another pause. "Double the usual." A longer pause. "I completely understand; but you can't just snap your fingers to get somebody like that. And I'm only making a simple introduction between two businessmen. Whatever you arrange with him is none of my concern." Labelle fell silent for a longer period before answering, "Yes... but I won't send my best. I told you what happened last time." A momentary pause. "Maybe, but I'm not taking any chances. So, after six o'clock tonight? ...Okay. Yes, I have the address. See you later."

The recording ended and I stared at the speaker, a trickle of fear chilling my heart. I had to clear my throat so my voice wouldn't come out in a croak.

"I'm meeting Riel for dinner at six o'clock tonight."

"Indeed." Stemp inclined his head. "Be careful. Dismissed."

Down the hall, I tapped on the open door to Spider's office and poked my head in. He looked up from his computer with a smile.

"Aydan! Come on in!" As I settled myself into his guest chair, he added, "I missed you this week. I always worry when you're assigned to a mission. Is everything going okay?"

"Thanks, Spider. I'd much rather be here, believe me. And I guess it's mostly going okay..." The lie stuck in my throat, and I swallowed hard and went on, "So, what have you got for me?"

"Here's your network key." He held up the tiny cube containing the circuitry that allowed me undetectable access to any brainwave-driven network. "How do you want to carry it?"

"Um..." I frowned. "It's so tiny, I'm always afraid I'm going to lose it. I don't dare put it in my wristwatch this time." I hid a shudder at the memory of how close I'd come to disaster the last time I'd carried it to Harchman's. "Do you have any suggestions?"

"Well, we could put it in a necklace again," Spider said slowly. "Not the big emerald one, but maybe in an unobtrusive pendant..." He hesitated. "But I've never seen you wear a necklace, and if they've been gathering data about you, they'll know that."

I sighed. "Yeah, I think that's a little too obvious. It would be better if it was part of something that I always wear."

"We could... um..." A tide of colour reddened his face. "...could we hide it in your, um...?"

"In my bra! That's a great idea! It's so tiny I could just open up a little bit of the underwire seam and tuck it in." Resisting the mischievous urge to lift my T-shirt and demonstrate just to see his blush turn purple, I took the key from him. "I'll do it as soon as I get home."

"Oh..." The word puffed out in obvious relief as his flush drained away. "Okay, great. And here's the network generator." He handed me a USB stick. "If there's a virtual reality network running, you can use the generator to contact me via the internet." He eyed me worriedly. "But you won't be able to switch networks without triggering your pain response."

I shrugged, hiding my dread. "It doesn't matter. It's not like it's anything new."

Spider's eyes darkened with concern. "I know, but I just hate that it hurts you so much."

"Thanks, Spider." My smile came easily, warmed by his friendship. "So how will I contact you? I don't know what time of the day or night I might be doing this."

"Just appear in the virtual file room in our network. I've set up a monitoring program that will send an alert to my phone as soon as you become visible."

"Okay. Then what?"

"Well..." He hesitated. "If it turns out they are running a virtual reality network, you'll need to install a program on their server. It'll create a secret back door into their system that only I can access."

Uh-oh.

"So, um... you're saying I can't just go in through the virtual network and install some spy software that way?"

"Well, no." Spider gave me a regretful grimace. "That's the problem; you can't transfer information from one network to another without some kind of connection. So you'll have to find Harchman's physical server and plug this into it. It'll automatically install my back-door program." He handed me a second USB stick. "Give it about ten seconds. This little red LED..." He pointed to the end of the stick. "...will blink while it's transferring the files. When it stops blinking and goes solid red, it's done and you can pull it out."

"But first I have to sneak into the secured server room and find the right server," I finished, fear twisting my stomach into cold knots. "Great. Fabulous. No problem."

Spider's face lit up. "You're such a great agent! Anybody else would be freaking out!"

"Um..." I couldn't help it; I had to burst his bubble. "Sorry, Spider, I was being sarcastic. I am freaking out a bit. Harchman's got a fingerprint scanner to secure his server room, and as far as I know he's always got a guard in the room watching the closed-circuit security feeds, too. I have no idea how to get in; and if I do somehow get in and get past the guard, I have no idea how to find the server that's running the virtual reality network. He's got a bunch of computers in there."

"Oh..." Spider's face fell, but a moment later his smile returned. "Well, I can get you through the door. I knew about the biometric security from your report last year, so I had the lab make up some silicone fingertips with Harchman's prints on them. And once you're in, you can just plug that USB stick into all the computers you find. It won't do any harm if it's not the right computer, and it'll only take a few seconds to transfer the files. Here are the fingerprints."

He handed over a small envelope. When I peeked inside I had to squint to see the clear silicone caps. Extracting one, I pulled it carefully over my fingertip.

"Wow, it's so thin and clear I can't even see it!" I studied my fingertip.

"Well, um..." Spider shifted, pink rising in his cheeks. "Actually... maybe you should put your glasses on. I can see it from here. But of course I'm looking for it," he added tactfully. "If somebody else just glanced at your hand they likely wouldn't notice."

I delved into my waist pouch for my reading glasses, and he was right; the edge of the silicone was visible but unobtrusive.

"Thanks, Spider." I stowed the glasses and the envelope of fingerprints in my waist pouch with a sigh. "I don't even want to know what else I'm not noticing without reading glasses, but I just can't bear to wear bifocals fulltime. You only have to get hit in the face once before you get really damn tired of getting cut up by the frames."

He let out a small incredulous laugh. "Getting hit in the face once would be more than enough for me anyway, glasses or not."

"Well, yeah; it is kind of an overrated pastime. Anything else I need to know?"

"No, I think that's it."

"Okay." I started to rise, then sat back again. "Wait, one more thing..." I dug out my bug detector and handed it over. "Can you check this for me? I want to make sure it's still working right."

"Sorry, not here," he replied. "I'll have to take it back to my lab. But leave it with me and grab a new one from Stores. I'll run a diagnostic on this one later, and if it passes I'll return it to Stores." He frowned. "Do you think it's defective?"

"Um... no... not really..." I gave him a twisted smile. "I'm just feeling paranoid right now. Nobody's tracking me or listening in on me. It just seems... wrong."

He shook his head. "I really wouldn't want to live your life."

"Believe me, I'm not crazy about it either."

CHAPTER 22

I heaved myself out of Spider's guest chair and trudged down the hall, my heart thumping at the thought of confronting the guard in Harchman's server room. Even if I created some distraction outside the server room it wouldn't draw him out; it would only attract more of Harchman's security personnel. Top agents like Kane or Holt would undoubtedly have some brilliant plan to get in, but I was just a bookkeeper...

Realization struck. "No, dammit, I'm an idiot," I muttered.

"Not really; you're just a weirdo who talks to herself in public." The voice came from behind me, and I spun with a gasp to confront a half-melted nightmare of a face.

"Speak of the devil!" My voice came out a little shriller than I'd intended. "You scared the shit out of me."

Reggie Chow snorted, the undamaged side of his mouth twisting in a sardonic grin. "Fuck, Kelly, I scare the shit out of everybody, but I've never been called the devil before... to my face."

I patted my chest in an attempt to calm my hammering heart. "No, I said 'speak of the devil' because I'd just thought of you, and I'm an idiot for not thinking of you sooner."

"What, you're finally realizing what a prize I am and you

want to have my baby?"

I batted my eyelashes at him and leaned in. "Absolutely..." I breathed. Then I straightened. "Not."

His remaining black brow drew down in a scowl. "It's because of my left nut, isn't it?"

Continuing our long-running joke, I deadpanned, "No, your nuts are fine. It's because you spend your days thinking up creative ways to kill people."

"Chickenshit," he growled, but wicked humour sparkled in his good eye. "At least you're still thinking about my balls."

"They're never far from my thoughts," I assured him. "But believe it or not, I actually managed to tear my attention away from them for a minute..."

"...which makes you an idiot," he finished smugly.

I dropped the banter with a sigh. "Yeah. That part's not up for dispute." One of the civilian analysts emerged from the stairwell at the other end of the hall and I added, "Can we talk in your lab?"

"Sure." Chow fell into step beside me, his prosthetic legs giving him a slightly springy gait.

"Wearing your blades today?" I inquired, nodding down at the high-tech footpads.

"Just finished my lunchtime run."

"How's it going? Are you in your final ramp-up for the Paralympics yet?"

"Not yet. I've still got nine months. I'll be ready." He gave me penetrating glance. "So why are you beating yourself up?"

"Oh..." I grimaced and admitted the truth. "I'm so used to reacting to crises without backup, I keep forgetting that sometimes I can ask for help."

"Hm." After a few silent strides he added, "More like you don't ask for help because you're trying to prove you can handle everything, plus you have serious trust issues."

I gave him my best poker face. "As a shrink, you make a great head of weapons research."

Chow returned his distorted half-grin-half-grimace. "I'm better than a shrink. I've been there."

We halted in front of the door to the secured area and he leaned down to activate the retinal scan. When the door to the time-delay chamber closed behind us, he stepped forward to trigger the next scan. Fighting claustrophobia in the tiny space, I closed my eyes and concentrated on keeping my breathing steady.

"So, did you kick the shit out of Holt yet?" Chow asked.

My eyes flew wide open. *"What?"*

"Did you kick the shit out of Holt yet?" he repeated. "Come on, say you did. I've got good money riding on this."

My mouth opened and closed soundlessly, fighting off shock and debating whether to tell the truth.

"Sorry," I equivocated at last. "You're not going to get rich this week."

"Damn." The chamber door unlatched, and Chow shot a triumphant glance over his shoulder as he bounded down the stairs. "Made you forget about your claustrophobia, though, didn't I?"

"Asshole." I softened the epithet with a grin and followed him.

When we stepped into the Weapons lab a doleful-looking man looked up from his work at one of the counters, brightening at the sight of me.

"So?" he asked. "She didn't, did she?"

Chow shot him a disgusted look. "No, West, she fucking

didn't. But you can wipe that stupid grin off your face. It's not over yet. It could still happen."

"You seriously do have a bet?" I demanded.

"Yep," Chow confirmed. "So hurry up and smack that asshole. I'll split my winnings with you if you do. Fifty-fifty."

"How much are we talking?"

"Twenty bucks."

I raised a cynical eyebrow. "So I'd make ten bucks for committing an assault on a fellow agent that would probably send me to jail. Or get me dead. You know Holt's a martial arts expert."

Chow shrugged. "So? You've got a gun. Go on, you know you want to belt him. Think of the ten bucks as icing on the cake."

"Don't do it," Murray West urged, eyes wide and hound-dog jowls quivering with sincerity. "I *told* Reggie you were far too good an agent to do that." He turned an accusing gaze on Chow. "She's a true professional. You don't have a hope of winning this bet." Returning his attention to me with a smile that looked frighteningly like hero-worship, he added, "It's really good to see you again, Aydan. You did such a great job of testing our last inventions! Can we do something to help you this time?"

"Get back to work, West," Chow growled. "Come on, Kelly, we can talk in my office." He jerked his head toward a door in the corner.

I followed him inside, and he made a point of swinging the door shut behind us. "Sorry about West and his fanboy hard-on," he said. "He has a major thing for smart competent women."

"Like his wife?" I dropped into the guest chair, hiding

my small glow at Chow's implied compliment.

"Don't worry, he's completely devoted to Melinda." Chow took a seat behind his desk. "He doesn't want to bone you, just worship at your feet."

"Don't want to know. So, down to business..."

Chow grinned. "Don't tell me; let me guess. You want to sneak that ultrasound weapon out of here and liquefy Holt's brain."

I shuddered. "I can't even joke about that."

"Wussy."

"You're a sick twisted son of a bitch," I said mildly. "Which is why I'm consulting you right now."

"Ah, flattery will get you everywhere. Are you sure you don't want to have my baby?"

"Very sure. But I want to have your puke-pen."

"I hope that's a dirty euphemism."

"Keep hoping." I stretched out my legs, the unwholesome badinage easing my tension. "I'm talking about your nice little fake ballpoint pen that makes people fall down and vomit uncontrollably."

"Hm." Chow leaned back, frowning. "It's not in production yet. I still only have the prototype."

"So it needs testing, right? I could do that," I wheedled.

He laughed. "Oh, sure, hit me in a weak spot. How long will you need it? And where are you taking it?"

"I'd only need it for a day or two, and I'd be down around Calgary. I need to sneak into a manned server room. I've got fake fingerprints to get me through the biometric security, but I need to create a distraction once I'm inside."

"The ultrasound pen isn't a good choice for that," Chow argued. "You might as well just yell out 'hey, look at my classified weapon' if you walk into a room and point it at a guy and he promptly falls down vomiting."

"Yeah..." Inspiration struck and I gave him a hopeful look. "Don't you have a smoke bomb or something I could stick under the door so he sees the smoke before he sees me? If it was thick enough he'd just run for the door without even noticing me or the pen..."

Reality intruded and I slumped. "...oh. Shit. Never mind. It's a server room; it'll have a fire suppression system. At the first whiff of smoke it'd set off alarms and inert gas and sprinklers and God knows what else."

Chow leaned forward to plant his elbows on the desk, clearly switching into analysis mode. "Why not just use a crowd-control gas grenade that would cause vomiting all on its own? Those are standard-issue, and you could wear a gas mask. That way if he pulled an alarm or something, anybody who responded would be too busy puking to bother you, too."

I grimaced. "With my luck, I'd accidentally set it off in my room and gas myself. And if somebody searched me, a grenade would be hard to explain. At least the pen is unobtrusive."

His brow drew down. "If there's that much risk of being searched, you shouldn't carry classified tech. And you were thinking of carrying a smoke bomb anyway."

"Yeah, but not a gas mask. And anyway, the smoke bomb is a no-go."

"Why not just trank him? You don't even need to make him vomit."

I sighed. "I thought about that, but it's a small room and the aerosolized trank from the shot would knock me out as well. And the trank guns are classified tech, too, so unless I got lucky enough to be able to shoot without him seeing me,

I've got the same problem. Plus, the trank injected by the dart lasts too long. If he stays out cold for twenty minutes, ambulances get called and people get suspicious. If he's dizzy and vomiting for ten minutes and then he slowly recovers, that looks natural."

"Hmph." Chow regarded me in silence for a few moments. "I still think the gas mask and grenade is a better solution. You wouldn't have to use one of the big crowd-control grenades; we've got another type in production that's about the size of a cigar. Slip it in the door, wait a few seconds, then go in with your gas mask. The guard's on the floor puking; you do your thing; pick up the empty gas canister on your way out, and nobody knows what happened. Perfect."

"Except for the gas mask sticking out like a third tit under my T-shirt while I escape."

Chow snickered. "Well, that's it; if you're a three-titted freak, I'm not having a baby with you." He sprang up and headed for the door. "Seriously, though, you're thinking about a World-War-Two-era gas mask. We've got something 'way better than that. Come on."

Grinning at his infectious enthusiasm for all things weapon-related, I followed.

"Check these out," he commanded a few minutes later, dropping a couple of small foam cylinders onto my palm.

"Um... I need a gas mask, not ear plugs," I said cautiously.

"You whined about not wanting a third tit..." Chow gave me his scar-twisted grin. "...So stick it up your nose."

"Seriously?"

"Yeah. Obviously they're no good for contact irritants like tear gas, but they'll filter out the nauseating gas as long as you don't accidentally breathe through your mouth. And they're extremely discreet. People can walk right up to you and never even notice them."

I eyed him suspiciously. "Or maybe you just want to watch me stuff a pair of cheapo earplugs up my nose."

Chow guffawed. "That'd be almost worth the pain you'd inflict on me later."

"Almost?" I prodded.

Murray West sidled over wearing an ingratiating expression. "It's okay, Aydan, they really are nasal filters. I'd never let him play a trick like that on you."

Bestowing my best smile on him, I said, "Thank you, Murray," and gingerly inserted a plug in each nostril. While I inhaled, Chow turned to West. "Let off one of those godawful cabbage farts you do so well. Might as well make it a good test."

West went crimson. "I... I... don't..."

"Ignore him, Murray, he's a jerk," I said, my voice sounding slightly congested. "Damn, there's not a lot of air flow in these things..."

"There is a bit of restriction," West agreed hurriedly. "You may want to wear them for a while to get used to them so you don't accidentally suck in a mouthful of gas when you're using them for real."

Clamping my lips shut, I breathed slowly through my nose. It wasn't as bad as having a head cold, but nonetheless the first fingers of claustrophobia gripped my throat.

Slowly suffocating...

I fought the fear, closing my eyes to concentrate. It would only be for a few minutes. I could do this.

Slow breaths. In... Out... Just like ocean waves...

"Never mind; take them out, Kelly." Chow's voice made

me twitch, and I gasped a mouthful of air as my eyes popped open. "I can give you something else," he added.

Trying to figure out a graceful way to extract the plugs without sticking my fingers up my nose, I panted a few grateful breaths through my mouth. Then I abandoned dignity and plucked the filters out. "I really hope these are disposable."

"Ah, just lick 'em off and they'll be as good as new," Chow wisecracked.

"That's disgusting!" My loyal Murray held out a garbage bin. "Here, Aydan. Of course they're disposable."

"Thanks." I discarded the plugs and turned back to Chow. "You have something else?"

"Nothing as unobtrusive as that, but I do have another compact option." He jerked his chin and I followed him to another counter. "This is good for half an hour, less if you're trying to breathe something really nasty." He reached into a drawer to withdraw a cupped oval patch. "It's self-adhesive and disposable; just slap it over your nose and mouth and seal the edges to your skin." He held it out to me. "Give it a try."

I sealed the patch over my nose and mouth as directed. Exhaling was easy, but on inhalation the patch sucked back against my nose and mouth, restricting my breath almost as much as the nasal filters but with the added bonus of recalling the sensations of being bound and gagged. My pulse spiked in response and I fought panic.

Settle down, for chrissake...

Chow reached over and ripped the patch off.

"Ow!" Sucking in a breath, I patted the stinging areas and glared at him. "What the hell? Could you at least leave me a *little* skin?"

"You were having a panic attack."

"I was not."

"Bullshit. You went white, your pupils dilated, your respiration increased, and that little vein in your throat popped out like a garden hose. It was 'way worse than the nasal filters."

I shook my head stubbornly. "I would have been fine. I was dealing with it."

Gripping my elbow, Chow steered me around a corner out of West's sight and lowered his voice. "You don't have to be a fucking hero here. When you're in the field, you're going to have heightened anxiety and increased heart rate and respiration on top of whatever issues you're dealing with now. You really want to take a chance on sucking in a lungful of gas and getting caught puking your guts out right beside the guard? Or trying to deal with a panic attack in the middle of an op?"

"No, but I need to get in there and I can't think of another way. Can you?"

"Exactly what have you got to work with?"

"Windowless room, manned 24 hours, one exit controlled with biometric security. End of story."

He scowled. "Fine, I'll lend you the pen. But take a set of the nasal filters just in case. If things go sideways and you end up having to trank him after all, they'll protect you from the aerosolized gas."

My relief came out on a long breath. "Thanks, Reggie."

"You're welcome." He studied me for a moment, the gaze of his good eye disturbingly keen next to the blank stare of his prosthetic one. "I get the whole trust-issue thing, believe me. But don't bullshit me again. I'm a fucking weapons genius, but I can't make stuff work for you if you won't tell me when you're having a problem."

Heat rose in my cheeks. "Sorry," I mumbled. "I don't do trust very well."

Chow grunted. "You don't do it at all. I'll get the pen. Just don't let anybody see you using it." He headed for one of the secured rooms.

Waiting, I drifted around the corner again only to come face to face with Murray West's eager basset-hound features.

"Aydan..." He leaned in confidentially. "I just wanted to mention, if you ever need anything... any kind of specialized research... just let me know and I'll do it for you. I sometimes help Melinda with the research for her books; in fact, she used some of my work in her latest bestseller. Of course, she's so brilliant she doesn't need my help, but..." He drew himself up. "I'm the one who told her about the short-beaked echidna's four-headed penis and long fast tongue, and she used it for one of her alien sex scenes..."

Chow mercifully returned with the pen and a fresh set of nasal filters, so I limited my response to a choked, "Thanks, Murray, I'll keep that in mind", and hurried for the door.

Chow trailed me, grinning. "Let me guess, West just dropped the quadruple-cock story on you."

Shaking my head in an attempt to dislodge the thought, I muttered, "That's a mental image I just didn't need to have."

Chow snorted. "Hell, try sharing a lab with him and Melinda. I swear, every time I turn around they're fucking in the supply closet. I'm so traumatized that even when I'm at home, I still look away before I open a closet door."

"Better you than me," I said without sympathy. Halfway out the door, I paused and turned back. "Reggie..." I raised the pen. "Thanks. I, um... I do trust you, you know."

His mouth softened for an instant before curling into his

usual sardonic half-smile. "Nice try at sucking up, Kelly, but your ass is still going to be in a sling if you lose that pen."

I grinned and faked confidence. "I won't."

CHAPTER 23

A quick trip to Stores provided me with a replacement bug detector. On impulse, I also requested a set of bump keys. They didn't have Holt's magic O-rings, so I dropped by the local hardware store before steering my car back to my farm.

There I scanned my house, garage, and car with the new bug detector. Its light remained obstinately green, and at last I put it away with a sigh that wasn't quite relief.

After a check-in with Nichele and a quick lunch, I spent a few minutes researching bump keys on the internet, then used one of my new ones to open my front door lock almost as rapidly as Holt had broken into Dante's house.

Shit.

I was shopping online for secure door locks when my burner phone vibrated on the desk beside me.

Probably Riel. Let him leave a voicemail. Then I'd have time to figure out my response instead of making a decision on the spot...

With a start, I realized it wasn't Riel. It was the other phone.

Kane.

I scooped up the phone. "Hello?"

Kane's voice was taut. "We have a situation."

"What..." I began, but he was still talking.

"Meet me where you ran through the spider web," he rapped out, invoking our code from long ago. "Today. The number of times we've slept together."

Before I could gather my thoughts, the line went dead.

"Wait, hang on!" I protested into the silence. "...Shit."

I pressed the callback button but he didn't pick up, and after twenty rings I disconnected and stood staring at the phone in my hand.

Had he been attacked and overpowered? Or had he simply ditched the phone as a precaution?

Swallowing hard, I turned the phone over and over in my hands as if it might magically disgorge instructions for what to do next.

Should I call Spider and have him trace the phone? Get on the highway and drive like a bat out of hell to Alicia's house? To Kane's condo?

But he hadn't sounded as though he was in danger. Just... terse. In secret-agent mode. And he'd obviously planned his message so that even if it was intercepted, nobody would know when and where we were meeting.

I leaned back in my chair, frowning. Hell, did I even know? The 'where' was easy enough. But when?

"Today; I got that," I muttered. "But 'the number of times we've slept together'? I guess that would correspond to hours on a clock. Like six times would be six o'clock..."

I trailed off, staring into space. But how was he counting? Times we'd actually slept together in the same bed? That would make it...

I counted in my head. Four. If I ignored the technicality that he'd been the only one sleeping while I lay awake having panic attacks.

But what if he meant the number of times we'd had sex? Muttering, I enumerated the list on my fingers. "In my bed that first time when I thought he'd been killed; in the woods; in his bed when he seduced me at his place; twice when we thought we were going to die in that plane crash; three times at his place in Silverside when I thought I'd have to marry him..."

I suppressed a shudder at the memory of how messed up I'd been then. Thank God Arnie had rescued me. And now, after months of therapy and soul-searching, I knew that if Kane and I ever had another relationship conversation I could be completely honest with him.

Probably.

Mostly.

But he was with Alicia now, so that wouldn't happen...

Pulling my thoughts back to the situation at hand, I frowned at my fingers. "Eight. So, eight o'clock. He couldn't mean the number of orgasms I had. There aren't enough numbers even on a twenty-four hour clock."

My mind drifted again to memories of his muscular body hard against mine; his hot mouth and hungry hands...

I shook myself back to reality and sat up. "Okay, so it's either four or eight. Well, that narrows it down. Not."

Unable to sit still any longer, I dragged myself to my feet to pace around and around my small office.

"I bet he means four," I muttered after a few laps immersed in thought. "He'd want to meet as early as possible. But hell, if I'm wrong, we're hooped. By eight I'll be with Riel. He'd better mean four, dammit!"

Door locks forgotten, I hurried to my bedroom to pack. Dress-up clothes for dinner with Riel and a stay at Harchman's fancy spa. Black yoga pants and a baggy T-shirt for loungewear that would conceal a waist holster and also be unobtrusive if I was sneaking around in the darkness. Jeans and hiking boots in case I had to crash through the bush again.

Should I take formalwear, too, just in case?

I glowered at the half-packed suitcase. "Why don't I just bring my entire fucking closet?" I snarled. "And why can't the rest of the world just get over itself and let me wear jeans all the time?"

The suitcase made no reply, and after another moment of indecision I added a cocktail dress, heels, stockings, and jewellery, muttering imprecations under my breath.

A glance at my watch accelerated my pulse even more. One-thirty already. I barely had enough time to get back to Calgary and drive across town to get to Kane's meeting place at four.

I restocked my supply of secured phones, tossed a couple of extra magazines for my Glock and trank pistol into my suitcase, and hit the road.

My mind fully occupied with anxious speculations, I had been driving for nearly an hour when I remembered my 'date' with Hellhound.

Shit.

Pulling over, I punched in his number and waited.

It rang repeatedly on the other end, finally going to voicemail.

"Hi, Arnie," I said. "I'm sorry, something's come up and I'm not going to get to see you this afternoon. I'll catch up with you later, okay? Take care."

I almost added 'I love you', but settled for ''Bye'. If my

enemies somehow got access to his voicemail, I didn't want them to know how much he meant to me.

Steering back onto the highway, I stared anxiously out the windshield. He had said he'd be there. He was expecting my call. So why hadn't he answered? And if he'd been busy at the moment I called, why hadn't he called back?

Maybe he was with another woman. I tried to comfort myself with memories of his wicked grin the other times I'd accidentally walked in on one of his trysts.

But somehow I couldn't imagine him hitting the sheets with somebody else when he knew I was on my way. And anyway, I was pretty sure he hadn't been skirt-chasing as much lately...

A sudden horrible thought made my guts clench.

Oh, God, what if something had happened to him? What if he'd been attacked or abducted? Was that what Kane's 'situation' was?

I drew a deep breath and let it out slowly.

It would take an army to overpower Hellhound. And if Kane knew his best friend was in danger, he wouldn't mess around with an encoded message; he'd tell me right away...

My phone vibrated and I nearly drove off the road in my rush to pull over. The number on the call display was unfamiliar, and I answered with a cautious, "Hello?"

"Hey, darlin'..."

"Hi, Arnie!"

My initial relief vanished when he kept talking over me, his words fast and tight. "...Sorry I can't see ya today; somethin' came up. Watch your six. Love ya."

The click of his disconnect shattered the fragile dam I'd constructed around my worries, and they cascaded over me like icy water.

His wording told me he hadn't gotten my earlier message, so he wasn't at home. The unfamiliar number confirmed that. And that terse 'watch your six'... Was it general advice to watch my back, or did he know something bad was coming my way?

I dialled the number back, but it rang and rang without an answer. My heart thumped harder. Maybe he'd had to ship out on an unexpected job.

But Dante had made one call from a burner phone before he disappeared. What if this was Arnie's one call?

Had his 'love ya' carried extra meaning this time? Were those the last words of a man who knew he was going to certain death?

"Oh, God, no," I quavered. "Arnie, please be okay."

By the time I parked at the coffee shop where I was to meet Kane, my shoulders were aching with tension. Peeling one tight finger after another off the steering wheel, I leaned my head back against the headrest and attempted some yoga breathing.

In... out...

In...

My breath hitched at the sight of a black Expedition pulling into the parking lot, but the narrow-shouldered man who got out couldn't have been Kane even in disguise. Nothing could hide that spectacular build.

I consulted my wristwatch for approximately the tenth time. Only a few minutes before four. How long should I wait?

A peevish voice from the past spoke in my memory. *"How stupid are you? If he wasn't there at the appointed time, he obviously had to abort. You don't hang around attracting attention."*

"Thanks, Kasper, you dickhead," I muttered. "I'm glad I shot your stupid face off."

But he had been correct at the time; and he was probably correct now, too. If Kane didn't show up by five after four, I shouldn't stick around.

Five after four came and went, leaving me jittering in the driver's seat. Dammit, he must have meant eight...

Sudden realization struck me, and I groaned. Shit, I'd counted wrong. I'd forgotten that time he'd been drugged and ended up sleeping in my bed after our first explosive round of sex. He must have meant five. Or maybe...

Clenching my fists in my hair, I redid the tally yet again. What if he'd included the time at the commune when Hellhound and I had dragged his mattress over beside ours to soothe his nightmares while he slept?

Six.

Dammit, I couldn't make it at six; I'd be sitting down to dinner with Riel.

Which was more important?

My heart cried 'Kane' with all its might, but I muffled it with cold facts.

Hundreds of innocent lives might be on the line. And Kane had sounded tense but not frantic. He was a top agent. I had to trust that he could deal with his 'situation'; just like he had believed I could take care of myself last summer.

I drove away resolving to come back at five just in case, but the knowledge that he almost certainly wouldn't be there weighed in my belly like a cold stone. He must have meant six o'clock.

But what if he *had* meant four o'clock, and something

had prevented him from coming?

Had Riel set up our dinner date so he could gloat that all my lovers were hostages?

Or worse, so he could tell me they were all dead and watch me shatter?

A cold wave of fear swamped me. I hadn't heard from Holt all day, either.

Nichele.

"Oh, no. No, no, no..."

CHAPTER 24

Trembling, I pulled into the nearest parking lot and dialled Holt's number.

The phone rang once.

Twice...

"Greg Holt, Realtor. It's a great day to sell your house!"

"Hi," I croaked, then cleared my throat and tried again. "Can you meet for coffee in twenty minutes?"

"Sure thing," he said breezily. "The usual place?"

"Yeah. See you there."

I disconnected and sat staring at the phone. Should I call Stemp?

No. I had no new facts to report except that I apparently couldn't count; and Hellhound had stood me up. Not exactly a useful update.

I tried Arnie's burner number again but there was still no answer. Blowing out a tension-filled breath, I put my car in gear and headed for my meeting with Holt.

My mind flitted like a distracted sparrow, pecking at each possibility only to drop it and jump to the next.

What if Labelle had hired an assassin to pick me off as I went into the restaurant tonight? Or worse, abduct me and torture some critical piece of information out of me? Should I get Holt to come to the restaurant for backup?

But if Kane had something urgent to tell me, somebody needed to meet him. And with hundreds of innocent civilian lives at stake, I couldn't ditch my mission.

And what about Arnie and Nichele and Dante?

Dammit, I needed to meet Kane...

When I arrived at the coffee shop, the red Audi with its Realtor signs was already in the parking lot. Inside, Holt rose to greet me with one of his shit-eating grins and a hearty handshake.

I dragged my lips into an answering smile and chose an herbal tea before seating myself at the table Holt had claimed in a quiet corner.

"Is Nichele okay?" I asked as my butt landed in the chair.

"Yeah. Nobody following her but me."

I flopped back in relief. "Thank God. At least that's one less thing I have to worry about." Hugging my paper cup, I reported Labelle's worrisome arrangements for six o'clock as well as my conversations with Riel and Kane, conveniently omitting the details of Kane's time-counting code. "...so I can't meet Kane at six and I don't have a clue what his 'situation' is," I finished. "It didn't sound good, though."

Holt scowled. "That's not related to our mission. Kane's a civvie now. Let him deal with his own shit."

I held onto my temper and kept my voice level. "James was following him and words were exchanged. James is related to our mission."

"That doesn't make Kane related to our mission. And there's no evidence that James has anything to do with it, either. Just because Riel and Tawny Harchman know him, that doesn't mean squat. They probably know a shitload of people." Holt crossed his arms and leaned back, his scowl deepening. "You want to know what I think?"

"No, but you're probably going to tell me," I muttered, but he was already talking over me.

"I think you've got a hard-on for James because he beat the hell out of you and your friends. I get it; the guy's a fucking waste of skin and you want to see him go down. But leave your personal shit out of this, Kelly. Focus on the mission."

"I am focused on the mission," I snapped. "Listen, Kane wasn't just calling to say 'Hi, let's get together for coffee'. He used a secret code from our first op together. He wouldn't have done that without a damn good reason."

Holt's frown turned thoughtful. "Huh." He sat in silence for a moment before adding, "Okay. I'll meet him. But you damn well better not get yourself killed while I'm doing it. Stemp would have my ass."

I snorted. "If I'm busy getting killed, your ass will be the least of my worries."

"So have you reported Kane's call to Stemp?"

"Um..."

Holt scowled. "You haven't, have you?"

"I haven't had time," I began, then stiffened my spine. Dammit, I wasn't going to let Holt intimidate me. "And I don't intend to unless it turns out to be relevant," I said firmly. "I'm trusting my gut, but I don't have enough to report yet."

"Huh." He eyed me levelly. "Yeah, okay. I always trust those gut feelings, too. If you're sure."

I hesitated. If Kane only wanted to vent about Alicia or talk about Daniel, I was risking my life and my tenuous reputation as an agent for nothing.

But surely he wouldn't have used that code unless he needed to discuss something critical.

"Good. Thanks," I said. "Let me know as soon as you talk to him. Nobody's been listening in on me yet, but I'm sure that'll change once I'm with Riel. So if you need to get in touch with me you'll have to be creative. I'll check in with you as soon as I'm clear of Riel after dinner."

At least if something disastrous happened to me at six o'clock, Holt would know within an hour or two...

Somehow that thought wasn't as comforting as I'd hoped.

"No problem," Holt replied. "After I make contact with Kane I'll use the Realtor phone and leave you a message that I have a potential buyer for Dante's house and for you to call me ASAP."

"Perfect."

I was just beginning to rise when Holt asked casually, "So how long have you been screwing him?"

"What?" My knees gave way and I plopped back into the chair. "What the hell did you just say?"

Holt gave me a long-suffering look. "How long have you and Kane been screwing? Hell, Kelly, I know how it goes. You work a few ops together and get close; shit happens, right?"

"Wha..." I closed my flapping jaw with a glare and snapped, "What, you screw all your female partners so you figure everybody else does, too?"

"Not all of them." He gave me an appraising look as though gauging my potential as a bedmate. "Most, though. It just seems to happen that way."

"It just happens?" I summoned up some righteous indignation in an attempt to hide the truth. "Well, news flash, Romeo: it's not going to happen this time. Keep it in your pants, and I won't cut it off." I rose. "I'll text you from

Harchman's when I can. If you don't hear from me by ten tomorrow morning, the shit's hit the fan and I need backup."

Holt leaned back, amusement glinting in his eyes. "Nice redirection. Well played, Kelly. Talk to you later."

I marched out under his knowing gaze, back straight and cheeks flaming.

Driving toward Kane's meeting place again in time for five o'clock, I tried to reassure myself with positive thoughts. He'd be there. Maybe he'd only been late before, and I'd left just before he arrived. He'd find some way to communicate...

A fast survey of the parking lot a few minutes later made my heart sink. No black Expedition.

But maybe he was driving a different vehicle. Dammit, why hadn't I thought of that an hour ago? What if he'd been waiting here and we'd missed each other because I was too dumb to go and stand at the designated place?

Muttering curses under my breath, I parked and trotted over to the back door of the coffee shop. Leaning against the wall and trying to look unobtrusive, I made a mental note to buy a pack of cigarettes for situations like this. At least if I had a cigarette in my hand, I'd have a reason for loitering outside in the chill of the rapidly-approaching dusk.

I compromised by pulling out my phone as if texting somebody, but I still felt far too conspicuous. The rancid stink of a nearby garbage dumpster made my stomach shift uneasily.

At five after five, I had to admit defeat. I'd missed him. Or he hadn't come at all.

Or wait; maybe he'd left a message for me...

After a glance around the parking lot, I made a quick hop, skimming my fingertips across the top of the door frame beside me; then hopped again to check for anything on top of the wall-mounted light fixture.

All I gained was a layer of gritty filth on my hand.

Sighing, I trudged back to my car. I had exactly enough time to drive to Arnie's place, change my clothes, and get to the restaurant in time to meet Riel...

Hope flooded me. Maybe Arnie was home by now. Or maybe he'd left a message for me with Miss Lacey.

Heart beating fast, I swung into my car and hit the gas.

"No, I'm sorry, Arnold didn't leave you a message." Miss Lacey's sharp black eyes measured me. "He merely said he had to leave on another job and asked me to care for John Lee until he returned."

"Did he say when he was coming back?"

"No, his work is unpredictable and generally takes him away for several days at a time. Is there anything with which I may assist you?"

"No." The word fell between us like a tepid lump, and I attempted a smile and added, "Thank you, though. But... did you notice, was he with anyone when he left? Or was he carrying anything?"

Her brow furrowed. "He was alone and carrying his rucksack as usual. May I inquire why you're asking? Is anything wrong?"

My tension eased. He hadn't been abducted. Thank God.

"N-no... I don't think so. It's just... he sounded odd when he called me and I'm worried."

Her face softened. "Aydan... I don't know how to put this tactfully, so I shall be blunt and hope you understand that I mean no offense. Arnold has longstanding emotional issues which make him irrationally afraid of commitment. You are the only woman he has ever allowed into his life, even peripherally; and it may be that he is withdrawing because he fears you are becoming too close. You would be wise to give him space."

I drew a deep breath. "Thanks, Miss Lacey. I know about his commitment phobia and we have an arrangement that's comfortable for both of us. I don't think it's that..." I trailed off.

Hell, maybe it was. Maybe he'd been lying about being okay with me staying at his place and doing his laundry. Maybe he was running scared.

"No, I really don't think so," I said, half to myself and half to Miss Lacey. "If he was running scared, he wouldn't have said he loved me before he hung up."

A small choking noise interrupted my reverie, and I blinked back to the present and Miss Lacey's goggle eyes. "He... he said he loved you?" she demanded. "My heavens! My... My dear, that is... simply... marvellous!"

"Oh. No, it's not what you think," I assured her. "We both know there's no commitment attached to that. Nothing's changed between us. He lives his life and I live mine. No strings attached."

A smile softened her lips and her eyes were bright. "Unconditional acceptance is love in its truest form. I never thought I would live to see my beloved Arnold find that level of trust with anyone. You have made this old woman very happy today."

I shuffled my feet. "Well, um... I'm glad, I guess, but..."

"Try not to worry." She patted my hand. "I'm sure Arnold will return in time for Remembrance Day. It is a meaningful time for him, and he always takes me to attend the service at Battalion Park. In all the years I've known him, he has never missed it."

A chill slithered down my spine. "Um... Miss Lacey... have you been following the news lately? Maybe you should skip the Remembrance Day service this year."

"Of course I read the news, dear." She straightened, black eyes snapping and mouth firming. "And I most certainly shall not allow some cowardly terrorist to prevent me from expressing my respect and gratitude to those who offered their lives in exchange for my freedom and safety."

"But do you really think those veterans would want you to risk your safety now?" I pleaded. "Maybe this year you could-"

She held up a fragile blue-veined hand. "Excuse me for interrupting you, Aydan, but please save your breath. At my age I have little left to lose except my self-respect. I would rather die than surrender to craven fearmongers."

I drew a deep breath. Maybe Arnie could talk her out of it, or simply refuse to take her to the service. Or maybe he wouldn't get back in time.

Or maybe he'd never come back...

I fought off the tightening of my throat and held my voice level. "Okay, I won't argue with you. So... I might be staying at Arnie's place for the next few days. Don't worry if you hear me coming and going. I'm sorry I won't be here reliably enough to feed Hooker, though."

"It's quite all right, dear." She smiled. "I enjoy my times with John Lee. He is an agreeable companion."

"Yeah." I glanced at my watch. "Well, I'd better get

going. I'm sorry to have bothered you."

"It's no bother at all. If Arnold returns I shall tell him to contact you immediately. Have a pleasant evening."

"Thanks, Miss Lacey. You, too."

She withdrew into her apartment and I crossed the hall to Arnie's door, anxiety tightening my neck and shoulders. Hooker made his usual break for freedom, and I scooped him up and deposited him unceremoniously on the mat inside the apartment, closing the door behind me.

When he made for the kitchen with purposeful meows, I shook my head. "Sorry, big guy. Miss Lacey will be giving you supper in half an hour, and I barely have time to get changed and get out of here."

I skinned out of my jeans and donned slacks and a blouse under his indignant yellow gaze, then let myself out before I could change my mind.

My car clock read five-fifty as I circled the block around the restaurant, searching for potential threats and a parking place with equal vigilance. After shoehorning my car into a spot that would likely require a can opener to extract it later, I drew a deep breath and consulted my bug detector again.

Its green light glowed as steadily as ever.

Still nobody tracking me.

But why would they? Riel knew exactly where I was going to be.

I cast a nervous glance around me. Crammed between a panel van on one side and a half-ton truck on the other, my car would be almost invisible unless somebody walked right up to it.

And if somebody planted a bomb under it while I was

eating dinner, the blast would be nicely contained by the surrounding vehicles...

"Cut it out," I admonished myself. "Riel doesn't want to kill you. He still wants something from you. Labelle could have been making a deal for six o'clock with anybody. It might have been sheer coincidence."

Wishing I could believe that, I unfastened my seatbelt and cracked open my door.

Struck by a sudden thought, I closed the door again and leaned back in my seat.

It wouldn't matter if I was a few minutes late, and by then Holt would have met Kane at six and I could get his report in solitude instead of trying to disguise my conversation in front of Riel.

Not to mention that it might put a crimp in Labelle's plans if he'd scheduled an attack on me.

The minutes dragged slowly past.

My anal-retentive bookkeeper's persona squirmed at the embarrassment of being late without calling, but I squashed her determinedly. Patience.

At ten after six I was completely out of patience and almost at the end of my scant store of endurance when my phone rang at last. The call display said GHoltRealtor, and I punched the Talk button with a shaking finger.

"Hello?"

"This is Greg Holt, Realtor calling. I waited as long as I could, but that potential buyer didn't show up. Let me know if you hear from him again, okay? We can arrange a showing for him at another time."

My heart turned to lead and plummeted to the pit of my stomach. "Oh... That's, um... too bad. I'll... I'll let you know if I hear from him... but..." I squeezed my eyes shut in chagrin. "Maybe I got the time wrong. Maybe it was eight, not six."

"What?" Holt's voice rose in irritation. "How could you mistake eight for six?"

"It was a bad phone connection and I was having trouble hearing," I croaked. "I'm sorry. Could you please try again at eight?"

"Of course." The words sounded as though they were being strained through his clenched teeth. "The customer is always right. I'll be in touch."

I disconnected, my mouth dry. Why hadn't Kane come? Had I totally misinterpreted his message?

Or had he vanished after a single phone call like Dante and Arnie?

CHAPTER 25

After a few moments of fearful hesitation, I squeezed out of my car and sidled along the narrow gap between it and the panel van. I couldn't see a damn thing beyond the two tall trucks. I could be stepping out into a hail of bullets.

Or somebody might be hiding under the panel van, waiting to grab my ankles and yank me underneath...

Heart hammering, I snapped a glance under the van.

Nothing.

The sound of footsteps on concrete in front of the truck made me catch my breath. Was a gunman coming for me?

Should I confront him or turn and flee?

Dammit, in this narrow gap I couldn't even reach my ankle holster easily...

The footsteps carried a well-dressed woman in front of my car, and I clenched my teeth and strode forward. Surely if she was strolling along without a care in the world, there couldn't be thugs lurking just beyond my field of view.

When I emerged from the gap, nobody was in sight. With a sense of anticlimax mixed with relief, I scuttled to the door of the restaurant.

Inside the foyer, I paused to take a long slow breath in an attempt to dissipate my adrenaline.

Made it. Not dead or abducted.

Yet.

I straightened my spine and put on a pleasant expression before striding up to the reception station.

"I'm meeting someone for dinner," I informed the suit-clad young man. "Benoit Riel?"

"Yes, ma'am; he's here already. This way, please."

I followed him, my mind whirling with half-baked strategies. Should I pretend nothing was wrong? Or confront Riel and demand what he knew about my disappearing men? A brief but glorious vision of my hands around Riel's throat while he choked out answers made me smile as we rounded the corner.

Riel rose from his table with an answering smile. My heart sank at the sight of Frederick Labelle beside him, giving me one of his big insincere grins, too.

Dammit. Was this part of his six-o'clock plan? And with Labelle here, would Riel clam up?

"Allô again, Arlene," Riel greeted me. "You honour us with your presence."

He bowed over my hand and courteously remained standing while the maître-d' seated me. As he and Labelle resumed their own seats, I made my decision.

Concentrate on the mission. Betraying my concern over the missing men would only endanger them further. Arlene Widdenback was a stone-cold bitch, so she wouldn't care enough about anyone to make a scene if they'd disappeared.

Of course, I'd already spoiled that impression by demanding Dante's whereabouts from James at gunpoint; but I conveniently ignored that inconsistency.

I focused on Riel with my best fake smile. "I'm sorry I'm late. It took longer than I expected to find a parking spot."

"It is quite all right. The parking here, it is very difficult, no? And expensive. Even in Montréal it is not so dear."

I nodded. "I try to avoid coming downtown if I can."

After a few more banal pleasantries, we settled down to peruse the menu. I stayed silent, my mind racing while I skimmed the offerings without seeing them.

How should I approach this? With Labelle here, I'd have to wait for Riel to make the first move in the weapon negotiation. What could we talk about? My handy-dandy spy courses had recommended that I build rapport or fake a sexual attraction, but neither of those seemed like a good idea. Arlene Widdenback didn't give a shit about building rapport with anybody; and Riel wasn't giving off a sexual vibe, despite his charm. And I sure as hell wasn't going to cozy up to Labelle.

"I 'ope there is something on the menu that appeals to you." Riel's pleasant voice interrupted my thoughts. He made another of his self-deprecating sad faces. "I would be most sorry if I had made this restaurant to be so wonderful, only to find you do not like any of the food."

"No, that's not the problem at all." I gave him my best smile. "My problem is that everything looks good and I can't decide."

Inspiration struck. He makes people like him by pretending he needs help.

I could do that.

I laid down the menu and added, "I'll put my fate in your hands. I'm sure you know all the best dishes, so please choose your favourites for me. I like everything, so you can't go wrong."

Surprise and pleasure warmed his expression. "Ah, you honour me again with your trust. I shall not disappoint you."

When the waiter arrived Riel ordered both our meals. I

leaned back in my chair and concentrated on keeping a pleasant expression on my face while trying to develop a strategy that would advance both my assigned mission and my personal one.

Riel opened the conversation with a discussion of the food he had ordered, and soon we were chatting about gourmet cooking. Even though both Labelle and I made subtle attempts to steer the conversation during the meal, Riel remained charmingly convivial to me and ignored Labelle except to respond to his sallies with replies as brief as basic politeness required.

When dessert arrived at last, I scowled at the delicate meringues on my plate. The meal was almost over. I'd have to say something about the weapon despite Riel's obvious reticence. Once we got to Harchman's, I'd be simultaneously watching my own ass and spying on their network. I wouldn't have any brainpower left for verbal jousting.

"Is something wrong with the macarons?" Riel inquired with concern.

I summoned a smile. "No, they look delicious. I'm sorry; I have a lot on my mind at the moment."

"Ah." After a polite pause, he added, "Can I 'elp with anything?"

Finally, an opening. Start with something easy...

"I don't know. Maybe. You said James Helmand is your friend, but how well do you really know him? I think he had something to do with my friend Dante's disappearance."

"Ah." Riel sat back in his chair. "You are very... 'ow shall I say it...? Honest?"

"Straightforward. I don't like playing games."

Labelle looked as though he was about to make a snide comment, but instead he took a large mouthful of his dessert and leaned back in his chair.

Riel gave me a sorrowing look. "But it is all about the game, is it not? Like the 'ockey, it is both strategy and brute force, no?"

I didn't know how to respond to that, so I shrugged and took a bite of my dessert, eyeing him steadily.

He sighed as though I'd disappointed him. "My friend James, he is also very... 'ow did you say it? Straight ahead. Too much, sometimes. And after this prison term, he is now... not the man I knew before. I may ask him, but he may not tell me."

"I'd appreciate it if you'd see what you can find out." I held eye contact with him. "I like to know who my enemies are."

Riel chuckled, obviously unfazed. "Yes, and the enemies of Arlene Widdenback, they do not live long."

"Coincidence, I'm sure." I took another bite of dessert. It really was delicious. Too bad I was too nervous to enjoy it.

"Yes, coincidence, no doubt." Riel savoured a bite of his own dessert with a beatific expression before adding, "This Dante must be very dear to you."

Alarm bells clamoured in my brain. He was fishing to see what kind of leverage he could gain. Thank God I hadn't mentioned Kane or Hellhound.

Willing my pulse to steady, I returned a wry smile. "Not particularly. We were introduced by a mutual friend for a blind date last year. It didn't turn out, and I haven't seen him since. But the friend who introduced us is very fond of him, and..." I let my smile sharpen. "...I don't like to have my friends upset."

"Ah, of course not. And this is why I would prefer to be your friend." Mischief sparkled in his eyes. "But your blind dates, they seem to not go so well."

I forced a laugh and nodded toward him. "Particularly the fictitious ones."

Labelle's brow furrowed, obviously confused by our in-joke but unwilling to ask for an explanation. Riel's attention was solely focused on me and I took his cue, ignoring Labelle's frown to continue, "But Dante is a nice guy; we just didn't..."

"...click," Riel and I finished simultaneously, and Riel smiled and offered me a half-bow from his seated position. "It is his great loss." He turned his attention to his dessert for a few more leisurely bites before adding, "But maybe he had no chance. When I saw you at Nichele's office, it seemed your affections were perhaps already spoken for?"

A bite of meringue stuck in my throat and I momentarily stopped breathing, forcing myself to reach calmly for my water glass and sip. While the lump moved reluctantly stomach-ward, I regarded Riel over the rim of my glass with a half-smile.

"I'm afraid I don't have much in the way of affections," I said after a moment, thankful that my voice didn't come out in a squeak or a croak. "I do enjoy a pleasant distraction, though."

"Ah, yes," he agreed. "I believe I recognized your distraction. John Kane, was it not?"

Shit.

He wouldn't talk about the weapon, but he'd blab about Kane in front of Labelle? Bastard.

I held onto my smile. "You've done your homework."

"But of course. Though, I am curious." Riel leaned forward, his eyes alight. "Your... 'ow shall I say it... alliance... with Monsieur Kane? My 'omeworks tell me it is..." He tilted his hand from side to side. "...sometimes on, sometimes off. Is 'e one of your... 'ow shall I say it... trusted ones?"

"Trusted?" I raised a sardonic eyebrow. "Trust is overrated. He's convenient at times."

"Ah." Riel leaned back, studying me. "You are an interesting woman. So warm and yet so cold. And this is 'ow you control him, yes? With such promises that he cannot resist."

I shrugged, conscious of Labelle's attentive presence. "He could easily resist, but he doesn't have any reason to. It's a convenient arrangement for him, too."

"Ah, you underestimate yourself." Riel gave me a courtly inclination of his head before continuing, "My 'omeworks also tell me your arrangement with Monsieur Kane was in place last Christmas when you went... 'ow shall I say it? Shopping...? Together?"

My pulse ticked up. Maybe he'd talk about the weapon after all.

But he'd already indicated subtle disapproval of my bluntness...

I chose to stall. "Is that so? I'd be interested to know who started that rumour."

"My friend James said 'e became friends with a Monsieur Barnett and a Monsieur Parr..." Riel raised an eyebrow before finishing, "...before they died. Apparently your Christmas toys made quite a... 'ow shall I say it? ...impression... on Monsieur Barnett."

So Riel knew I'd claimed to have the lethal ultrasound weapon last Christmas, and he also knew about the so-called 'torture weapon' I'd used to trick Barnett.

God, his screams still haunted my nightmares.

I converted my shudder into a contemptuous shrug. "Barnett made some bad choices. And he was an asshole."

Labelle leaned forward, his avid posture at odds with the casual tone he affected. "Those must have been quite the Christmas toys."

"Or per'aps Monsieur Barnett was... impressionable," Riel said dismissively. "Shall we 'ave coffee?"

I finished my last bite of meringue. "No thanks. You go ahead."

The words had just left my mouth when the monitor in my wristwatch vibrated, sending a surge of adrenaline through my veins.

Somebody had breached the perimeter of my farm.

Whipping out a burner phone so as not to draw attention to my wrist, I toggled to the monitoring app and switched to streaming video. Sure enough, two men in dark clothing were approaching my back door, crowbars in hand.

"Excuse me," I added, holding my voice steady with all my might. "I have to take this call." Punching the speed dial as I rose from the table, I hurried toward the washrooms.

When Stemp answered on the first ring as always, I rapped out, "Somebody's breaking into my house through the back door. Can you send a team to pick them up and hold them until I can question them?"

"Stand by."

While dead air filled my ear, I toggled back to the video display. The two men had wasted no time with my back door, and I swore quietly. Another fucking repair. They were probably trashing my house right now. Stemp's team had better get there pronto.

"The team has been deployed." Stemp's crisp voice soothed my nerves. "Perhaps this is what Labelle was arranging earlier. Any other developments? We're not getting audio from our bugs."

"No, Riel has dropped hints that make it plain that he knows I had the weapon, but he doesn't seem to want to talk in front of Labelle."

"Interesting. And when do you expect to return to question your visitors?"

"Um... I don't know. I'll likely have to go to the spa tonight as planned and hope Riel and I get a chance to talk. Let's plan for tomorrow afternoon. And I'll want to question them as Arlene Widdenback."

Cold humour tinged Stemp's voice. "I will ensure that their accommodations are up to Ms. Widdenback's standards."

My lips peeled back in a wolfish grin. "Thank you very much."

"My pleasure, I assure you."

The grin still tugged at the corners of my mouth while I made my way back to the table.

Labelle remained seated but Riel rose graciously, smiling in return. "Good news?" he inquired as we reseated ourselves.

"Maybe. We'll see."

"Ah." His eyes sparkled with interest. "Very mysterious." The waiter arrived with an insulated carafe and Riel declined a coffee refill and requested the cheque. "The spa calls to me," he said as the waiter departed. "Let us not waste our precious relaxation time."

The cheque arrived promptly and after a brief wrangle which I didn't try too hard to win, he prevailed and paid the bill.

Labelle sat sullenly silent throughout our exchange and

avoided eye contact.

Hmm. What had he and Riel discussed while I was gone? Or not discussed? Or maybe Riel had confronted Labelle about stalling our deal.

When we stepped out into the cold evening, Labelle muttered, "See you there," and strode away.

"Are you sure I may not drive us?" Riel asked. "I would most appreciate the company on such a long and dark drive."

Making himself sound vulnerable again. Oh, he was smooth.

"Sorry, but I really don't know when I might need to leave," I said. "I'll meet you there."

Riel looked flatteringly disappointed, and we parted with mutual expressions of fake goodwill.

When I slid into my car and activated my bug detector, it still registered all-clear. Then I clenched my teeth and twisted the key in the ignition, half-expecting it to be the last thing I ever did.

The car didn't explode. Trembling, I laid my head back and switched to yoga breathing in an attempt to calm my pounding heart.

God, I could barely make it through a meal without letting my fears show. How would I manage an overnight stay among enemies? What if I woke up screaming, as I almost certainly would? That wasn't the image I wanted for Arlene Widdenback at all.

But if I stayed awake all night, my trembling hands and dark-circled eyes would betray me in the morning.

Shit, shit, shit!

My positive attitude of the previous day was long gone. Good agent, my ass. I was a pathetic imposter whose friends were being picked off one by one; and my only strategy was to have dinner with my nemesis and then meekly follow him out into the middle of nowhere, probably to my doom. But, dammit, what else could I do? I had to stay true to my undercover role...

Pulling out a secured phone, I stared at it with my finger quivering over the speed dial button. Should I call Stemp and ask for advice? That would have been unthinkable only a few short months ago, but now...

My hand dropped back into my lap. Nope, it was still unthinkable.

And I sure as hell wouldn't ask Holt. His jab from the previous night was still smarting, probably because it was true. I hadn't done anything to earn his respect.

I thumped a fist on the steering wheel. So do something.

Hissing out an angry breath between my teeth, I texted him 'Had a nice dinner, going to the spa now', and pulled out of the parking lot to head for the highway.

About halfway to Harchman's my phone vibrated. GHoltRealtor.

Hope ballooned in my chest as I pulled over to the shoulder. Please let it be good news...

My optimism was dashed by Holt's tone, a blend of tension and irritation. "That buyer didn't show up at eight o'clock, either. Have you been able to reach him? What's his problem, anyway?"

My heart shrivelling, I cleared my throat but my voice still came out thin and uncertain. "I haven't heard from him. I don't know what his problem is. I hope he hasn't..." I gulped, choosing my words carefully for the unsecured line. "...lost interest. If I hear anything I'll let you know."

"What about the homeowner? Have you heard from him yet?"

"No."

Holt blew out a breath. "Well, we shouldn't even be showing the house until the homeowner has signed a listing contract with me. Call me as soon as you hear from him; and let me know if you hear from the potential buyer again, too."

"I will."

I hung up and stared out the windshield, my insides as cold as the night that surrounded me.

No matter how I counted, that meeting time couldn't have been later than eight o'clock.

Oh, God. Had I lost Kane, too?

CHAPTER 26

The blackness pressed in on me while I navigated the hills and bends of the narrow highway, alternately dazzled by oncoming headlights and blinded in the darkness of their passing.

With only my worries for company, I had second-, third-, and fourth-guessed myself in the past half hour. By the time the gatehouse to Harchman's estate glowed ahead, I was convinced that I should have played hardball with Riel and demanded information...

No, I should have had the analysts at Sirius trace both Kane's and Hellhound's calls...

No, I should have...

"Good evening, ma'am." The gatehouse guard's deferential voice interrupted my scattered thoughts.

I shook myself back to the situation at hand. "Um... hi. I'm Arlene Widdenback. Lawrence and Tawny invited me to their spa...?" I tried to sound confident, but the statement came out sounding like a question anyway.

"Yes, of course. Please drive up to the main turnaround and the concierge will meet you there." He gave me a half-bow and gestured me forward as the gate swung open on silent hinges.

The winding drive up to the turnaround gave me more

than enough time to review the many ways this could go wrong. My secret network key and the silicone fingerprints were safely tucked into my bra, but what if they searched my briefcase and looked too closely at the pen or USB sticks? And would they believe that the nasal filters were earplugs that I needed for sleep?

The concierge's small shelter appeared in my headlights and I squared my shoulders. Too late to do anything about it now.

Heart pounding, I stepped out of my car and attempted nonchalance while I handed the keys to the valet. The concierge offered me the staff's trademark half-bow and transferred my suitcase and laptop case to a baggage cart.

As he wheeled it toward his shelter, my nerves got the better of me.

"I'll take those up to the guesthouse myself." My voice came out slightly higher than normal. "I need to do a bit of work right away."

The concierge paused, clearly scandalized by the thought of a guest carrying her own luggage. "They will be in your room before you get there," he promised. "One moment, please..."

He ducked into his shelter while I silently berated myself for my faux pas. Way to look as though you're carrying something suspicious, idiot. And taking my bags to my room by myself wouldn't ensure their security anyway. I had to leave the room sometime, and of course Harchman and his staff would have passkeys. Damn.

The concierge emerged again, bearing a cardkey which he handed over with another half-bow. "You will be in Suite 108," he informed me. "Please follow the blue lights in the path to your destination."

He withdrew a small remote from his pocket and pressed the button, illuminating a trail of blue LEDs embedded in the low stone wall that flanked the walkway.

"You are welcome to retire for the evening if you wish," he added. "But Mr. and Mrs. Harchman would be pleased to receive you for drinks in the salon if you are not too tired. Press this button..." He indicated the one on the remote marked with an 'S'. "...to illuminate the path to the salon. Or, at any time, please feel free to press this larger button..." He indicated one with a pictogram of a bellhop. "...and one of our staff members will come to wherever you are and escort you personally."

"That's great, thank you," I murmured, making a mental note to leave the thing in my room. Innocent civilian guests might be delighted by the novel technology, but I recognized it for what it was. If Harchman couldn't see a guest on one of the many surveillance cameras, he could just track the fob. Ignoring the shiver that crept down my backbone, I summoned a smile for the concierge and left my bags to their fate.

I had only followed the twinkling blue LEDs a dozen or so paces when a wash of cold adrenaline nearly paralyzed me. Shit, I'd left the extra magazines for my Glock and trank pistol in my suitcase. They'd find them for sure...

Sucking in a breath, I forced my rigid muscles to keep moving. Settle down. I was Arlene Widdenback the arms dealer. They'd be suspicious if I *didn't* have spare magazines in my suitcase.

But should I have even brought the classified trank pistol? If it fell into enemy hands...

Stifling a groan, I hurried toward the guesthouse. Why hadn't I asked Stemp before I'd left? I had studied the protocol manuals until I knew them backward and forward, but protocol and field experience were two totally different things.

The doorman gave me yet another half-bow and smile as he opened the guesthouse door for me, and I stifled the urge to tell him to cut it out. All this deference was making me nervous.

Well, more nervous than I already was.

"Whatever," I muttered, and headed for number 108.

When the door opened to my cardkey, I stepped into the room and froze, staring. The concierge had been as good as his word. My suitcase already rested on the luggage rack, my laptop case beside it.

"How the hell...?" I said aloud, then clamped my mouth shut with a paranoid glance around the room.

Sidling into a travertine-paved bathroom that could have easily accommodated a medium-sized dance troupe, I studied the cavernous space. Would they have cameras and bugs in here?

Choosing the toilet enclosure as the area least likely to be under video surveillance, I slipped in and activated my bug detector.

Its light glowed steady green.

I gaped at it.

No way. They had to be listening, or watching me, or both.

I gave the device a little shake but its all-clear indication didn't waver.

Hissing a breath between my teeth as I sank onto the toilet seat, I glared at the bug detector. It couldn't be malfunctioning; I'd just gotten it from Stores. So either I wasn't under surveillance at all, or else they'd figured out some non-electronic method of watching or listening.

Maybe a one-way glass panel?

I stood again and approached the giant ornately-framed mirror. A wary-looking middle-aged woman stared back at me.

Then her anxious expression dissolved and our shoulders relaxed simultaneously. It couldn't be a one-way glass panel. The living area of the suite was on the other side.

"Okay, fine; it's not that," I muttered, and exited the bathroom to stand considering the mystery of my magically-transported luggage. I hadn't wasted any time getting here. I knew the route and I'd walked briskly. No staff member had passed me with a luggage cart.

So they must have a service tunnel between the concierge's shelter and the guesthouse, allowing them to zip directly between buildings instead of following the meandering arcs of the above-ground pathways. And there were probably service tunnels between the other buildings, too.

Note to self: Don't try outpacing any of the staff between buildings. And remember that someone might pop out of a concealed corridor at any time. Great, just great.

I sank into one of the luxuriously upholstered armchairs, frowning at the ceiling while I paged through my memory of the floor plans. There hadn't been any tunnels on those drawings. Damn. How the hell was I going to avoid all the surveillance cameras and subterranean staff while I sneaked over to the server room?

I was nowhere near solving that problem when my cell phone rang. The call display showed Riel's number, and I braced myself and accepted the call.

"Allô, Arlene," he said in his usual pleasant tones. "The 'Archmans 'ave invited us to meet them for drinks in the salon. Would you honour us with your presence?"

Wishing I could just hide in this well-appointed room and let them play their games without me, I forced an equally pleasant tone. "Thank you, I'll join you shortly. I just need a few minutes to freshen up."

"Ah, good, then I will see you soon. Au revoir."

My 'freshening-up' consisted of standing in front of the bathroom mirror and exhorting myself to suck it up and show some backbone. The lecture didn't increase my courage any, but at least it left me irritated enough to slip easily into Arlene Widdenback's hardass persona.

Checking my ankle holsters, I smoothed my slacks over my Glock on the right and the trank pistol on my left. Then I extracted the spare trank magazine from my suitcase and tucked it into the large handbag that held my waist pouch. The innocent-looking gold pen followed.

If someone searched me and confiscated my weapons, so be it; but at least I'd done my best to safeguard the classified technology.

I blew out a quivering breath and departed.

The walk up to the main house felt like a march to the gallows. My feet dragged while possibility after possibility played out in my mind, each more frightening than the last.

Shaking my head to dispel the mental image of stepping through the salon door into a storm of automatic weapon fire, I concentrated on the most probable outcome.

I had already scoped out the salon at the party so there was nothing new to be learned there. Harchman would either be revoltingly chummy or peevish and uncooperative. Tawny would play the bubblehead, and I'd have to remind myself not to be fooled by her act. Riel would be his usual charming and evasive self, and Labelle would be as slimy as ever. I'd accomplish absolutely nothing except to raise my own blood pressure.

And that was the best-case scenario...

I hesitated outside the salon door trying not to think about automatic weapons, then stepped inside.

The little cluster of people around the bar looked lost in the huge room. Tawny wore yet another skintight dress and too much makeup, Harchman was overdressed in an obviously expensive suit, and Riel and Labelle looked suave and sophisticated in slacks and casual blazers. But I barely registered them as my gaze locked onto the one person I wouldn't have expected in a million years, my breath catching in shock.

Kane.

CHAPTER 27

Even though his face was concealed as he stared at the floor, there was no mistaking Kane's short dark hair, towering height, and massive arms and shoulders. Both hands were behind his back.

Cold fear stabbed my heart. Was he a captive, his hands bound?

Tawny stroked one of his bulging biceps, gazing up at him as she spoke softly. I couldn't hear what she was saying, but Harchman looked distinctly ticked off.

My feet carried me forward as if they were under someone else's control while my mind ping-ponged frantically between snatching out my Glock or playing ice-cold Arlene Widdenback.

A moment later Kane looked up and spotted me, his face relaxing into a smile. "Arlene," he said warmly.

Closing the distance between us in a few long strides, he pulled me into a passionate embrace and kissed me, devouring my lips like a starving man.

Nope, he definitely wasn't bound. Big hot hands spanned my back, pulling my body tight against all those magnificent muscles.

My own hands reacted instinctively, roaming the rock-hard contours of his chest and shoulders while my mind scrambled to catch up.

What the hell? Why the public display of affection when he should be distancing himself from me? And why was he here at all? I would have bet my life that he wouldn't leave Daniel and Alicia for anything...

He broke the kiss and smiled down at me, still holding me close. "Nice to see you again."

"Uh... yeah," I croaked. "Hi." Turning my attention toward our audience, I managed a feeble smile. "Hi, everybody."

Riel's eyes sparkled with amusement. "Bonsoir, Arlene."

Labelle and Harchman each offered me a stiff nod, and Tawny gave me a brief venomous glance before turning on the smiles and bubbles and draping herself over her husband.

Harchman brightened, wrapping her in a possessive embrace. With one hand locked on her ass, he turned a reluctant gaze to me. "May I offer you a drink?" he inquired unenthusiastically.

"Um... sure... thanks." Disengaging myself from Kane, I accepted the wineglass Harchman handed me and downed a swallow before realizing it was the vile oaked Sauvignon Blanc that he considered a special treat.

I held my best neutral expression. "So, this is a surprise," I said, nodding toward Kane.

"What, you're not happy to see your partner in crime?" Harchman sniped, his acrimony poorly disguised by a jocular tone.

I summoned a noncommittal smile, my mind completely devoid of an appropriate answer.

Fortunately Riel spoke up with his usual tact. "I am most pleased you arrived safely. That is a long and dark drive, is it not?"

"It is," I agreed, hoping I'd concealed my relief at his interruption. "It's not bad now, but it wouldn't be much fun during a snowstorm."

"Indeed, no." He turned to Harchman. "Do you find it tiresome in the winter, to live so far away from the city when the roads are bad?"

Harchman shrugged, puffing out his chest as though he couldn't resist the temptation to flaunt his wealth. "It doesn't bother me a bit. I have drivers."

"Ah, yes, of course," Riel murmured. "You 'ave the... 'ow shall I say it? The touch of gold, yes?"

"The Midas Touch." Harchman puffed up even more. "I certainly do. I have the highest net worth of anybody in Canada." He waved an expansive hand at the palatial surroundings. "This is just one of my properties. I have small pied-à-terres in Calgary, Edmonton, Vancouver, Toronto, and Montreal, too... only about four thousand square feet each." He smirked at his own attempt at humour.

When Harchman mispronounced 'peed-a-tares' in his Anglicized accent, Riel's eyelid twitched but he maintained his warm and friendly demeanor nevertheless. "Most impressive. All this wealth and a lovely wife, too." He offered a gallant nod to Tawny before continuing, "And you are 'aving another big success with your latest software, no?"

"Not yet," Harchman demurred with false modesty before reverting to his true obnoxiousness. "But when it's released next week it's going to be huge! Everybody's going to buy it, and why wouldn't they? My marketing is brilliant. It plays on everybody's biggest fears: terrorists, unpredictable attacks... that's what makes people buy, you

know.   Fear or reward, but fear is by far the strongest
motivator."

My heart thumping, I asked, "Terrorists? What are you
talking about?"

Harchman clammed up with a suspicious glance at Kane
and me, but Riel saved the conversation again. "Ah, yes, you
arrived too late at the gala for the software presentation.
Monsieur Harchman has developed a most ingenious app for
phones, called Terror Watch."

I drew a secret breath. At the gala. Before the terrorist
threat had been announced.

"I told you before, Benny; call me Lawrence. We're all
friends here, right?" Harchman said. He slapped Riel's back,
apparently oblivious to another twitch of Riel's eyelid.

As if unwilling to relinquish the limelight despite his
mistrust for Kane and me, Harchman babbled on, "Terror
Watch, it's brilliant! It monitors all the emergency broadcast
systems and media-"

"Pookie-Poo," Tawny interrupted.   "Let's not bore
Aiding with-"

Harchman kept talking over her, completely absorbed in
trumpeting his own brilliance. "...and if there's a terrorist
attack or mass shooting or any kind of violent crime, it pings
and pops up a map showing the location. You can preset the
area you want to monitor..."

"Pookie..." Tawny dug her red talons into his arm.

He patted her hand absently, still talking. "...or choose
several locations, or even have worldwide coverage. People
are going to eat it up! The ones that are scared of terrorist
attacks will use it to avoid the hotspots..." He bestowed an
unpleasant grin on us. "...and the looky-loos will use it to
run to the scene for a glimpse of blood and dismembered

bodies. It'll make millions..." As if recollecting himself, he adopted a grave expression and serious tone. "And it'll save innocent lives. That's what's really important. Right, Sweetums?"

Excitement fizzed in my veins. Terror Watch. How convenient for Harchman's marketing if there were a terrorist attack only a few days after its launch. And if Harchman's app made millions, Tawny would reap the benefits, too.

No wonder she was trying to shut him up. He must have told her about Kane and me trying to steal his drilling software over a year ago. She wouldn't want us anywhere near this.

As Harchman focused on Tawny at last, her expression of tooth-grinding frustration vanished behind another bimbo-smile. "That's right, Pookie," she cooed. "You're such a humanitarian."

"Well, I have to carry on the family tradition, don't I?" he said, patting her ass indulgently.

"Oh? And what is this noble family tradition?" Riel asked.

Both Tawny and I shot him an 'oh-God-don't-get-him-started' look, but it was futile. Riel remained oblivious to our psychic message and Harchman was already running off at the mouth.

Tawny caught me watching her and turned away to regard Harchman with rapt adoration, or an excellent facsimile of it. I transferred my attention to Riel. He was listening to Harchman's account of his illustrious forebears with his usual attentive charm, nodding and exclaiming in all the right places. Only his tiny sidelong glances betrayed the fact that he was more interested in the interactions between the group than in Harchman's interminable story.

Labelle stood with a fixed smile on his face, staring through Harchman with the unfocused gaze of a man bored beyond endurance but trying not to reveal it.

Beside me, Kane observed in silence, too, with only a slight stiffening of his shoulders when Harchman heaped praises on the late elder Harchman, an army general who had 'saved so many lives in the Korean War with his brilliant leadership'.

Knowing that Kane considered most high-ranking officers to be megalomaniac paper-pushers who caused more casualties than they prevented, I moved a little closer, brushing my elbow against his.

"...and I made a *very* generous donation to the Poppy Fund this year..." Harchman blathered on, "...with the condition that I'd get to lay the first wreath at Battalion Park and make a speech about my father and today's War On Terrorism. It'll be perfect PR for my Terror Watch app; I'll get huge publicity..."

Kane's hand clenched around mine and I squeezed his in return, clamping my teeth on my tongue to prevent myself from lambasting Harchman for being such a slimy self-serving little prick.

The grip on my hand softened and the pad of Kane's thumb lightly caressed the sensitive skin inside my wrist. Startled, I glanced up to see his gaze fixed on me with heated intensity.

I suddenly became aware of how close he was standing.

His arm grazing my right breast, stimulating every nerve to tingling alertness...

The intoxicating spicy scent that was pure Kane...

And the fact that although Riel was still nodding and

prompting Harchman to further excesses of egotism, his attention was fixed on us.

Leaning into Kane, I let hot memories resurface, warming my face. Let Riel think we were totally wrapped up in each other. Better that than blowing my cover if he realized I'd made the connection to the Remembrance Day terrorist.

Kane turned toward me, closing out the rest of the group and gazing down into my eyes. His fingertips lightly traced the line of my jaw and even though I knew he was only acting, my breath shortened and my lips parted in unconscious invitation.

I vaguely registered Riel's polite attempt to include us in the conversation. "And 'ow about you, Monsieur Kane? 'Ave you any noble family traditions?"

Kane feigned deafness, relinquishing his grasp on my hand to wrap his arm around my waist and pull me closer.

"Monsieur Kane...?" Riel repeated.

"...uh?" Kane did a creditable imitation of a man awakening from a trance. He dragged his gaze away from my face just long enough to include the rest of the group in a cursory attempt at politeness. "I'm sorry, it's been a long day." His glance at Tawny held a hint of accusation, but before she could react Kane went on, "I'm exhausted, and Arlene and I have some catching up to do. Will you please excuse us?"

"Yes, sorry," I agreed. "Thank you again for the invitation..." I recalled too late that I hadn't thanked them in the first place, but ignored that technicality and forged on. "...I don't want to be rude..." Okay, that was a lie as well; I wanted to be extremely rude. "...but I'm exhausted, too." I topped off my bullshit sundae with a fake smile. "Can we talk tomorrow?"

"Sure!" Tawny assured us with far too much enthusiasm, and Harchman nodded eagerly, too. "Brunch is at ten. Good night!"

Riel looked nonplussed for an instant before regaining his composure. "But of course. I wish you good evening. Per'aps we will meet in the spa tomorrow morning? I plan for a time in the mineral pool around eight-thirty."

"Maybe we'll see you there," I agreed, and followed Kane's gentle pull toward the door.

We left the house without speaking, but as soon as we were safely on the pathway outside I turned to whisper at Kane. "What are you doing here?"

He stopped and turned to face me, using the movement to disguise a tiny headshake.

Shit, he knew something I didn't. My pulse ticked up.

"Meeting you, of course," he said smoothly, and pulled me into his arms.

I forced a chuckle. "Bullshit. But..." I snuggled closer. "I like where this bullshit is going. As long as you don't interfere with my business it's all good."

"Do I ever?" He trailed a line of kisses down my neck.

"Mmmm... nope, not yet. You're a smart man."

"I know."

"And modest, too," I teased.

"To a fault," he agreed. "Wait until I get you alone, and you'll see how modest I really am." He nibbled the sensitive spot between my neck and collarbone, and I sucked in a breath.

"Well, what are we waiting for?" I purred, and led the way back to the guesthouse.

As soon as we were inside my room, I moved close to

Kane again, slipping my bug detector out of my purse. Holding it concealed between us, I sneaked a quick peek.

My heart gave a hard thump. Flashing red light.

Kane and I exchanged a single wide-eyed glance before he seized me in his arms, pushing me back against the door and kissing me hard.

I let out an aborted yelp that I converted hastily to a moan, and stuffed the bug detector back into my purse before returning the kiss with interest.

Growling low in his throat, Kane dominated my mouth, his hands roaming hungrily over my body. I gave a few more fake moans and upped the ante with some heavy breathing, doing some hand-roaming of my own. The knowledge that somebody was listening and/or watching gave me a creepy sensation, which intensified when I realized that warmth was pooling in parts of my body that should have been clenched with anxiety.

Kane's scent filled my senses, generating fiery memories that weakened my knees and my willpower. Unbidden, my hands followed the ridges of muscle down his backbone to clutch an ass that should have been immortalized in marble.

His knee pushed between mine and I rode his thigh, the rough friction igniting heat from my belly button to my toes.

"John..." My voice came out in a ragged gasp.

His teeth clamped onto my collar and he jerked his head. The top button of my blouse opened with a pop, quickly followed by more pops as he nipped a tingling trail across to my shoulder. Pinning me against the door, he traced the line of my bra strap with little flicks of his tongue, working slowly down to my cleavage.

"Oh God John..." Pressing a hand down between us, I found the hard ridge in his pants and massaged it until he groaned and pulled me against him.

"Condoms," he grated between harsh breaths. "I have condoms in my suitcase."

"Hurry." The whimper of need tore from my lips.

"Come with me." Peeling us both away from the door, he dragged me outside and a few doors down the fortunately abandoned hallway.

As Kane jammed his cardkey into the lock, I registered several things simultaneously.

He had a room and a cardkey. Definitely not a prisoner.

He had a suitcase. He had known he was coming here.

He had condoms. Who had he intended to share them with?

And his hands were trembling.

Was it red-hot passion... or something else?

He yanked me into the room.

CHAPTER 28

"Do you have any lube?" Kane growled, his voice rough with hunger while his gaze flicked meaningfully toward my purse.

"I... I..." Swallowing hard, I rummaged through it. "Um... I don't know... Maybe."

He moved closer so that when I activated the bug detector inside my purse we could both see the flashing red light.

"Is it in your luggage?" he prompted.

"Uh..."

"Go and check. I'll be right there."

He turned to ransack his suitcase, and after an instant of dazed incomprehension, I brained up and hurried back down the hall.

Stepping inside my room, I checked the bug detector again. Solid green light.

"What the hell?" I muttered.

As I stood staring at it, the green light changed to red. A long interval stretched between the first and second flash, then shorter between the second and third, followed by shorter and shorter intervals as though it was a timer counting down to an explosion...

A thump on the door made me bite back a cry and spin,

my hand swooping toward my holster. More thumps followed, and I gasped a silent breath of relief when I realized it was Kane knocking.

And the bug detector was flashing the same rapid cadence as when we had stood here together.

He was bugged.

"Dammit," I breathed, afraid to speak aloud in case the bug was sensitive enough to hear me through the door. "I'll be right there," I called, then stood immobilized in thought.

Was it only an audio bug, or video as well? Was it even possible to make a camera small enough to hide on a person without their knowledge?

Or maybe he knew about it. Was he intentionally wearing or carrying a recording device? Was he working undercover? If so, for whom? It couldn't be for the Department; Stemp would have briefed me if he'd known...

Kane knocked again. "Hurry up... or have you changed your mind?" he asked playfully.

I gulped. "Sorry, I'm coming..."

No, I sure as hell wasn't coming. Not tonight, and not with him. But I still needed to keep up appearances for the sake of our audience. And having him in my bed might keep me from screaming in my sleep. Maybe.

I drew a deep breath and opened the door.

He stepped inside and swept me into another embrace, and a few more scorching kisses weakened my resolve.

I trusted him, didn't I? He wouldn't make me the unwitting star of yet another humiliating porn video. If he knew we were under video surveillance he wouldn't undress me.

...Would he?

His fingers fumbled at the front of my blouse,

unbuttoning it down to my waist. Kicking off his shoes beside the door, he walked me slowly backward across the huge room, kissing me all the way.

The backs of my knees hit the bed and I sat abruptly. He rolled onto the bed beside me, pulling me over on top of him.

"What did you find in that giant purse of yours?" he inquired huskily.

Somehow I managed a teasing grin. "Wouldn't you like to know?" I opened the purse slowly as if tantalizing him, and reached inside.

When the red light of the bug detector flashed, I gaped at it.

Slower cadence. The bug was farther away.

Inspiration hit.

"Here, you dig for it," I instructed, passing Kane the purse and palming the bug detector. "I forgot to lock the door."

Hopping off the bed, I hurried toward Kane's shoes. As I turned the deadbolt lock with a heavy clunk, I swooped the bug detector down toward the shoes. Sure enough, the light glowed solid red.

"Oh, gross, there's a giant spider!" I yelped.

Kane was off the bed in an instant. "Where?"

"It went under your shoe!" I raised my voice to a frantic squawk, gesturing with the hand that held the bug detector. "Oh! There it goes! God, I hate spiders! Squish it!"

Kane dropped to his knees, turning his shoes this way and that. Tucked unobtrusively near one of the tongues we spotted the small electronic dot.

Kane dropped the shoe upside-down, likely making our listeners wince in pain. I spared an uncharitable hope that they were wearing headphones and they'd just lost an eardrum or two.

"Got it!" Kane exclaimed. "Wow, it's a big one. Hand me a tissue and I'll flush it."

I bent, holding the bug detector next to the shoe. It still glowed solid red, but at least now I knew it was audio-only.

I slumped in relief. Nobody was watching us.

As I reached for the bugged shoe, Kane clamped a hand on my wrist. Surprised, I looked up to see his headshake. He waited for my nod of understanding before releasing me, then strode across to the bathroom. A moment later the toilet flushed and he returned, smiling.

"Now, where were we?" he asked, his voice deepening into a seductive rumble.

"Um..." I hesitated.

He had known he was bugged. So who was on the other end? I imagined somebody like Holt listening with cynical amusement, and the memory of his knowing grin dried up the last vestiges of my desire.

"That was, um... kind of a buzzkill," I mumbled. "I really hate spiders."

"Oh." Kane managed to infuse the syllable with a heavy dose of disappointment. "Well, now I hate spiders, too." He heaved a sigh, then ducked back into the bathroom to emerge moments later with a bottle of the rich lotion that was one of the guesthouse's many amenities. "Come and lie down." He rolled the bottle between his fingers, giving me a look that sizzled with invitation. "I'll give you a massage that'll make you forget that spider ever existed."

"If you can do that, I'll be amazed."

"Prepare to be amazed." He led me toward the bed.

"Actually..." I halted a few paces away and rebuttoned my blouse. "I'll take you up on that a bit later. I need to do some work, and then a massage will feel twice as good."

I reached for the small pad of paper and pen that lay beside the suite's phone, but Kane forestalled my attempt at written communication by sweeping me into another kiss.

Frustrated, I pulled away just far enough to mouth, "Why not?" at him.

He gave an almost-imperceptible headshake, and kissed me again before turning me loose.

"All right," he said aloud. "I'll give you half an hour, but after that you're mine. You work too hard. It's time to play a bit."

I channelled Arlene Widdenback the hardass. "I'm not yours or anybody else's, and I'll work as long as I want." His smile faded into an unreadable mask, and I added teasingly, "It likely won't be more than half an hour anyway, and after that you're mine. Go warm up that bed."

"Hmm." The seductive rumble was back. "I see we need to review the power structure here. You can have your half hour. But after that..." His voice deepened and hardened to a tone of effortless dominance that chased a shiver down my spine. "...you *will* be mine."

"We'll see about that." My words came out in a feeble croak and I turned away to set up my laptop, hoping he couldn't see my hands shaking.

Dammit, what game was he playing?

My stomach dropped in sudden realization. Of course; he was playing the bad-guy role I had assigned to him 'way back when we had first gone undercover at Harchman's nearly a year and a half ago. My own damning words replayed in my brain.

He forced me to do the most perverted things, you can't imagine. And he hurt me...

Oh, shit.

With Kane's veiled threat echoing in my brain and his silent presence looming on the bed behind me, I spent several minutes staring blankly at the screen before I recovered enough presence of mind to concentrate. Finally I gave my head a shake and considered Kane's actions.

If he didn't want to take a chance on communicating in writing, that must mean he still suspected we were being watched.

Chilly fingers of fear brushed my spine.

From where? And by whom?

But we couldn't be. I had cleared the room. There was no wall or panel that could conceal non-electronic surveillance; and if Kane was tagged with any other bugs, the bug detector would have maintained its fast cadence close to him. The audio-only shoe bug had to be the only one.

So why the hell wasn't he trying harder to communicate with me? He knew damn well I was in the middle of an op and I'd need all available intel.

And why was he here at all when he had been so adamant about being there for Daniel? It was well past eight o'clock. Daniel would be screaming for his father...

I sneaked a glance over to where Kane reclined comfortably on the bed, arms tucked behind his head.

Watching me, with a tiny smile quirking the corner of his mouth.

Unnerved, I turned back to my screen and pretended to read.

He had been a top agent. He must know what he was doing; I just had to trust him.

Just trust him and concentrate on my mission.

I squared my shoulders. Time to go looking for a

brainwave-driven virtual reality network, if there was one.

Then I stared at the screen some more, procrastinating while I tried to screw up my courage. If there was a network and I got into it, coming out was going to hurt like hell. And what if I discovered another horrific torture simulation in progress?

A shudder shook me.

A touch on my shoulder made me start and corkscrew around to discover Kane's concerned face behind me. "How's it going?" he inquired, with the subtext of 'Are you okay?' clear in his expression.

I blew out a breath that was half relief, half tension. "Not great."

"Why don't you lie down for a while?" he offered. "I'll give you a massage and then you can go back to work with a fresh eye."

Inspiration dawned. When I came out of the network I could muffle my pain-filled obscenities in the pillow. I gave him a grateful "Okay" and headed for the bed.

As I was about to lie down, strong hands landed on my shoulders and the heat of Kane's body warmed my back. "Just slip off your blouse," he coaxed, brushing a few convincing kisses down the side of my neck. "Here..."

He unbuttoned my blouse and eased it off my shoulders.

"Um... thanks..." I pulled away and flopped facedown on the bed, hoping with all my heart that I was right and nobody was watching.

Squirming into a comfortable position, I bunched the pillow under the side of my face so I wouldn't suffocate when my body went slack on entering the virtual network. The mattress dipped as Kane swung astride my hips, settling himself lightly.

But if he wanted to immobilize me, he could do it in an instant by simply shifting his weight...

I swallowed hard and fought the irrational fear. This was Kane. I had trusted him with my life over and over. I could trust him now.

"You won't need your bra, either," he murmured, unhooking it.

Twisting around, I shot him a look over my shoulder. He gave me a tiny calm-down wink in return. Nothing to worry about. Just playing to the audience.

I settled myself again, mortifying memories of my fake porn-star career making me cringe inwardly. If we were being recorded and this hit the internet, I'd have to move to a mountain in Tibet that was only accessible by yak-train...

Kane warmed a small amount of lotion between his palms before applying it to my back in long smooth strokes.

It didn't take any acting ability to react appreciatively. "Ohhhh... my... God... That feels so good..." I groaned and sank deeper into the luxurious bedding, remembering not to bury my face in the pillow in case I smothered.

As his stroking changed to gentle kneading, I allowed myself a few moments to drift in sheer bliss. Then my eyes popped open.

"What?" Kane asked.

"Uh?"

"You tensed up."

"Oh. Sorry. Just thinking..." I subsided on the pillow again as he switched back to long relaxing strokes.

Eyes wide, I checked and re-checked the logic of the plan I'd just hatched. If Harchman was running an internal virtual reality network, and if his other internal networks were accessible from it, I might be able to knock out the surveillance cameras covering the route to the server room. And if I did have to sneak down there, I had just figured out how to conceal my departure from my room, too.

But I really didn't want to implement my plan...

Stop procrastinating.

I closed my eyes and sought the familiar white void, concentrating on being invisible.

When I stepped into it, my virtual stomach clenched. Damn Harchman. I had been clinging to the hope that I wouldn't find anything. That I wouldn't have to make the perilous trek to the server room at all.

But no; the little shit *was* running an unauthorized brainwave-driven network, and now I had to find out why.

I eyed the featureless white corridor that represented the network and swallowed hard. The doors that lined the virtual corridor each gave access to a simulation that might or might not be active. What was inside?

Innocent spa users?

Kinky porn?

Gruesome torture and violent death?

Steeling myself for what I might find, I drifted soundlessly to the first door and willed a small transparent window into it. A quick peek inside revealed only a blank white room.

I let out a virtual breath that I didn't actually need to draw or release, and drifted to the next door to repeat the process.

Then the next. And the next.

When I discovered an active sim a few doors down, I jerked back from my viewport wishing I could unsee what I'd just seen: Harchman and Tawny in the throes of passion. Ew. She really was 'the best wife ever' if she let him do what he was currently doing.

Then comprehension dawned and my lips turned up in a grin that was half cynicism, half admiration. Tawny was friggin' brilliant. She'd probably never slept with Harchman at all.

Instead, she could use a real-life kiss to distract him while she stuck one of Fuzzy Bunny's special network access keys on him. That would pop him unknowingly into a sim, where he could satisfy all his twisted cravings with a construct that looked exactly like her. She wouldn't even have to participate because the construct would react according to Harchman's expectations. He'd never know it wasn't real.

Clever, clever girl.

And let that be a reminder not to underestimate her.

Sobering, I moved on.

The next few sims were inactive, but I soon came upon another occupied room. This time it was Riel, and I watched for only a few moments. He was receiving a massage from an impossibly gorgeous scantily-clad woman, and I recognized her Barbie-doll-like proportions as one of Harchman's spa-sim constructs.

Unlike Harchman, Riel didn't seem interested in taking advantage of the situation. Eyes closed, he lay enjoying his massage like a perfect gentleman, the towel across his hips undisturbed by any sign of arousal. Either he didn't know he could have his every fantasy fulfilled here; or else an expert massage *was* his fantasy.

Lucky I hadn't tried to seduce him. If he was behaving himself in private with Masseuse-Barbie, I wouldn't have had a prayer.

Storing that knowledge away for future reference, I

moved on.

When I peeked into the next room I recoiled, my heart hammering at the sight of its occupants.

Kane again.

CHAPTER 29

Shaking my head to dislodge the memory of what I'd just seen, I backed away from the sim.

It wasn't really Kane in there. If it had been, his physical body would have been blank-faced and immobile. And he'd been giving me a nice massage only a few minutes ago...

Oh.

Shit!

Diving back toward the entrance portal, I cursed my lack of forethought. As soon as I had entered the network, my physical body would have gone limp. Kane didn't know what I was doing. What if he thought I'd passed out?

Although if I was lucky, he'd figure it out fast when I came out of the network...

I stepped out of the virtual portal into a world of pain.

"Cocksucking-motherfucking-sonofaaaaargh!" I clenched my head in both hands in an attempt to keep it from splitting in two.

Shit, I shouldn't have been able to do that if I'd been muffled by the pillow as I'd planned...

"That'll teach you," a rough voice snarled in my ear. "You won't give me any more backtalk, bitch."

Keening under the relentless pain, I cracked one eye half-open to see Kane's scowling face inches from mine.

"Right, bitch?" he repeated, seizing my head in a gesture that probably looked violent to any observers but in fact eased the pressure points in my skull.

The pain combined with the vicious contempt in his voice made my stomach roll with nausea. "Ow... Goddammit... ow... yes," I croaked. "Whatever you say... Ow..."

"Say it!"

Why was he so angry? I groaned, squeezing my eyes shut to keep them from exploding. "Say what?"

He shook me; not hard, but it was enough to send another bolt of blinding pain through my temples. "Say you're sorry, bitch!"

"I'm sorry, I'm sorry!" I cried, ineffectually trying to pull his hands off my head.

"You're sorry, what?" he grated.

I thought as fast as my throbbing brain would allow. What had I done to deserve... oh.

Was this a dominance play for the sake of the bug?

"Um..." I clenched my teeth and forced myself to say it. "Master." Sickness climbed my throat, my skin crawling with revulsion at the demeaning words. "I'm sorry... Master."

"That's better. Roll over."

I rolled onto my stomach and he swung astride me again. His strong fingers found the burning knots in my neck and temples, massaging them away.

"Why do you make me do this?" he asked in reasonable tones. "You know I don't like hurting you, but you keep making me do it. This is all your fault. Why do you treat me so badly?"

His words were so eerily like my abusive long-ago-ex-husband's that my roiling stomach clenched into a knot and I shuddered under his hands.

His massage slowed and he brushed aside my hair to softly kiss the nape of my neck. I couldn't help it; I shrank from his touch.

Firm fingers gripped my chin, gently turning my face to his as he leaned down beside me. With an effort I met his gaze.

Strong square features. Steady grey eyes soft with regret.

I sucked in a breath. Not Steven.

This was John Kane, a man I trusted with my life. He had been covering for me, making my outburst of agonized profanity sound plausible to our listeners. Only an act.

I went limp with a sob of relief that I muffled in the pillow.

As he stroked my hair I turned to face him again, letting him see the understanding in my eyes before I kissed him.

"Again," I breathed, hoping he'd understand what I was doing; and hoping that if the bug was sensitive enough to catch the word, our listeners would think I was enjoying myself and asking for Round Two.

Kane kissed me in return, his chin dipping in comprehension.

Silently blessing his quick thinking, I stepped into the network again.

I whisked down the virtual corridor, rechecking the sims I'd already passed and finding everything as before. At the one that contained Kane, I slowed to a halt. Feeling like a sleazy voyeur, I recreated my invisible viewport and peeked in.

Tawny was in the sim, too, but she was clearly the one controlling the action.

And some action it was. Eyeing Kane's magnificent nakedness, I had to admit that she had an excellent eye for detail.

Oh.

And an excellent imagination.

...Wow.

I blinked, warmth rising in my cheeks.

Well then. Moving right along...

I tore myself away from the sim and wobbled down the corridor, flapping an invisible hand in front of my face to dissipate the heat.

The rest of the sims were unoccupied, and at the end of the corridor I turned, considering my next move. Was this network connected to the security server?

Nobly resisting the temptation to peek in and get a comprehensive sex education from Tawny's imaginary tryst with Kane, I bypassed the sim doors and drifted toward a blank corridor wall.

As I had hoped, a brick wall wavered into existence when I approached. Firewall. Perfect.

Unstoppable and undetectable, I slipped through it.

On the other side, streams of data packets zipped past. I hovered for a few moments to study them before diving into the nearest one.

Chasing data bits, I assembled and assessed the information. Email server. Nope. Next.

I switched streams and absorbed few sentences of a private journal on a backup server. Nothing helpful there, but somebody had a serious attitude problem.

The next stream felt more primitive. Low-level machine-language instructions jostled past, and I realized I'd found the automated controls for the heating and cooling systems.

Possibly useful later, but not what I wanted at the moment.

Switching streams again, I would have let out triumphant cry if I'd been capable of it in my current form. Security data at last. Surfing along the data stream, I identified one feed after another, all converging on the main server.

I could take down the whole security system from here, including the surveillance cameras.

But I'd do it later; around two AM when everyone was asleep except the guards. The staff likely wouldn't wake Harchman to report that the surveillance system was down.

I hoped.

Or maybe they'd raise a huge outcry and scramble all personnel to patrol the place until the security server was restored...

Dammit.

I turned for the portal, then hesitated. My top priority was to get to the server room and plug in Spider's program so the Department could monitor it. But with all our resources consumed by the terrorist threat, how long would it take for the analysts to get to it? If people were being tortured right now, how could I live with myself if I let it go on for even another hour?

I couldn't.

Mentally bracing myself, I dove into the vast repository of the archive server.

I started with the smallest files. Only video clips, they panned around people in various poses; standing, sitting, reclining, reaching up, reaching down. They were all smiling and attractive, their garb ranging from Harchman's conservative staff uniforms to suggestively tight clothing to explicit sex gear. And...

I stared in disbelief.

...a pornographic zebra costume...?

Okay, then.

This must be the source material for Harchman's spa sims. Skimming through the last of them, I found no torture or evidence of anyone forced to do anything against their will. Then I turned to the full-length sim records.

Measureless time later, my senses had been deadened by a parade of pornography. Harchman and his guests didn't seem to be using the sims for anything else, and my investigation consisted of an unending cycle of dipping into sim records only long enough to catch the first glimpse of naked flesh and hear the first moan of passion.

But at least it wasn't torture.

When an unusual record came up at last, I was out and on to the next one before my exhausted brain processed the absence of nudity.

Had that flash of crimson been blood?

Oh no...

Rolling back the record, I watched it from the beginning.

A Remembrance Day service, dark clouds looming ominously above the Battalion Park cenotaph. Poppies glowed against the sepia-toned winter landscape and a military honour guard stood to attention. Elderly veterans with canes and wheelchairs held themselves as tall and proud as they were able. A solemn group of men, women and children surrounded them.

A short man advanced to the cenotaph bearing a wreath, and with disgust I recognized Harchman's smirking face.

The contemptible little slimeball must have created a sim of his expected moment of glory so he could replay it time and again for his own enjoyment. The crimson I had glimpsed earlier had been the poppies on his wreath.

Revolted by the depth of his self-absorption, I was on the verge of closing the sim when it exploded in a maelstrom of red.

I gaped at the carnage, unable to react or even to think.

Nothing remained of Harchman but a crimson mess on the concrete. His dismembered right hand lay several feet away, still attached to the tattered remains of the wreath.

Corpses sprawled everywhere. None left standing.

A little girl's body lay motionless in her pink coat and white tights, a tiny broken doll among the dark scattered lumps that used to be men and women.

A single poppy floated silently down to settle on the base of the cenotaph.

The sim ended.

I hung paralyzed in cyberspace, my nonexistent stomach roiling, my virtual heart pummelling my chest.

Just as I was beginning to recover, the next sim began.

A Remembrance Day service...

Immobilized with horror, I watched the sim play out again. This time the explosion seemed to come from a different angle. Again Harchman was obliterated. Different splatter pattern this time. Only his lower leg and foot remaining. Everyone else dead.

Then the next Remembrance Day sim began.

And the next.

After three more scenarios with varying angles of destruction for Harchman, the porn resumed.

My mind still reeling, I watched the entwined limbs and bouncing body parts without seeing them.

No surprise that somebody hated Harchman enough to blow him up. But all those innocent people...

Icy nausea gripped me.

What psychopath had created that sim? Someone cold-blooded enough to not only depict the innocent lives they'd snuff out, but also to revel in horrific details like a dead child in a little pink coat.

It didn't take a leap of intellect to identify Tawny as having the best motive to kill Harchman. She'd probably inherit part if not all of his vast wealth.

But how could she contemplate killing all those people? Surely evil that monstrous should show some outward sign. I hadn't gotten that vibe from her.

But it had to be her. The centre of each blast seemed to be Harchman himself, and only Tawny would have that kind of access to him. She must be planning to slip an explosive into his pocket or something.

I studied the file attributes of the Remembrance Day sims. They had been heavily encrypted and the user data was encoded, but that couldn't stop me. Fading into invisibility, I slipped into the data stream, then searched out the sim file and absorbed its secrets.

Only minutes later I popped back into the sim repository, a feral grin of triumph stretching my lips. James Helmand. Got the bastard. He'd made the sim, but I'd be willing to bet Tawny had given him access to the system. They must be conspiring to murder Harchman and split his vast fortune.

And maybe Riel was involved, too. They would want the ultrasound weapon to wipe out the crowd...

I fought the urge to dive out of the network immediately and report to Stemp. Stay calm. Remembrance Day wasn't until Monday, so there was still time to stop the slaughter. I'd check the rest of the sims, in case that wasn't the worst of them...

Nerves strung tight, I rocketed through the remaining sims. They played out without further bloodshed, and at last I dragged my virtual self out of the archive server.

Dreading what was to come, I retraced my steps to hover at the virtual portal.

Time for the next phase of my plan. If everything went well, it would get me in and out of the server room undetected. Once that was done I could report the murder sim when I connected with Spider via the network...

My heart clenched. But if I got caught infiltrating the server room and couldn't report to Stemp, all those people would die.

Dammit, I'd have to make the terrifying virtual trip to Sirius twice.

I stifled a whimper and stepped through the portal.

Pain crashed through my head, jerking me into a swearing ball.

"Just a reminder." Kane's harsh voice penetrated my pounding brain like a hammer-drill. "This is what happens when you cross me."

His tone was so ugly and hate-filled that terror and pain short-circuited in my defective emotional wiring to explode into violent anger.

Mustering every ounce of control, I forced myself to choke out the humiliating words between sobs of agony and fury. "I'm sorry... Master. I'm sorry... I won't do it again..."

"Enough." Firm hands massaged my throbbing temples. "I forgive you. This time. Let this be a lesson to you."

Trembling with suppressed rage, I concentrated on the slowly-easing pain and faked a grateful tone. "Oh, thank you!"

Breathe. Let it go. It's only a cover story.

Unclenching my teeth, I closed my eyes and switched to yoga breathing while Kane's expert massage did its work.

A few minutes later both the pain and my anger had subsided, and I rolled off the bed and plugged the network generator stick into my laptop.

Giving Kane a resigned shrug, I lay down on the bed again and slipped into the internet before I could chicken out.

CHAPTER 30

As I sped along data tunnels, I obsessively marked each node of my path with a tiny data flag invisible to everyone but me. Sirius's servers were notoriously hard to find, and if I got lost...

If I had been capable of it in my bodiless state, I would have shuddered at the thought of being trapped forever in a purgatory of consciousness without form.

Don't think about it.

Just keep looking...

At last I found my destination. Now for the worst part.

Bracing myself for terrifying dissolution, I surged forward, visualizing my consciousness surfing in on a wave of data.

My wave smashed against the breakwater of their security, shattering me into data bits and tumbling me out of control.

Fighting terror, I dragged my tiny spark of consciousness to the edge of the data stream. Slowly, painfully, I regrouped, seeking out my scattered bits and pulling them back together.

Oh, God, it had been months since I'd done this. What if the analysts had beefed up their security and I couldn't get in at all?

Don't think about that.

Keep trying.

It took three more nerve-shattering attempts before I finally popped into visibility in the safe haven of Sirius's file repository.

Spider burst in only a few seconds later, making me jerk with surprise.

"Jesus!" I patted my avatar's nonexistent heart. "I didn't expect you to get here so fast."

"Sorry," Spider apologized. "I'm working late again. We're still digging for intel on this terrorist." The dark smudges under his eyes told me exactly how hard he'd been working, and for how long. He probably hadn't gotten any more sleep than I had. "Have you gotten into Harchman's server room already?" he added, a hopeful smile illuminating his tired face. "You're amazing!"

"Um, no. I didn't get into the server room; and I'm not amazing. Unfortunately. But I do have an important update and this was the best way to report. Is Stemp still here, too?"

"Probably." Spider conjured a virtual keyboard out of thin air and typed rapidly.

Moments later Stemp's avatar strode in, already speaking as the door closed behind him. "Webb said you have an update?"

"Yes, and a question. First I need to know if Kane is working for you. He's at Harchman's right now, and he's bugged. Is the bug one of ours?"

"No." Stemp's reply was immediate and unequivocal, his face hardening. "Kane is a civilian. He was very clear about cutting all ties with the Department. If he is at Harchman's, it is at his own behest. Find out what he's doing and intervene if necessary. The mission is your top priority."

I suppressed a shiver at his unspoken meaning. Kane had been debriefed when he resigned and all our protocols had been updated, but he would still pose a major security threat if he were captured by enemies, or worse, turned. If things went sour at Harchman's, my next command from Stemp might be a kill order.

I drew a deep breath and switched topics. "Harchman is running a virtual reality network. I checked the sim archives and it looks as though Tawny and James Helmand are planning to plant a bomb on Harchman and blow him up at the Remembrance Day service where he's scheduled to speak. In the sim, the blast vaporized Harchman completely and..." My throat constricted and my words came out in a dry croak at the memory of the carnage. "...killed everybody there." I cleared my throat and took a slow breath. "Tawny must have given Helmand access to the network so he could create the sim. But at least we've got time to stop it."

"How certain are you about the maker of the sim?" Stemp demanded.

"It was encrypted, but I'm positive it was James."

"Very well. Webb, when your backdoor program becomes active, have Brock and Mellor pull the sim for evidence. I'll contact the anti-terrorism teams and advise them to check the area to make sure no explosives have been planted in advance."

"Okay." I let out a breath of relief.

"You said Harchman was blown up," Stemp added. "Not the bloodless death that our Remembrance Day terrorist promised."

"No..." I said slowly. "And I checked all the sims. There was no sign of an ultrasound weapon or anything that even looked bottle-shaped. But Harchman just released a new app that pinpoints acts of violence so people can steer clear of them. Tawny might be planning to use his murder to boost publicity for the app. She'd inherit Harchman's estate, and all the extra money from the app along with it. But I feel like there's something missing in that theory. If she is the Remembrance Day terrorist, why would she put inaccurate information in the threat?"

"And you said Riel asked about the weapon," Stemp prompted.

"Yes. Were you listening in on the bug?"

"Not personally. The analysts will have the record."

"Right, I'll want to listen to that later." I switched back to the topic at hand. "At our dinner tonight Riel hinted that he knew about the weapon and what it could do, but he wouldn't go into detail because Labelle was there. I think Holt was right; Riel doesn't trust Labelle. I was trying to get more information out of Riel when the alert came in about the intruders at my house. Did you get them, by the way?"

"Yes. They are awaiting your questions. Not very comfortably."

"Good." I gave him a smile. "Thank you." My smile slipped. "So, back to our terrorist. Even though everything points to Tawny and James, I'm still not convinced that Riel isn't somehow involved. Or maybe Riel is actually our terrorist, and Tawny and James are copycats. Maybe they heard about the threat and decided it was a perfect opportunity to get rid of Harchman. Everybody would assume it was part of the terrorist attack so they wouldn't be looking for murder suspects. Or who knows? Maybe they're all working together; or maybe the original threat came from somebody else entirely. Is there any news from the other counterterrorism teams?"

"Not yet," Stemp said. "We'll update you if anything develops. Is there anything else?"

"That's all for now. I'll report in again later after I've gotten into the server room..." I secretly crossed my fingers for luck. "...but I wanted to make sure this intel got passed on right away."

"Very well." Stemp gave me a small smile. "Good luck."

"Thanks. Talk to you later."

Slipping into invisibility, I dove back into the internet.

To my surprise, my markers were still in place and the trip back to Harchman's went smoothly. In the portal, I hesitated for only a moment before bracing myself and stepping through.

Once more, Kane snarled abuse at me, foul words that flayed my raw nerves. Rage and pain choked my faked contrition into hisses as the demeaning words forced themselves out between my clenched teeth.

I fought the unreasonable anger.

It's only a cover story. Let it go.

Despite my efforts, my heart shrivelled with shame at the thought of someone listening and believing my act. I squeezed my eyes shut, trying to force away the thoughts.

Let it go, dammit.

Kane lay down on the bed beside me and took me into his arms, still gently massaging the base of my skull as he guided my head onto his shoulder. I battled the urge to pull away; to yell and slam him with my fists until he apologized.

Or begged.

Let him see what it was like to crawl and snivel...

Pressing a kiss to the top of my head, Kane continued to massage my scalp. The knotted muscles resisted him while I lay tensely in his embrace.

Breathe. Relax.

The pain slowly eased, and my anger ebbed with it.

Kane would never treat me that way in real life. This was strictly a cover, and a good one at that. I was lucky to have him with me; lucky he was a top agent who could think on his feet.

Or on his back.

My lips turned up at the thought, amusement banishing the last of my dark emotions. Kane cuddled me closer and pressed another kiss to the top of my head.

Limp with reaction, I melted against him. Laying an arm over his chest, I took comfort from the steady reassuring beat of his heart. His contempt and anger might be far too real when he discovered what I was about to do.

I allowed myself a few precious moments, then returned to duty with a sigh. No turning back now.

I let my hand roam across the hard planes of his chest. "I'm really sorry. Can I make it up to you?" I murmured.

His hand stilled on my neck. "I don't know. Can you?"

"May I try?" I hauled myself up onto one elbow to look down at him, gliding my hand down over the corrugations of his abs.

Heat kindled in his eyes. "You may."

I was committed now.

Probably should be committed to a mental institution, because this was pure craziness. I summoned up every exhibitionist fantasy I'd ever read about and slid my hand lower.

Kane growled satisfaction as I fondled him through his pants, his erection hardening under my hand.

He would stop me if he didn't want to do this, wouldn't he?

Or would he hate me for forcing him to choose between blowing our cover or playing out this scene for our observers?

His arm tightened around me and I slowed my stroking. Did he want me to stop?

Apparently not. His free hand moved to the waistband of his pants.

Undid the button and slid the zipper down.

My mouth went dry.

Taking my hand, he placed it on the hard muscle below his navel. The landing strip of coarse hair tickled my palm, enticing my hand lower. My fingertips made small circles, creeping inside the warmth of his clothes, under the elastic of the snug black underwear that never failed to turn me on.

Despite my discomfort at the thought of an audience, heat grew between my legs. Hellhound's rough whisper from long ago echoed in my memory. *"You're all hot an' slippery, darlin'. Ya like the danger, don't ya? Ya like knowin' ya might get caught."*

God, maybe he was right.

Or maybe I was just so pathetically eager to get it on with Kane that I didn't care who listened in.

I rejected both thoughts. Irrelevant. This needed to happen, or my plan wouldn't work. Duty first.

Yep, duty. That's what this was...

My fingertips searched lower, encountering steel hardness encased in hot velvet skin. Kane groaned as I traced his contours, his hips thrusting up to meet my touch.

His hand clamped on the back of my neck. "Suck it." The harsh dominant voice was back, but this time it sent shivers cascading down to tingle in every erogenous zone.

I had only a moment to wonder whether this was the

true Kane or if he was still playing the bad-boy part I'd assigned him. With one hand he freed himself from the confines of his pants, his other hand fisting in my hair and shoving my head downward.

After that first rough gesture he didn't push me. His hand remained buried in my hair, tightening while I slowly explored. Savouring the taste and feel of him, I reveled in his groans and intakes of breath while I alternated hard suction with teasing flicks of my tongue.

His body tensed under me. "Stop." The word came out in a guttural growl. "Strip."

Heart thumping, I slid off the bed, making sure I stood near my discarded purse to drop my pants. They puddled around my ankles and I crouched as if to fumble with them. My phone was mercifully accessible near the top of the purse and I reached in just as Kane sat up to tear off his clothes.

"Hurry." Kane knelt on the bed, rolling on a condom and giving me a sizzling up-and-down scrutiny.

"My pants are caught on my guns," I muttered. "I'll take the holsters off..."

"Leave them." His teeth bared in a savage grin. "They're sexy. Get naked except for your weapons."

I didn't have to fake the trembling of my hands as I worked my pant legs over the holsters. Lucky Riel already knew I was armed.

The thought of Riel watching this little show made me hesitate in my bra and thong. Exposed, my ass tingled as though I could actually feel the eye of the camera on it.

Dammit, stop thinking that. There were no cameras. I had checked. I *knew* it.

And anyway, it was too late to stop now. I grabbed my phone and flicked on its recording app, hiding the movement behind my thigh as I stood.

Kane pulled me onto the bed. Tossing me roughly onto my back, he covered my body with his, allowing me a perfect opportunity to conceal my phone under the pillow with only its microphone exposed.

A surge of gratitude for his perceptiveness mingled with sudden excitement at the hard contact of his body. He pressed hungry kisses on my lips, my throat, my cleavage. A tidal wave of lust suffused me and I writhed under him, every nerve electrified.

Shameless now, I pulled off my bra and cupped my breasts, offering them to him and moaning in bliss while he licked and sucked. His teeth closed lightly on one nipple with a gentle tug that fired jolts of sensation to the centre of my being. Arching up to him with an inarticulate cry, I rode the fiery updraft of pleasure, my hands greedily devouring the iron contours of his arms and shoulders.

Scattering kisses down my body, he moved lower in bed, then paused. In an instant of eye contact, he asked and I answered.

Yes.

God, yes.

He pushed my thong down to my ankles, leaving them bound by the soft elastic while he lifted my legs over his head and nibbled down the inside of my thigh.

Panting, I let him press my knees up and apart, my body blazing with hunger. The first touch of his mouth left me molten, my moans rising while he pinned me to the bed and teased me with the same light strokes of his tongue and hard hot suction I'd inflicted on him.

Each time I tensed on the edge of orgasm he drew back, barely touching me; then urging me on again until I was blind and deaf to everything but the fire in my veins and the sound of my own begging.

Again the hot tension surged up; again he pulled back, leaving me quivering on the edge.

"Please..." My voice was only a ragged gasp. "Please... please..."

His hot mouth descended and my world detonated in glowing shards of pure sensation. Wave after wave of ecstasy submerged me, slowly subsiding to leave me limp and panting.

Before I could catch my breath Kane flipped me over, strong hands clamping on my hips to pull me to my knees. Opening my legs, he entered me with slow strokes, easing in only to back out; pressing in tantalizingly farther each time.

Whimpers of need escaped me. "Please... John... please... now... *now*..."

At last he filled me with a long thrust.

"Mine," he growled over my hiss of satisfaction.

Another slow withdrawal, my body clenching around him in protest at the loss.

A harder thrust, burying himself to the hilt and setting off fireworks of pleasure.

"...You..." He pulled slowly out again and I whimpered and rocked backward in an attempt to hold him. "...Are..." He drove deep inside me, wrenching a cry of rapture from my throat. "*Mine!*"

His tempo quickened. Hard deliberate thrusts awakened every nerve, igniting brilliant sparks of sensation.

"John... omigod..."

Hands braced on the headboard, I slammed back to meet him over and over. The sparks coalesced into pools of heat spreading and spiralling back in on themselves, glowing ever brighter.

Electric tingles raced over me, my cries rising and quickening.

Every muscle tensed.

Sensation amplified.

Contracted to a single incandescent point...

Exploded with supernova brilliance.

I soared mindless on the expanding edge of the shockwave, my senses filled with Kane's scent, the slap of flesh on flesh, my own raw-throated cries beyond words.

Before the first wave could ebb another orgasm blasted me; a volcano erupting into earthshattering cataclysm as Kane drove home again and again, his fingers digging into my hips, his harsh breaths mingling with mine.

White-hot, all thought vaporized.

I was everything. Nothing.

Pure sensation.

Kane roared like a wild beast.

His thighs steel-hard, he strained me to him, surging inside me for long moments before falling forward to wrap his arms around me. I collapsed and we lay panting facedown, our bodies still joined.

And I slid my hand under the pillow and ended the recording.

CHAPTER 31

Kane's hand glided down my arm, a sensuous caress that followed my wrist under the pillow to close around my hand and the phone.

Nuzzling kisses along my shoulder, he positioned his head beside mine. I took his cue and lifted the edge of the pillow just enough so we could both see underneath, my heart contracting with guilt.

This was the part where he realized I'd used him...

At the sight of the recording app, he dropped another soft kiss on my shoulder, then nudged me with his chin.

Emboldened by what I hoped was acceptance, I cued my alarm clock app and set it to two AM.

Kane's hand patted mine under the pillow, then deactivated the alarm.

"Go to sleep," he said softly.

He rolled off me and sat up to remove the spent condom, then reclined on one elbow watching me with that small smile again.

My muscles slack, my face half-buried in the pillow, I blinked an eyelid that felt as though it weighed ten pounds.

"This bed is eating me alive," I mumbled. "I can't move."

Kane chuckled. "You don't have to."

Rolling me from one side to the other, he freed the

covers, then lay down and pulled them over both of us. He tucked me against him with my head pillowed by the sweet spot between his chest and shoulder, and when we were settled he stroked the tangled hair away from my face and dropped a kiss on my forehead. "Good night."

Fighting the urge to give in, I widened my eyes at him. He gave me the tiniest of nods in return. "Go to sleep."

A leaden blanket of exhaustion weighed me down.

Kane would look after me. He would wake me when it was time.

I struggled against the seductive comfort.

Too many unanswered questions. Why was he here? What was his agenda? Who was listening to the bug that he wouldn't let me destroy?

I shouldn't count on him...

A warm hand caressed my shoulder and I purred with satisfaction, caught between a delightful dream and a sense of nervous urgency I couldn't define.

Shit!

My eyelids popped open, encountering blackness. I tensed, swivelling my head to take in my surroundings. Was I imprisoned?

The hand tightened on my shoulder and a black-on-black silhouette loomed closer. The sandpaper of Kane's five o'clock shadow brushed my chin as he pressed a kiss to my lips.

Letting out a breath of relief, I collapsed back onto the pillow. The glow of the clock radio provided the only illumination in the room. Two AM.

Kane must have stayed awake all this time, watching

over me and soothing my nightmares before they began. My heart warmed.

I pulled him closer and kissed him deeply, then took his hand and placed it over my lips. I felt his nod in the darkness.

Hoping the network key in my bra was still close enough to function, I closed my eyes and visualized the network.

The white void popped into existence around me, and I squared my invisible shoulders.

I could do this.

All I had to do was knock out their security server...

No; wait a minute.

Knocking it out entirely would alert them that something was wrong. I could do better than that.

With a surge of gratitude for the few hours of sleep that had cleared my head, I floated through their firewall and hovered over the currents of data streaming to the security server.

What if that data went in a circle instead?

I insinuated myself into the flow, gradually altering it and testing the results.

Yes.

A few more circles; a couple of pinches in the data stream to divert power from the electronic locks...

I eased back and regarded my handiwork with satisfaction. All locks between the guesthouse and server room were temporarily disabled, and for the next twenty minutes the cameras between the guesthouse and the server room would display a continuous loop. I could travel unseen.

Now I only had to avoid the guards in person.

After one last check of the system, I turned reluctantly

back toward the portal.

Gritting my virtual teeth, I stepped out into pain.

Kane was ready for me with another vicious display of verbal dominance. I fought the agony in my head and the red-hot need to lash out at him while I choked out the degrading apologies. At last the pain diminished to a bearable level and I went limp in his arms.

But only for a few moments.

Pushing myself up on one elbow, I broke his embrace to lean down and kiss him. "Fuck me again," I growled. "Fuck me hard. Fuck me 'til I scream."

His hand clenched on the back of my neck, dragging me down into a ravenous kiss. Concealed by the fall of my hair, I tapped his cheek once. Pay attention.

He growled and pulled me closer but his lips stilled, his body tensing to alertness under me.

Tap-tap-tap-tap-tap...

I raised the count to twenty, hoping he'd understand.

Twenty minutes for me to get to the server room and return.

I pressed my phone into his hand and drew back, making little moans of simulated pleasure. He replied with a harsh breath that was almost a groan, a sound so sexy I nearly jumped back into bed and abandoned my mission altogether.

Instead I yanked on my clothes, hoping their rustle would sound like action under the bedsheets.

Kane must have been thinking along the same lines. Rhythmic rustling came from the direction of the bed, like a couple beginning to make love.

Or like a man unhurriedly pleasuring himself.

Lust punched me low in the belly and I sucked in a breath, imagining Kane's big hand wrapped around his thick luscious...

I swallowed hard and made for the door.

When Kane cued the recording and our first moans and gasps of passion began, I slipped into the hallway with my heart beating fast.

If I was wrong about the video surveillance, that brief sliver of light as I stepped outside had just blown our cover.

Sending a heartfelt prayer skyward, I hurried for the exit.

Only a few paces later a surge of adrenaline stopped me dead as I recognized the giant gap in my planning.

How the hell was I going to get past the doorman?

My feet went into motion again. Don't stand around; somebody might come along.

I strode purposefully down the hall, my mind hurtling through possibilities.

There were three other exits but they were all marked with signs saying 'Fire Exit Only – Alarm Will Sound'. And I hadn't disabled the fire alarms, dammit.

My decisive strides carried me to the end of the hallway far too quickly. Still devoid of ideas, I stared in despair at the cardkey lock on the service door.

Why hadn't I asked Reggie Chow if he had anything to crack a cardkey lock? Or I could have asked Holt Of The Magic Bump Keys. Or hell, I could have asked at Stores.

But no, I hadn't thought that far ahead...

...Hang on.

I stared at the cardkey reader.

Its light was green.

Thank God. I hadn't realized the service corridor locks were controlled by the same circuit as the locks I'd disabled between the guesthouse and the server room.

Sometimes you win.

I stepped through the door praying that none of Harchman's staff were lurking on the other side.

My prayer was answered. On my left was an unoccupied alcove containing lockers, shelves of linens and housekeeping items, and a laundry cart. On my right, a long straight corridor stretched in the direction of the main house.

Hard to get lost.

Easy to get spotted.

Dammit.

Ducking into the alcove, I rapidly inventoried the contents of the lockers, finding nothing but a couple of abandoned uniforms.

Next I rooted squeamishly through the laundry cart, trying not to think about the things people did in their hotel beds and showers; but unless I wanted to construct a slightly soiled toga there were no options for disguise available in there.

Reluctantly turning back to the uniforms, I hissed out a breath. Better to wear the livery than my own clothes. Even if a uniform didn't fit, its colours would make me unremarkable if somebody glimpsed me at a distance.

I whisked Chow's pen-weapon and Spider's USB stick out of my purse, then appropriated a clean sheet from the housekeeping shelf and dropped it on top of the laundry cart. Skinning out of my pants and blouse, I laid my purse on the sheet along with my clothes and rolled the whole thing into a bundle.

The first uniform was impossible. The pants stuck at my hips, and when I fastened the jacket it cut off the circulation in my arms and gaped in ugly scallops that revealed my bright red bra and pasty white belly between the straining buttons.

The other uniform apparently belonged to a descendent of André the Giant. What the hell; did Harchman hire only circus freaks? Where were the uniforms belonging to all the normal-sized staff I'd seen around here?

Even at my 5'-10" height, the pants came nearly to my armpits. I folded the waistband over and over to bring it down to my waist, then rolled up the pant legs and submerged myself in the huge jacket.

A glance in the locker room mirror made me stifle a groan. Even at a distance it just wouldn't work. I looked like an ill-dressed marshmallow, and the pants wouldn't stay up despite the extra bulk of the rolled waistband. If I had to run I'd trip and break my damn leg.

And time was ticking away. A glance at my watch clenched my teeth. Seventeen minutes.

I flung off the oversized clothing and added my ankle holsters and their contents to the bedsheet before turning back to the tiny uniform. With some profanity-laden squirming and struggling I managed to work the pants up over my hips. Buttoning them was out of the question and the zipper stuck halfway up, but at least my ass was covered. Three inches of bare ankle stuck out the bottom of the skin-tight legs. With a few stiff contortions hampered by the tourniquet pants, I managed to get my shoes back on.

Coiling my hair into a quick French twist, I anchored it in place with Chow's pen and a couple of ballpoints from the supply shelves. The jacket was next. Fortunately it was long enough to cover most of the gaping front of the pants, but the too-tight sleeves ended two inches above my wristbone and hampered my arm movement. I crammed the USB stick into one of the pockets, creating an ugly bulge.

Fifteen minutes.

Go.

Wincing as the jacket sleeves bit into my arms, I seized the handle of the laundry cart and wheeled it down the corridor as fast as I could go without actually breaking into a run.

The corridor branched approximately where I thought the turnoff to the concierge's station should be, and I veered left toward the main house and hurried on.

Fourteen minutes. Almost there.

The passageway turned a few yards farther on, and I hustled around the corner only to stop dead, my heart banging my ribcage.

I was only a few feet away from an employee lounge. A liveried man sat at one of the tables, his forehead already creasing into a frown as he looked me up and down.

"Where do you think you're going?" he demanded. He hooked a thumb toward the guesthouse. "Housekeeping is back that way." His eyes narrowed. "Hang on, you don't even work here. I never forget a face."

Shit!

Why hadn't I worn my regular clothes and brazened it out aboveground where everybody knew I was an invited guest? If I got caught down here, they'd know I was up to no good.

Stupid, stupid...

His frown deepened and he reached for his phone.

"Um... I'm new," I stammered frantically.

Think, think!

"You're right," I went on. "I don't know what I'm doing. But they told me to come here. With this." I nodded at the laundry cart, hoping he couldn't see my hands shaking. And hoping he wouldn't ask who 'they' were. "At least I think this is where they wanted me," I added uncertainly. "Maybe I got it wrong. I'll go back..." I took a few backward steps.

"Hold on there." He was on his feet now.

Dammit, that must have been his spare uniform back there in the locker. At least seven feet tall, he towered over me with his shaved head only inches from the low ceiling and his huge shoulders causing a near-total eclipse.

He was too close. Could I get to my gun inside the rolled-up sheet?

Should I even try?

"I'm sorry," I squeaked. "I'll just go."

A hand the size of a baseball mitt clamped onto my wrist. "No."

CHAPTER 32

I drew myself up and made my best attempt at a commanding voice. "Let me go."

Amazingly, the mountainous man released me and backed off a pace or two with his hands raised as if trying not to scare me.

Too late for that. In another couple of seconds my stolen pants were going to need the services of my laundry cart.

"Sorry, I didn't mean anything by it; I just didn't want you to run off." He surveyed my pornographic uniform. "You're one of those acting students, aren't you? Let me guess: Auditioning for a chambermaid scene?"

A tiny hope stirred. "...Yes...?"

His frown was back. "Shouldn't you be in the guesthouse or the spa? And shouldn't you have been here at two PM, not two AM?"

I swallowed hard, hoping my voice wouldn't come out sounding like Minnie Mouse. "They said two AM. I was supposed to take the service tunnel to the main house and somebody would meet me." I gave him a nervous smile, which wasn't much of an acting achievement under the circumstances. "I'm sorry, I've never done this before and I really don't know..."

He shook his head and blew out a breath as he sank back

into his chair. "Nothing surprises me anymore." He surveyed me from top to toe. "Don't take this wrong, but I can't believe anybody would think that looks sexy."

I grimaced. "It sure doesn't feel sexy."

"Well, don't worry; it could be worse." He chuckled. "Last week there were two blondes running around in nothing but the front and back half of a zebra costume. People are weird, you know?"

Enlightenment dawned as I nodded in sincere agreement.

Acting students; of course. I'd been right about those video clips being created for sims. And that explained the pornographic zebra, too.

The man-mountain leaned back and clasped his hands behind his head as if settling in for a good chat. "I didn't have a clue what this gig was going to be like when I hired on. I've been with the Harchmans for five years next month, and y'know, I think I've seen just about everything."

Urgency hammered at me. How much time had I lost?

"I'll bet you have." I gave him a timid smile. "I wish I had time to hear about it all, but..."

He waved me toward the exit. "It's okay. Go on, don't keep 'em waiting."

Barely able to believe my good fortune, I took my bedsheet from the laundry cart and tottered toward the door. "I'm just going to leave the cart here until I find out where I'm supposed to go."

"No problem, I'll make sure nobody moves it on you." He smiled, his kind brown eyes bracketed by laugh lines. "Break a leg."

"Thanks." I cranked the wooden corners of my mouth into the best imitation of a smile I could muster, and stepped through the door.

A guard was striding down the hall only a few paces away. Clutching the bedsheet to my chest, I hurried in the opposite direction. My back crawled with the expectation of a sudden shout or a restraining hand descending on my shoulder, but nothing happened.

Heart pounding, I sneaked another glance at my watch. Eleven minutes.

Why hadn't I taken more time with Kane? I could have teased him longer; slowed him down, dammit.

The memory of his roar of passion made me shiver. Or maybe not.

Shut up and focus.

The trip through the convoluted corridors seemed to take forever. Each time I came to a corner I braced myself for a confrontation, but none came. At the server room door I checked my watch again. Ten minutes left.

No time to put on Harchman's fingerprints. Thank God I'd already disabled the scanner from inside the network.

Using a corner of the sheet to shield the door handle from my own fingerprints, I eased the door open a crack and peeked in. Between the shelves of rack-mounted servers I glimpsed the uniformed guard sitting in front of the security console, his attention glued to the screens.

Shit, had he noticed that some of them were on a continuous loop?

Fumbling Chow's magic pen out of my hair, I rotated the clip and inserted the point through the crack before pressing the activation button.

A one-second burst should do it...

Nothing happened. The guard yawned, stretching and scratching his head.

I tried again.

Still nothing.

Shit, was the battery dead? Tension knotted my belly.

One more attempt netted no results.

Dammit!

I must be outside the ten-foot effective range. Or maybe the beam was being blocked by the server racks.

I couldn't keep trying. Only seven more uses left in the pen.

My back prickled as though there was a target on it and I shot a frantic glance around me. I couldn't hang around out here; I'd get caught for sure.

But if I went in and the guard spotted me he'd be able to identify me when he recovered.

And even if I shot him in the back with the trank pistol he'd remember the impact of the dart, and the Harchmans could easily figure out which of their guests was most likely to be carrying some kind of designer weapon.

And once they realized I'd been in their server room, they'd double-check everything and find Spider's back-door software. My cover would be blown, along with Kane's; and maybe even the entire Department's. Not an option.

Dammit!

Ransacking my bedsheet, I extracted Chow's nasal filters and stuffed them up my nose, then drew the trank pistol and fitted its muzzle to the crack of the door. Heart pounding, I aimed for the back of the guard's chair and pulled the trigger.

He went limp, and I spared a moment of thankfulness for the hum of the servers that had hidden the 'pfft' of the gun's propellant and the pop of the trank chamber exploding against the back of his chair. He'd never know what had happened.

I checked my watch again. Nine minutes left. The aerosolized trank would keep him down for three to five. Maybe that would be enough.

Clamping my lips shut, I slipped into the server room and closed the door behind me.

The suffocating sensation struck immediately. Sucking air desperately through the filters, I pulled the spent dart out of the chair and positioned the pen beside the guard's head.

Two-second burst this time, just to be sure.

Nothing happened.

My pulse ratcheted up even higher and sparkles appeared in the edges of my vision.

Heart beating too fast. Need air...

I drew harder through the nasal filters, fighting panic.

USB stick. Into the nearest server. Red light flashing.

Oxygen...

My mouth opened involuntarily, sucking in life-giving air. The floor rushed up to meet me.

I never felt the impact.

Dizziness rocked me and I groaned, blinking blurry eyes. My nose felt stuffed with cotton and I pawed at it with uncoordinated hands.

What...?

A jolt of memory drove me up to my hands and knees.

Server room.

The guard still sprawled unconscious in his chair.

I squinted at my watch, concentrating fiercely on numbers that wavered in and out of focus.

Five and a half minutes left. I hadn't gotten a full dose of the trank mist, thank God. It must have dissipated by the time I took my first breath.

I staggered to my feet and shoved Spider's USB stick into the next machine, clinging to the rack to balance my still-shaky legs.

After the longest ten seconds in history, the red light stopped blinking and I repeated the process with the next server. While I waited I plucked out the nasal filters. After a moment of indecision, I tucked them into my bra to dispose of later.

Beside my knee, the guard's dangling hand twitched.

Come on, buddy, stay down. I didn't dare fire another dart in the enclosed space. I'd have to press one into his skin to inject the longer-acting tranquilizer...

Next server.

Then the next.

The guard groaned.

Shit shit shit...

With trembling fingers, I ejected the trank magazine and took out a dart.

Twenty minutes of unconsciousness was far too long. Somebody would come in, try to rouse him, and get suspicious.

But I couldn't let him see me.

The guard's eyes were still closed. Next server.

Only one left...

Another groan sent my heart rate into the stratosphere and I inched closer to the guard, dart poised.

The USB stick stopped flashing and I chanced a quick lunge to pull it out and stuff it into the last server.

"Wha...?"

I spun in time to see the guard's eyelids flutter. Then he fell out of his chair and landed face down on the floor, spraying vomit in all directions.

The fucking pen *had* worked, just not while he was unconscious.

I'd punch Reggie Chow for not telling me that little detail.

A few seconds later the file transfer was complete and I snatched up the USB stick. The guard lay motionless facedown, groaning between retches and, with any luck, oblivious to everything but his own misery.

My bundled bedsheet lay inside the splatter radius. Avoiding the vomit-smeared parts as best I could, I scooped it up, stuffed my weapons into it, and slipped silently out the door.

Three and a half minutes.

Afraid to attract attention by running, I powerwalked back to the service entrance clutching my soiled sheet. I was almost to the service door when another guard approached in the hallway.

"Hey, what are you..." he began.

Face turned away, I thrust the malodorous bundle toward him. "Sick guest."

He recoiled and I scurried past, heart pounding.

When I jerked open the service door and dove through it, my brown-eyed man-mountain looked up from the dregs of his coffee.

"So, how did it..." he began.

"You were right, I was supposed to be in the guesthouse!" I squawked. Pitching my bundle onto the laundry cart, I seized its handle and sprinted down the corridor.

At the two-minute mark, I slammed the cart back into its berth in the service alcove.

God, what if I'd miscalculated the length of the recording? If it reached its noisy conclusion before I sneaked back into the room, there would be nothing to conceal the sound of the door opening and closing.

I peeled off the torturous jacket, wincing at the abrasions on my arms.

Shoes off.

Pants.

The zipper stuck.

"Fuck!" I jerked at the recalcitrant tab, then abandoned the effort and clenched a side of the waistband in each fist. With a gargantuan yank the zipper parted and I peeled the pants down, hopping and staggering while I flailed my feet out of them.

One minute.

No time.

I stuffed the ruined uniform under the dirty laundry and flung the soiled bedsheet on top. Tearing into it, I grabbed my purse, weapons, and clothes, then snatched up my shoes. A moment later I burst out the door in my underwear, snapping a wild glance around the quiet corridor.

No witnesses. Thank God.

Run.

Panting up to Suite 108, I seized the door handle, then let out a whimper.

Locked out. My temporary bypass had ended.

My cardkey was in my purse.

I fell to my knees to ransack it.

The surveillance cameras would come back online in seconds. Please don't let me get caught kneeling out here in my underwear...

Thank you, Lord, my hand clenched around the cardkey.

Resisting the urge to slam it into the reader, I kept my movements smooth and quiet.

A slow turn of the latch; a quick shimmy inside clutching my clothes and weapons; a soft closure of the door behind me...

A savage roar from the darkness nearly stopped my heart.

CHAPTER 33

A moment later I realized the roar had been the recording of Kane's mighty orgasm.

Heart hammering, I shuffled toward the sound of my own subsiding moans as rapidly as I could, completely blind after the bright light of the hallway.

Goddamn this giant room; I had no idea where...

My toe smashed into something hard and I bit down a yell of pain. Found the chair.

Bed would be to the left and farther along...

Limping hurriedly in what I hoped was the right direction, I panted open-mouthed, trying to keep silent. The moans were fading now. In a few more seconds the recording would end.

My knee slammed into the edge of the mattress and I pitched forward onto the bed.

Kane's strong arms found me, pulling me under the covers. His naked skin burned against my sweat-chilled body, and he held me closer to run hot hands over my arms and back.

"So..." His voice was a sexy tease. "Ready for another round yet?"

I gasped out a laugh of sheer giddy relief. "Not quite yet." I pressed my head under his chin, clinging to him until my galloping heart slowed and my breathing steadied.

As soon as I'd regained a measure of control, I slipped out of bed again. My eyes had adjusted enough that I could make out my laptop's power LED glowing on the desk, and I vectored toward it and fumbled the portable network generator into the USB port by feel, then padded to the bathroom to generate a convincing toilet-flush.

When I slipped back into bed, I reached for Kane's hand. This time I pressed it a little more firmly over my mouth.

Come on, John, figure it out. Keep me quiet when I come out of the network.

I felt his nod against my hair.

Steeling myself against the upcoming fear and pain, I closed my eyes and concentrated on finding the familiar white void.

When I stepped into it, I paused, suddenly uncertain. Was I in Harchman's network or my own?

Did it matter?

Theoretically if Spider's backdoor program was working, I'd be able to find the Sirius network either way.

I gave a virtual shrug and dissolved into the vast complexity of the internet.

Once again I left a trail of markers behind me, but Sirius's servers remained elusive. My path looped and crossed, leaving a confusing maze behind me while I hunted.

At last I found Sirius. Hovering in the data stream, my consciousness felt thin and weak, attenuated by distance and fatigue. Data packets rushed by, buffeting me in their slipstream while I braced myself for the shattering effort of breaching their server.

Do it.

I flung myself at the firewall, imagining bodysurfing with

all my might.

Tumbling into terror and chaos, I anchored the tiny remaining spark that was me, then sought out my scattered remains one bit at a time.

This time I'd make it.

I tried again, then again. Each time regrouping was more difficult; my reactions slower.

Electric fear shivered through me.

I was exhausted, my control fading. What if I couldn't do it?

And the more time I spent battering myself against this implacable wall, the harder it would be to find the path back to my physical body.

I could be trapped forever...

Panic swelled and I fought it down.

Maybe I should explode into Sirius's network in a holocaust of destruction while I still had enough energy. It was possible; I'd done it before. But that time Spider had been able to roll back the damage. Who knew what critical data I might accidentally destroy?

I couldn't chance it.

Try again.

Again...

At last I made it through, my consciousness diminished to a thin thread wavering in the smooth stream of internal data. When I found the comforting familiarity of the file repository at last, I oozed into an invisible puddle in the corner and simply existed in mindless gratitude for long moments.

Finally I regained enough composure to create a visible avatar and a chair. Flopping into it, I leaned my head back and waited for Spider.

Only a few minutes later he appeared. With a superhuman effort I managed to control a spurt of hysterical laughter.

"Hi, Spider," I said, my voice coming out slightly strangled despite my best efforts. "I'm sorry I woke you."

Smothering a yawn behind his hand, he mumbled, "It's okay...", then glanced down at his rumpled Star Wars pajamas and bare feet, his eyes widening and face flushing crimson. "Omigod!" His hands flew down to cover his crotch despite the fact that his modest pajamas provided complete coverage. "I'm sorry..." he stammered. "I'm sorry, I'll fix it... right away..."

His flush deepened to purple as his pajamas slowly faded away, exposing a scrawny torso and bony knees.

"I'm sorry, I'm sorry!" he cried frantically. "I can't..."

I stood and turned my back, partly to give him privacy and partly to hide the laughter I couldn't suppress any longer. "Spider, take a breath," I commanded. "It's only a sim. You're fine. Just think of being at work."

"Oh... Oh, right..." A moment later he let out a breath. "Okay, you can turn around now."

When I faced him again, he wore his usual work garb of khakis and button-down shirt. His cheeks were still glowing with embarrassment. "I'm sorry," he mumbled. "I just... I wasn't quite awake yet." His flush deepened again. "It was like those dreams where you have to write a final exam but you're naked-"

"Don't say that," I interrupted. "Or it'll be like trying *not* to think of a pink hippopotamus and we'll both end up..." I stopped myself before I could repeat the word 'naked', and a large pink hippo popped into existence in the corner.

I banished it with a stern chopping motion. "Spider." I

spoke firmly to focus our attention. "I just finished loading your backdoor software over at Harchman's. Can you get into it?"

"Oh, awesome!" he exclaimed, waving a laptop into existence. In moments he was clattering keys, his poise completely restored.

I drew a breath of relief and tried not to think of being naked. Or of anybody else being naked. Especially not Kane...

A suspiciously flesh-coloured cloud formed in front of me, and I hurriedly thought about a pink hippo.

Spider looked up at the sound of its grunting and laughed. "You must be tired, too."

I fell back into my chair. "You have no idea."

He sobered. "Are you... safe? I mean... right now, where your physical body is?"

"I think so. John's with me, so if there was an emergency..." I trailed off. "Shit. If there was an emergency he'd have to choose between dragging my useless body around with him or pulling me out of the network by hurting me, and having me thrash around and scream my head off."

I jumped to my feet. "I need to get back there. I don't even know how long I've been gone. What time is it?"

"Quarter to four. I just need you to stay until I get this connection. It'll only be a minute..." Spider's voice faded as he resumed his rapid typing.

"Okay." I sank back into the chair and tried not to fidget.

A few minutes later Spider gave me a smile. "Perfect. My programs are working. I'll get Brock and Tammy to go through Harchman's data tomorrow, so you shouldn't have to go back into the network again."

"Thanks, Spider," I said with sincere gratitude. "See you

later."

As I faded into invisibility he cried, "Wait!"

I popped back into existence. "What is it?"

"Just..." He hurried over to throw his skinny arms around me. "Be careful."

I returned his hug, my heart warming. "Thanks. Talk to you soon."

The return trip through the internet was almost as long and frightening as the outbound one. When I finally stepped through the portal, the pain seemed magnified by my stress and fatigue.

Involuntary profanity spewed from my lips as I hugged my splitting head. As the suffering slowly eased I realized that Kane wasn't muffling me as I'd hoped.

Instead, his rough angry voice pounded my aching eardrums, spitting ugly abuse.

White-hot rage detonated behind my eyes.

In an instant I was kneeling astride him, my forearm crushing the repellent words to silence in his throat.

My face inches from his, I snarled, "Don't you EVER talk to me like that again!"

His hands clamped onto my elbow and wrist, effortlessly bench-pressing my weight off his throat. "You said that's what you wanted."

My voice came out in a menacing growl. "If you ever even *think* that shit again, I'll rip your balls off and shove them down your throat."

"Arlene." The reminder of my cover identity and the warning in Kane's voice jolted me out of my berserk rage, but fury still boiled in my veins. "You asked me to dominate you," he said evenly. "You said you liked it."

"Maybe we should switch places." I spat the words at

him like bullets. "See how you like it."

"Is that what you want? You want me to play submissive?"

Something in his voice snuffed out my anger. With the bug active, he would probably do it if I said yes. I imagined his pride broken, his dignity violated, his gaze downcast while he begged...

Nausea twisted my stomach and I slid off him, propping my throbbing head in my hands.

"No." My voice came out small and weary.

Remember the bug. Be Arlene Widdenback.

I snorted. "I can make any man crawl. There's no novelty in that. But I'm done with the dom stuff, so cut it out. It was only fun for a while after we scammed Harchman."

"All right." Kane sounded cautious. "But maybe next time you could say something like, 'By the way, John, this isn't working for me; let's not do it anymore' instead of crushing my throat and threatening to castrate me."

Be hard-ass Arlene.

"By the way, John," I mimicked him mockingly. "We're not having a relationship here and I don't do touchy-feely talks. You're good for exactly two things; and if you're not fucking me silly or supplying me weapons, I have zero use for you. Remember that."

"I will," he said stiffly. "Maybe I should go back to my own room now."

"Don't let the door hit you in the ass on your way out."

Clicking on the lamp, he got out of bed and dressed, his expression cold and remote. After he had put on his shoes and departed I listened for the sound of his door closing down the hallway, then activated the bug detector.

Green light.

I buried my face in the pillow and fought the urge to burst into tears.

CHAPTER 34

After a couple of hours of fitful sleep broken by violent nightmares, I gave up. Trudging into the echoing stone cavern of the bathroom, I fought to focus on the bright side.

At least I hadn't slept well enough to get deeply into my nightmares, so I hadn't woken up screaming. And maybe Kane would be safer now that our listeners knew he meant nothing to me.

Or maybe they'd just kill him since he was no use as leverage.

Don't think about that.

I turned the water on full blast.

A long hot shower left me almost awake, and by the time I'd finished drying my hair I had forced myself to concentrate on my next goals. Figure out Riel's game, and find out why Kane was here and what he was doing. And find Dante. And Arnie.

The mineral pool with Riel would be my first stop. Meanwhile, though, I was starving.

The small refrigerator held Perrier, grapes, cheese, and crackers. Not exactly my breakfast of choice, but it would have to do. At least I wouldn't pass out from sheer hunger and drown in the pool.

My makeshift breakfast half-eaten, I froze. What if they

had drugged the food?

I drew a deep breath and let it out slowly.

Why would they?

And anyway, it was a little late to worry about it.

Alert to any unusual sensations, I finished eating. When I hadn't keeled over ten minutes later I grabbed my bathing suit and headed for the spa.

It was eight AM when I arrived, and the pool was deserted. In the luxuriously-appointed changing room I slipped into a spacious cubicle, suspiciously surveying the walls and ceiling for hidden cameras.

I didn't spot any, but nevertheless I changed as quickly as possible into my one-piece suit and wrapped myself in one of the thick white terry-cloth robes hanging behind the door. I rolled my pistols and holsters into a second robe and tucked the bundle under my arm before cautiously leaving the cubicle.

Padding barefoot to the pool area, I took stock as I shed my robe and approached the pool. Soothing instrumental music complimented the trickling of a pebble-and-bamboo water feature in the corner, and the creamy tiles were warm under my feet.

More importantly, there were three exits: the one I'd come through from the main house into the spa reception area; another marked 'Employees Only'; and the third leading out through a wall of glass that overlooked the frost-rimed landscape. In summer it would be beautiful with the footpath meandering downhill flanked by gardens, and the water fountain playing in the pond beside the ornate gazebo. Today the dead-brown gardens looked cold and dismal and the half-frozen pond matched the sullen grey of the clouds.

I shivered and stepped into the pool, letting out a long

breath as the hot silky water lapped around my legs. Lowering myself onto one of the submerged benches, I leaned my head back and draped my hair over my bundle of weapons like a makeshift pillow. Narrowing my eyes against the wisps of steam, I considered my strategy.

Should I confront Riel and demand information about Dante and Arnie? Get up in his face and tell him to stop wasting my time and talk business?

Or just keep playing his game, whatever it was?

I remembered his attentiveness to the group dynamics last night and his expression of disappointment when he'd reminded me that 'It is all about the game'.

Slouching lower so the water covered my shoulders, I pondered the enigma that was Riel. Gang member; but he dressed and acted like an affable businessman. Charming and attractive except for that brief hard-eyed moment; but no hint of lust or even sexuality. Non-smoker. Non-drinker. Opposed to drugs.

With none of the usual vices, he must get his gratification from more cerebral pursuits.

Shit, it really was all about the game for him. I could push him and he might comply if he wanted the ultrasound weapon badly enough, but he'd lose respect for me. And if he wasn't our terrorist and I antagonized him enough to make him take his future business elsewhere, the chain of command might decide I was more use to them as a prisoner doing decryptions than as a field agent.

Dammit.

"Bonjour, Arlene." The object of my contemplation came through the spa door and hung his robe beside mine before approaching the pool with a smile. "'Ow nice that we 'ave the pool all to ourselves. I must apologize for Monsieur Labelle last evening. He... 'ow shall I say it? Broke our fête...?"

"Crashed our party." I gave him an encouraging smile.

"Yes, 'e invited himself and I did not wish to be rude. Did you sleep well?" he asked as he stepped into the water and submerged himself opposite me.

Conservative black swim trunks and no tattoos. He just didn't suit the image of a gangland arms buyer at all.

I dragged my tired mind back to his question. What the hell, Kane's intentions had been pretty clear when he dragged me out of the salon last night.

I gave Riel a wicked smile. "I slept well, but not for very long."

"Ah." Amusement sparkled in his eyes, along with something else I couldn't quite identify as his gaze flicked to the abrasions on my arms, glowing livid red in the heat of the water. "It was a good evening, then."

Was that a knowing look? Had he been listening to our bug?

I shrugged. "Good enough. And did you enjoy your evening?"

"Yes, I 'ad a wonderful massage. Monsieur 'Archman's staff, they are... most accommodating."

I gave a noncommittal 'mm'. Had he taken advantage of Masseuse-Barbie after all?

"What are your plans for the rest of the day?" I inquired.

"I 'ave a manicure and pedicure booked at nine. Do you care to join me?"

"Um. No." I nearly admitted that people wielding sharp objects around my fingers completely freaked me out, but I stifled myself in time. "I'm going to go for a massage," I extemporized instead. "If they can fit me in."

"I am sure they can," he said. "And what of Monsieur

Kane?"

I kept my face expressionless and my tone neutral. "I don't know."

A brief silence stretched between us.

Nope, buddy, that's not going to work. I'm not going to keep talking just to fill the silence.

"Ah," Riel said after a few moments. "So you are not bothered that Monsieur Kane and Madame 'Archman are together."

Together? What the hell did he mean by that? Had Tawny's sim been based on real-life experience instead of imagination?

Oh, God. My stomach tightened.

Breathe.

"Nope." I sank lower in the pool, leaning my head back against my bundle of guns and holding onto my poker face for all I was worth. Thinking fast, I added, "I told him to stay out of my business, so I don't expect any trouble from him. That's all I care about. And speaking of business... I can supply the item we discussed, if the price is right."

There, that's your opening. Talk business now, Riel.

"Ah," he said again. Silence fell.

Asshole.

God, I was tired. Questions and demands hammered in my brain, but I gave a yawn that was only partly simulated and let my eyelids droop half-closed. The next move was his. Arlene Widdenback wouldn't look eager.

The bamboo fountain trickled quietly through the soothing flute melody. The delicious warmth of the mineral waters softened my aching muscles to the consistency of warm molasses. I oozed lower in the water, my breathing slowing to match the unhurried pace of the music...

My head dropped forward and I jerked awake to face Riel's indulgent smile.

Had they drugged me after all?

Was he going to wait until I passed out and then drown me?

Adrenaline ignited my veins, driving my pulse into rapid drumming. Wide awake now, I gave Riel a sheepish smile. "It's very relaxing here."

"Yes, that is why we came." He eased lower in the water, stretching his arms along the edge of the pool. "One needs these small vacations from such a busy life."

"You're lucky to be able to take the time off." I tried to sound casual. "How long will you be able to stay?"

"As long as I wish." He smiled, stonewalling me again.

Okay, fine. Maybe he suspected surveillance here and didn't want to chance a conversation about weapons. But at least I could work on Dante's disappearance.

"Have you heard from James Helmand?" I asked. "My friend is still missing."

"Ah. That is most unfortunate." Riel gave me a convincingly sympathetic look. "I 'ave not 'eard from James. I called and left messages, but it seems he is... 'ow shall I say it? Off the ground...?"

"Fallen off the face of the earth?" I suggested.

"Ah, yes. He did not return my calls."

"I wonder if he's returning his parole officer's calls?" I speculated aloud.

"I do not know." He eyed me curiously. "Why are you so certain that James is behind your friend's disappearance?"

I blew out a breath. "I'm not. It's just that he's the most likely suspect if Dante's disappearance has anything to do with me. But who knows, maybe it's completely unrelated.

It's just suspicious timing, that's all."

"Indeed," Riel murmured. "Well, I 'ave a feeling your Dante will be found safe soon, if all goes well."

My mental threat-detector sprang to attention. What the hell did he mean by that?

Before I could demand clarification, Riel rose and stretched luxuriously. "I must change to be ready for my manicure. Will I see you at brunch?"

"Yes," I said, the word coming out sharper than I'd intended. "See you later."

He left, and after a few minutes of intense thought I hauled my waterlogged carcass out of the pool and into the changing room again.

Dammit, what was going on here? Were Riel and James working together to threaten my friends? Or was I reading threats into Riel's conversation that weren't there? I needed advice.

Kane would know what to do.

But I couldn't ask him with the bug in place. And I especially couldn't ask him if he and Tawny were...

I shook off the thought.

No. Kane wouldn't screw Tawny. In the first place, she was married. In the second place, she wasn't his type at all.

At least, not as far as I knew. Hell, what did I really know about his preferences? Maybe he liked the slutty look. Or maybe he didn't care as long as he got the information he wanted. Seduction was just another tool for him when he was undercover.

Was he trying to trap Tawny with the bug?

Or was he working for someone else to trap me?

No, dammit, he wouldn't betray me. And anyway, if he'd been trying to get information from me he would have started conversations that would draw me out instead of shushing me at every turn.

Unless he hadn't expected me to use my bug detector because I trusted him. Then if he wanted to keep my trust he'd have to pretend he was as dismayed by the bug as I was...

My exhausted brain rebelled at the convolutions of logic, and I dragged on my clothes and trudged back to the spa reception area.

The perky young receptionist assured me that several massage therapists were available and ushered me to a softly-lit room containing a pillowy reclining chair.

"Please make yourself comfortable," she urged. "Would you prefer a male or female therapist?"

"Doesn't matter."

I seated myself and she activated the electronic reclining mechanism. Circling behind the chair, she murmured, "I'll send in the therapists and you can choose the one you want. Meanwhile, just relax." She deftly slipped a pillow under my head, and if I hadn't been expecting the barely-perceptible press of Fuzzy Bunny's network access key on the side of my neck I would never have noticed it.

She, or rather a construct of her, withdrew from the room. I sighed and shifted in the chair as if making myself comfortable, but I prodded the chair with an experimental finger as I did so, willing the small area to be insubstantial.

Sure enough, my finger passed right through it. She'd put me into a sim.

Okay. After my marathon session in the sim archives last night, I knew what to expect.

Moments later there was a tap at the door and five beautiful young people filed in, three men and two women.

They all wore the white uniforms of the spa, but there the similarities ended. Apparently Harchman was big on variety.

The men were a dazzling selection of chiselled bodies and jaw-droppingly handsome faces. The man at the end would have movie directors falling all over themselves to cast him as an elf-king or celestial deity with his clear azure eyes and long silky blond hair bound with a leather cord. Next to him, a broad-shouldered hunk gave me a wink, his chocolate skin a mouthwatering contrast to his white uniform. The third was a boy-next-door type with brown hair and a square jaw, his hazel eyes sparkling with naughtiness.

The women were equally varied: A busty blonde and a petite Asian girl whose slim fingers looked as though they would snap like twigs if she attempted to work out the knots that were currently wound up in my shoulders.

I recognized them all from the video clips. Did they know how their footage was being used? Had they been told that their simulated selves could be made to do literally anything, and that it would be recorded for anyone to see?

I hid a shudder at the knowledge that somebody could be watching this sim right now. Waiting for me to choose my fantasy man and get naked...

My shoulders knotted up even harder at the thought, and I blew out a breath. A massage would be heavenly right now, but it wouldn't do me any damn good since my physical body was currently sprawled in an armchair staring into space.

Anybody could be watching me there, too. And I'd never know.

My stomach clenched.

"I've changed my mind," I said. "I'm not in the mood for a massage after all. I'm going to go back to my room and do some work."

The receptionist appeared immediately. In fact, her appearance was a little too immediate since she winked into existence without actually opening the door. I pretended not to notice, and she dismissed the dream team and hurried over to my chair.

"Is anything wrong?" she inquired worriedly.

"No, nothing. I'm just going to go back to my room." I made as if to stand up, and she pressed me back in the chair.

"Oh, just wait a moment, please, I'll fix the chair..." She hurried around behind me and I waited while she fumbled with the controls.

Obviously the spa employees weren't used to people backing out. I'd taken her by surprise and she needed time to set everything up in the real world for a seamless re-entry.

Thank God Fuzzy Bunny's network keys gave me a painless exit from the sims. If only I could hack and decrypt using their keys, too, the past twelve hours would have been a whole lot more comfortable.

"There," the receptionist said a moment later as the chair hummed into its upright position. "May I bring you a cool drink?"

Another subtle poke at the chair arm assured me that I was in the real world now.

"No, thanks. I'm just going to go back to my room." I headed for the door, fighting disorienting uncertainty as to whether it was real or simulated.

When I stepped back into the reception area I touched the vibrant green leaves of the bamboo plant on the desk. Despite my concentration on making them insubstantial, they remained stubbornly tangible between my fingers.

Okay. This was reality.

But what if they'd found a way to overcome that

limitation of the sim? What if I was in a sim even now?

They could lock up my body and hold me in a sim forever, my life unfolding exactly according to my own expectations, never knowing I was a prisoner...

Heart pounding, I hurried out.

CHAPTER 35

The sense of unreality slowly faded while I trotted back to the guesthouse, suspiciously testing each door handle. Everything remained solid, and by the time I let myself into my room again I was convinced that I was truly in the real world.

My bug detector still indicated all clear, and I sank onto the bed with a sigh. The memory of those few blissful hours of sleep in Kane's arms made me stifle a whimper of self-pity.

My eyelids dipped in spite of me and I shook myself back to wakefulness.

Think.

I dragged myself off the bed to pace in tight circles.

I was getting nowhere with Riel.

Well, fuck him. If he was 'all about the game', we could play by my rules for a while. If he wanted the weapon by tomorrow, my departure should shake his complacency.

I paced another circuit.

But Riel as the terrorist just didn't make sense. If he needed the weapon in time for Remembrance Day, he would have made an offer by now. What the hell was I missing?

Blowing out a breath of frustration, I grabbed my phone and texted "1 PM coffee" to Holt's burner phone. Stemp likely would have told him about my check-in last night, but

Holt might still be expecting the contact I'd originally promised. I could only imagine his contempt if I screwed up something so basic.

I tossed the phone back onto the bed and paced some more. At least brunch would give me one more chance to observe Kane and Tawny together.

What the hell was Kane doing? Should I offer him a pretext to leave? Or was he secretly hoping I'd go away so he could conduct his business with Tawny?

And what business might that be?

And what if Stemp decided Kane's presence here posed too much of a security risk?

Don't think about that.

Blowing out a breath, I headed for the bathroom to attempt a presentable appearance for brunch.

When I strolled into the salon at ten AM doing my best imitation of confidence, I discovered that my acting skills had been wasted. Nobody was there.

A table in the corner of the huge room was laid for six, so I drifted in that direction. A moment later one of the uniformed staff hurried out of a swinging door.

"Good morning, Ms. Widdenback," she greeted me. "Won't you please sit down? May I bring you coffee, tea, or juice?"

"Green tea, please. And orange juice. Thank you." I selected a place that positioned my back against the wall while giving me a view of all the entrances, and slid into the chair.

My tea and juice arrived in minutes, along with a menu hand-written in calligraphy with scrolls and flourishes. I was studying it with my mouth watering when Riel strode in.

"Allô again," he said with a smile as he took the seat

beside me.

Without asking his preferences, the server placed a cup of black coffee and a glass of tomato juice in front of him. "Don't worry, I washed your cup and glass separately by hand," she murmured.

Riel thanked her graciously before turning back to me. "The food is all wonderful, but the smoked salmon eggs benedict..." He closed his eyes in an expression of rapture. "...they are magnifique."

I eyed him for an instant, wondering whether he had doubts about the cleanliness of the kitchen or only some weird obsession with clean glassware, but I couldn't think of a polite way to ask him.

Forget it. Stick to the mission.

"Mmm, I was looking at that," I agreed. "But this fresh fruit and custard crepe sounds delicious, too."

"It is. Have both." He smiled. "The chef is most accommodating. He will do half-portions. Or even one-third portions, if there is another thing you desire."

"Oh..." Skimming down the menu, my gaze snagged on a roasted asparagus and goat cheese frittata with wild mushrooms. "Uh-oh..."

Riel chuckled. "Yes?"

"Oh, yes."

I surfaced from the menu before I could find anything else to tempt me. After the server had departed with my three-part order and Riel's single one, I leaned back and cradled my tea, my smile almost genuine at the thought of the delectable food to come.

"You know, I've never had a desire for any of..." I made an encompassing gesture at the grandeur that surrounded us. "...this. But I could get used to the food."

"Ah, indeed." Riel sipped his coffee, smiling. "Money, it is not everything, but it is... convenient. So tell me, if it is not money you desire, then what is your... 'ow shall I say it...? Your first love?"

My defensive shields sprang up, but I held onto my pleasant expression and kept my posture relaxed. "There you go talking about love again. I don't do love. Too much desire for anything is a weakness."

He leaned forward, his gaze intent. "That is true. Very few people understand that."

My pulse quickened. Maybe we were getting somewhere. Was this his opening gambit in price bargaining?

"Bring me coffee!" Harchman's peevish voice shattered our moment of rapport as he bustled into the salon.

Dammit, his timing couldn't have been worse. If I'd had a bomb I would have been tempted to blow up the little shit myself.

"*Coffee!*" His voice rose to a whiny shout.

The server hurried out to proffer a steaming cup.

Harchman took one sip, then pitched the cup across the room where it shattered, spraying the dark fluid across the carpet and up the wall. "What is that swill?" he snapped. "Bring me *fresh* coffee. And clean up that mess."

"Yes, Mr. Harchman, right away. I'm sorry." The hapless server rushed back into the kitchen.

Riel's face betrayed a single flash of contempt before smoothing into his usual pleasant expression. "Bonjour, Lawrence," he said. "Are you 'aving a difficult day?"

"No." Harchman dropped into the chair at the head of the table, scowling like a petulant child. "Everything's fine."

"Ah." Riel sipped his coffee as if to swallow a comment he might regret voicing. In his most charming tone, he added, "I 'ope you will excuse our rude behaviour. Arlene and I 'ave ordered our food already. But we would be pleased to 'ave the chef wait with it until you 'ave ordered and Madame 'Archman and Messieurs Kane and Labelle arrive."

"It's fine." Harchman waved an irritable hand. "Go ahead and eat. They're not coming, and I'm not hungry."

"Ah," Riel repeated without inflection, and returned his attention to me. "It is so nice to find someone who shares my appreciation of fine food. If you are ever in Montréal..."

We discussed gourmet dining for the rest of the meal, ignoring Harchman's sulky presence. I barely tasted the food, my nerves strung tight.

Where was Kane? Was he safe, tucked away doing who-knows-what with Tawny and causing Harchman's pique in the process? Or had something gone terribly wrong?

And would I make it better or worse if I interfered?

"...Arlene...?" Riel's voice intruded on my thoughts.

I blinked back to the present. "Sorry, I zoned out for a second. I have some pressing business on my mind. What did you say?"

Riel smiled his pleasant smile. "It is quite all right; it was nothing important. I only asked if you 'ad enjoyed your massage."

"Oh. No, I didn't have time for it; I had to go back to my room and work. In fact..." I stood. "...I'm afraid I need to get back to Calgary."

Riel politely rose with me. "So soon?"

"Yes. Business. You know how it goes." I gave him an insincere smile. "Thank you for inviting me. Enjoy your spa vacation."

He laid a hand over his heart, giving me his sad face.

"The joy will be gone without you."

I held onto my smile. "I'm sure you'll survive."

Harchman made no move to rise or even to acknowledge my departure, so I walked out and left him glowering into his coffee cup.

Senses on high alert, I headed for the guesthouse trying to look relaxed and confident. This was too easy. Were they just going to let me leave?

Maybe they would. After all, I was Arlene Widdenback, badass arms dealer...

"Hey, hold on there!"

My heart shot up to vibrate in my throat as I turned. Glock on my right ankle; trank on my left. Which would I need?

A uniformed giant loomed up, and adrenaline burned my veins. Shit. The guy who never forgot a face.

He smiled down at me. "So how did it go last night?"

"Oh, hi." I cleared my dry throat, stalling. "You're still on duty? That's a long shift."

He shrugged. "Midnight to noon. I like it. That's when all the good stuff happens."

I raised an eyebrow. "Like zebra blondes and chambermaid seductions?"

"Yep. So, you look a bit more comfortable today." He nodded at my slacks and sweater.

"Um... yeah."

Shit, now he'd seen me twice. What if he mentioned my foray into 'acting' to Harchman, or worse, Tawny? They'd immediately recognize my description. How could I get him to keep quiet?

"I, um..." I dropped my gaze as if embarrassed. "It didn't go very well last night. I kind of... quit. Well... got fired, actually." I darted a glance up at him, hoping I looked as uncomfortable as I felt. "I wouldn't do what they wanted. They gave me a guest room so I didn't have to drive back in the middle of the night, but I'm leaving now. So, um..."

Was I laying it on too thick?

I straightened and met his gaze. "I'd appreciate it if you didn't tell anybody you saw me last night. This was a big mistake and I'd rather just put it behind me."

He shrugged. "No problem. Don't feel bad; these gigs aren't for everybody. You'll get a better one." His kind face split in a grin. "And I won't remember you when you get your big break and you're accepting your Oscar."

My relief spilled over into a smile and I took his huge hand and squeezed it. "Thank you! You're the best!"

"No problem. I told you I'd seen it all..." His eyelid drooped in a wink. "...but I don't tell."

"Thanks," I repeated. I was turning away when an idea struck me. "Uh... can I ask you something?"

"Sure."

"One of my friends was here last night, too. A big guy..." I gave him a playful look, theatrically shading my eyes as I gazed up at him. "Not as big as you."

He laughed. "Nobody's as big as me. What does your friend look like?"

"About six-four, bodybuilder, dark hair, grey eyes. Have you seen him?"

"Yeah, I saw him this morning with Mrs. Harchman."

I bit down the urge to snap, 'Where were they and what were they doing?' Instead I kept my tone casual. "Oh, good. I wanted to tell him I was leaving this morning but he wasn't at brunch. Where did you see them? Or..." I hesitated. "Did they look... busy? Should I just call him later?"

"No, they weren't... busy." He matched my meaningful inflection with an uptick of his eyebrow. "They were just going into the spa. But that was around nine. I haven't seen either of them since."

"Oh. I left the spa around then, so I must have just missed them. Well, I guess I'd better get going. Thanks again."

"You're welcome. Have a good day." He gave me the trademark half-bow as though it was an unconscious habit, and I managed a feeble smile before heading for the guesthouse.

Shit, shit, shit.

If he was so willing to disclose details like the zebra blondes and Tawny's and Kane's whereabouts, how good was his promise not to tell anybody about me?

And worse, Tawny and Kane had been together at the spa two hours ago and nobody had seen them since. What were they doing?

Innocently enjoying the mineral pool and massage?

Not-so-innocently enjoying each other?

Or was Kane a prisoner, suffering barbaric torture while I pigged out on gourmet food?

Stomach churning, I hurried for my room.

A quick scan with my bug detector showed a reassuringly green light. I threw myself on the bed, mentally reaching for the white void of the virtual reality network.

A rapid survey of the virtual sim rooms showed nothing active, and I dove through the firewall and into the archive server, checking timestamps as I went.

Nothing.

Nobody had created any sims since my aborted massage experience.

So what the hell were Kane and Tawny up to? And where had Labelle gone?

Dammit.

I stepped out of the sim into my usual firestorm of pain. Hands clamped around my temples, I swore and battered my head against the pillow until the misery subsided. Then I lay motionless, my headache thumping while I tried to formulate a plan.

Surely Tawny couldn't harm Kane here in the real world. In the first place, my man-mountain was living proof that most of the staff were just innocent people doing their jobs. Tawny wouldn't blow her cover by attacking Kane where there might be witnesses.

And even if she did attack him, Kane's deadly martial arts skills would prevent her from getting the upper hand unless he actually wanted her to have it.

I could look for them in the spa, but even if I did find them I still wouldn't know what to do.

I'd just have to trust Kane to take care of himself. If he had needed help he would have found a way to signal me last night.

...Unless he *had* signalled me and I'd been too dense to pick up on it. What if he was counting on me to know some secret protocol that only top agents used?

What if my inexperience killed him?

Hissing out a breath, I rolled off the bed. I'd memorized every single protocol manual, dammit. I hadn't missed anything. Like it or not, I'd have to leave Kane to his mysterious mission and get on with mine.

My worries weighed in my belly like cold lead while I packed.

As I left the guest house, the sun was blotted out by a

mountain of uniform as my friendly guard fell into step beside me. "Just wanted to let you know, I found out your friend checked out a couple of hours ago," he said. "He left around ten-thirty."

"Oh." The word sounded hollow, and I followed it up with a bright smile and a perky tone. "Maybe his gig didn't go well, either. Thanks for telling me."

"You're welcome. Take care, and good luck with your acting career." He smiled and strode off down the path, leaving me to trudge up to the concierge's booth accompanied only by my own worries.

So Kane had left without telling me.

Was that good or bad?

CHAPTER 36

After half an hour of driving back roads, I considered myself free of any physical surveillance. Pulling over, I checked my bug detector one more time before using a secured phone to dial Spider's number.

His 'Good morning' didn't sound quite as energetic as usual.

"Hi, Spider, it's Aydan," I said. "Sorry for the late night last night."

"Oh! Hi, Aydan! It's okay. Are you, um...?"

"I'm out of Harchmans and calling from a secured phone," I assured him. "Did your team get back to you with that information I requested?"

"Yes, I've got a list of those properties."

"Great, could you please send them to me with a copy to Holt?"

"Sure. And everything's still working fine with the program."

I let out a breath. "Good. At least one thing's going according to plan. What about that Remembrance Day service? Have Brock and Tammy found the evidence yet? Has Battalion Park been searched?"

"Yes, we need to talk about that. Will you be coming in soon?"

"I'll be there this afternoon around..." I considered for a moment. "Three? Maybe three-thirty? I need to talk to Holt first."

"Okay, great. See you soon."

My conversation with Riel in the hot tub echoed faintly in my brain, and I added hurriedly, "Hang on! Are you still there?"

"Yes, what is it?"

"Did Riel own any of the properties on the list you're sending?"

"No, none."

"How about... sorry, Spider, I know how busy you are right now, but could you please check to see if Riel is currently renting any property in Calgary?"

"I can, but it'll take a while. Scraping data from private servers is slow; and if we have to search for lease records from all the landlords in the city, individuals as well as management companies..."

My heart sank as I realized what a huge task that would be.

Spider went on, "...it would take a lot of resources. What's the priority level?"

My conscience jabbed me. I couldn't risk slowing the terrorist investigation, potentially sacrificing hundreds of lives just to save Dante.

"Um... Low." The word choked out sounding as defeated and helpless as I felt.

"Okay." Spider hesitated, then added, "I can set up a quick automated scan that will check the major property management companies and hotels, if that would help. It wouldn't consume any of the analysts' time and we have processing power to spare."

Gratitude warmed me. "Thanks, Spider, that would be great. I'll let you get back to work now."

I disconnected and sat staring through the windshield for a few moments, guts twisting. What if Dante was found dead, but he could have been saved if I'd acted sooner?

Blowing out a breath, I jerked my mind back from that thought. I had done what I could, for now. Concentrate on the next problem.

When I got back to Sirius Dynamics Stemp would undoubtedly quiz me about Kane's activities. I had half an hour to spare before my meeting with Holt. Maybe I could appease Stemp by dropping by Alicia's place, so I could say I'd searched for Kane and tried to find out what he was doing.

Hell, Kane might actually be there. He wouldn't leave Alicia and Daniel unguarded...

My heart rose in sudden hope. Kane wouldn't have left them yesterday unless he was sure they'd be safe. Hellhound would be his first and most trusted choice to protect them.

Of course. That made perfect sense. Kane or Hellhound, or both, would be at Alicia's place. And if Kane was there, surely he would have ditched the bug by now and I could get a full explanation.

Or even if he wasn't there, Arnie would know what was going on. This was all just a big misunderstanding. After we explained it to Stemp, everything would be fine.

I steered back onto the highway and headed eagerly for Calgary.

When I pulled up in front of Alicia's house, my optimism wavered. It looked abandoned. The blinds were closed and the only vehicles in sight were in front of the neighbours' houses.

But maybe the vehicles were in the garage. And Arnie would keep everybody away from the windows. They could still be here...

I got out and strode around to the side gate, holding onto hope. If they were pretending not to be home, they wouldn't answer the front door in full view of the neighbours, but Arnie would let me in the back when he identified me.

When I rounded the corner, a shock of adrenaline burned my veins.

The back door was open.

Swinging in the cold breeze, it closed slowly, then opened again as though admitting an invisible presence.

A shiver tracked down my backbone. The yard was barren except for a swing set, the empty seats swaying as if occupied by ghostly children. The tall fence blocked the views from all the neighbours' houses.

The door banged shut, making me jump. Then it eased open again, a stealthy movement that made me look for malevolent eyes peering through the crack.

"Fuck *off* with the imagination," I muttered.

Then I drew my Glock, just in case. Holding it down beside my leg, I crept toward the door.

It swung wide again.

Come on in, little girl. Just like every horror movie ever made.

Swallowing hard in an attempt to get some moisture into my suddenly-dry mouth, I moved forward, half-expecting to hear creepy music start up.

Dammit, I was not going to call Holt and ask him to come and hold my hand because I was afraid of a door.

I wasn't afraid. Just... alert.

Yeah, that was it.

The stairs creaked ominously as I climbed them, and I flattened myself against the house. After a few breathless moments of waiting for an attack that didn't come, I resumed my slow climb.

Shouldering through the door when it swung open again, I sidestepped to put my back to the wall, Glock at the ready.

A few dry leaves swirled in the middle of the kitchen floor, rustling like evil whispers. The only other sound was the rumble of the furnace while it fought to maintain a semblance of warmth in the crypt-cold house.

Dammit, that imagery wasn't helping.

I shook my head to dislodge the scary thoughts. Focus. Clear the house.

Basement first.

The dark staircase yawned to my right like an entrance to hell, the impression enhanced by the heat wafting up from below. Hoping that the windows I'd seen from outside would allow some daylight into the basement, I inched down the stairs as silently as possible.

The air temperature increased as I descended, accompanied by the hot metallic smell of the overworked furnace. As I reached the bottom it wheezed to a halt, cooling with sharp pings like tiny bullets ricocheting in the ducts.

Thank God, Alicia was a tidy housekeeper. Even in the dimness of the small windows, it only took a few minutes to search the unfinished basement.

All clear.

As I climbed the stairs the furnace groaned to life again, responding to the icy current of air that met me on the main floor.

The kitchen offered no place for anyone to hide, and I sidled toward the living/dining room. Pausing with my back to the wall, I drew a deep breath, then pivoted around the corner gun-first.

I snapped a fast glance around the open space. Nothing moved.

Not even the pair of denim-clad legs on the floor, just visible on the other side of the sofa.

My heart slammed against my ribs, accelerating to jackhammer tempo.

The rest of the room was unoccupied. The legs were very still.

Glock at the ready, I crept forward.

The legs were attached to a bulky body clad in a black leather jacket.

Oh, God.

Not Arnie.

No, no...

My knees wobbled. Panting open-mouthed, I fought to hold my gun steady.

Move.

Forward.

I took the last step that would give me a sightline to the face and my legs gave way altogether. Dropping hard to my knees, I hunched forward to get more blood to my brain.

Do *not* pass out.

No question about the cause of death. His body lay on its stomach, but the contorted face stared up at me, head twisted a full hundred and eighty degrees on a broken neck.

James Helmand.

The roaring in my ears gradually abated, allowing me to

hear my own whimpers. "Thank-God-oh-thank-God- thank-*God*..."

I stifled myself and heaved back to my feet.

Check the rest of the house.

My hands shook so violently I could barely hold my gun. Disciplining my breathing, I forced calm. Through the lungs, the shoulders, the arms, the hands...

Calm...

My hands steadied and I crept forward again, heart still pounding.

Three bedrooms, five closets, and two bathrooms later, I let out a long slow breath and tucked my Glock into the back of my pants for fast access if necessary.

My fingers were still trembling, and I fumbled out a text to Holt's burner phone with the address along with the instruction, "Use back door & gloves." Thank God the coffee shop where we'd planned to meet wasn't far away.

So what was Helmand doing here?

Even though he was obviously dead, I still had to marshal my courage to approach the body. He looked so angry. As if he was just waiting for me to get close enough so he could jump up and attack me.

I nudged one of his legs with the toe of my boot.

Stiff.

So he'd been dead for a while, and his assailant had fled the house leaving the door open.

My mind gradually re-engaged.

His assailant.

Someone capable of snapping the neck of a very large and angry man without leaving any other mark on him.

Someone who lived in this house and had recently threatened James.

Someone who'd killed another man exactly the same way only a few months ago.

Someone who had called me yesterday about 'a situation'...

Shit, I shouldn't have texted Holt.

A slide show flitted through my imagination: Helmand arriving and threatening Alicia and Daniel. Kane reacting, fast and deadly. A quick snap of James's neck, his body abandoned where it landed. Hellhound rushing Alicia and Daniel into hiding while Kane went to eliminate some other unforeseen threat...

A tap at the back door jolted my adrenaline into emergency production all over again.

"Hello? It's Greg Holt, Realtor. Is anybody home?"

I hurried toward the kitchen, not sure whether to ward him off or ask his advice, but the decision was made for me when he rounded the corner. His innocuous business clothes and empty hands might have fooled an unwary observer, but I identified the combat-ready stance of an experienced martial artist.

He took in the motionless legs with a single glance. "House clear?" At my nod, his shoulders relaxed and he ambled the rest of the way into the room, eyeing Helmand's body. "Huh. Looks like Kane had a situation after all."

"We don't know that Kane had anything to do with this..." I began, but Holt was already crouching beside the body and peering down at its right hand.

"Know anybody with short hair who dyes it dark brown?" Holt shot me an accusing look.

My stomach sank. Putting on my reading glasses, I squinted at Helmand's index finger. Under the nail was a single short dark hair with a tiny glint of silver at the root.

"I'm sure Kane didn't do this," I said with more certainty than I felt. "In the first place, he might want to beat the hell out of James but he wouldn't kill him. In the second place, even if he did kill him, he's far too much of a professional to just leave the body lying here with such obvious evidence under its fingernails. And in the third place, even if there was some situation so bizarre that he killed Helmand and didn't have time to clean up, he'd still close the door when he left. This is a frame job."

"Huh." Holt rose, frowning. "Or maybe your boyfriend decided to do you a little favour and now you're covering for him."

Irritation flooded me but I kept my voice level. "He's not my boyfriend; and if I'm covering for him I'm doing a hell of a shitty job of it, considering I texted you as soon as I found the body."

Holt sneered. "Or maybe you're just covering your own ass and letting him take the rap."

"Fuck *off!*"

His brows snapped together, his jaw jutting as he took an aggressive step toward me. "Make me, bitch!"

My own jaw jerked down, my fists knotting as rage boiled into my veins.

With all my might I fought the urge to lash out.

Don't do it.

He'd kick the living shit out of me.

"Anger... management," I gritted through clenched teeth. "I feel... as though... you're deliberately... trying to *piss me off!*"

The last words came out louder than I'd intended, but Holt relaxed with a short bark of laughter. "Good call, Kelly." He punched the speed dial button on a secured phone and waited for Stemp's answer before rapping out, "Somebody murdered James Helmand in Kane's ex-wife's house. Snapped neck..." He prodded the body with a toe. "...still in rigor, so more than six hours ago but probably not more than a day or two. Looks like one of Kane's hairs under his fingernail, and Kane called Kelly and said he had a situation yesterday. Guess now we know what it was."

"Hey!" I barked. "I told you, somebody's obviously trying to frame him!"

Ignoring me, Holt went on, "The back door was open and the main floor of the house is cold even though the furnace is going full blast, so it's probably been open since yesterday. Guess that's when the killer left."

He listened to the crackle of Stemp's voice for a moment, then responded, "Right. Alive if possible? ...Right. Hang on, she's right here." He passed the phone over to me.

"Kelly," I snapped.

"Come to Silverside immediately for additional briefing and to question your intruders. After that you'll return to your original mission with Riel. Tell Holt everything about your recent interactions with Kane and his possible whereabouts."

Heart plummeting, I muttered, "Okay", and disconnected before he could demand Kane's head on a platter. If he hadn't already.

I turned my scowl on Holt. "What are your orders regarding Kane?"

"Bring him in for questioning, alive if possible. But if he resists..." Holt shrugged.

CHAPTER 37

Holt eyed my balled fists and added, "Take a pill. Stemp will have my ass if I kill Kane before we can question him. Come on, we need to get out of here. Stemp's calling in an anonymous tip to the cops about the back door hanging open, so they'll be here pretty soon. Meet you at the coffee shop."

Still seething, I followed him out and strode to my car.

By the time I got to the coffee shop I had my temper more or less under control. Antagonizing Holt wouldn't help Kane. And anyway, Kane didn't need help because he hadn't done anything wrong. There was a perfectly good explanation for all this.

I hoped.

I heaved a sigh and got out of the car.

Holt had staked out a quiet table in the corner, and I dropped into the chair across from him with a groan.

He surveyed me with one eyebrow raised. "You look like you need a coffee."

I glowered at him. "Coffee makes me cranky."

He snorted, but there was a curl of humour at the corner of his mouth. "Wouldn't want that. What can I get you, then?"

"Chamomile tea. Thanks. And the biggest chocolate

chip muffin they've got."

By the time he returned to his chair my eyelids were drooping.

"Look sharp, Kelly," he commanded. "Spill everything you've got on Kane."

I shrugged, choosing my words carefully. "There's not much. The last time I talked to him, he was moving in with his ex and son and being a dad. Then all of sudden last night he was at Harchman's, and we couldn't talk because he was bugged."

"Bugged." Holt set down his coffee cup, frowning. "What the hell?"

"That's what I thought. I don't know who the bug belonged to, and I didn't want to mess with it in case Kane was undercover and I screwed something up."

Or something like that, anyway.

I went on, "Kane and I had faked a love-hate relationship the last time we were undercover at Harchman's, so we put on a show for the bug and then called it a night. I didn't see him again, but I found out he left this morning at ten-thirty."

"Huh." Holt sipped his coffee, narrowing his eyes as if to read between the lines I'd handed him. "Love-hate, eh? So you were up all night playing hide-the-salami. No wonder you look so bagged."

"Fuck off." I didn't have energy to spare, so the words came out flat and weary.

Holt acknowledged the half-hearted insult with a casual middle finger, and persisted. "Why was he at Harchman's? Who did he talk to? Who did he avoid?"

"Don't know. We weren't with the others long enough. Tawny and Lawrence Harchman were there, along with Labelle and Riel. Tawny was talking to Kane and feeling him up, but I'm pretty sure she does that with all the guys. He dropped her like a hot potato as soon as I arrived, but that might have been part of his cover."

"You think he was expecting you?"

"Haven't a clue." I gulped down the last of the muffin and sipped my tea. "I sure as hell didn't expect him."

"But he had a room of his own."

I suppressed a sigh. "Yeah."

"Well, Stemp said the wiretap on Riel's phone picked up a call this morning around eleven-thirty. Just a short conversation; Riel said 'She just checked out', and somebody that sounded a whole lot like Kane said 'Don't worry, I have it under control'."

My stomach clenched as a thought that had been niggling at my subconscious flared into comprehension. Riel had said he was going for a mani-pedi at nine-thirty AM, but when I'd checked the network right before I'd left, there were no new sims.

So either he'd had a real-life manicure; or else he'd skipped the whole thing because he was otherwise occupied.

Maybe meeting someone... like Kane?

No. That just didn't make sense.

I kept my voice level. "Lots of guys sound like Kane."

Not true; that velvety baritone was his alone.

I followed up that flimsy defense with another one, equally flimsy. "And even if it was him, he's bugged and obviously undercover so he'd have to say whatever Riel wanted to hear."

"Get your head out of your ass, Kelly." Holt scowled at me. "You're compromised. He's got you wrapped around his little finger, and you're swallowing his bullshit whole." He leered. "Along with anything else you might've swallowed last night."

A jolt of anger straightened my tired spine. "Listen, asshole-"

"No, *you* listen, dumbass! Your boyfriend is in serious shit here, and if you don't show some objectivity, you're going to go down with him when this all shakes out." His eyes narrowed. "Unless you're already double-crossing the Department..."

"Fuck *off!* I just passed my fucking lie-detector test, okay? And so did Kane!" I reined in my temper with an effort. "I'm not compromised; I'm just telling you the facts as I see them. We both know Kane's record as an agent, and we both know that after a career like that, it's pretty damn unlikely that he'd turn." I glared at him. "Unless you're saying you'd consider it yourself."

Holt bristled. "You know damn well I wouldn't!" I flung out my hands in a 'well, duh' gesture, and he acknowledged it with a shrug. "Okay, fine, I'll give you that; for now. So that's all you know?" He eyed me suspiciously. "Where did he go when he left this morning?"

"Don't know. I didn't even know he'd left." I didn't mention that he'd last been seen in the company of Tawny Harchman. No need to fan the flames.

"Huh." Holt frowned at me some more. "Okay, so tell me about his personal life. Where does he hang out, and who with? Give me bars, restaurants, hobbies, drinking buddies, ex-girlfriends, everything."

"How the hell should I know?" I scowled at him over my mug. "I told you, we're not seeing each other. I know he was living at his condo here in Calgary-"

"Address?" Holt interrupted.

"It's in Sundance, but I don't know the actual street

address. Stemp would have it."

"Okay. What else?"

"Like I said, as far as I know he was living at his condo until he moved in with Alicia, and he's been volunteering at Daniel's school during lunch periods. That's about it."

"Don't give me that bullshit," Holt snapped. "You're a fucking agent. Your life depends on observing people. You're lying to protect him."

"I am not!" I jerked forward to growl at him. "Look, I don't get close to people, okay? He works out. I don't know which gym. He volunteers at Daniel's school. I don't know the name of the school. He calls his dad in Winnipeg sometimes. He visits Hellhound sometimes. He likes cars and kids and gourmet cooking, and he gets up at five-thirty AM. That's all I know about him. I don't know his friends. I don't know what he does in his spare time. I can't name his favourite restaurant or bar. I don't know his daily routine, or if he even has one. I never asked; he never told; and I haven't spent enough time with him to find out."

Holt stared at me in silence. "That is really fucking sad," he said at last.

"Welcome to my life." I downed a slug of tea in an attempt to fill the sudden emptiness in my chest.

He scowled. "Staying detached is part of the job, so suck it up. What I meant was, that's a fucking piss-poor job of observation. You expect me to believe you can't do any better than that?"

My fingers closed in a stranglehold on my mug in lieu of throttling him and my voice came out hard and level. "I don't give a shit what you believe. If you're such a fucking hotshot, go dig up Kane's background yourself. Good luck."

He sneered. "I don't need luck. Unlike you, I've got

observational skills."

"Right, Mr. Top Agent." I gave the title a sarcastic curl of my lip. "So what's my favourite restaurant? Daily routine? Ex-boyfriends? Hideouts? Secret contacts? Go ahead, dazzle me with your brilliant observational skills."

Holt glared. "How the hell should I know? I only see you when we're working. I'm not investigating you."

"Well, duh. Same with Kane and me."

"It's not the same at all. You're screwing him. Women get attached as soon as there's sex involved."

I jerked forward, fists clenching, and he held up a restraining hand and kept talking. "Settle down, Kelly; I'm trying to help you. I'm just saying, you can't trust a spook. He's been playing you all along, and he's playing you now. You're just his patsy until he decides to stick a knife in your back, and then you're his dead patsy. I don't want to see that happen, okay?"

I bit down the angry tirade that begged for utterance and kept my tone measured. "Thanks for your concern, but he could have done that a dozen times over, and he never did. You're wrong, Holt. Believe me, I get the whole professional paranoia thing, but you have to trust somebody sometime."

The irony of those words coming from my own mouth made my lips twist in a bitter smile.

"What's so goddamn funny?" Holt demanded.

"You wouldn't get it."

"Probably not." He shrugged. "Good thing I don't give a shit. So what were all those addresses Webb sent me?"

"Oh..."

My brain booted into emergency justification mode. With his new mission to capture Kane, Holt wouldn't waste any time looking for Dante. But maybe I could slow his pursuit of Kane and help Dante at the same time...

"Those addresses are all the properties around here owned by Lawrence or Tawny Harchman, Labelle, Riel, and James Helmand," I said with all the confidence I could muster. "I was originally thinking they might be helpful with my mission with Riel..." I kept talking, hoping he wouldn't ask for clarification of that vague statement. "...but now they might be worthwhile investigating if you're looking for Kane, too. I'm positive that he's not doing anything illegal, but if he's mixed up in this case somehow, those are some other places he might be."

Holt gave me a level look.

I sipped my tea, hoping he couldn't smell the bullshit I'd just spread in front of him.

"It's a long shot," he said slowly. "I'll check out the more promising leads first, but it's good to have those just in case."

Keeping my face expressionless, I hid a sigh of relief. Time to escape before he realized I'd snowed him.

I gulped the last of my tea. "Are we done here? I have to go back to Silverside for a briefing and to question the two dirtbags who broke into my house last night, and then I have to get back to Riel."

"Another break-in? Shit, Kelly, how many times have you had to fix your house now?"

I scrubbed my hands over my face. "I'm trying not to tally it up. At least I won't have to scrape up frozen blood this time." A sudden yawn nearly turned me inside out, and I dragged myself to my feet before I could succumb to the urge to curl into a ball and sleep for a week. "Here's my latest burner number."

Holt rose, too, and we exchanged numbers and headed for the door.

At my car, I reached for the door handle only to have Holt's hand land on top of the door, preventing me from opening it. When I turned a frown on him, he said, "You're too tired to drive safely. Pull off somewhere and grab a half-hour nap. I'll check in with Stemp in half an hour and tell him you just left."

Gratitude thickened my throat. "Thanks," I muttered, and got into the car before I could reveal the emotion.

Despite my nap in an abandoned roadside rest area, I fought sleep interspersed with worry all the way to Silverside.

What if Holt lost his temper and shot Kane instead of bringing him in for questioning? He'd only have to say Kane had resisted arrest. If Kane really didn't want to be brought in, his lethal martial arts skills would make deadly force the only option.

I sought comfort in the knowledge of Kane's expertise. He was the better agent of the two. If Kane didn't want to be found, Holt wouldn't find him.

But Kane didn't know Holt was hunting him. And I didn't have any way to warn him.

A sliver of Holt's suspicious paranoia prickled under my skin. Should I even be thinking about warning Kane?

What if I'd been wrong about him all along?

Goddammit.

By the time I parked in the Sirius Dynamics lot, my face hurt from yawning and I was in a mood foul enough to make Arlene Widdenback look like Pollyanna.

I stomped up the stairs and into the lobby, mustering a tight-lipped smile for the security guard while I signed in. Going directly to Stemp's office, I tapped on his open door and stuck my head in.

"I'm ready to question those guys now," I growled. "Where are they?"

Stemp looked up from his computer. "In my garden shed."

"Your...?"

I must have looked as confused as I felt, because Stemp smiled. "It's a useful shed, quite secluded and soundproof." He tossed me a set of keys attached to a fob, which by some miracle I managed to snag out of the air without fumbling.

"Press the red button before you go in," he explained. "It will fill the shed with tranquilizer gas. Press the green button on the back of the fob to activate the screen for video surveillance. After the occupants lose consciousness, press the blue button to exhaust the gas from the shed and replace it with safe air. That takes approximately sixty seconds."

"Okay," I confirmed as I turned over the fob to check the button and tiny screen, feeling slightly more cheerful.

"If they tell you what you want to know, gas them again but leave the door open so they can escape. I'll send video footage of them breaking and entering at your farm to the RCMP, who will coincidentally receive an anonymous tip saying two men were seen behaving suspiciously in my back yard. By the time the police arrive, our friends should be conscious and ready to be arrested."

"Perfect."

"If they don't tell you what you want to know, you may leave them where they are for another day." Stemp eyed me for a moment in silence before adding. "Keep in mind that video surveillance will be active the whole time, and I'll be watching the live feed."

"Of course," I agreed, as if I would never consider any method of interrogation that wasn't strictly legal. "Who have they seen so far?"

"Nobody identifiable. The retrieval team was masked and the prisoners were tranked immediately. They haven't seen another human being for nearly twenty-four hours. Please return here for briefing as soon as you're finished."

I gave him a nod and departed, making a stop at Stores for a ballistic trank pistol in case I needed to convince my captives that Arlene Widdenback wouldn't hesitate to kill.

On the short drive to Stemp's quiet neighbourhood, my curiosity rose. I already knew his outwardly-modest home contained some unusual security features; but the garden shed was a revelation. Holt must have searched it when we investigated last year, but he hadn't mentioned it to me.

So either the shed's special features were well-concealed; or else Holt considered it perfectly normal to have a high-tech jail cell in one's back yard.

Damn, now I was envious. I needed to beef up my farm. My secret room in the basement was good and so was my video surveillance system, but I needed better locks on the doors; and a secure holding shed seemed like a fine idea.

I heaved a sigh as I parked in the alley. When I'd bought my farm nearly two years ago, I had been innocently anticipating the joys of a custom-built garage. Who knew I'd end up coveting a high-tech interrogation facility?

"Fuck my life," I muttered as I got out of the car, my renewed bad mood settling on my shoulders like a dark and thorny cloak.

CHAPTER 38

Slipping into Stemp's back yard, I approached a small rundown building nearly swallowed by a cluster of dark spruce trees. About eight feet square, it canted to the southwest on a crumbling foundation. One of the rain gutters hung half-detached, its sagging line contributing to the neglected appearance. Beside Stemp's immaculately-kept brown bungalow, the shed looked as though nobody had entered it in years.

Once again my estimation of Stemp rose. What a brilliant psychological manipulator. Everything about the shed sighed, "Nothing interesting here." Nobody would give it a second glance.

I pressed the red button, then flipped the fob over and pressed the green button in time to see two men topple off a plastic bench onto the floor. I gave them a few more seconds, and when neither moved I pressed the blue button.

While waiting the prescribed sixty seconds, I reflected that Stemp's choice of décor was diabolically effective. The interior was barren except for a bucket in the corner and a single light bulb enclosed in a steel cage on the ceiling. The bench was long enough for a man to lie on, but not wide enough to accommodate him unless he lay on his side. And the floor sloped so that even if a prisoner did manage to fall asleep on the bench he couldn't relax fully. Not to mention there were two prisoners and only one bench.

When I unbolted the door and stepped inside, the interior was damp and chilly but not cold enough to cause hypothermia. I had expected a stench from the commode bucket, but there was none. It must have some kind of flushing mechanism. The setup had obviously been calculated to fall just short of inhumane; but any occupant would certainly be miserable in short order.

Making a mental note to avoid pissing Stemp off, I bent to check the prisoners' restraints. They were secure, and I propped myself in the corner beyond the reach of their leg chains.

A few seconds later I drew the ballistic trank pistol. After all, first impressions matter.

Pointing its muzzle at the floor so they wouldn't notice the small aperture for the tranquilizer dart under the larger bore for the blood-coloured paint pellet and noise-making blank, I waited.

The bigger man groaned and stirred about five minutes later. After a couple of failed attempts, he dragged himself into a slumped position against the wall, sluggishly blinking eyes the colour of mud. A few seconds later he registered my presence.

His gaze locked onto my gun, his eyes widening. "What the...?" he croaked.

His skinny straw-haired counterpart dragged himself over onto his back, his groans drowning out the last of Mud-Eyes's question.

I waited until Straw-Hair was sufficiently conscious to notice my weapon, too. He said nothing; just stared fearfully at the gun.

I snapped, "Why were you breaking into my house?"

"I never broke into no house," Mud-Eyes grumbled. "You got the wrong guy."

"Don't fuck with me, dipshit," I growled. "My guys picked you up, *in my house.*" I let the pistol drift up to aim at his crotch. "I want to know *why.*"

"I don't know nothin'," he protested. "I don't even know who the hell you are."

"Then it sucks to be as stupid as you," I said, and pulled the trigger.

The report of the blank was deafening in the small space. Mud-Eyes screamed, the sound abruptly cut off as both he and Straw-Hair passed out from the aerosolized tranquilizer. Holding my breath, I slipped out and closed the door behind me, then pressed the blue button again.

Sixty seconds later I stepped back into the shed, my ears still ringing from the shot. Another key on the fob opened Mud-Eyes's leg chain, and I unlocked it from the shacklebolt in the floor and hauled his inert body out, making sure the blood-coloured paint smeared artistically across the floor.

Thankful for the deep cover of the spruce trees and Stemp's tall fence, I laboriously dragged Mud-Eyes behind the shed and relocked his leg chain around a tree just in case. He should be out for at least twenty minutes from the injected trank, but I wasn't in the mood for surprises.

I plucked the spent tranquilizer dart out of his red-stained pants, then slumped against the back of the shed to catch my breath, sweating and glaring down at him.

Asshole.

I probably shouldn't have shot so fast, though. Hard to ask questions afterward.

Anger management. Stay cool.

My hearing was still blunted when I returned to the shed, and I sank down on the bench and massaged my ears. How many more close-quarters gunshots could I experience before my hearing suffered major damage? And would I even notice the loss until the day somebody sneaked up behind me and slit my throat?

I groaned and scrubbed a hand over my damp forehead as another thought struck me. Was shooting a guy in the nuts with a trank dart and paint pellet considered unreasonable force?

Probably.

But then again, I was supposed to be a badass arms dealer. Arlene Widdenback didn't acquire her reputation by being mild and gentle. Maybe I wouldn't be in too much trouble...

Another groan refocused my attention on the situation at hand. Straw-Hair was waking up, flopping and twitching in an attempt to get farther away from me even before his eyes were fully open.

"Don' shoo'..." he slurred. "Tell you... 'nything... y'wanna know..."

"See, you're a smart guy," I said encouragingly. "Lucky for you, too, 'cause otherwise I was going to chuck your buddy back in here and see how many days it took before you got hungry enough to eat him." Straw-Hair whimpered, and I added, "Just a word of advice: If that ever happens, start eating right away. They get stinky pretty fast."

"I'll-tell-you-I'll-tell-you!" He scrambled backward in an attempt to cram himself into the farthest corner. Flattened against the wall, he quavered, "Wh-What d'you wanna know?"

"Why were you breaking into my house?"

"We were s'posed to look for some bottle." He stared up at me, eyes wide. "Some white bottle with a silver bottom. Or... the guy said it might not look 'zactly like that but it'd be heavy glass. I dunno how we were s'posed to find it when we didn't know what it looked like, but the guy paid good so what the hell."

"Do you know who I am?" I gave the words my best menacing intonation.

Straw-Hair shook his head, looking as though he might burst into tears.

"And you never thought that there might be a reason why the guy was paying so well for such an easy job?" I aimed the trank pistol at him. "Maybe you're not as smart as I thought."

"Don't shoot!" His voice pitched higher as my pistol drifted below his belt, his words running together in a squeal of fear. "...*I-can-tell-you-about-the-guy!*"

"Ah." I lowered my gun. "You are smart after all."

Straw-hair swallowed hard, his gaze locked on the weapon. "Tall guy, fancy suit, brown hair, brown eyes, an' he talked like some guy on the radio."

Labelle.

Ha.

"Good job," I said.

Straw-hair gulped again, still staring at the pistol as if afraid it would jump up and shoot him if he stopped watching it. "You can trust me," he babbled. "I never saw nothin', I never heard nothin', I don't know you, I never even saw you or nothin'..."

"Oh, it's okay," I assured him with a feral grin. "I'm Arlene Widdenback, and you're definitely going to remember you saw me."

Straw-Hair closed his eyes with a moan, and I went on, "But don't worry, I'm going to let you go so you can spread the word that nobody fucks with me."

His eyes popped open, fear and hope mingling on his face.

"So here's the deal," I informed him. "I don't care who you tell about what happened here, because I can make a body disappear and nobody will ask questions. But I don't ever want to see you again. I'm giving you three hours to get out of town and never come back. If I or any of my guys see you after..." I consulted my watch. "...eight o'clock tonight..." I glared at him and hefted my pistol. "...We'll be the last thing you ever see. Got it?"

Straw-Hair nodded vigorously, gaze still glued to the weapon. "Okay. No problem. I'm gone. Gone an' never comin' back. I'm so gone, I'm already halfway to Vancouver."

"Good." I pulled out my phone one-handed and punched Stemp's speed dial, still watching Straw-Hair over the gunsights. When Stemp answered I said, "One of our guests is leaving now. I've given him safe passage out of the city until eight o'clock tonight so don't kill him unless you see him after that."

"Very well." Stemp's tone was dry.

I hung up and pointed the pistol at Straw-Hair while I unlocked his leg chain. Then I backed out of the shed and jerked my chin at him, still keeping him covered. "Go."

"B-but what about..." He tugged against the handcuffs. "C-can you take off the cuffs? An' I dunno where I am, or where my car is..."

"You'll figure something out." I shrugged. "Or I could just shoot you and end your troubles." He shook his head frantically, sidling past with his gaze locked on the gun. "Fine," I growled. "Get lost before I change my mind."

He ran for the gate, then stopped short. When he turned back to me, his face was a study in terror. "I c-can't..." He twitched his hands behind him, indicating the gate latch well above his reach. "P-please..."

"Oh, *fine*," I snarled as though it was the pinnacle of inconvenience, and opened the gate for him.

He fled without a backward glance.

When I was sure he was out of earshot I dialled Stemp again.

"I take it you got what you wanted," he said instead of a greeting.

"Yeah, Labelle sent them. But I don't want to arrest the guy I just released. If he's handcuffed and focused on getting out of town in a hurry he'll have enough to worry about and won't cause any more problems; and I don't want him to run into his supposedly-dead buddy in jail later."

"Indeed. And what of the supposedly-dead buddy with the unattractively stained crotch?"

"He should be knocked out for another five minutes at least, so I'll unlock him and leave him here. When he wakes up and gets out of the yard we can go with the original plan to have him arrested."

"Very well. Secure the shed and return immediately for briefing."

Obeying the spirit of Stemp's command if not the letter, I detoured to the secured weapons lab after signing in again at Sirius.

When I strode in, Reggie and Murray looked up from

their work with interest and eagerness respectively.

"You didn't punch Holt, did you?" Murray asked before I could speak.

"No." I marched over to Reggie and socked him on the arm, not very hard. "But I'll punch this asshole."

Reggie let out a yelp of protest. "Ow! What was that for?"

"For not telling me that this thing..." I slapped the ultrasound pen down on the table in front of him. "...doesn't work on unconscious people."

"Of course it doesn't. The vestibular nervous system is pretty much irrelevant when you're out cold." He scowled. "Why the fuck would you use it on somebody who was unconscious anyway?"

"Because..." I blinked. "Um... well, it sounds kind of stupid when you say it like that; but... shit." I hung my head. "Sorry. It was a high-stress situation and I thought it made sense at the time." I held out my arm. "You can punch me back if you want."

"I'll let you get away with it if you'll tell me what happened," Reggie replied, his good eye bright with interest. "I never thought to test it on somebody who was unconscious." He grimaced. "Scientific bias; there's nothing worse than being 'absolutely certain'..." He made a one-handed air quote with his good hand. "...of what you know."

Hiding my gratitude for his unexpected tact, I grinned. "Well, it did actually work, just not until the inhaled trank wore off and the guy woke up. He puked his guts out as soon as he opened his eyes about five minutes later."

"Ah." Reggie's expression went thoughtful. "But I wonder if it would still have been effective if he'd been down for twenty minutes? The vestibular disruption dissipates after ten minutes; so would recovery take place while he was unconscious, allowing him to wake up with no ill effects? Or would it kick in for the full ten minutes after he woke up?"

I shrugged. "I didn't stick around to find out. I was on a pretty tight timeline."

"Hm. Well, that was an interesting test anyway. Worth a punch in the arm." He gave me his distorted grin. "Besides, now I've got something to guilt you out with, punching a poor defenceless cripple. You'll have to have my baby out of pity now."

"Defenceless cripple, my ass! You could run circles around me and still have enough energy to kick the shit out of me. You'll have to come up with something better than that."

He frowned. "Actually, you did hurt me quite a bit. I just had a skin graft taken from that arm for some more repair work on my scalp."

Horror clenched my stomach. "Ohmigod, I'm so sorry! I didn't-" I broke off at the sight of his evil grin. "You just made that shit up, didn't you?"

"Maybe," he said with satisfaction. "Now will you have my baby?"

"No, you prick. I can't have children. I had a hysterectomy years ago, and it's really insensitive of you to keep harping on it when I've been deprived of the joy of motherhood; my heart broken again every time I see someone else's baby..." I summoned up a convincing sniffle.

He paled. "Jesus, Aydan, I'm sorry, I didn't know..." I let a small smile sneak through and he stopped, eyeing me worriedly. "Please tell me you were joking."

"Of course I was joking. I hate kids. Horrible little disease-bearing vermin. They're not even human; they're just small vicious aliens."

"Methinks the lady doth protest too much," he said quietly.

Uncomfortable, I waved away his seriousness. "No, I was just exaggerating for dramatic effect. I don't actually hate children, but I'm not sorry I never had any." I grimaced. "They probably would have grown up to be axe-murderers if I had. So I hate to break it to you, but your baby is a no-go. A pity fuck would be the best I could do."

The wicked sparkle reappeared in his eye. "How many times do you have to punch me before I get a pity fuck?"

"Far too many times for it to be worth the pain."

We grinned at each other, the balance of the universe restored.

Then I sighed and took my leave to plod upstairs for what would undoubtedly be more bad news.

CHAPTER 39

When I slid into the guest chair in Stemp's office he eyed me in silence for a moment, his reptilian features betraying no emotion.

Shit, was I in trouble for shooting Mud-Eyes?

Or maybe Stemp was just organizing his thoughts, and any disapproval was being manufactured by my own guilty conscience. Resisting the urge to blurt out justifications or confessions, I met his gaze with my best poker face.

"So... Labelle," Stemp said at last. "What was his intent?"

"The guy said Labelle told them to look for the ultrasound weapon. Maybe Riel was the one who hired Labelle to have these guys break into my house at six o'clock. I had told him I could get the weapon, so maybe he was checking to see if I was dumb enough to keep it at my house. After all, why pay for what you can steal? And Labelle obviously offers full-service arms brokering with thugs à la carte."

"Yes." Stemp considered for a moment. "Although after you dispatched Labelle's previous thug a few months ago, one would think he'd be more cautious."

"That would make sense of Labelle's comment about not sending his best. These guys weren't the brightest, and it didn't seem as though they had any prior relationship with him. Maybe he just scooped them off the street thinking it would be an easy job. After all, he knew I'd be two hours away at the time. Although..." I fell silent, frowning while puzzle pieces shifted in my mind.

Stemp didn't rush me; just sat waiting until I spoke again.

"When I got the alert from my surveillance system, I left the table to call you," I went on. "When I got back, it looked as though Riel and Labelle had disagreed over something and Labelle was looking pouty. They would have guessed what that call was about, and if Labelle had supplied the thugs he'd be pissed off that they'd gotten caught."

"Logical," Stemp agreed. "Unfortunately we can't confirm their conversation. We still aren't receiving consistent audio from our bugs. All we've caught was Labelle's call yesterday and Riel's call to Kane this morning."

I gulped down my chagrin and attempted a non-confrontational tone. "Do we know for sure it was Kane?"

"Yes. The voiceprint analysis was definitive."

"Shit." The word popped out before I could stop it, and I hurriedly added, "I know it looks bad, but I'm positive Kane's still on our side. He helped me out quite a bit at Harchman's."

"We shall see." Stemp's expression gave away nothing.

Trying not to betray my anxiety, I held my voice steady. "Has Holt had any luck tracking him down yet?"

"Holt hasn't called in, so I presume that to be negative." Stemp's gazed pinned me to my chair. "Where do you think Kane is?"

Thankful that I didn't have to lie about it, I said, "I don't have a clue", and changed the subject. "I'll call the numbers

Riel and Labelle gave me and leave messages. They'll likely check their voicemail so maybe we can pick up something with the bugs while they're using those phones."

Stemp nodded, and I went on, "Riel's definitely interested in the weapon, but it's just not making sense for him to be the terrorist." I blew out a breath of frustration. "I told him I could get the weapon. He didn't make an offer, and the Remembrance Day services are less than eighteen hours away. I can't see him making plans that hinge on getting it from me before eleven o'clock tomorrow. Have any of the other teams made progress on the terrorist threat?"

"No, there is no intel indicating that anyone else is even aware of the existence of the weapon. However, I did inform the civilian authorities about the murder threat against Harchman. Battalion Park has been thoroughly searched. No explosives were found; and the area is under guard and will remain so until after the service ends tomorrow."

"But the ultrasound weapon can't be detected with regular weapons scanners." I ground my knuckles into the tense muscles at the base of my skull. "Somebody could carry it in tomorrow and we'd never know until everybody dropped dead. Can't you get them to cancel the service?"

"I tried." Stemp pinched the bridge of his nose as if attempting to subdue a headache of his own. "The organizers had already announced that the Battalion Park service would be cancelled, and many other services across Canada had also been cancelled as a precaution after the threat was issued. But the public will not be intimidated. Have you heard of the EndTerror hashtag?"

"Um... no... I haven't had time for social media lately."

"There was an enormous social media backlash after the cancellations were announced. Thousands of people posted and tweeted that they would be assembling at the cenotaphs at eleven hundred hours on the eleventh as a show of solidarity against terror, and as a gesture of respect to the veterans who had braved such threats in defense of our freedom." Stemp let out a small breath that might have been a sigh. "Intel indicates that we'll have the largest-ever public turnout for Remembrance Day services this year."

I groaned. "Oh, for shit's sake! I mean, it's great that people don't want to give in, but... but..." I let out a sigh of my own. "Shit."

"Precisely. However, due to the specific threat against Harchman, the organizers cancelled his appearance; both for the public's safety and his own."

"They cancelled Harchman's speech?" A smile spread unbidden over my lips. "No wonder he was so pissy this morning. Did they explain to him that they were trying to save his miserable hide?"

Stemp's tone turned even dryer than usual. "Apparently he loudly questioned the effectiveness of our military if they couldn't even protect him with a full assembly. The organizers took offense. Harchman's speech is permanently cancelled, regardless of the presence or absence of any bomb threat."

My grin widened. "Couldn't happen to a nicer guy. Is it wrong of me to wish he'd get blown up anyway?"

A quirk of humour tugged at the corner of Stemp's mouth, quickly suppressed. "Yes. It is definitely wrong of you."

"Okay, I take it back." Sobering at the memory of the horrible sim, I added, "I was kidding anyway. I wouldn't wish that on anybody."

"Understood."

A glance at his eyes assured me that he truly did understand. I gave him a half-smile and went on, "But now that James Helmand is dead, Harchman's probably pretty safe anyway. Did Brock and Tammy decrypt that sim?"

"Yes, and Brock agreed with your initial assessment, that James Helmand created it. However, I'm not convinced that James's death negates the threat. Although we have no evidence pointing to Tawny Harchman, she has the best motive and opportunity to murder Harchman. If she colluded with James to test the effects of an explosive in the sim, then she might have also acquired the explosive from him. Perhaps she eliminated James after she had what she wanted."

I frowned. "If she's already got a bomb, Harchman is going to be strawberry jam sooner or later; whether he speaks at the Remembrance Day service or not. She could slip it into his pocket anytime."

"True."

"So can't we just arrest her?"

"No. In the first place, we have no evidence pointing to her; and in the second place, even if the sim did contain hard evidence incriminating her, we couldn't admit that we had it without revealing our clandestine operations." Stemp surveyed me in silence for a moment before dropping the bombshell. "So you'll need to protect Harchman."

"Wha... *me?*" My jaw dropped, my mind rebelling at the thought. "Protect *him?* That disgusting little-"

"Innocent civilian," Stemp finished my sentence, deadpan. "Yes."

"But you said we weren't in the bodyguard business," I protested.

"We are not. But you will be present to keep Riel under

surveillance, and also to determine whether Tawny is involved in the Remembrance Day threat. That is your stated mission; and with it comes the usual responsibility to avoid collateral damage. That would include Lawrence Harchman."

"Fuck." The f-bomb popped out before I could stop it, and I pressed my lips together. "Sorry," I added as soon as I was sure no other obscenities were going to slip out. "I'll see if Riel can get me invited back to Harchman's. I checked out of their guesthouse this morning, and they sure as hell won't invite me back of their own accord."

"Very well. And if Kane contacts you at any time, report to me immediately." Stemp held my gaze and I resisted the urge to squirm. "That is a direct order," he added, his words as precise as a scalpel. "Failure to comply will have serious consequences."

"Got it," I muttered. "Are we done here?"

"Not quite. Have you seen Helmand lately?"

I blinked. "Um... not since I found his body."

"Arnold Helmand," Stemp clarified.

"Oh. Sorry, I'm really tired." I rubbed my gritty eyes. "No. The last time I saw Arnie was Saturday morning around eight-thirty AM. He called me after lunch that day..." My heart sank as I made the connection between the timing of that call and James's estimated time of death, but I kept talking without a pause. "...and I haven't heard from him since. I don't know where he is, either."

"Interesting timing," Stemp murmured.

Damn his brilliant mind. I should have known he wouldn't miss something like that.

I shrugged, keeping my tone casual. "Maybe; maybe not. He had a mission a few days ago so he might be doing something related to that. Or..." My throat tightened. "Maybe he's been abducted, too. Maybe that was Kane's 'situation'."

"Perhaps." Stemp studied me, eyes narrowed. "But I also happen to know about your loyalty to both men. Perhaps I should ask you these questions with the lie detector activated."

Weariness overcame me, and I slid lower in the chair with a yawn. "Knock yourself out."

After contemplating me in silence for a moment, Stemp said coolly, "Very well, I shall." He dialled the phone and said, "Dr. Travers, please bring the lie detector to my office immediately. Thank you."

A knot of anxiety lodged itself under my breastbone, making my heart beat a little harder as I sat up. "You don't believe me?"

"I don't believe anyone. The best way to catch a liar is to lull them into a false sense of security. I have taken your word many times in the past. I believe my trap has been adequately baited." He dipped his chin a fraction in my direction, expressionless. "No offense intended if you are telling the truth."

I swallowed to prevent my voice from coming out in a dry whisper. "None taken. And I am telling the truth."

He nodded and sat back in his chair. Heavy silence blanketed the room. My pulse thumped in my ears and all the moisture in my mouth seemed to have migrated to my palms.

I resisted the urge to rub my clammy hands on my pants.

I *was* telling the truth, dammit. Why did he always make me feel so guilty?

Probably because I had bent the truth in his office far too

many times, the small unhelpful voice between my ears reminded me.

Shut up and look honest.

I leaned back in my chair and made a show of smothering another yawn.

An eternity or possibly five minutes later, a tap at the door heralded Dr. Travers's arrival. At Stemp's 'Come in', she entered with a worried glance at me and set the portable lie detector unit on the corner of Stemp's desk.

"Thank you, Dr. Travers," he said. "Please prepare Agent Kelly and then wait in the corridor. This will only take a few minutes."

She complied without speaking, but I read her concern in the small crinkle of her flawless forehead as she secured the crown of electrodes around my temples.

After she had closed the door behind her, Stemp activated the machine and lobbed the first question my way. "Is your name Aydan Kelly?"

"Yes."

My heart rate stepped up to double-time, and I glanced compulsively at the indicator. Green light.

Get it together. I knew my own name. Calm down.

"And did you pass your previous lie-detector test with Dr. Travers this past Thursday?"

"Yes." I swallowed in spite of my best efforts to prevent myself. Where was he going with this line of questioning?

"Have you done anything between then and now to cause you a guilty conscience?"

I stared at him open-mouthed.

A few seconds later I found my voice; and with it, my temper. "Are you kidding me? I'm undercover. Everything I do gives me a guilty conscience!" My voice rose. "I caused the abduction and possible murder of an innocent man! I broke into some poor shopkeeper's store and stole fancy designer clothes! I terrorized people at a party with a firearm and ran from the police! I lied to so many people I can't even remember all the shit I said! I shot a guy in the balls! I had happy thoughts of blowing up an innocent civilian! *Yes, I have a fucking guilty conscience!*"

It was Stemp's turn to stare, incredulity warring with a twitch at the corner of his mouth that looked suspiciously like an attempt to keep from laughing.

"Very well," he said in a slightly strangled tone. "Let's proceed." His deadpan façade descended again. "Do you have any idea why Kane was at Harchman's?"

"No." Irritation still sizzled in my blood, making my voice hard and level. The green light flashed as if it was afraid to do anything else.

"Do you have any idea where he is now?"

"No."

"Do you have any idea what his plans were or are?"

"No."

"Do you have any reason to suspect that he may have been compromised?"

"No."

"Can you think of any reason why he would be communicating with Riel?"

"No."

"What about Arnold Helmand? Do you have any idea where he is?"

"No."

"Do you have any idea what his plans were or are?"

"No."

"Do you have any idea if he and Kane were in contact

prior to Helmand's disappearance?"

"No."

"Do you have any idea if either of them conspired to murder, or actually murdered, James Helmand?"

"No."

Stemp surveyed me, one eyebrow cocked quizzically, and I stared back, daring him to push me just a little bit farther.

Go ahead, asshole...

"Very well," he said, and turned off the lie detector.

CHAPTER 40

After Dr. Travers had unhooked me from the lie detector and departed with it, Stemp leaned back in his chair again and regarded me over steepled fingers.

"Thank you for your patience with the test," he said. "I'm quite pleased with your anger management. You didn't even call me a dickhead."

"Yay, me," I muttered, still annoyed.

He studied me for a moment longer. "The formal part of this briefing is complete. But... may I ask you a personal question?"

"I can't stop you," I said flatly. "Do you want to hook me up to the lie detector again?"

"That won't be necessary." His expression eased into something a little closer to human. "And you are under no obligation to answer. I'm simply... curious. Do you really feel guilty over those things?"

"Of course I do. I'm a bookkeeper, for shit's sake; my life is all about honesty and accuracy. And now I lie and cheat for a living." I sank my face into my hands. "Never mind that; I lie and cheat to stay alive. I hate this fucking job." The last sentence choked out past the emotion that suddenly clogged my throat.

I gulped it down and straightened, giving Stemp a

defiant glare. "Happy?"

"No," he said, regret softening his face. "I know the toll this job takes on one's heart and soul, and I wish it could be otherwise for you."

"Thanks," I said quietly, and fled before I could burst into tears.

Damn sympathy.

A brief sojourn in the ladies' room stiffened both my spine and my resolve, and I hurried into my office to file my reports before striding out to my car. Shivering in the biting wind, I slid into the driver's seat.

I would nail Riel, dammit. And I would prove that Kane was innocent. And protect Harchman, and incriminate Tawny, and find Dante and Arnie, and save hundreds of innocent civilians...

The weight of it bowed my shoulders, but I fought off despair.

One thing at a time. Call Riel and get invited back to Harchman's. I pulled out my burner phone.

Its voicemail light was glowing, and when I played back my messages Labelle's rich voice flowed from the speaker.

"Hello; it's Frederick Labelle calling. I was sorry to have missed you at brunch this morning. Benoit and I have some business to discuss with you, and we were hoping you could meet us for brunch at ten AM at my home tomorrow morning." He reeled off the address and finished, "Please call me as soon as possible. Thank you."

I let out a long breath. Finally, something was going right. At least I didn't have to cudgel my exhausted brain into creating a plausible excuse for returning to my enemies' lair.

And he'd called me from his own phone. Maybe our

makeshift bug was working again.

With my fingers crossed for luck I dialled his number, but the call went to voicemail. I left a message saying that I'd attend his meeting, then hung up and stared through my windshield into the deepening twilight.

That was too easy. Was I just walking cooperatively into Labelle's trap? I should be chasing the bad guys down instead of waiting for their invitations. Bearding them in their dens and forcing them to confess...

I blew out a breath. No, that was Holt's stupid action-hero attitude. Thank God I'd had Kane for a mentor. Undercover work meant long hours of staying meticulously in character and collecting evidence, not charging around antagonizing the suspects.

Dragging my tired body out of the driver's seat and back up to Stemp's office, I reported the upcoming meeting with Labelle and Riel, feeling only slightly guilty about my relief at being able to avoid Lawrence Harchman for a few more hours.

Back in my car, I devoured a granola bar from my stash in the glove compartment before leaning my head against the headrest with a sigh.

Now that my official mission was back on track, I could use the remainder of the evening to hunt for Dante. A slow chill spread through my belly as I counted back the days since his abduction. James Helmand had been dead since sometime yesterday. So his captives, if any, had been without food or water for at least a day and a half. By the time I got back to Calgary it would be after eight PM and pitch dark. I was exhausted already, and I likely couldn't search all of the eleven addresses on the list Spider had provided.

And tomorrow morning I'd be occupied with Labelle and Riel.

More than two days. A person could die after three days without water. Especially if they had been tortured; their ravaged bodies succumbing to shock...

"Dammit, dammit, *dammit!*" I slapped the car into gear and accelerated out of the parking lot.

A few miles out of Silverside, a flash of light focused my attention on my rearview mirror.

A single bright headlight bobbed behind me, closing rapidly. Some hardcore motorcycle rider must be taking advantage of the snow-free highways despite the cold. He or she must be frozen to the bone, especially at that speed.

The bike was only a dark blur as it flashed past. Its taillight had diminished to a dot in the distance when it flared into sudden brightness. The rider was tapping the brakes, rapid flashes in an odd rhythm.

Adrenaline spiked into my veins when I recognized the pattern. Three short, three long, three short. SOS.

I slowed, realizing I was gaining on the biker. As I closed the distance between us, the motorcycle pulled off to the side of the road and stopped, still flashing SOS.

A trap?

Or an earnest call for help?

Holding my breath, I pulled over well behind the bike and drew my Glock.

The rider dismounted and strode back toward me, black leather and full-face helmet blending into the dusk. As he approached, more details appeared in my headlights. Very tall; very broad-shouldered...

My heart leaped as I recognized Kane's smooth powerful gait, and I holstered my weapon and sprang out of the car to meet him.

As I hurried forward he made a slicing gesture across his throat.

Still bugged. We couldn't talk.

But he was holding a white object in his hand. A folded piece of paper...

Headlights blazed behind us. Coming fast, then braking hard.

Kane flung the paper at me and ran. A gust of wind whisked the white scrap into the ditch and I dashed after it, not sure whether I was chasing the paper or hiding from whomever Kane was trying to evade.

Holt's shout came from a few yards back. "Stop or I'll shoot!"

Kane's stride altered to an erratic zigzag. A few paces later he jumped astride his motorcycle and kicked it into gear.

Gunshots shattered the country silence, the muzzle flashes from Holt's pistol splitting the dusk.

"STOP!" The scream tore my throat as I pivoted and sprinted up the embankment toward Holt.

Kane's big bike snarled and rocketed into the night.

Holt swore and dove back into the driver's seat. Seconds later he screeched to a halt beside me, bellowing, "Get in!"

Too stunned to argue, I flung myself into the passenger side only to be slammed back in the seat as Holt floored the accelerator. The Audi gave a snarl of its own, and I grabbed for the seatbelt.

"You can't catch him," I gasped, sneaking a fearful glance at the speedometer as my seatbelt clicked into place. A hundred and twenty kilometres per hour and accelerating fast. "That's a BMW K1300R. Major muscle bike. Zero to a hundred in about two seconds; tops out around three hundred."

"This is an Audi Quattro," Holt grated. "Zero to a hundred in six-point-two seconds, top speed around two-forty. He only has to make one mistake and I'll catch him. Especially if he smears himself all over the road. I've got four wheels; I don't have to worry about keeping my balance."

Drymouthed, I watched the speedometer climb over two hundred kilometres per hour.

"I drive this road all the time," I quavered over the thumping of my heart. "There are a lot of deer. Especially at dusk..."

"Good." Holt pushed the car faster. "Maybe he'll hit one."

"Or we will." My voice came out in a squeak, my knuckles glowing phosphorescent white in the dashboard lights. "Slow down! There's a rise here-aaaaaaAAA!" My words turned into an inarticulate yell as we topped the rise and the car took air.

Holt swore. The highway briefly disappeared, then reappeared in the headlights as the car slammed back to the pavement. A yellow curve sign flashed past. Holt braked hard, throwing me forward against the seatbelt.

"Fucking asshole!" Holt roared. "That *asshole*..."

Our tires shrieked as the car skidded into a four-wheel drift. Too terrified to even blink, I braced my arms and legs against the interior, my heart battering my ribs.

"*Asshole!*" Holt snarled. Suddenly we were facing the direction we'd come and Holt hammered on the gas again. "He hid under that rise and backtracked!"

Sure enough, a red taillight was fading into the distance.

"You can't catch him," I repeated, trying to hyperventilate and sound authoritative at the same time. "That bike's 'way too fast and he knows this road like the back of his hand."

"So do you," Holt snapped. "Make yourself useful."

Up over two hundred kilometres per hour again.

Holt was clearly an excellent driver, but this was far too dangerous. Just one old farmer dawdling along the highway in a pickup truck, and we'd kill an innocent civilian. And ourselves.

Enough of this shit.

I conveniently failed to mention the tiny back road through a ravine that I was pretty sure Kane would take.

Holt continued to push the Audi into the gathering night, but after several miles it was obvious that we'd lost Kane. Holt slowed to a decorous hundred and thirty kilometres per hour.

"Where the fuck is he?" he snapped. "There's a back road around here, isn't there? You didn't tell me!"

"Give it up. You know as well as I do that you can't catch a bike with a car; and anyway, it's too dangerous to drive like this. We'll kill some poor civilian. Slow down, and take me back to my car."

Holt shot me a murderous glare. "You let him get away! You fucking traitorous bitch! I should shoot you right now!"

Fear and adrenaline blazed into violent rage. "YOU FUCKING ASSHOLE!" I slammed both hands into his shoulder, making the car swerve dangerously. "WHAT THE FUCK IS YOUR PROBLEM! YOU FUCKING STUPID..." I couldn't think of a vile enough epithet so I just kept yelling. "He was giving me an update! He dropped a paper, which is now probably somewhere in fucking Saskatchewan thanks to this wind! You blew the whole fucking op! YOU FUCKING MORON!"

Holt slammed on the brakes, catapulting me forward against my seatbelt. A few seconds later the Audi slid to a halt on the gravel shoulder and I was staring into the muzzle of Holt's gun.

CHAPTER 41

"That's a whole lot of fucking," Holt said, his voice dangerously quiet. "Probably because that's all you've got on your mind. I've got news for you, honey: Your boyfriend is wanted for murder and treason, and you're looking a whole lot like an accessory to me."

Too furious to consider the consequences, I jerked forward, ramming his gun into my sternum. "Listen, shithead," I snarled. "Stemp just questioned me about Kane in a lie detector test less than half an hour ago. I passed. And if you'd stop trying to be Mr. Hotshot Action Hero for a nanosecond, maybe we could keep some innocent people from dying!"

The pressure of Holt's gun slackened. "Stemp made you take a lie detector test?"

"Yes!" I glared at him in the glow of the dashboard lights. "Now get your fucking gun out of my face!"

He holstered his weapon, leering at my chest. "If that's your face, I want to pat your cheeks."

I fell back in my seat, vibrating. After a few moments of speechless fury, I drew several deep breaths and managed to hold onto my temper. "You're such a fucking pig." My words came out sounding conversational.

Holt produced a remarkably realistic oink.

Sudden hysterical giggles climbed my throat.

"Cut it out." I tried for a commanding tone, but my voice came out choked by suppressed laughter. "I said, cut it out!" I repeated as the oinks came thick and fast. "I'm still pissed as hell at you!"

Holt eyed my quivering lips with a devilish gleam in his eye. "Laugh your ass off, Kelly," he commanded. "You know you want to."

With a supreme effort I controlled the giggles. "No, I actually still really want to kill you." Anger welled up again and I barked, "What the hell were you thinking, shooting at Kane? What happened to 'alive if possible'? And how the hell did you know he was going to meet me there? *I* didn't even know."

"I wouldn't have killed him. I was aiming low. Legs or bike tires. If you hadn't jumped into my line of fire I'd have gotten him for sure." Holt's lips curled into a predatory grin. "And I didn't have to know where or when he was going to meet you; I only had to follow you until he did. Just like I figured he would." His grin widened. "Brains, Kelly. That's why I'm a top agent."

"Too bad your so-called brains just blew this case," I growled. "Now you can help me search a few thousand acres in the dark to see if we can find the paper he was trying to give me."

The smile drained from his face. "Seriously?"

"Yes, seriously. Let's go. And step it up. Maybe we'll get lucky and find it snagged on something in the ditch."

We didn't get lucky; in any sense of the phrase.

After an hour of fruitless stumbling in and out of furrows

and ditches in the cold darkness, I reluctantly gave up.

"It's gone." I slumped against my car, barely resisting the urge to curl into fetal position. "Jesus, I wish I knew what it said. I have to meet Riel and Labelle tomorrow morning at ten. What if Kane was warning me not to go?"

Leaning on the car beside me, Holt kicked the gravel with his heel, his cockiness subdued for once. "Sorry. I was following Stemp's orders."

I sighed. "I know."

We stood in glum silence for a few moments.

"So what are you going to do now?" I asked. "Keep hunting Kane?"

Holt scuffed harder at the gravel. "I pretty well have to, don't I? Those are my orders."

"What about your orders to back me up?"

He dealt my tire a vicious kick. "How the hell should I know? Are you going to run out and get yourself killed if I don't?"

"Probably," I muttered.

"Nice positive attitude, Kelly."

"Bite me."

He snorted. "Maybe later, if you're really nice to me."

"In your dreams."

"In yours, you mean." Holt heaved himself upright. "Well, enough of this shit. I'll follow you. If Kane went to that much trouble to make contact with you, he'll keep trying. I can follow both sets of orders at once."

My heart sank. Great. Just what I needed: Holt watching me while I bumbled around like an idiot. I hadn't even spotted him tailing me. Hell, I hadn't spotted Kane, either. What a sorry excuse for an agent.

"All I'm doing is checking those addresses Spider gave

us," I said. "If you want to follow me around, fine, but we could split up and cover them in half the time."

"I don't think so." Holt glowered at me. "I'm not putting my career on the line by ignoring both sets of orders. Especially if you're planning to get yourself killed on my watch."

"Fine. Then brace yourself for a stimulating evening of poking around real estate in the dark." I got into my driver's seat and drove into the night.

I fought sleep all the way to Calgary, my eyelids dragging to half-mast only to waver open again. At last the glow of big-city streetlights welcomed me, and I navigated to the first address on the list.

Twenty minutes later I stared up at a twelve-storey office building, my heart sinking. Even if I could have sneaked past the security desk on the main floor and picked all the locks on the other floors, it would still take me forever to search the offices and service areas.

I let out a groan and let my head fall forward to rest on the steering wheel. Not a chance.

Do *not* curl up and cry.

I pulled myself upright again. An office building would be a dumb place to hide a hostage anyway. Too many tenants and maintenance staff poking around. Maybe the next address would be a smaller building.

It wasn't.

I gazed up at the sheer granite wall of a highrise, fighting despair all over again.

Body throbbing with exhaustion, I pulled away from the curb and steered toward an address farther away from the downtown core. A small residential building would be an ideal place to hide a captive...

Parked in front of the last address more than two hours later, I slumped in defeat. Like all the other properties on the list, the expensive-looking fourplex had discreet security decals, obvious video surveillance, and a locked vestibule. Unless I had a camera jammer, preternatural lockpicking skills, and/or plastic explosive and a complete disregard for stealth and personal property, I wasn't getting into any of these buildings tonight.

I hadn't glimpsed Holt's car since he'd pulled up behind me at the first property, which only disheartened me more. Pretty pathetic, when I knew for sure he was following me and I still couldn't spot him. Who else might have been following me all those times I'd driven around thinking I didn't have a tail?

Blinking away blurriness that might have been fatigue or tears, I was about to put the car in gear again when a nondescript grey sedan pulled up beside me. From the driver's seat, Holt gave me a 'now what?' lift of his eyebrows.

He'd changed cars, the bastard. No wonder I hadn't spotted him. I'd been watching for the red Audi.

That made me feel both better and worse. At least I hadn't been too blind to spot a bright red car following me; but neither had I been smart enough to watch for any other tails.

I mimed sleeping, palms together beside my tilted head. Holt nodded and drove away, leaving me to trail back to Hellhound's place alone.

Hellhound's parking slot was still empty, and I crept into

his apartment feeling as though nothing would ever be right again.

I was trudging toward the bedroom when my secured phone vibrated.

"Oh, God, now what?" I whimpered. Punching the Talk button, I managed a more or less professional-sounding, "Kelly."

"Hi, Aydan, it's me." Spider's cheerful voice lifted my spirits only slightly.

"Hi, Spider, what's up?"

"Guess who's been staying at the Macleod South Holiday Inn Express since Wednesday?"

I sucked in a breath. "Seriously?"

"Yep. Benoit Riel checked into Room 316 on Wednesday afternoon and his room is still occupied."

"Well, isn't that interesting!" I straightened, my fatigue falling away like a sodden overcoat. "Funny how he needs a hotel room when he's enjoying the swanky digs at Harchman's."

"I thought so, too," Spider agreed. "But he might be just using the room for a home base while he's in Calgary, to save travelling back and forth to Harchman's."

"Maybe. And maybe not. Thanks, Spider." I consulted my watch. "It's after midnight. Why are you still at work?"

"I'm following a lead on this terror case. It doesn't look too promising, but..." His sigh floated over the line. "I need to know for sure. If I went home now I wouldn't sleep for thinking about it." A smile warmed his voice. "Anyway, look who's talking. You're going to the Holiday Inn as soon as you hang up, aren't you?"

"Well... yeah."

"I knew it." His tone went solemn. "Be careful."

"I will. Thanks. Go home and get some sleep."

I was almost to the hotel when I realized I'd forgotten to check in with Holt. Dammit.

Should I call him for backup?

I'd be stupid not to.

I blew out a sigh. My petty inner child really wanted to one-up him. If he was such a hotshot agent, he should still be following me. After all, I was his assigned mission.

But I had told him I was quitting for the night, so I couldn't really blame him for wanting to grab a few hours of sleep. And how stupid would I look if I stumbled into trouble and he had to rescue me? Or worse, if he didn't rescue me in time?

Despite some internal foot-stamping and pouting from the less-mature me, my adult self prevailed and I pulled over to call Holt's burner number.

His brisk answer on the second ring sounded just as wide-awake as if it was the middle of the day, and I had to control a surge of irrational irritation.

"It's Aydan," I said. "I'm on my way to Room 316 of the Holiday Inn Express on South Macleod."

"What, you're making another porn video?"

"No, smartass, I'm checking it out because Riel's been renting it since Wednesday."

"What's your ETA?"

"I'll be knocking on the door in five minutes."

"Fuck!" Rustling and some thumps bespoke Holt's speedy departure, and when he spoke again the uneven cadence of his voice indicated he was running. "Can you make it fifteen minutes?"

Successfully squelching the desire to refuse, I said, "Okay, fifteen", and hung up with a childish glow of satisfaction at catching Holt The Magnificent with his metaphorical pants down. Hopefully not his actual pants. I didn't really want to think about that.

Fifteen minutes later I was on my way up to the hotel room. Holt hadn't appeared, but he was undoubtedly somewhere nearby doing his invisible-superspy thing.

Pulse pounding, I strode down the hallway. This was likely a dead end. Riel was probably just keeping the room to use during the day. I'd knock on the door and nobody would answer; and that would be the end of my investigation, since I didn't know how to bypass an electronic cardkey lock.

Holt probably did.

Dammit, I didn't want to defer to him again.

I halted in front of 316.

Maybe I should wait for Holt. What if somebody answered my knock with a shotgun blast?

I squared my shoulders. That was really unlikely. And the longer I hung around in the hallway, the more suspicious I'd look on the security cameras.

Before I could second-guess myself, my hand rose and knocked on the door.

Pulse thumping in my ears, I waited.

No answer.

Halfway between relief and disappointment, I knocked again, the sharp raps echoing in the quiet corridor. I could almost feel the other guests' annoyance focusing on my inconsiderate noise.

I pressed my ear to the door.

Was that a rustle of bedding? Or only my imagination?

I knocked once more, cringing at the thought of being that irritating person in every hotel who bangs incessantly on a door in the middle of the night...

The door jerked open and a shock of adrenaline froze me to the spot.

CHAPTER 42

My heart turned a jubilant cartwheel at the sight of six feet of perfectly-sculpted male muscles.

"Dante!" I flung myself at him and he staggered back under the onslaught of my hug, his hands flying up as if to defend himself. Ignoring his apparent discomfort, I hugged him even harder. "Thank God..." I could barely form words around the enormous relief expanding in my chest. "Thank God... You're okay! What..."

Holt's cynical voice interrupted me. "So you *are* doing a porn video. Where's the camera?"

I released Dante and stepped back a pace, heat rising in my face as I took in the rumpled bedcovers and the mostly-naked man in front of me. Dante's sleep-tousled black hair and five o'clock shadow made him look even more breathtakingly handsome than usual, and the bruised cut on his cheekbone gave him a deliciously rakish air. Generously filled bikini briefs riding low on his perfect hips completed the sex-god image.

After a moment of sheer mindless appreciation, I remembered my spy training and drew a breath of chagrin mixed with relief. Thank God the bathroom door was open and the rest of the room offered no place for anyone to hide. It was only dumb luck that I hadn't jumped into a room full of enemies who were using Dante as bait.

"Who is he?" Dante asked, indicating Holt with a hesitant gesture. His slightly-accented voice was as sexy as ever, but anxiety sharpened its edges.

"It's okay, he's a friend," I said hurriedly.

Dante backed away. "I've had enough of your 'friends'. Please leave now."

Holt leaned one shoulder against the door jamb, eyeing Dante. "What's that supposed to mean?"

Dante spared him only a glance before turning back to me. "Did James Helmand send you?"

"No, he's dead." The words were out of my mouth before I could consider whether a lie might serve me better.

"He's..." Dante staggered backward to sink onto the bed. After a deep breath he finished, "...dead?"

"Yeah, dead," Holt confirmed. "As in, cold, stiff, and not breathing. What's it to you?"

"He... uh..." Dante shook his head as if recovering from a punch, then focused on Holt. "Would you please either leave or come in? At least close the door."

Holt slouched farther into the room, letting the door swing shut behind him. "You're a famous underwear model. Why so modest all of a sudden? Aren't those your working clothes?"

Dante glanced down at himself, frowning. "It's not the same..." He shook his head. "Never mind. Aydan, who is this... person? Why are you here? Did Benoit send you? Or John?"

Holt's gaze sharpened. "John who?"

My stomach clenched. Please don't say what I think you're going to...

"John Kane," Dante said with an accusing glance at me.

"Your ex."

"Oh." I couldn't think of anything else to say. The single syllable floated small and alone on a sea of silence. My heart felt equally small and alone in my chest.

"Benoit has been checking on me every day," Dante went on. "But he couldn't make it this morning so John came instead. I suppose he told you I was here. I should have known not to trust him."

I still couldn't speak.

Holt took over, his cover identity slipping smoothly into place. "Yeah, that's why we're here. I'm Greg Holt, Realtor, and I'm a friend of Aydan's." He stepped forward to shake Dante's unresisting hand. "Benoit and John couldn't come tonight, so they sent us instead."

"To tell me James Helmand is dead," Dante repeated as if he couldn't quite believe it. "And I'm safe. I can go home now."

"Sure. You just have to check in with the police first," Holt said. "They've been looking for you since Friday when you didn't show up for your photo shoot."

"Oh, no." Dismay crinkled Dante's forehead. "Benoit said he would tell the police that James had kidnapped me and threatened to torture and kill me. He said he'd let me know as soon as James had been arrested and it was safe for me to go home. He must have..." His frown deepened. "...forgotten to report to the police? But that doesn't make sense... oh, no!" Fear paled his cheeks. "Could James have killed Benoit for rescuing me?"

"No, Benoit is fine," I said automatically. Then my beleaguered brain caught up with his last statement. "Wait, *Benoit* rescued you?" I demanded.

"Yes. James pushed into my house and beat me..."

Dante's fingertips brushed the bruise on his cheek with a shudder. "...and forced me to go with him. Just a few minutes after he'd locked me in a room, another man sneaked in. He said his name was Benoit and he was there to rescue me. He brought me here, and he's been keeping the room under his name ever since so I could stay hidden. I was only waiting until after James had been arrested," Dante repeated worriedly. "I didn't know what else to do. Benoit said James would find me if I contacted anybody else." He returned his gaze to me, his tone cooling. "Especially you."

"Why 'especially' Aydan?" Holt prompted with interest.

"Because that's why James kidnapped me. He said he was going to torture and kill me to get revenge on Aydan." Dante shot an accusing look my way. "If I'd known he was interested in you I wouldn't have been so... forward... last year. You should have told me."

"I... I'm... sorry..." I choked, unable to think of any plausible excuse that didn't include classified information. "I, um... As far as I knew he was only interested in Nichele. I don't know what his problem was."

Dante frowned. "I'm sorry to say this, Aydan, but please don't call me again, and stay away from me from now on. I don't like the company you keep."

Bitter laughter tried to leap from my mouth. If only he knew.

"I'm really sorry this happened to you, Dante," I said instead. "And I promise I'll stay away from you."

"It might be smart not to tell anybody about John coming here, or about Aydan finding you, either," Holt added, sounding convincingly concerned. "If you mention their names it might bring you more trouble from their weirdo friends. Just tell the police you saw on the late news that Helmand had been murdered so you knew it was safe to come out of hiding."

"Thank you," Dante said gratefully. "Please go now, and I'll call the police right away."

I moved toward the door, my mind still reeling. What had Kane been doing here? This didn't look good...

"I'm so sorry about all this," I repeated.

"I forgive you." Dante's tone was cool. "Goodbye."

Head hanging, I trailed out behind Holt.

In the parking lot, he turned to me with a nasty grin. "Good job finding your boyfriend. One of your boyfriends, anyway. It's too bad this one dumped you, though, 'cause your other boyfriend's going to prison for a long, long time."

Too tired and disheartened to wrangle with him, I mumbled, "Lucky I've got a third boyfriend for backup, then", and trudged off to my car, leaving him standing there open-mouthed.

All the way back to Hellhound's apartment I wrestled with my conscience. Holt had undoubtedly already called in to Stemp, so it wouldn't help to leave Kane's involvement out of my report.

Maybe I could spin it somehow, so it didn't look so incriminating.

But should I?

What if I had been wrong about Kane?

No, dammit, there had to be a good explanation. I knew it.

Back in Hellhound's apartment, I cuddled Hooker for moral support while I hit the speed dial for Stemp.

When his crisp voice came on the line after the first ring I said, "It's Aydan. I'm sorry to bother you so late; Holt's probably already told you everything..."

"He did check in," Stemp agreed. "But I've been waiting for your report. Please go ahead."

I began with the motorcycle chase and told him everything exactly as it had happened. It felt like a betrayal of Kane but I did it anyway, salving my stinging conscience with the knowledge that falsifying my report wouldn't change what Stemp already knew anyway.

When I was finished, Stemp said, "So, since Kane did not indicate to Olivieri that James was dead-"

"I bet he didn't know!" I interrupted eagerly. "I told you somebody was framing him for James's murder!"

"Or perhaps Kane did actually kill James but chose not to inform Olivieri," Stemp said, his tone as detached as always. "Kane was clearly acting at Riel's behest, and they might have been conspiring to hold Olivieri as potential leverage on you."

"But..." I began, but Stemp kept talking.

"At this time we must assume Kane has been compromised. More than twenty-four hours have passed since you discovered his involvement at Harchman's. An agent of his calibre would have found a way to check in by now if he was, in fact, acting in our best interests."

"But he did try to check in, and Holt screwed it up!" I clenched a fist in my hair, wishing it was Holt's throat. "Didn't he tell you?"

"Holt reported that Kane attempted to contact you, but Holt believes Kane is trying to compromise you, and that your judgement is clouded by your personal attachments."

"Holt's an asshole!" The words snapped out before I could stop them. I jerked my temper to heel and added, "Which is true; but he's also wrong. If Holt hadn't started shooting at Kane, we'd have that paper and we'd know exactly what was going on."

"Or you would have some marginally plausible excuse to cling to," Stemp said with surprising gentleness. "Tell me, what could Kane do to make you stop trusting him?"

Stricken dumb, I stared at the worn shelves sagging under the weight of Hellhound's vintage record collection.

When had I started trusting Kane so much that I believed in him no matter how egregious his actions seemed?

"I thought so," Stemp said after a moment. "Like you, I still want to believe that Kane is acting in our best interests; but unlike you, I will not wait for him to betray us in order to verify that. You are compromised by your personal feelings for him."

"I'm not-"

Steel entered Stemp's voice as he talked over my incipient protest. "Riel is attempting to obtain a classified weapon, and if Kane is aiding him in any way, that is treason. If the weapon is subsequently used against innocent civilians, it's treason, terrorism, and premeditated mass murder. And Holt reported that you obstructed his efforts to capture Kane. Twice. If Kane is proven guilty, you will be charged as an accessory and subjected to the full penalty of the law. Holt has orders to subdue and detain you if you interfere again."

Claustrophobic terror clamped an icy fist around my throat, and hot anger leaped up to combat it. "I did not interfere!" I barked. "I was nowhere near Holt's line of fire when he was shooting at Kane. And I didn't tell him about the side road that let Kane escape, because you'd just ordered me to avoid collateral damage to civilians. Holt was driving at two-forty on a rural highway in the dark. It's a miracle we didn't kill somebody. I had to let Kane get away, to end an unsafe pursuit."

When Stemp spoke again, he sounded weary. "That will be for the tribunal to decide, if it comes to that. Let us hope it doesn't. Meanwhile, I'm placing Holt in charge of your mission. If you fail to follow his orders, you will be charged with insubordination and obstructing justice in addition to any other charges you may face regarding your collusion with Kane."

The click of his disconnect sounded like the closing of a prison door.

CHAPTER 43

After a fitful sleep punctuated by violent nightmares, I pulled the pillow over my head when Miss Lacey arrived to feed Hooker at seven AM. When she was gone I lay in bed a while longer, but sleep eluded me.

What was Kane doing? He couldn't have turned against us. He had given his entire life to national defense and law enforcement. It simply wasn't in his nature to betray it.

But why hadn't he reported to Stemp?

What if Holt was right? What if Kane had just been using and manipulating me all along?

"Shut up," I growled, and hauled myself out of bed.

I was drying my hair after my shower when my cell phone rang. When I answered, Nichele's excited voice burst from the speaker.

"He's okay! Dante's safe! He's okay, he's okay!"

"I kno- Ohmigod, *really?*" I converted my incriminating words in the nick of time. Dammit, I'd almost blown my cover. Too tired to think straight. "That's fantastic!" I added with fake excitement. "Thank God! What happened? Where is he?"

As Nichele poured out the story I interjected questions and exclamations, hoping they sounded sincere.

"...and Hotty Benoitty is such a hero," she gushed.

"Imagine him hiding Dante like that and even getting him a burner phone, just like in the movies! What a sweetheart! I wish he could have told me Dante was okay; but I get it, really I do. It was all about keeping Dante safe, because the police couldn't do anything to protect him as long as James was at large."

I snorted. "Bullshit. If Dante had just called the police, they would have arrested James on the spot. He was on parole, and he committed assault and kidnapping, and uttered threats to torture and murder. He would have been back in jail so fast it would have made his head spin."

"They only could have arrested him if they found him in time," Nichele said earnestly. "And he might have killed Benoit as well as Dante. Benoit was really brave to take that chance."

Clamping my tongue between my teeth so I wouldn't tell her the real story, I drew a slow breath and choked out the only truth I could. "Yeah, Dante was lucky."

"But Aydan," she went on. "Dante said James was going to torture and kill him to get revenge on you. What did you ever do to James? You only talked to him that one time in the bar, and I don't remember you saying anything that would make him mad enough to kill somebody."

"I don't have a clue," I lied. "He must have been nuts. Who knows what sets people off? Maybe he had some kind of vendetta against redheads or something."

"That's just scary." She hesitated. "I feel really guilty saying it, but I'm glad he's dead. I feel safer now."

"I'm glad, too," I replied with utmost sincerity. "At least now when you come home from your trip with Dave, you won't have to be constantly looking over your shoulder."

"Yes, we're leaving in a few minutes, but I just wanted to

let you know Dante was safe. And, um..."

"Um, what?" I prompted when she didn't say anything for a few seconds.

"Well, um... Dante said... he doesn't ever want to see you again. So if he and I are going out for drinks or whatever, I, um... kind of can't invite you."

I sighed. "I don't blame him. Tell him I'm really sorry and I'll stay away from him forever."

"He's not trying to hurt you," Nichele apologized. "It's just that he was really scared; and he's not going to be able to work until his face heals, and he's afraid to take a chance on something like this happening again..."

"It's okay. I totally understand. I'd feel the same way if I were him. Listen, Nichele, thanks for calling, but I have to go. I've got a meeting this morning. Have a good trip, and say hi to Dave for me."

"Okay, thanks, Aydan. He says hi back."

I detected a waver of worry in her voice and added, "You guys are going to have an amazing trip. Trust me, I know it."

She laughed. "Thanks, girl. I know it, too. Now we just have to find a great guy like Dave for you."

My heart contracted around a stab of pain. I had two great guys; one suspected of treason and the other missing in action.

"Maybe someday," I choked out. "Take care. 'Bye."

When she disconnected I sank onto the toilet seat and stared at the floor, feeling utterly alone in the world.

Scratching roused me as a large furry paw appeared under the door, questing back and forth before withdrawing. A few moments later the paw reappeared, followed by a fluffy leg as Hooker stretched to his limit, whiskers pressed to the crack under the door.

I opened it and looked down into his beseeching yellow eyes, a lump rising in my throat.

"Poor guy," I whispered. "You miss him, too, don't you?"

Picking him up, I cuddled him close as I headed for the bedroom to get dressed.

After breakfasting on a few handfuls of dry cereal from the sparse offerings of Hellhound's cupboard, I punched in Holt's number.

He picked up with a curt, "Holt."

Trying to hold the rancour to a minimum, I asked, "So what's up, oh mighty leader? Do you still want me to meet Riel and Labelle this morning?"

Mercifully, he didn't rub it in. "Yeah. Where are you meeting them?"

"At Labelle's place." I gave him the address and added, "I checked it on the computer. It's a pretty big place, fenced and gated. Are you going to come along?"

"No, it's still your op. I'll be close by for backup."

I kept the surprise out of my voice with an effort. "Okay, thanks. Anything else?"

"Nope. Good luck." He disconnected, leaving me staring at the phone and wondering if I'd dialled the wrong Holt by mistake.

Or maybe he was just giving me enough rope to hang myself.

I stifled a groan and headed for the door.

In the driveway of Labelle's mansion I said my name into the intercom with my best smile for the closed-circuit camera, and the gates swung open soundlessly.

My hands quivered on the wheel, a fine tremor born of

nerves and exhaustion. A quick check in the rearview mirror confirmed that for once in my life I'd managed to apply makeup skillfully enough to camouflage the pallor of fatigue and the dark circles under my eyes. Nichele would be proud.

Unfortunately, if I lived through this I couldn't tell her about it; and if I died today she'd only see the undertaker's makeup job, not mine.

I sighed and parked the car, then straightened and assumed my Arlene Widdenback persona with an effort. Calm. Confident. No bullshit.

Controlling my breathing, I willed the trembling out of my hands. This was it. We weren't going to be interrupted by Harchman this time. Maybe Riel would finally give me an arms order; and then I could hand it over to the Department and go back to my nice safe desk job for a while.

...Or maybe he'd kill me.

Stop it. Positive attitude.

The weight of the Glock in my ankle holster reassured me as I stepped out of the car, and the hardness of the trank pistol at my waist felt like a bracing hand concealed by the soft folds of my sweater.

I could do this.

Hell, I had to. I didn't have a choice.

As I strode up to the front door, it opened and a dark-suited butler stood aside to let me enter.

"May I take your coat?" he inquired.

Thankful that I hadn't concealed any weapons in it, I relinquished the garment and followed him to a bright room where a table for three had been laid. Labelle and Riel occupied wing chairs next to the window, the picture of gracious living with flutes of orange juice in their hands. They both rose as I entered.

"Bonjour, Arlene," Riel greeted me. "'Ow nice to see you again."

"Yes." I gave him a thin smile. "Nice to see the hero of the day. No wonder you were so certain Dante would be found safely."

"Ah." His answering smile dissolved into contrition. "You are angry, and I do not blame you. I am sorry, but I feared for the safety of your friend if anyone knew where he was."

"Bullshit," I snapped. "You were holding him in case you needed leverage on me."

Riel held a hand to his heart as though grievously wounded. "I would never do such a thing."

"Yeah, right." I scowled at them both. "So what's this business you want to discuss? You've wasted enough of my time, so spit it out."

Riel swallowed the mouthful of orange juice he had taken, looking revolted. "Spit it? I would not offer such insult to Monsieur Labelle's food."

"Knock off the 'I don't speak English well' act," I snapped. "You know why I'm here. Do you want that item we discussed, or not?"

"Please." Riel gave me a pained look. "Let us not spoil our meal with such things. Monsieur Labelle has gone to great trouble..."

He indicated the table, where two young women in black dresses and white aprons were placing silver chafing dishes on the table. It was already crowded with luscious-looking sliced fruit and an assortment of cheeses and breads, and as one of the servers whisked the lid off the chafing dish the mouthwatering aroma of bacon made my stomach growl.

I clapped a hand over it, embarrassed despite my Arlene

Widdenback persona. "'Scuse me," I muttered. "I only had dry cereal for breakfast."

"Ah, no wonder you are out of sorts," Riel soothed. "Come, let us eat, and then we can discuss our business more pleasantly."

Labelle looked put out that Riel had usurped his duties as host, and he rose and poured out his most mellifluous voice. "Benoit is right, of course. Please come to the table." He gave us a gracious 'after you' gesture, and strode to the end of the room to turn on a large-screen TV and pick up the remote. "I normally wouldn't have the TV on during a meal," he assured us. "But this terrorist threat has been on my mind, and I want to see if anything develops."

"But of course," Riel agreed. "It is a most upsetting thing. I 'ope nothing comes of it."

I slid into my assigned chair at the table, wondering what game they were playing. Were they as much in the dark as everyone else? Or did they have something terrible planned and they wanted to see it unfold?

But if they were the terrorists, why was I here? It was far too late for me to supply the weapon now.

I suppressed the urge to frown, and kept a neutral expression on my face while Labelle took his seat and plied the TV remote to adjust the volume.

The food was good, but not as good as Harchman's. Riel's usual volubility seemed to have deserted him, and the conversation limped along. The talking heads on television only added to my tension with their anxious speculations about what might happen in thirty minutes.

Then in twenty minutes.

Ten...

At five minutes to eleven we abandoned all pretense of

eating or conversation, and simply watched the TV in silence. The servers cleared the dishes away and vanished, leaving the three of us alone in the room.

The news coverage displayed video clips of various cenotaphs across the country.   Toronto,   Montreal, Vancouver...

When Calgary's Battalion Park appeared on the screen, a chill shivered down my spine. Déjà vu. Veterans standing to attention; gloomy overcast sky; solemn crowd...

My breath caught as the camera panned across the crowd and I glimpsed two familiar figures. Apparently the news crew was looking for a poignant shot, and they'd found it. The camera zoomed closer to frame a fragile elderly lady standing straight and proud, holding the arm of a grizzled veteran three times her size.   Hellhound stood to rigid attention, his somber gaze locked on the horizon and his hand gently covering Miss Lacey's on his arm.

Dammit, I must have missed him by minutes. I should have left him a note; told him to keep Miss Lacey away from the service.

The camera pulled back to a larger view of the crowd and cenotaph again as the first heartwrenching notes of the Last Post sounded. My pulse thumped harder. Please, please, let everything be okay...

A flash of pink at the edge of the crowd made my blood run cold. No, it couldn't be-

The screen flared crimson.

Then slowly cleared to a skewed view of motionless bodies and debris fluttering down.

I heard Labelle's and Riel's gasps as if from a great distance. Clearly audible, yet miles away.

Heart frozen in my chest, I stared at the culmination of

my nightmares, unable to look away.

I couldn't breathe.

Couldn't think.

Couldn't comprehend how anyone could do such a monstrous thing.

Couldn't accept that I'd lost my cherished friend and lover.

After an eerie moment of total silence, the television station cut to a chaotic babble of reporters.

I was still paralyzed when Labelle punched the button on his remote and the screen died to the same black emptiness that gaped in my chest.

"Who did you sell it to?" he snarled.

I stared at him, uncomprehending.

"*You bitch, who did you sell it to?*" he roared, jolting me back to a semblance of intelligence at last.

"I didn't," I croaked. "I still have it."

Across from me, Riel's face was sheet-white, his rapid breaths edged with faint wheezing.

"You didn't?" Labelle demanded incredulously.

"No." Too stunned to lie, I added, "I thought Riel wanted it. I thought you guys were the terrorists."

Riel was still white-faced, his wheezing more pronounced as he patted his pockets with trembling hands.

Labelle smiled, a slow chilling display of teeth. "Looking for this?" he asked Riel, and drew a EpiPen from the pocket of his blazer.

Riel nodded. "Yes... must 'ave... been peanuts..." His words came out jerkily between wheezes, and suddenly I understood his worry over the dishes at Harchman's.

Labelle's smile widened. "Yes, there were. I hope you enjoyed your last meal."

"Please..." Riel reached across the table with a trembling hand. "I... must... 'ave..."

"What, this little thing?" Labelle removed the blue cap, then slammed the orange tip onto the table. Fluid squirted out, and Riel let out a feeble cry.

"Shit, do you have another?" I yelped.

Riel's lips were swelling and darkening. He swayed in his seat as he gestured toward Labelle, his breath coming in laboured gasps.

"Give him his goddamn EpiPens!" I yelled, belatedly grabbing for my Glock.

"No." Labelle's gun was already in his hand.

Staring into its muzzle, a small hopeless voice sounded in my head.

Too late.

Too late for everything.

CHAPTER 44

Riel toppled out of his chair and hit the floor with a sickening thud.

Labelle smiled at me over his gunsights. "Please take your weapons out slowly and put them on the table." As I moved to obey, he added, "All of them, please. The guns at your waist and your ankle, and also the small knife in your purse. In fact, I'll take the whole purse, just in case."

He hooked a foot under my purse and tossed it across the room, his pistol never wavering. As I laid my weapons down, his smile widened. "This is a nice change. I really do prefer it when I'm the one holding the gun. Now, if only I had a bear-infested wilderness in which to abandon you."

He pulled my guns over to his side of the table and thumbed the intercom. "Please send Mr. Kane up."

As Labelle settled back in his chair with a self-satisfied smirk, Riel's breathing wheezed into silence. After a few convulsions his body went still, his face mottled and contorted under the spittle trailing from swollen bluish lips.

My heart hammered so hard it hurt my chest.

Focus.

Fall apart later.

I fought off the horror of the Battalion Park slaughter and the enormity of my loss.

Why hadn't I kept Reggie's puke-pen? A burst from it might have bought me enough time to grab Labelle's gun.

Think.

Kane was coming. Maybe we could still turn this around.

Caught between terror and hope, a cold composure settled on me.

A tap sounded at the door and Labelle's gaze flicked in that direction as he called, "Come in."

Good, he was distractible. Maybe I could disarm him...

Kane strode in, briefcase in hand. A small grim smile twisted his lips as he surveyed the situation.

"Do you have it?" Labelle demanded.

"Of course." Kane reached into the briefcase and withdrew a horribly familiar white ceramic bottle with a silver base.

My heart stopped.

No.

No, it must be a replica. He's setting a trap for Labelle...

"Though apparently my original buyer doesn't want it anymore," Kane added with a nod toward Riel's corpse.

"No, he won't be needing it. You can leave it with me," Labelle said, his nauseating butterscotch voice rich with satisfaction.

"And my payment?" Kane inquired.

"In the case by the sideboard, the full amount you originally negotiated with Riel."

Kane hefted the large case onto the table and popped its latches to reveal stacks of hundred-dollar bills. His small smile reappeared. "Thank you. But before I go I have some unfinished business." He picked up the bottle-weapon again.

This was it. When he made his move, I'd be ready.

Poised to lunge for Labelle's gun, I held my face

expressionless.

Kane flipped open the targeting cap and pointed the lethal silver base at me. "You really should have fallen in love with me the way you were supposed to," he chided. "We would have been good together."

I stared at him, not speaking; not even breathing.

He would turn the weapon on Labelle, and when he did...

His aim unwavering, Kane fired directly at me.

In the instant before darkness claimed me, Holt sprang through the doorway, guns blazing in both hands.

Shots echoed distantly in the expanding void between my ears.

Red exploded from Kane's chest and forehead.

Holt, the consummate professional. Double-tap. No hesitation, no second chances.

Kane's body fell as if in slow motion.

Lost.

All was lost...

Death's dark wings obscured my vision.

CHAPTER 45

...I wasn't dead.

The surface under me was too hard and cold to be heaven, and I wasn't in enough pain for hell.

But maybe hell wasn't physical pain. Emotional pain?

Yes, surely this was hell.

Somebody was whimpering, thin helpless cries like a dying child.

Maybe it was me.

I should check. Feel my mouth and throat.

My arms felt too heavy to move and I didn't care enough to try.

At last I dragged my eyelids open. The ceiling circled slowly above me, white spattered with red.

I squeezed my eyes shut, then reopened them. The ceiling stabilized.

I might be in danger. I should get up. Grab my gun.

But why? To save my own life so I could suffer longer?

After a few long moments the whimpering got annoying.

I hauled up an uncoordinated arm to paw my face, but I actually wasn't the one making that sound.

I let my arm fall back to the floor. I was beyond whimpering. Far beyond any expression of the monstrous grief that smothered my soul.

When nothing happened after a few more moments I sat up, bracing myself against waves of vertigo.

Blood everywhere. Labelle's body lay on its back a few feet away, a messy hole in its head and a matching one in its chest. Kane's body was mercifully facedown. The weapon and suitcase full of money were gone, and so was Holt.

He had double-crossed us all.

The thought felt like a hammer striking an anaesthetized thumb. No pain, just a dull impact that would be excruciating later.

I should crawl over to Kane's body.

And do what? He had betrayed me in the end, too.

I squeezed my eyes closed.

It didn't help.

After a while I opened them again and staggered to my feet to collect my weapons from sheer force of habit. Trank pistol at my waist; Glock at my-

"So you're finally up." Holt's voice was obnoxiously cheerful, and I turned slowly to see him regarding me from just inside the doorway. "What the hell were you thinking?" he demanded. "That was a fucking stupid rookie move, letting Labelle get the drop on you like that."

As if guided by someone else, my Glock swung up in a smooth arc and my finger squeezed the trigger once, twice; my hands rock-steady.

No hesitation.

No second chances.

Holt hit the floor with a yell, rolling and twisting to come up in a shooter's crouch with his gun pointing at the sprawled corpse that lay where he had stood only seconds before.

He eyed the wicked-looking knife clenched in the

corpse's hand and swallowed hard before bellowing, "JONES! WHAT THE FUCK, YOU SAID THE PLACE WAS CLEAR!"

"Sorry, sir, there was a concealed room," a faint voice replied. "We're double-checking now."

"YOU'D FUCKING BETTER TRIPLE-CHECK!" Holt roared. "FUCKING IDIOT!" He lowered his voice. "Thanks, Kelly."

I nodded. The Glock felt good in my hand. Safe and normal and right. Not like the rest of my world.

A man clad in black fatigues escorted the two servers out and the whimpering ceased at last. I stood staring at Holt in the silence.

"Oh," he said as though suddenly enlightened. "You don't know what's going on, do you?" He nudged Kane's body with a toe. "I shot him with the ballistic trank. The mist knocked you out, too. He should wake up in a few minutes."

"He... wha...?"

Holt's words registered and I dropped to my knees beside Kane, mostly because my legs wouldn't hold me anymore. My fingers trembled to his throat, finding the strong steady pulse that should have sent a surge of joy through me.

"Oh. That's good," I said stupidly, and sat on the floor with a thud.

"Fuck, Kelly." Holt crouched to study me with concern. "Did you hit your head or something?" He waved a hand at the scattered bodies. "It's all good. When you didn't respond to your 'call home' text and the bug picked up Labelle's and Kane's conversation, I brought in the cavalry." He nodded at Riel's body. "That didn't quite end according to plan; but whatever. At least nobody important died."

My heart shattered.

"The terrorist attack at Battalion Park," I whispered. "How many...?"

I couldn't say the word 'dead'.

Holt's eyes widened. "What terrorist attack?"

"It was on TV. Live news feed. That's how Labelle got my weapons. I couldn't..."

Words failed me again.

"Goddammit, we were infiltrating the house then..." Holt lunged to his feet, snatching out a secured phone and jabbing at the speed dial button. "It's Holt!" he barked. "Battalion Park! What happened! How many casualties?"

Face hard, he listened to the crackle of Stemp's voice on the other end of the line.

Kane groaned and flopped over onto his back, his hand going to his forehead. "Didn't have to take the head shot," he mumbled grumpily. "Could've lost an eye..." His eyes opened and he squinted at his red-smeared hand. "Dammit..."

Reaching up to the table, I grabbed one of Labelle's crisp white linen napkins and handed it to Kane.

"Thank you." His gaze sharpened as though his vision had just come into focus. "Aydan, you're all right. Thank God." His hand closed around mine.

"Kelly, step away!" Holt's hand hovered dangerously near his holster.

"What-" I began.

"Move it! Now! Opposite side of the room!" Holt raised his voice to a shout. "Jones!" One of the fatigue-clad men appeared in the doorway and Holt jerked his chin at us. "Take their weapons."

My hand tightened reflexively on the Glock I still hadn't holstered.

Holt's gun was trained on me in an eyeblink. "Don't do it, Kelly," he warned.

"What the hell?" I protested.

"Put it down! Do it now!" His finger hovered over the trigger.

"Okay, okay. Jeez, take a pill." I laid the Glock down carefully. "Trust me, if I was going to shoot you I would have done it days ago. Or a few seconds ago."

Holt shrugged. "You're a spook. I don't trust you any farther than I could throw you." As Jones pocketed my weapons and turned to frisk Kane, Holt directed a glare at Kane and added, "And I sure as hell don't trust him. Now, get over to the other side of the room like I told you. Nice and slow."

As I dragged myself to my feet to comply, Kane rose, too, holding his arms away from his body so Jones could complete his search.

"I'll cooperate," Kane said mildly. "But not unless I see my son first. I just have to make a call to arrange it, and I only want a few minutes with him. After that I'll do whatever you want." His gaze bored into Holt. "But that gun won't do you any good at all if I decide not to cooperate."

Holt's jaw hardened as his weapon locked onto Kane. "Big words from a guy I tagged twice before he could even move."

Kane dabbed the shallow bleeding gouge in his forehead where the dart had struck him, his movements slow and deliberate. "I didn't move because I didn't trust your aim. Taking the head shot was dangerous grandstanding. If you'd blinded me I would have killed you with my bare hands when

I woke up."

Holt's eyes blazed, his knuckles whitening on the gun's grip. "*If* you'd woken up, asshole. I could've used real bullets and shut your fucking mouth permanently. Maybe I still will."

All my tension and fear detonated into a full-throated shout. "SHUT UP!"

Into the moment of shocked silence I barked, "Knock off the pissing contest, both of you! Holt, do what you have to do, but let Kane see his son for a few minutes. Dead civilians are a hell of a lot more important than your fucking ego. Let's get back to Sirius and nail whoever did this."

Holt's nostrils flared, his jaw jutting; but after a few steady breaths he nodded tightly. "Fine. Jones, give him his phone back, then get a team of four and secure these prisoners." He turned his glare back to Kane. "One call. Keep it short, and don't try anything."

"Dead civilians?" Sudden tension vibrated in Kane's voice. "How? What happened?"

The terrible memory struck like a battering ram and my throat closed. With all my remaining strength I forced myself to speak. "There was... a terrorist attack... at Battalion Park." The words came out in a rusty croak, as though I hadn't spoken for decades. "Everybody died. Arnie..." My voice broke, my eyes filling.

"Arnie what?" Kane stiffened. "What are you talking about? What happened to Arnie?"

"He... he was there."

"No." Kane shook his head. "That's not possible."

"Yes. I saw him on TV. He..." My voice wavered at the memory of his proud posture and the stern beauty of his ugly face. "He was there... with Miss Lacey..."

I couldn't say any more.

"No, he couldn't have been," Kane repeated. "He's guarding Daniel and Alicia. He said he'd guard them with his life." His voice rose, his shoulders going taut as he punched the speed dial on his phone. "He wouldn't have gone to Battalion Park," he repeated as though his words could make it true.

Hoping against hope, I listened to the buzz of the phone at the other end. As the ringing continued, Kane's knuckles whitened on the phone. "He wouldn't have gone," he said forcefully to me. "He couldn't have been there."

The crackle of a voice at the other end of the line made my pulse leap, but Kane's expression went grim. "It's Kane," he said into the phone. "Call me as soon as you get this message. It's urgent."

He disconnected and we stared at each other, desperate hope and sickening fear reflected in each other's eyes.

"Holt." My voice came out in a dry whisper. "Were there... any survivors?"

Holt frowned. "Don't know yet. There are crazy conflicting reports coming in..."

Kane's phone rang.

Holt's gun flicked up, drawing a bead on Kane's chest. "Try anything and you're dead," he snapped.

Ignoring the weapon, Kane punched the Talk button and barked, "Kane!"

A second later his shoulders eased, his expression slackening into relief. "You're all right?" he asked.

Wild hope blazed into my veins and I lunged at Kane, nearly bowling him over in my effort to shove my face close to the phone.

"Arnie? Arnie, is that you?" I cried.

"Yeah, what's wrong, darlin'?" he rasped.

I collapsed against Kane. "Thank God!" My voice came out in a squeak, short-circuited by the selfish joy ballooning in my chest.

Hundreds might have died in the attack, but not Arnie.

Not my Arnie.

"Thank God," I repeated, my tears overflowing into Kane's shirt.

"No, it's all right; she's fine," Kane reassured Hellhound. "And this whole mess is over. Take Alicia and Daniel home. I'll meet you there in about half an hour-"

"That's enough," Holt interrupted. "Hang up. And you..." He jerked his chin in my direction. "Get off him. I told you, opposite sides of the room."

"See you soon," Kane said into the phone, his voice calm and level. Then he pressed the disconnect button and held out the phone, his movements smooth and unthreatening. "Do you want this, too?"

"Put it on the floor," Holt snapped. "Kelly, move it!"

Jones had been muttering commands into his shoulder mike, and as I moved across the room four large fatigue-clad men with assault rifles arrived. In moments my hands were bound tightly behind my back and claustrophobia clutched my throat.

"B-But..." I quavered. "If Stemp trusted Kane enough to lend him the weapon, why are we prisoners?"

"Stemp didn't give him the weapon." Holt shot a hard glare at Kane. "He had another prototype."

My stomach dropped and I gave Kane an imploring look.

"Where did you-" I began at the same time as he said, "It's not-"

"No talking," Holt snapped. "Jones, keep them

separated. Let's go."

Kane and I were escorted out by two burly men each, our arms pinned in their grasp. Holt followed with his gun in ready position.

Outside, a large black van waited. Our guards bundled Kane and me into the back and chained us to opposite benches before taking seats on both sides of us.

Holt inspected our restraints and turned to our guards. "Don't let them talk. Not one word, to you or to each other. If they try, trank them. In fact..." He reached into a locker at the rear of the van. "I don't even want them looking at each other." He yanked a black hood down over Kane's head, and a moment later a matching hood blotted out my vision, too. "Stay sharp," Holt admonished the guards. "Consider them extremely dangerous."

The van door slammed.

The hood clung to my face, already warm and stuffy with my rapid breathing. The restraints bit into my wrists and terrifying memories flashed behind my eyes.

Panic flared. My heart rate spiked, my breath accelerating into shallow panting. With all my will I fought the compulsion to scream and struggle.

If they'd just lift the hood enough so I could breathe...

"Could you-" I began.

A jab in my thigh.

Then nothing.

CHAPTER 46

I struggled up through ponderous darkness, already fighting my bonds.

Escape. I had to escape.

Hard hands clamped on my arms and I lashed out with a foot, letting out a cry of pain when something bit into my ankle.

The clank of the door latch and Holt's voice brought me back to full comprehension. "Okay, here's how we're going to-"

"Take her hood off, for God's sake!" Kane's voice sounded strained. "She's only semi-conscious and she's claustrophobic. She doesn't know where she is."

"Take him out," Holt said flatly.

"Take her hood off!" Kane barked.

"As soon as you're out. Move it!"

The jingle of chains and rocking of the van's suspension marked their exit, and a moment later my hood was whisked off with a painful jerk of my hair.

"Ow! Fuck!" I glared up at Holt from my uncomfortable position, half-crushed by my two big guards. "Get them off me!"

Holt nodded at them and they eased their weight off to sandwich me tightly between them instead of leaning on me.

"What the fuck, Kelly?" Holt demanded.

"What the fuck yourself," I snarled. "I just wanted them to lift the hood enough so I could breathe, and they tranked me as soon as I started to ask."

"As per their orders," Holt retorted. "So shut up or they'll trank you again." He turned on his heel and got out, slamming the door behind him.

"*Asshole!*" I bellowed, but one of my guards held up a trank dart with a warning look, and I shut up.

Outside, Kane spoke again, his voice only slightly muffled by the van's closed door. "What did you do to her?"

"Nothing. She's just a cranky bitch. Do you want to see your kid or not?"

After a moment of sullen silence, Kane growled, "Yes. I would like to see my son. And I don't intend to do it wearing shackles."

There was a brief tense pause, and I braced for an explosion from Holt.

Instead, when he spoke his voice was hard and even. "Okay, here's how it's going to happen. We'll remove your restraints. You'll have three automatic weapons trained on you at all times. You won't go into the house. You can talk to the kid on the doorstep. One wrong move and the bullets will fly; and if your kid happens to be in the crossfire, well..."

Imagining Holt's shrug, I barely prevented myself from yelling obscenities through the door.

"Unacceptable," Kane said, his voice dangerously flat. "Daniel's safety is not negotiable."

"I'm not negotiating," Holt replied. "If you don't try anything, your kid will be perfectly safe. That's the only deal going. If you don't like it, you can get back in the van right now."

A familiar gravelly voice said, "Hey, what the fuck's goin'-"

Scuffling and loud thumps against the van made my guards bolt to attention, their hands flying to their weapons. A surge of adrenaline kicked my heart into overdrive.

An instant later the van door burst open and two small flat reports plunged me into blackness again.

"Wha... whaddafuck...?" I mumbled, straining to push the weight of the guards off me.

"Hey, darlin', it's okay." Hellhound's gentle rasp sounded close to my ear.

I dragged one eye half-open. Above me, his beloved battlescarred face wavered in and out of focus.

"You're okay, darlin'," he assured me. "Ya don't hafta fight. I got ya."

Going limp in the safety of his arms, I let my eyelid fall closed again.

Sleep. I could sleep here forever...

"Shit!" My eyes popped open and I struggled into sitting position. "What happened? Where am I? Where's John?"

"We're in the Sirius van, an' he's right there." Hellhound nodded out the window to where Kane stood on Alicia's front lawn holding Daniel.

"Oh..." I relaxed into Hellhound's embrace, my heartstrings tugging at the sight of Kane's smile. He held Daniel close, his gentleness obvious despite the power coiled in his bulging muscles. Daniel nestled in his father's arms, both hands curled into Kane's T-shirt and his face pressed to Kane's shoulder. Alicia stood on the doorstep frowning, but she didn't interfere.

"Thank God..." I began as I turned back toward Hellhound. "*...Jesus Christ!*" I yelped, recoiling from Holt's murderous close-range glare.

Behind a gag that looked suspiciously like one of the blackout hoods, Holt growled words that were probably capable of igniting the fabric in his mouth, if he had been able to enunciate them properly. His hands and feet were bound with Sirius-issued restraints and the seatbelt had been tied through both, trussing him in the driver's seat with remarkable effectiveness.

"Sorry 'bout that, darlin'." Hellhound's grin was unrepentant. "Hate to make ya look at that ugly mug, but I didn't know where else to put him."

More inarticulate invective leaked out around Holt's gag as I stared open-mouthed at him.

"Wh... What... exactly... happened?" I asked.

"He pissed Kane off," Hellhound said cheerfully. "Ya really don't wanna do that."

"Um... what about the guards?"

"They're havin' a nap in the back. They got the darts an' you only got the inhaled trank, so they oughta be down for a few more minutes."

"B-But... what...?" Words failed me as I imagined the repercussions.

Oh, God.

We'd defied orders. Obstructed justice. Attacked officers of the law.

We were going to jail.

Unless...

An even scarier thought occurred to me.

What if Kane really had gone rogue? What if he left Holt and his team tied up in the van and went on the run? Or worse, made a stand? If he decided to fight, it would be a bloodbath...

"It's gonna be okay," Hellhound said as if reading my mind. "Come on, let's get outta here. Don't wanna look at that ugly fuck any longer." He jerked his chin at Holt's rage-purpled countenance.

My knees buckled as I stepped out of the van, and Hellhound's strong arms caught me.

"Easy there, darlin'." He eyed me worriedly. "Ya okay?"

The memory of the motionless bodies at Battalion Park surged back, slicing my heart open to sear it with the bitter acid of failure. Tears flooded my eyes and I buried my face in Arnie's chest, clinging to him as if his solid presence could somehow bring all those innocent people back from the dead.

"Hey." He held me tightly, stroking my hair. "Hey, Aydan, what's wrong?"

"I'm so... glad..." I drew a hiccupping breath. "...you're okay..." The grief of all the people who would never be able to hold their loved ones again crushed my soul. "Oh God... all those poor people..." Sobs wrenched my chest.

"Whoa, hang on. What people, darlin'?"

"At B-Battalion P-Park..."

"What...? No." His hands closed on my shoulders, strength schooled to gentleness as always. "No, Aydan. Hey, look at me." He held me away from him, ducking down to look me in the face. "Darlin', it didn't happen. It was fake news. Some fuckin' sicko spliced a video clip into the live feed. Nobody died. They announced it on the news just before ya got here."

"Nobody..." My knees went weak. Tremors spread through my body until I was vibrating in his grasp. "...F-

Fake...?"

"Yeah." Arnie closed his arms around me again, enfolding me in comfort and safety. "Everybody's fine. No casualties."

Pressed tightly against him, I let the glorious heat of his body melt the icy chill in my chest.

"It's all... okay?" I asked again, afraid to believe it.

"Yeah. It's all okay, darlin'." He pressed his lips to my hair, rocking me while I clung to him. "It's okay, everythin's okay."

"Well, maybe not quite everything." Kane's voice intruded on our moment. When we pulled apart, he gave us a regretful grimace. "I'm afraid we'll have to pay the piper now."

Leaning past us, he opened the passenger door and eyed Holt's furious face. "I'm going to untie you now," he said evenly. "And I'm going to let you put the restraints back on me, and I'll get in the back of the van and cooperate with the guards so you can deliver me to Sirius as per the original plan. You've been watching us the whole time, so you know Aydan and I haven't communicated in any way. It's up to you whether you want to put this in your report. I'll own up to it if you do; and I'll pretend it never happened if you don't. Your call."

He reached in and pulled the gag off Holt.

Braced for a deluge of obscenities, I dared a peek into the van when all was silent. Holt and Kane had locked eyes, both wearing their impenetrable cop faces.

"You goddamn prick," Holt said. "This is going to make me look like a fucking idiot, but..." He hissed out a breath. "I'm not going to falsify a report. It's going in, and we're both going to have to take whatever Stemp dishes out." He turned a sardonic smile on me. "Kelly, of course, comes out smelling like a fucking rose since she was unconscious. Well played, Kane. Asshole."

Kane shrugged, the small grim smile twisting his lips again. "Thank you." He turned back to us, but Hellhound spoke before he could.

"I'll stay with Lish and Dan, Cap. I'll protect 'em with my life."

"Thank you." Kane briefly clasped Arnie's shoulder before going around to the driver's side to release Holt. Then he turned his back, holding his arms behind him.

Holt bound his wrists with a fresh set of restraints. "For all the fucking good it'll do," he grumbled. "Stay here. I'll let the boys out of the back and keep them from killing you." He turned to me. "You need to come to Sirius, too. No talking. Hoods on. But I'll make sure your nose and mouth are uncovered."

"Thanks," I said in a small voice, my pulse bounding up in renewed fear.

"It's gonna be okay, darlin'," Hellhound said, but I could see the worry in his eyes.

CHAPTER 47

Blindfolded with my hands bound behind me, the two-hour trip to Sirius felt interminable; but it was nothing compared to my wait in the holding cell. Eyes closed, I slouched on the small hard bench and fought panic with slow even breaths.

In...

Out...

Slow like ocean waves...

Not hurrying along in a frantic rhythm like my pulse...

By the time the guards arrived to take me to Stemp's office, I was ready to confess to crimes I hadn't even committed. As we marched along the hallway, my heart thumped in double-time.

What had happened to Kane? Had they been interrogating him all this time?

Or was Stemp just using his knowledge of my weaknesses to soften me up? Letting me go slowly mad in captivity?

Damn that twisty bastard. He knew how claustrophobic I was, but since I'd been downplaying it in my psych reports I couldn't even accuse him of using it to manipulate me.

At last the guards deposited me in Stemp's guest chair and withdrew. Holt sat in the other guest chair, giving me a look almost as unreadable as Stemp's own. The lie detector machine crouched on the corner of the desk, an unpredictable beast poised to attack.

"Please tell us your version of today's events," Stemp said.

I poured out my story, careful to report everything exactly as it had happened. "...and I never did get the 'call home' text," I finished. "My phone was in my coat pocket and the butler took it."

"Ah, so the butler did it," Holt interjected. "Classic."

"Smartass." The word popped out before I could stop it, and I bit my tongue and faced Stemp. "Sorry."

"No need to apologize to me," he said. "Holt is the injured party."

I glanced over at Holt's smug expression and the devil spoke with my mouth. "Not sorry. You are a smartass."

Holt turned a scowl to Stemp. "See what I have to put up with?"

"Indeed." Stemp gave me his reptilian stare, then pressed the intercom button. "Dr. Travers, we're ready for you now."

Wired up to the lie detector a few minutes later, I drew a breath and let it out slowly in an attempt to calm myself.

Stemp began with the usual questions. "Is your name Aydan Kelly?"

Instead of being reassured by the familiar procedure, my heart pounded harder.

My voice came out in a croak. "Yes."

The green light seemed to take longer than usual to appear.

After a few standard questions, Stemp got to the point. "Was everything you just reported true, complete, and accurate?"

"Yes." The faint breathless voice didn't even sound like me.

But glory of glories, the green light flashed its vindication.

"Did you omit anything at all from your report?"

"No."

Green light.

"Did you conspire with Kane to attack Holt and his team?"

Oh God. They'd charged Kane with assault and resisting arrest. Sick despair dragged my belly down to my toes.

"No."

One small word in a small voice. Enough to free me and incarcerate Kane. The green light taunted me with its cheerful glow.

"Do you know where or from whom Kane obtained the weapon he was carrying today?"

Hope died.

They had charged him, and with good reason.

He was a traitor.

"No." The word came out sounding strong, a denial of Kane's guilt as much as response to Stemp's question.

Kane wasn't a traitor. I couldn't believe it.

I *wouldn't* believe it.

"Did you know he had agreed to sell the weapon to Riel and Labelle?"

"No." The word floated out on my last evaporating wisp of hope.

How could I have been so wrong about him?

"So you were completely unaware of Kane's motives and activities?"

Stemp's words sounded like an accusation. How could a so-called professional agent be so blinded by her feelings that she didn't even see what was going on under her nose?

He was going to rescind my agent's status and imprison me forever...

"Yes." Devoid of hope, the word came out utterly flat and expressionless. "I was completely unaware."

Stemp eyed me for a long moment, his face giving away nothing. A snake about to strike.

"Very well," he said coolly. "Debriefing in the meeting room in ten minutes." He pressed the intercom again. "Dr. Travers, you can take away the lie detector now."

CHAPTER 48

Unwilling to face my fate, I closed myself into a cubicle in the ladies' washroom for the entire ten minutes. When I couldn't delay any longer, I sucked in my gut, squared my shoulders, and tottered to the sink to wash my hands.

Dammit, I wouldn't go out snivelling.

I would stand tall while they delivered my sentence.

And I would find a way to die if they locked me up.

The white-faced woman in the mirror stared back at me with haunted eyes.

I straightened, anger warming my belly. No, dammit, I *wouldn't* die. I would fight for my freedom. I would fight to remain an agent.

And I would damn well win.

Head high, I strode out into the hallway.

In the doorway of the meeting room my stride faltered. I had expected Stemp, Holt, and Spider.

I hadn't expected Kane. At least not without an armed guard.

Hope quickened in my chest, but I squashed it. They probably just wanted to squeeze as much information out of him as possible before they imprisoned him.

Or maybe this was one more of Stemp's manipulation tactics.

Holding my face expressionless, I slid into a chair with my back to the wall.

Stemp acknowledged my presence with a fractional nod, then turned to Kane. "You may begin."

"All right," Kane said, and I let myself sink into the warm velvet of his voice. It might be my last chance...

"Aydan had used me for a distraction when she first spotted Riel in Nichele's office," he began. "So I was aware of the situation with James Helmand and all the other players. What I didn't know was that Helmand had come to my... uh, Alicia's... house a couple of days earlier and introduced himself to Alicia; undoubtedly hoping I'd take his visit as an implied threat to my family. Alicia forgot to mention it to me until late Saturday morning. That was the 'situation' I called you about around noon..."

My heart sank as my imaginary scenario played out in my head again. James appearing unanticipated at the door, Kane reacting instinctively...

"...so when Tawny Harchman arrived at two o'clock on Saturday to warn me that James Helmand intended to cause trouble, it was completely unexpected," Kane finished.

"Wait, *Tawny* showed up at your door?" I demanded. "Was she doing her bubblehead bimbo act?"

"Yes. She said if I came with her to their home, she would mediate between Helmand and me, and we could resolve our issues peacefully."

"Well, sign the girl up for a Nobel Peace Prize," I muttered.

"I played along," Kane went on. "Which was why I missed my check-in with you. I'm sorry about that."

I managed a feeble nod, and he continued, "I accepted her invitation and told her I would be there shortly. As soon as she left I called Hellhound to take Daniel and Alicia into hiding, and I set up surveillance cameras in the house."

He gave us a thin smile. "Cameras which subsequently recorded footage of Labelle's men dumping Helmand's body in the living room. I discovered later that Riel had hired a hit on Helmand, who was becoming increasingly unbalanced and threatening his transaction with Arlene Widdenback. Framing me for Helmand's murder was his backup plan, to force me to help him acquire the weapon if Arlene Widdenback didn't deliver."

"So that's why you were at Harchman's," I said. "Waiting for Helmand, who never showed up because he was already dead. Did Tawny know?"

"She seemed puzzled and annoyed that Helmand was a no-show." Kane shrugged. "But she's a very good actress, so who knows?"

"And the bug?"

"It belonged to Riel, I figured out later. At the time I assumed it was Tawny's, so I didn't want her to know we'd found it. Then later I discovered that Riel had asked Tawny to come and collect me, and the bug was his. I didn't dare compromise it because I wanted him to be convinced I'd turned against you." His lips twisted. "I didn't realize Labelle was planning to double-cross him and kill both of you to take the weapon for himself."

"He must have found another buyer who paid better than Riel," I guessed. "That must have been why he was stalling our deal."

"So where the hell did you get the other weapon?" Holt demanded. "I asked Reggie Chow, and our weapon never left the lab."

"I didn't have another weapon. That's what I was doing

Sunday afternoon." Kane smiled. "Building a fake weapon out of a Malibu coconut rum bottle and some aluminium foil. It took forever to sand off the glaze and label, and to get the foil looking right."

Released tension folded me into a slump of relief. "So you never had another weapon at all."

"No, of course not." Kane frowned. "If I'd had an active weapon, I wouldn't have pointed it at you. I knew you'd know that."

"Right," I said faintly.

Holt leaned back in his chair. "Huh. Lucky I'm a top agent. When I saw you pointing that thing at Kelly, I came this close..." He held up his fingers millimetres apart. "...to ventilating your brain for real."

Kane touched the reddened scab on his forehead. "You almost did anyway. I'm glad you trusted me enough not to use real bullets, but it's a good thing I trusted you enough to hold still and let you take the shot."

Holt snorted. "I didn't trust you at all. I just wanted answers before I blew your brains out. And I could have made that shot even if you were running across the room."

Kane didn't dignify his boast with a response. Instead, he turned back to me. "I was hoping to catch Labelle off guard with our infighting. I could see you were ready to take him, and I wasn't expecting Holt to show up shooting." He turned to Stemp. "Didn't you find the report I left for you last night? I was sure you'd see it on the windshield of your car this morning."

"Of course I saw it," Stemp said imperturbably. "I watched you break into my garage and leave it there when you triggered my silent alarms at zero three thirty. Your lock-picking was nicely done, by the way. I must upgrade my locks again."

Kane inclined his head in acknowledgement of the compliment, and Stemp went on, "However, I decided not to share all the details of your report with the team. Instead, I told Holt to expect you at Labelle's, and ordered him to bring you back alive and uninjured for interrogation. I thought everyone's actions would be considerably more... revealing... that way. And so they were."

My blood chilled with the realization of exactly how dangerous our situation had been. Holt had been right. Stemp had been testing us, with potentially fatal consequences for failure.

Kane, Holt, and I exchanged an uncomfortable glance and Kane cleared his throat. "Is there any word on who faked the terrorist attack?" he asked.

Spider sat up eagerly. "Yes! You're not going to believe this..." He paused dramatically. "It was Lawrence Harchman."

"What?" I stared at him, slack-jawed. "Why?"

"It was publicity for his new app. He wanted to scare people into thinking they needed it. He didn't have a clue that a weapon like ours actually existed; he just made up a weapon that didn't leave a mark because it was easier than simulating bomb injuries in a crowd. So he hired a programmer to use last year's footage from the Remembrance Day service..."

"That's why Hellhound and Miss Lacey were there!" I exclaimed. "It was last year's footage! Goddamn Harchman, that slimy little shit! I'll twist that pimple of a head right off his shoulders..."

Suddenly realizing I'd just uttered the intent to commit murder in a room full of law-enforcement personnel, I backtracked hurriedly. "I mean, I won't really, but I'd sure as hell love to-"

Spider saved me by interrupting, "So anyway, he hired James Helmand as an explosives consultant because he wanted convincing footage of himself getting blown up. He thought nobody would suspect him if it looked as though he was the intended victim. Then he had his programmer set up everything to splice the altered footage into the live news feeds, and gave the programmer an all-expenses-paid vacation in his Montreal home so the programmer could take the threat letter with him and mail it from there to deflect suspicion from Calgary."

"That's why Harchman was so pissed when they cancelled his speech," I deduced. "He wasn't going to get his dramatic death and all the associated publicity."

"Yes, and that's how we caught him." Spider grinned, the predatory look out of place on his boyish features. "He phoned the programmer to tell him to cut his murder out of the faked footage, and if it had ended there he would have gotten away with the whole thing because we weren't monitoring his phone. But after the altered footage went live, the programmer emailed Harchman the updated video file, and my back-door program caught the email. It's a lucky thing you installed the program on all his servers, not just the sim server."

I concealed my surge of satisfaction in a nod as if I'd planned it that way all along, and sent a psychic message toward Stemp: See? I'm a valuable agent. Please don't lock me up...

Then slow realization dawned.

My words came out on a wave of enlightenment mixed with trepidation. "Tawny will take over Harchman's empire." I stared at the frowning faces around the table. "So she wins in the end. Do you think she engineered the whole thing?"

"There's no evidence of it," Stemp said. "But if she is as smart as we think, she would have played the bimbo and manipulated Harchman, letting him believe the entire plan had been his own invention. Ms. Harchman may prove to be a formidable adversary, should she choose to act against us."

My heart sank. Oh God, not a reprise of Fuzzy Bunny...

The rest of the debriefing went by in a blur of fatigue, dread of Stemp's punishment, and an incongruously buoyant happiness that kept lifting my heart despite the gravity of the meeting.

When the last administrative details had been completed, Stemp's customary cool demeanor chilled by a few more degrees.

"Now," he said. "As to the issue of assault and forcible confinement of an agent, resisting arrest, and..." He turned his icy gaze on me. "...insubordination and obstructing justice-"

"Aydan didn't do anything wrong," Kane interrupted. "She followed Holt's orders, and she was tranked the rest of the time."

"That's true," Holt seconded, much to my surprise. "And she saved my life." Resentment glittered in the glance he shot at Kane. "Kane's the one who caused the problems. Him and his buddy Hellhound."

Fear chilled my heart. Oh, God, had I gotten my men back from the dead only to lose them to prison?

"Hellhound didn't do anything," Kane snapped. "He only came around the van and asked what was going on."

"Serving as a distraction," Holt growled. "And I'm pretty

sure he's the one who chucked the other guys in the back of the van and tied me up while I was unconscious."

"Enough," Stemp said in a quiet voice that sent a chill down my spine.

Stemp eyed Holt and Kane in silence. Holt slouched in his chair with the corner of his mouth curled in a cocky smile, but I was pretty sure it was only an act to hide the stinging of his pride. Kane sat ramrod straight, wearing his impassive cop face.

"Holt, can you say definitely that Hellhound attacked or restrained you?" Stemp said after a few moments.

Redness climbed Holt's neck. "No," he mumbled. "I was knocked out."

"Did your team see anything?"

The flush reached Holt's face. "No. They were knocked out, too."

"So." Stemp turned to Kane. "Since Hellhound's involvement can't be proven and Holt and his team are uninjured, it is highly unlikely that assault charges against you or Hellhound would be upheld in civilian court. And since you are no longer an agent I have no disciplinary power over you. I see no point in pursuing this matter further."

He directed a narrow gaze at Holt. "This incident will be classified as a training exercise on your record. You allowed yourself to be distracted and overpowered even though you and your team outnumbered your assailants. Take a lesson from the experience, and be glad the only injury was to your ego. Dismissed."

He rose and strode out.

Holt muttered "Asshole" under his breath, but he looked relieved.

I turned to face him, my happiness finally bursting out in

a grin. "I told you I could trust Kane." I reached over to squeeze Kane's hand and was rewarded with a smile and hand-squeeze in return.

"This time, maybe," Holt grumbled. "But he's still a spook, just like the rest of us. Spooks will always play you sooner or later."

"You're such a cynical prick," I said cheerfully, joy bubbling up inside me. I turned my smile back to Kane.

Tall, dark, incredibly hot Kane.

My smile widened.

He wasn't an agent anymore. There were no rules that prevented me from fraternizing with him.

And life was too damn short.

I leaned over and kissed him on the lips.

Holt groaned. "Christ, get a room." He rose and made for the door, followed by Spider, who gave me a conspiratorial grin.

When only the two of us remained, I turned back to Kane, still clutching his hand. "I knew I could trust you."

The smile slid off his face. "Aydan... we need to talk."

CHAPTER 49

The short drive to Kane's small bungalow in Silverside felt like hours. With my driving skills on autopilot and my heart quivering in fear of a death-blow, I manufactured and discarded scenario after scenario.

Maybe he'd decided to try again with Alicia, and he was dumping me.

Or maybe he was furious with me for making him put on a sex show for Riel's bug. Or for choking him and threatening to rip his balls off. That was a distinct possibility.

Or... good God, maybe he was going to confess to a torrid affair with Tawny.

Or he hated me for endangering Daniel.

Or he'd discovered he had some deadly sexually transmitted disease that passed through condoms...

By the time I parked in front of his house my hands were trembling and nausea churned my guts.

Walking up to his front steps, I drew deep calming breaths. Settle down, stomach. Don't hurl all over his welcome mat...

When Kane opened the door, he took one look at my face and whisked me into his living room. "Sit," he said, pressing me onto the soft leather sofa. "Head between your knees.

Slow breaths."

Bent double with Kane's warm hand making gentle circles on my back, I breathed slowly in time with his coaching.

"In... two, three, four. Out... two, three four. In..."

After a few minutes I straightened, not sure whether the heat in my face was embarrassment or increased circulation.

"Sorry," I said. "I haven't been sleeping lately, and I missed lunch."

"Just rest here," he commanded. "I'll make you something to eat."

"No, that's okay. I don't want anything. My stomach's a bit upset."

"I'll get you some ginger ale." He rose. "Just relax here for a while."

"No, I'm fine." I followed him to the kitchen, feeling anything but.

He filled a glass with ice and opened a ginger ale, his movements swift and sure.

When I was settled at the table with the glass fizzing in front of me, I took a steadying sip before throwing out the opening gambit. "You said we needed to talk."

"Yes." Kane sat abruptly in the other chair as though his knees had given way. "I... when we were at Harchman's..."

"I'm sorry about the sex," I blurted. "I didn't mean to use you, I just-"

"No, it's fine," he interrupted. "I mean... it wasn't only 'fine', it was mind-blowing. As it always is with you. But it's all right; I knew what you were doing and I was..." He hesitated and his voice softened. "Honoured. I was honoured that despite the bug, you trusted me enough to fall asleep in my arms."

"Oh."

I nearly added, 'It wasn't trust at all; I was just exhausted', but I silenced the lie before it could emerge.

I had trusted him then.

"Okay... and...?" I said instead.

"And..." He hesitated again. "Now here you are. Ready to talk. Not backing your chair away from me while pretending not to retreat. Not picking a meaningless fight to drive me away."

"Well..." I gave him a twisted smile. "I guess I've changed."

"Yes..." He studied me, his brow furrowed. "When you kissed me at Sirius just now... what was that?"

My old defensive shields flew up and my voice came out light and casual. "What do you mean?"

"I mean... don't take this the wrong way, but were you... was it just a ploy to rattle Holt?"

"Um..."

My cowardly heart seized the excuse with relief. I could laugh and pass it off as nothing more than a jab at Holt.

Or I could show some courage and admit the truth.

Go on, chickenshit. He can't hurt you any worse than you've already been hurt.

"I, um... I was just... happy that everything had turned out okay..." I equivocated.

Do it. Say the words.

"And, um..." I drew a deep breath and took the plunge. "This-whole-thing-made-me-realize-how-much-I-trust-you." I rushed the words out, already wishing I could take them back.

Kane paled.

"I mean, it was great to be working with you again," I

babbled, my heart pounding as though it would burst through my ribs and flee to safety. "I mean, not that we were really working together exactly, but I just-"

"Aydan."

I shut up, realizing I'd shoved my chair tight against the wall and my sweaty palms were clamped on the seat.

Forcing a shaky laugh, I let go of the chair and scrubbed my palms against my legs. "Sorry. I guess I haven't changed as much as I thought. Should I start a fight now?"

He didn't smile at my feeble joke. "No, please don't." He swallowed. "You may have ample reason to be angry with me soon enough."

I leaned back in my chair, as if those few inches of distance could protect me from what was to come. "That, um... sounds ominous," I whispered through dry lips.

"Yes," Kane said grimly. "I hope you'll hear me out, but stop me if you have questions." He drew a deep breath. "I... In the past couple of months I've discovered a lot about my own shortcomings." He barked out a mirthless laugh. "There's nothing like attending therapy sessions with your ex to uncover all your undesirable qualities."

"Ouch," I murmured in sympathy.

"Yes. There are things I can't reveal to Alicia or the civilian therapist. But I can reveal them to you. And... I need to do that, for both our sakes. It's probably..." His gaze wavered and he sighed. "It might mean the end of our friendship. But you deserve the truth, and I deserve to face whatever fallout there is."

My heart quivered but I held my face expressionless. "Okay."

Kane squared his shoulders. "I'll start at the beginning. I have only the barest inkling of what your first marriage was like, but it must have been hellish if even a strong, smart woman like you could be reprogrammed to believe that every moment of intimacy is a trap and a weapon to be used against her."

I shrugged, suppressing the urge to squirm.

He went on, "I, on the other hand... You know me pretty well, so you can probably guess what I was like in high school..."

I forced a chuckle. "A skirt-chasing jock. A highly successful skirt-chasing jock, according to the stories going around at your funeral last year."

He flushed. "Yes. I'm ashamed of it now, but when I was a teenager..." He shook his head. "Anyway, I learned early that women respond well to a take-charge guy."

"A take-charge guy who looks like you," I clarified with a gesture at his physique and a smile that felt wooden.

"Well... yes." He studied the table as though there might be a test later. "Anyway, in the army I was trained to identify objectives and develop tactical plans, and never to quit until I achieve the objective. Then when I went through training for clandestine operations, I learned emotional manipulation techniques..."

"And became damn near irresistible," I finished.

He flashed me a shamefaced half-smile. "I probably shouldn't take that as a compliment, but I do." Sobering, he went on, "I internalized those behaviours until I didn't even realize they were there. And then you came along, and my training kicked in. I'm not trying to make excuses, but..." He made a helpless gesture, both hands rising only to fall back to the table. "Thirty-one years of programming is hard to overcome. Especially if you don't even realize you're responding to it."

Fear trembled in my belly, but somehow I kept my voice calm and even. "You're preaching to the choir, remember? I've got more than enough fucked-up programming of my own. I get it, believe me."

He sighed. "Yes, of course you do. Anyway, to make a long story short and ugly... I played you. I've been playing you all along."

My breath stopped, my heart barely able to beat in the icy grip of bone-deep horror.

Holt had been right.

And I had been so, so wrong.

Kane added hurriedly, "Unintentionally. I didn't realize I was doing it until it was too late. You were so important to me I just... focused on the objective. Tried to be what I thought you wanted." He swallowed. "And instead I became the very thing you dread."

Kane stared at the wall and spoke tonelessly, as though reading a prepared confession before a firing squad. "At first I was my usual take-charge self. When that backfired, I switched to a sensitive-guy approach. That didn't work, either, so I played the 'vulnerable' card, which, to be honest, wasn't really an act at that point. I was so messed up after that mission..." He blew out a breath. "No excuse. It was exactly the kind of emotional manipulation you feared."

My heart clattered emptily into the dark abyss in the pit of my stomach, its echoes fading to nothing. Oxygen deprivation darkened the edges of my vision.

I managed a shallow breath.

In. Out...

"And then when you gave in and said you'd marry me, and I realized what I'd done..." Muscles rippled in Kane's jaw. "I felt... sick. But if I confessed, you'd hate me; and I was still reeling from my last mission, too much of a coward to lose you then. And if I backed away from our relationship without explaining, you'd feel as though I was rejecting you. That would have been worse."

He propped his forehead in his fists. "Thank *God* for Hellhound! He gave us both a graceful exit." He met my eyes at last. "I intended to come clean as soon as we'd both completed some therapy, but then Daniel came along..."

He broke off, then added, "Still no excuse. I do love you, as a person, not as an objective; but I realize I've betrayed any trust you might have had in me. I am truly sorry."

He bowed his head as if for the executioner's axe.

A chasm of silence gaped between us.

After a long moment, Kane muttered, "I'll... let you think things over."

He rose and headed for the hallway. As he disappeared around the corner, my throat unlocked at last.

"Wait," I croaked.

He reappeared, his cop face firmly in place, but his hands were clenched in white-knuckled fists.

I clutched the ginger ale glass between slick palms and swallowed hard.

"I don't hate you." My voice sounded stronger now. "I... I don't quite know what to do with this yet... but I don't hate you."

His expression eased to cautious hope.

I sucked in a deep breath and let it out slowly. "My first impulse is to assure you that everything's okay... but I'm pretty sure that's just my old programming, saying whatever it takes to smooth things over. So... I need to think about this."

"I should have been open with you from the start," Kane

said. "I should have understood what you'd been through and worked harder to avoid repeating your history."

I grimaced. "You couldn't have known. Even if you'd asked me, I wouldn't have told you the truth." We stared at each other in futile silence for a moment before I added, "But we've been through a lot together and I'm not willing to throw that away just yet."

Some of the rigidity went out of Kane's posture. "Thank you," he said quietly. "I promise to be completely truthful with you from now on." His face twisted in a bitter smile. "As if that promise actually has any value."

"It doesn't. Everything you've just said might be bullshit designed to convince me that your past behaviour was reasonable, so you can gain even more emotional control over me. That was my ex's best trick, too."

Kane's jaw hardened, pain flaring in his eyes, and I added, "But if it makes you feel any better, I've always known you were capable of that. You wouldn't be a top agent if you weren't." I reached out to him and he came closer, taking my hand tentatively.

"I think we're in the same boat," I added. "You don't have any reason to trust what I say, either. But I've been through a lot of therapy and soul-searching since the summer, and I meant it when I said I've changed. You still might be playing me, but... even if you are, I think..."

I fumbled for the right words. "I think... I'm strong enough to deal with it. And to walk away if I have to. And we have Arnie to watch out for both of us. So... maybe we could just... start again and see how it goes?"

Kane's voice softened. "Yes. A fresh start would be perfect."

"But are you sure that's what you want?" I asked.

"Because I'm still a bullet magnet, and you're still a dad. Every minute you spend with me is a potential risk to Daniel and Alicia. To your family."

"She's not-" Kane began, then bit off the words and tried again. "You're right, of course. She's my son's mother, and for his sake I need to protect her, too. But you... I..." He stared at me, frustration plain on his face. "I've said right from the start that I won't risk Daniel's safety for anything... but I can't... *won't*... choose between you."

I rose. "It's okay, we both have a lot of thinking to do. I'd better go. You need to get back to Daniel tonight." As I moved toward the door, I added, "Do you want to come over next weekend and help me tinker with the old Chevy? No heavy conversations, just a beer and bullshit session with a friend?"

"I'd like that very much." He smiled. "See you then... friend."

I returned his smile. "Okay... friend."

Turning away, I hesitated, then added, "John?"

"Yes?" His deep voice was very close behind me.

I turned to face him.

Reached up to trace the square contour of his jaw.

Let my hand drift around the back of his neck and pull his lips down to mine.

His arms closed around me, his embrace familiar but somehow different now.

After a sweet unhurried kiss, I pulled gently away.

He let me go, his eyes dark with hunger. "What..." His voice came out husky, and he cleared his throat. "Was that... 'goodbye'? Or 'hello'?"

I smiled. "It was 'life is too damn short'. See you next weekend."

Book 13 is available!

Visit my Books page at dianehenders.com/books for progress updates and announcements.

A Request

Thanks for reading!

If you enjoyed this book, I'd really appreciate it if you'd take a moment to review it online.

Here are some suggestions for the "star" ratings:
Five stars: Loved the book and can hardly wait for the next one.
Four stars: Liked the book and plan to read the next one.
Three stars: The book was okay. Might read the next one.
Two stars: Didn't like the book. Probably won't read the next one.
One star: Hated the book. Would never read another in the series.

You can help prospective readers by writing a few sentences about what you liked or disliked about the book.

Thanks for taking the time to do a review!

About Me

Before I started writing fiction, I had a checkered career: technical writer, computer geek, and interior designer. I'm good at two out of three of those. Fortunately, I had the sense to quit the one I sucked at (interior design).

When my mid-life crisis hit, I took up muay thai and started writing thrillers featuring a middle-aged female protagonist. ('Walter Mitty', you say? Nope, never heard of him.)

Writing and kicking the hell out of stuff seemed more productive than more typical mid-life-crisis activities like getting a divorce, buying a Harley Crossbones, and cruising across the country picking up men in sleazy bars; especially since it's winter most months of the year here in Canada.

It's much more comfortable to sit at my computer. And Harleys are expensive. Come to think of it, so are beer and gasoline.

Oh, and I still love my husband. There's that. So I stuck with the writing.

Diane Henders

And here's my "professional" bio, in case you need something more suitable for mixed company:

Diane Henders is the Kindle best-selling author of the NEVER SAY SPY series: Sexy thrillers packed with tension, laughs, profanity, and sometimes warm fuzzies.

The first book in the series, NEVER SAY SPY, has had over 450,000 downloads to date, and stayed on Kindle's 'Women Sleuths' Top 100 list for 60 consecutive months.

Diane enjoys target shooting, gardening, auto mechanics, painting (art, not walls), music, and martial arts; and loves food and drink almost as much as she loves her husband. They live in the wilds of British Columbia, Canada, where they get all the adrenaline rush they could ever want by growing fruit trees in bear country.

Want to know what else is roiling around in the cesspit of my mind? Drop by my blog and website at dianehenders.com, check out the extras, and don't forget to leave a comment in the guest book to say hi – I love hearing from you! Or you can connect with me on Facebook at:
https://www.facebook.com/authordianehenders.
See you there!